An *Heir of*

Deception

BEVERLEY KENDALL

An Heir of Deception
Beverley Kendall
Copyright © Beverley Kendall 2012
Published by Season Publishing
This is a work of fiction. Names, characters, places and
incidents are products of the author's imagination or are used
fictitiously and are not to be construed as real. Any
resemblance to actual events, locales, organizations, or
persons, living or dead, is completely coincidental.

All's Fair in Love and Seduction copyright © 2011 by
Beverley Kendall
Sinful Surrender copyright © 2011 by Beverley Kendall
A Taste of Desire copyright © 2011 by Beverley Kendall

www.theseasonforromance.com
www.beverleykendall.com
Cover Design © Hot Damn Designs

Dedication

To the love of my life, Ryan.
Mommy loves you always.

Acknowledgments

Grace, your edits are spot on. Thanks for your invaluable input. Anastasia, what can I say except thank you. A blind lady's maid was not what I intended. LOL!! Dawn thank you for holding everything else together while I wrote. You're the best sister a girl can have.

A BITTERSWEET REUNION

After a taut silence, he yanked his gaze from Charlotte's and turned to include her sister in his regard as well as his address. "I instructed Reeves not to disturb you when I arrived. I'm just here to retrieve some documents your brother left for me."

It was then Charlotte noticed the large envelope gripped tightly in his hand. A death grip.

"Um, Alex, Ch-Charlotte has ju-just now arrived."

Never had Charlotte heard her sister stammer so. Given the circumstances, it was *she* who should be rattled and out of sorts. She was all that and more. Utterly overwhelmed and buffeted by so many emotions, the paramount of which she still could not name.

"So I see," he replied in clipped tones, keeping his gaze averted from her. As telling and deliberate a gesture as she'd ever witnessed.

Charlotte knew then she would have to initiate any form of communication between them. And who else should do it if not her.

"Hello, Alex," she said, finding her courage and her voice. But never had two words taken so much effort to speak.

His jaw firmed, his nostrils flared and an ominous stillness settled over him. A moment later he gave her sister a brisk nod. "I shall leave you to your guest. Good day, Catherine." His gaze did not venture in her direction again. It was as if, to him, she'd ceased to exist.

Also by Beverley Kendall

The Elusive Lords Series

SINFUL SURRENDER
A TASTE OF DESIRE
ALL'S FAIR IN LOVE & SEDUCTION (Free Novella)

Note to readers

To everyone who has already read the sample chapters of An Heir of Deception, I urge you to read the book from the beginning. I made changes in the first three chapters during the edit process that impact other areas of the book. Unless you know what those changes are, parts of the book may not make sense. ☺

Prologue

A hushed silence greeted Alex Cartwright, the Marquess of Avondale, as he arrived in the large antechamber in St. Paul's Cathedral.

Attired in navy frock coats, precisely knotted neckties, and light-blue trousers, the Viscounts Creswell and Armstrong, and Rutherford, the Earl of Windmere, were certainly suited up well enough for the occasion. At least in dress if not demeanor, for their faces held the grayish cast of men bound for the gallows. And Rutherford's hair appeared as if it had been plowed more times than a seasoned whore.

Paused just inside the threshold, Alex let out a dry laugh. "Come now, gentlemen, it *can't* be as bad as that," he teased. "The occasion does not call for black dress or armbands. This isn't a funeral you're attending, but my wedding."

Such a comment would have customarily elicited a wry smile—at the very least—but received not so much as a blink. Another silence the weight of a ship's anchor descended upon the room, blanketing him in air as cold as London's fog was thick.

Determined that whatever their affliction, it would not spoil the most important day thus far in his twenty-nine years, Alex quelled the sense of unease beginning to unfurl in his gut.

Under a domed celestial frieze of cherubs and angels, Alex advanced toward the trio standing motionless in front of a large marble-topped table, his footfalls muffled by the carpeted floor.

He would have welcomed more noise, some sort of distraction from the somberness surrounding him, be it in human form or décor. Located in the south transept of the church, the chamber boasted dark-burgundy drapes of some thick, expensive fabric, and surrounding the black marble fireplace were three chairs crafted with enough gild, scrollwork, and velvet to satisfy royalty. But then, with the sudden death of his brother the year before—the much beloved son and heir to the Hastings dukedom—wasn't Alex now regarded as such? Despite his mother's vehement opposition to the marriage, when Alex had made it clear he'd marry Charlotte with or without her approval, she thrown her considerable ducal weight into ensuring his wedding would be the most celebrated event in Society for at least the next decade to come.

Halting in front of his friends, he quirked a brow. "Surely you're not commiserating over my nuptials?" Alex found light sarcasm served as a wonderful vehicle to lift a dour mood. "I would think not, as you all have walked," he executed a mock bow, "I stand corrected gentlemen—*vanquished* this course years ago."

And most assuredly they had, the three men happily married with nary a complaint regarding the oft-bemoaned rigors of the institution. Indeed, each had been passionate in its recommendation.

Armstrong shot Rutherford a look, one Alex instantly recognized. He'd seen it often enough over the course of an acquaintance numbering twenty-six years. In that instant, he knew something was terribly, perhaps tragically, wrong.

Panic bloomed and anxiety burned like acid in his throat. Alex's gaze flew to Rutherford. "It's Charlotte, isn't it? Something has happened to Charlotte."

The earl averted his gaze.

Alex grabbed Rutherford forcibly by the arms, bringing the two men practically nose to nose. Even if his friend's delay had been infinitesimal, it measured what felt like an eternity too long.

Alex held his friend in a vise grip and gave him a teeth-jarring shake. "Tell me, damn it. What's happened to Charlotte? Is she hurt? Where is she?"

Rutherford bent his imprisoned arm at the elbow. With obvious reluctance, he offered up the envelope. "She sent this for you," Rutherford said, his voice strained and hoarse.

With a cautious step back, Alex dropped his hands to his sides. At first, he could only stare at the innocuous rectangular paper, uncomprehending. Slowly, the fog released its hold on his senses.

His gaze darted to the sheet of paper crushed in his friend's other hand. She'd also written a letter to Rutherford and it was obvious he'd read his. Alex then recalled the footman hurrying down the hall. In that instant, he knew the man he'd passed with so little regard, so consumed with his own happiness, had been the bearer of the news that had sent his friends into such morbid melancholy. News that would assuredly send him someplace far worse.

Charlotte wasn't hurt. The evidence stood before him in the form of her brother. Had she been injured or taken ill, a stable full of horses wouldn't have been able to drag Rutherford from her side. But too swiftly on the heels of staggering relief nipped a growing fear, for penned in her signature slopes and curls was his name emblazoned across the front of the envelope. A letter from her on the day of their wedding could signify only one thing.

"She's not coming, is she?" His cravat—silk mulberry that his valet had fussed into an elaborate knot—felt as if it had a stranglehold on his words.

"Cartwright—"

Alex's head jerked violently in the direction of his friend, the set of his countenance effectively cutting Creswell off at the utterance of his name.

Armstrong sighed and ran his hand through a thatch of golden hair, regarding him with eyes filled with the kind of compassion no man should have to countenance on his wedding day. Sympathy was bad enough, but pity? Intolerable.

Directing his attention back to Rutherford, Alex stared at the envelope unclaimed in his friend's hand, knowing its contents promised to deliver him the felling blow.

"What does she say?" he asked, his voice a hollow imitation of his former self.

"I did not read it," Rutherford muttered gruffly, extending his arm so the tan paper touched the flesh exposed at Alex's wrist.

The fires of perdition could not have singed his skin more at the contact and Alex retreated several steps as he surveyed it with abhorrence.

"What did she tell you?" he asked quietly, dragging his gaze up to Rutherford's.

Three years ago when his friend had paced the halls outside his wife's bedchamber awaiting the birth of their twins, he'd worn the same expression he did at present, a helpless sort of fright.

"What does she say!" Alex's voice exploded like a cannon blast in graveyard silence. "Isn't it in the letter she sent to you?"

Isn't it in the letter she sent to you?

The echo transcended the room to storm the corridors of the prestigious church.

Rutherford appeared to be rallying his courage, swallowing and then drawing in a ragged breath before he said, "The footman brought the letters only moments before your arrival. I was coming—"

"God dammit, man, quit all your blasted blathering. Just tell me what she wrote!"

Rutherford made an uncomfortable sound in his throat before replying in graveled tones, "She wrote to beg my forgiveness for any scandal or shame her actions may bring upon the family but…says she can't marry you."

A roar sounded in Alex's ears as he grasped the back of a

nearby chair, the coolness of the metal frame muted by his silk white gloves. He blinked rapidly in an effort to halt the stinging in his eyes and swallowed to douse the burning in his throat. And a numbness such as he'd never known assailed him, turning his limbs into leaden weights.

"Where is she?"

Stark pain and fear flashed in Rutherford's pale blue eyes. "I do not know. She's quit the Manor but gave no indication as to where she's gone. She merely states she is safe and that we must not concern ourselves unduly over her."

The weight on Alex's chest threatened to crush every organ beneath it. But such destruction would do little to his heart, for it had already broken into a multitude of pieces.

Like that, with the flourish of a pen, she was gone.

Alex turned to the open door. Around him, he felt rather than saw his friends move in chorus toward him. He stopped abruptly, angled his head over his shoulder and met their gazes. "Let me be. I shall be fine." But he wouldn't lie to himself; he would never be fine.

The three men did not advance any farther.

Alex blindly put one foot in front of the other. With every step, he discarded a piece of the life he'd foolishly dreamt to have with her...until there were none.

He took his leave of the room, his leave of the church, to start his way back to a life obliterated to a pile of nothingness.

Chapter One

Berkshire, 1 March 1864

Her sister was gravely ill.

The knowledge plagued Charlotte Rutherford, consuming her with such fear that a proper night's sleep had been impossible since her dear friend, Lucas Beaumont, had informed her upon his return from England.

The news had catapulted her into a frenzy of activity for two days thereafter. In that time, she'd arranged passage to England and closed up her small townhouse in Manhattan. What came next required all of her endurance: an eleven-day voyage across the Atlantic Ocean.

With too much time to her solitary thoughts, she'd been wracked with inconsolable grief and the bitterest regret...and heart stopping fear that her presence there would open a Pandora's Box of a different sort.

Now two weeks to the day after she had learned of her twin's illness, Charlotte was here. The place she'd once called home. And after an absence of nearly five years, the reality of once again being on English soil—standing at the doors of Rutherford Manor—brought with it the heartbreak of old.

All of that, however, paled in the light of her sister's illness. For Katie, Charlotte would endure anything, even if it meant risking exposure and opening a wound that had never healed. One she feared might never *truly* heal.

With her heart in her throat and anxiety now a familiar—albeit unwelcome—companion, Charlotte lifted the knocker of the oak door and brought it down three times in rapid succession.

The ensuing seconds seemed to stretch on endlessly. Were

they home? She hadn't even considered that possibility when she'd arrived in Town and had proceeded directly to Paddington Station to catch the train to Reading. She shot a glance over her shoulder and regarded the carriage parked in front of her hired coach. Someone must be in residence, as it appeared they had company. Something else she hadn't considered.

Upon the opening of the door, she gave a nervous start and spun back around. Reeves, the Rutherford butler of thirty odd years, stood in the doorway, his tall, spare frame and lined visage reminiscent of happier times in days long past. But the advance of age had left its mark. Once possessed of a head of hair with equal amounts of gray and brown, his hair now rivaled the unadulterated white of Father Christmas. And his stature, which formerly would have been the envy of any uniformed man, now gently rounded at the shoulders, proving once again how time spared no one.

Given he was a man disposed to typical English butler demeanor, she'd never imagined he had it in his personal repertoire to blanch, but that is precisely what he did upon viewing her. He said nothing for several seconds, simply stared, his eyes wide and unblinking. Charlotte stifled a laugh—one of the nervous sort—fearing any attempt at speech would cause her to dissolve into a heap of polka dot skirts at his feet.

Behind her, a horse whinnied and stomped its hooves and birds continued their cheerful chirping while Reeves appeared to be struggling to find his tongue.

At length, he exclaimed softly, "Miss Charlotte." He spoke as if he believed she was but a vision and any undue noise would send her off into obscurity.

Charlotte managed a tremulous smile, tears pricking the corners of her eyes. "Hullo, Reeves. I-I'm delighted to see you looking so well." The greeting seemed hardly adequate, but she was at a loss to find something fitting to say after so long an absence. So sudden a departure.

Her voice appeared to galvanize him into action. Throwing open the door, he ushered her through an entrance hall as large as the ground floor of her townhouse and into the vestibule. She'd quite forgotten just how large an estate her brother owned.

"I fear we were not apprised of your arrival. Such a shame as, just this morning his lordship and her ladyship went into London with the children. However, Miss Catherine is in residence. She will be happy that you've returned."

In all the years Charlotte had known him, she could scarcely remember a time when she'd seen him looking anything less than unwaveringly stoic. At present his mouth curved into something close to a smile.

"I hadn't time to send word of my coming." She'd naturally assumed everyone would be home with her sister doing so poorly. She was more than a little surprised James had gone off to London and left Katie in the care of the servants—and no doubt the attending physician. Actually, it was inconceivable he would do so.

Charlotte pivoted sharply to face the elderly butler. She laid a restraining hand on his black-clad arm as he made a move to relieve her of her pelisse. "Reeves, can you tell me anything of my sister's condition?"

Reeves stilled at her touch. He lowered his hands to his sides, staring down at her with white furrowed brows. After a pause, the deep creases in his forehead eased. "If you're speaking of that rather nasty cold she fell ill with the month past, then I can assure you she has since fully recovered."

A cold? *The doctor has done all he can for her. If she recovers it will be by the grace of God.* She could hear Lucas's words as though he'd spoken them yesterday. Not even the severest of colds rose to that criticality.

Before she had an opportunity to question Reeves further, the scramble of feet and a high-pitched squeal drew her attention to the top of the double mahogany staircase.

Her sister stood in the middle of the first floor landing

clutching the balustrade, her form poised for flight.

"Charlotte, is that really you?" Katie cried.

Then in a blur of pale-green muslin, she took the right set of stairs with all the refinement of a horde of marauding boars. Her fingers skimmed and skipped over the polished mahogany banister as her skirt fluttered and quivered under the breeze of her stampeding steps.

Transfixed by the first sight of her twin in nearly five years as she flew down the stairs, Charlotte could neither move nor speak.

Lucas claimed to have received the information of her sister's illness on good authority, but it was clear he'd been grossly misinformed.

Katie was not ailing.

At least Charlotte had never seen a person whose survival was said to have hinged on God's mercy with so much bounce and pep, her cheeks flushed with the healthy hue of breathless excitement, not the ravages of fever. No, her sister looked as vital and healthy as any twenty-four-year-old woman could.

After a fortnight of anticipating the worst and ardent prayers that she'd arrive to find her sister at least on the verge of recovery, a tidal wave of emotion washed over her, and soon Charlotte was moving, her feet carrying her forward without conscious effort or thought.

"Oh Lottie, Lottie. You've come back," her sister cried before launching herself into her arms. "Lord, how I've missed you."

Charlotte choked out a sob at the use of her childhood name as they embraced at the foot of the staircase, clinging to one another under a deluge of shared tears. Joy, relief, and the pain of their long separation had Charlotte trembling uncontrollably. The last time they'd held each other this tightly, they had been frightened five-year-old girls just arrived at the boarding school. Save a father who'd ensured for only their financial welfare, they'd been very much alone in the world.

"Oh God, I thought you—" Charlotte broke off abruptly

when her sister turned a tear-stained face to her, her joy a living, breathing entity. How could she now admit she'd returned because she'd thought her near death's door? She simply could not.

"Thought I was what?" Katie asked in a voice choked with tears.

"I thought perhaps I would not find you home," Charlotte quickly improvised. "Oh Katie, how I missed you too, so very very much."

Katie's breaths came in pants and half sobs, her arms tightening around Charlotte's waist until she could scarce draw a breath. How long they stood holding each other, she didn't know. But for those finite moments, time seemed to stand still.

After she caught her breath, and her sister was no longer gasping as if she'd been running too hard and too long, Charlotte loosened her hold and drew back to take in a face so dearly familiar and identical to her own.

Sky blue eyes fringed with long, thick lashes gazed back at her. Eyes glassy with tears. In all the jostling and excitement, ringlets of burnished gold curls had come dislodged from what had to be a small army of pins securing her sister's chignon. How well Charlotte knew what it took to keep the thick mane properly tamed and presentable.

Katie reached out to cradle Charlotte's cheek in her palm, her touch almost reverent. "Where—when—why didn't you say anything about coming home in your last letter?"

"I decided at the last possible minute," Charlotte whispered in a voice equally thick with emotion.

After brushing the crest of Charlotte's cheek with her thumb, Katie dropped her hand to her side. "I hope you realize that James and Missy will be beside themselves when I send word of your return," she chided gently. "They're to stay in London a week. Of course, I'll have to send word express that you've returned. I expect they'll be home tomorrow or soon after. Christopher is touring the Continent. He's not expected back in England until the fall."

Charlotte was convinced that their half brother Christopher had vagabond blood running in his veins. He'd toured the Continent the summer he'd graduated from Eton. But whether she'd be here when he returned was still in question.

"I know and I'm disappointed too, but in a way I'm happy it's just the two of us—at least for today."

Katie smiled, her face flushed pink with pleasure. After several moments of contented silence, she took a step back and began a critical appraisal of Charlotte's figure, commencing at the ruffled collar of her blue-and-yellow wool traveling suit. Her expression sobered the farther her gaze continued downward. "You're too thin. Why, I must be a good half stone heavier."

"I have recently lost some weight." The stress of thinking one's sister hovered on the brink of death tended to kill one's appetite. Of course, that was something she couldn't now admit to her.

"We'll have to fatten you up a bit. It's obvious you haven't been taking proper care of yourself," Katie stated crisply, eyeing the ill fit of Charlotte's dress. Several weeks ago it had cinched her waist instead of hanging on her like a rooster's wattle as it did now.

"You haven't changed a bit, still just as bossy as ever," Charlotte teased, attempting to lighten the mood. Her sister would have time to reproach her on her inadequate diet later.

Desperate to hold off the questions sure to come, she turned to her surroundings. Her gaze swept the three-story vestibule and down the wide corridor of the picture gallery ahead. "Though the same can't be said of this place. I hardly recognize it anymore."

Katie came immediately to her side, hooking her arm through Charlotte's as if she couldn't bear any physical distance between them. She followed the direction of Charlotte's gaze. "Yes, Missy redecorated three summers ago. I'm proud to say I did have a small hand in the effort. I selected the chandelier." Her sister angled them toward the front and pointed at the elaborate crystal-and-glass light fixture soaring high above the entrance hall. "A fine choice if I daresay."

Charlotte nodded in agreement. Her sister had always had exquisite taste.

"Missy insisted on a décor more suited to children. The rugs were purchased when the floors met with one too many of her treasured Wedgwood vases. Marble tends to be terribly unforgiving that way." Her sister's laughter rang throughout the hall, ebullient and light. "But the alterations have added a warmth that was lacking before. Don't you think it looks and feels more like a home and less like a museum than when the dowager lived here?"

Charlotte nodded mutely as a frisson of fear coursed the length of her spine at the mention of her half brothers' mother. She did not want to think about her—could not bear to.

Slowly, she lowered her gaze to admire the Persian rug beneath her booted feet, and continued on to take in silk-papered walls done in dark green. Also gracing the hall were two walnut tables inlaid with a lighter wood, and several chairs with cushioned seats in which a weary bottom might actually find comfort.

"Yes, it certainly does."

Months after the death of their father, the dowager Countess of Windmere had moved to Devon and James had taken possession of the manor home. Charlotte had found the place as cold and sterile as its previous occupant. Although they had never been formally introduced, the dowager had made no secret of her intense dislike of her and Katie. But given they were the illegitimate issue of the woman's husband *and* born only months after Christopher, her youngest son, her feelings were understandable and expected. However, the dowager had carried her hatred too far. The letter and the threat had revealed how truly vindictive she could be.

"While I was sad for James and Christopher when she passed away, I must admit to a sense of relief knowing our paths would never cross again."

Charlotte's next breath emerged a serrated gasp. Her head snapped to the side and she stared at Katie, mouth agape. "She is dead?" She spoke in a hushed whisper as if terrified of waking the woman from her resting place.

Her sister sent her a puzzled frown, her winged brows collecting over a slender nose. "Surely you cannot be distressed?" Katie chided. "You know how I normally refrain from the use of clichés, but truly that woman was the bane of my existence. If you had remained, you would have been similarly affected. I'm certain if not for that wretched woman, I would have married ages ago. But no, despite the fact that James threatened to cut off her funds, she told everyone who would listen that we were James's sisters and not his cousins. Illegitimate and not at all good enough for their precious sons."

Charlotte didn't respond immediately, still trying to digest the enormity of what she'd just learned. With the dowager gone, so too was the threat she had posed. Which meant for the first time in years she could breathe easy.

"Wh-when did she die?"

"Early last year. I would have told you had I the correct address in which to send my correspondence," Katie replied with a note of censure in her voice. "I do not believe you ever used the same return address twice."

Guilt warmed Charlotte's cheeks. Lucas had posted the letters for her when he traveled to England on business. It had been the only way to ensure no one discovered her whereabouts.

But to learn the dowager had been dead an entire year made her wish for something solid to sit on.

Certainly if she had shared the information, something would have surfaced by now. And she could not fathom her brother taking his family to London with a scandal of that magnitude about his sisters raging within the drawing rooms of Mayfair. Dare she hope the woman had taken it with her to her grave as it appeared she had?

She shot Katie a glance. It would appear their secret was

safe.

"I imagine it must have been a very difficult time for James and Christopher." This Charlotte could say with all honesty.

Her sister gave her a sidelong look. "I feared you were going to start spouting empty platitudes about how sorry you are that she is gone. She was a simply horrible woman, and I have not missed her one little bit."

No, Charlotte could not have lied about that. The woman had been the cause of enough pain and heartbreak to ensure that three generations of Rutherfords wallowed in misery. "As I said before, *you* haven't changed a'tall," she said dryly. Her sister did not believe in being agreeable for propriety's sake.

Katie flashed an infectious grin. "And why should I change? As I recall it was the only way anyone could tell us apart. Should I become kind and agreeable, I could very well be mistaken for you."

"And we certainly wouldn't want that." Charlotte felt lighter than she had in years. Such a shame it was due to the death of someone close to the brothers she loved that had been responsible for relieving her of an enormous weight. "Although, that happened often enough when we first came to live with James."

For their newly discovered brother and his bride, telling her and Katie apart had come down to the simple matter of her sister's birthmark—a tiny mole on the nape of her neck. The memory of Missy craning her neck in a not-so-subtle attempt to determine the existence—or lack thereof—of said birthmark brought a small smile to Charlotte's face, eliciting a stark feeling of nostalgia.

"Yes, the only person who never confused us was Al—" Katie's eyes flashed wide with alarm. "I didn't mean to—I mean...."

Tears stung Charlotte's eyes and her chest constricted. She pulled her sister's arm tighter against her side and whispered, "It is fine. I shan't break at the mention of his name. Truly. In any case, it was I who..." She swallowed the lump that had

formed in her throat. "Alex has always been a big part of our—
your life. I certainly don't expect you to change anything to
suit me."

With a tiny nod, Katie drew Charlotte into the circle of her
arms for a gentle hug before setting her away. "Come, you
must be famished. Off with your cloak and I shall have the
cook prepare you something to eat. Then I can tell you
everything that has happened to me these last five years and
you can tell me everything you did not include in your letters. I
assume you hired a hackney from the station in town."

Without giving Charlotte an opportunity to respond, her
sister turned to Reeves, who stood far enough away as to allow
them privacy, but close enough to be summoned to duty
forthwith. "Reeves, please have the footmen retrieve my
sister's belongings from the coach."

"No!" The response sprang sharp and unbidden from
Charlotte's mouth. Even she could hear the panic threading her
tone.

Both Reeves and Katie treated her to a look of surprise.

"I mean not yet. Katie, there is something I need to tell
you—"

A movement, a figure, in the corner of her vision halted her
speech. Charlotte shifted her gaze. Her breath and her world
came to a shuddering halt.

Alex.

He rounded the stretch of hall leading from the study. Their
eyes met across a distance of some forty feet.

Her breath left her completely then. The air surrounding her
became charged and hot.

His stride might have faltered but he recovered so swiftly,
she couldn't be certain she hadn't imagined it.

Charlotte stood frozen, ensnared as deftly and completely as
a rabbit in the presence of a rattler preparing to strike. She
watched as he proceeded down the seemingly endless corridor
toward her.

Senses starved for the flesh-and-blood man greedily tried to take him in all at once, hoarding away every minute detail to take back with her to feed the lonely nights when dreams and memories were all she'd have…and yet still not enough.

Save the measured fall of his footsteps, silence reigned with a parasitic presence that made speech a novelty and breathing a luxury. Charlotte could do nothing but wait in statue-like stillness while her heart picked up its pace. To even blink would have created too much noise.

As he drew closer, she began to make out the subtle changes time had wrought in his visage.

In appearance, he looked much the same as the man she'd known and loved—loved still. With hair the black and shine of obsidian brushing the collar of his tan morning coat, and the delicious little dimple in his chin, he had always been surfeit in looks. But the Alex of old had possessed a wicked sort of charm. His smile, lazy and hinting at deeper passions, had caused the palpitation of many a female heart. Upon their betrothal announcement, the gossip sheets had stated the sound of those very same hearts breaking could be heard from Cornwall to Northumberland.

At present, however, it appeared no smile would dare venture near his lips. Faint lines bracketed his full mouth, the surrounding skin unforgiving in its tautness. And there was an iciness in his expression that pierced her heart with a corresponding blast of cold. He even carried his lean, muscular frame with an aloofness, tight and very controlled.

Any hope she would find in him a smidgeon of warmth, an inkling of the affection he'd once felt for her, wilted and died under his regard. Yet she remained resolute as he advanced upon her, awaiting the first words they would exchange since the day before what should have been their wedding day.

With his every step, her anxiety climbed and her heart stumbled over the hurdle an ocean and five years had created. Twenty steps separating them became ten and then five. He stopped just shy of an arm's length of her. Continuing to imprison her with his silver-eyed gaze, he finally spoke. "I see you have company."

Charlotte nearly wept at the sound of his voice, a smoky baritone. Perhaps that was the reason it took her a moment to comprehend he was speaking to Katie and not her. That it was she to whom he referred as *company*.

"Alex, I had no idea you were here," her sister said with an uncharacteristic catch in her voice.

After a taut silence, he yanked his gaze from Charlotte's and turned to include her sister in his regard as well as his address. "I instructed Reeves not to disturb you when I arrived. I'm just here to retrieve some documents your brother left for me."

It was then Charlotte noticed the large envelope gripped tightly in his hand. A death grip.

"Um, Alex, Ch-Charlotte has ju-just now arrived."

Never had Charlotte heard her sister stammer so. Given the circumstances, it was *she* who should be rattled and out of sorts. She was all that and more. Utterly overwhelmed and buffeted by so many emotions, the paramount of which she still could not name.

"So I see," he replied in clipped tones, keeping his gaze averted from her. As telling and deliberate a gesture as she'd ever witnessed.

Charlotte knew then she would have to initiate any form of communication between them. And who else should do it if not her.

"Hello, Alex," she said, finding her courage and her voice. But never had two words taken so much effort to speak.

His jaw firmed, his nostrils flared and an ominous stillness settled over him. A moment later he gave her sister a brisk nod. "I shall leave you to your guest. Good day, Catherine." His gaze did not venture in her direction again. It was as if, to him, she'd ceased to exist.

Charlotte turned to watch as his long strides carried him across the wool rugs on the marble floors, through the entrance hall, and out the front door.

Lord, he wouldn't even acknowledge her. She'd have

preferred he'd railed and cursed her. She'd rather he'd shaken her like a ragdoll. Anything would have been better than being so ignored.

The weight of her sister's hand settled on the curve of her shoulder, comforting and warm. "He is in shock. You must give him time to adjust to your...presence." Though the words were meant to placate her, Katie's tone held a hint of something else, a pained sort of despair. As if she herself was experiencing Charlotte's hurt.

But Charlotte knew he would never forgive her. The entire situation would simply grow ever more intolerable. The sooner she returned to America, the better it would be for everyone. To see him was to be constantly reminded of all she'd lost and all she'd had to walk away from. It would simply be too much.

"Where is he staying? The guesthouse? Have I just sent him in search of other accommodations?" Charlotte imagined he'd be departing the place shortly.

"Oh no, it's nothing like that. Alex purchased Gretchen Manor two years back. Do you remember it?"

Charlotte briefly lowered her lids, only able to dip her head in response. Of course she remembered the Palladian-style manor house with its portico, towering columns and lush, green lawns. She'd fallen in love with it on sight. The house was no more than ten miles down the road, an easy distance by carriage or on horseback. Alex lived but a stone's throw away.

"Oh Lottie, you mustn't look so cast down." Catherine nudged Charlotte's chin up with her fingertip. "So much has happened since you've been gone. Alex hasn't been the same since you left. You must be patient with him."

A blink sent a stream of tears down her cheeks. They landed on her sister's palm. "He despises me."

"Believe me, my dear, he does *not* despise you. Isn't it obvious he's still hurt by the whole affair? That itself says a great deal about how much he loved you."

Loved her. The past not the present. He didn't love her anymore. And would he still have loved her if he knew the truth? Who she really was?

"Come now, you look positively fatigued. First we must get some food in you and then you can rest. I'll have to put off my interrogation until later."

Her sister's words had her stomach clenching in apprehension. There was one secret she had no choice but to reveal now, for it would become known soon enough.

"Katie, I didn't come back to England alone. There is someone I'm most desperate for you to meet."

She is back.

Alex descended the front steps toward his carriage, his pulse pounding a staccato beat. After two years of sobriety, he wanted—no *needed*—a drink. He needed enough to wipe her image clean from his mind. Which meant he'd have to consume the whole damn bottle. But thankfully not a drop of alcohol existed at his residence. Today he was safe, temptation of that sort well out of reach.

Though not impossible to acquire should his resolve crumble, a voice inside him taunted. Alex ruthlessly quashed it. He'd come too far and worked too hard to be dragged down by that particular vice. By her.

Why the blazes had she come back? A damned eternity would have been soon enough to have to see her again.

Is she back for good? Is she married?

The questions crept insidiously into his thoughts, catching him unaware. Once, years ago, he would have sold his soul—and at times thought he had—for any news of her. How often had he lain in his bed and prayed she'd come back to him or wished he would wake up to discover his wedding day had just been a dream? A nightmare. Today the thought that only a few miles separated them made his blood run cold.

She is so damn beautiful.

Though unwanted, the observation was in no way a compliment to her. It was simply a statement of fact. And if he dared flirt with facts, he would have to concede she was even more beautiful than before. At nineteen, she'd been a flower on the brink of bloom. Well, she had bloomed and was certain to be a danger to the gentlemen in Society. No doubt she was a danger to men everywhere. Lord how he wished those four years, ten months and three weeks hadn't been so kind to her.

Suddenly, the plaintive cry of a child rent the quiet of the March midday. Just about to bolt into his carriage, Alex stilled, his gloved hand resting on the cold metal door of the barouche. Angling his head in the direction of the sound, he noted for the first time a hackney coach parked a fair distance behind his in the circular drive. No doubt *her* transport. And it appeared she hadn't come alone.

Without stopping to consider the injudiciousness of his actions, but compelled by a force beyond his control, Alex tossed the envelope onto the seat of his barouche and started toward the carriage, unsure of his purpose or what he hoped to learn.

He passed the idling driver without a glance, his mind preoccupied.

Whose child was it? Not that any of this mattered to him. It did not.

Despite his denials, he found himself peering into the dark green interior. Ensconced in the back was a woman, and tucked at her side sat a young boy, whom she spoke to in quiet, soothing tones.

"Is there something wrong with the child?" He was fully cognizant that he had no business asking the question and that the answer was none of his concern. None of that seemed to matter.

The woman's head snapped up at his voice, revealing a breathtakingly beautiful face belonging to a young woman of no more than seventeen or eighteen years. With brown spiraling curls peeping from beneath her bonnet and a complexion that resembled his own tanned several hours in the sun, it was apparent she was of mixed blood. A mulatto.

"No sir, we is—are waiting for his mama," she replied in an accent that proclaimed her American origins.

She had a child.

Although Alex had prepared himself for such an answer, upon actually hearing it, he stiffened, his breath escaping between his lips in an audible rush.

Swallowing hard, he stared at the boy who sat crowded against the girl, a fisted hand rubbing his eyes as if he'd just awakened. Then the boy tipped his head back to gaze up at him. Alex staggered back a step, his stomach feeling as if it had plunged clear down to his toes.

When he was five, his mother had commissioned a portrait of him and his older brother, Charles. Vivid in his recollection were the three lashes he'd received that day from his father for some small infraction. It had never taken much for him to raise his father's ire—it still did not. The portrait borne of that unhappy incident in his young life hung in the gallery at Windsor Place, the duke's seat and country estate. The child who peered up at him now, his blue eyes still drowsy with sleep, his hair a mop of blond, looping curls, could have been the six-year-old boy in the portrait.

The child peering up at him could have been his brother Charles.

Chapter Two

"Who do you want me to meet?" Katie asked, her voice
lowered to a whisper, ripe with curiosity. Then she gasped as if
a scandalous thought had just occurred to her. Her blue eyes
rounded as did her mouth. "Are you engaged? Have you a
fiancé waiting out in the carriage?"

Charlotte drew a deep breath, bracing herself. Her sister
wouldn't be happy. Above all else, this would be yet further
evidence of how much of her life she'd kept hidden from her.
"No, not a fiancé, but a—"

With the sort of timing only seen in a melodrama heavy
with suspense undertones, voices at the front entrance halted
her revelation. Charlotte turned and watched in shocked
disbelief as Alex, her maid Jillian, and Nicholas appeared in
the archway between the entrance hall and the vestibule,
Reeves currently nowhere in sight.

"I've found a child in need of his mother," Alex announced,
his gaze never wavering from hers as he approached.

Ever since Charlotte had made the decision to return to
England, she'd anticipated and prepared for this moment. Well
as much as a green soldier could prepare himself for the
realities of war. Nothing, however, could have prepared her for
the fear threatening to consume her whole. This was not how
she'd imagined Nicholas's introduction. She'd had a speech
prepared and had run through it a hundred times in her mind.
But like the only player on stage who'd lost their script and
forgotten the directions, she fell silent as her mind raced,
searching for the proper response. But search as she might, no
words would come.

"Mama." Her son's exclamation was accompanied by the

sound of tiny booted feet charging across the floor until he reached her side in a fever of breathlessness, his face stained with dried tears.

"Mama?" The same two-syllable word, yet her twin uttered it in an entirely different manner. "You have a son?"

Alex strode toward her with staggering nonchalance given he hadn't deigned to address her only minutes before. But his expression hadn't lost its cold inscrutability. His gaze darted to Nicholas, before settling on her.

Behind her, Katie sounded like an asthmatic trying to catch her breath but Charlotte could deal with only one calamity at a time. Alex had to come first.

Alex had always come first, a voice inside her whispered.

Settling her hands protectively on her son's shoulders, she met Alex's stare as air inched its way into her lungs.

I can do this. I must do this.

"When I heard him crying, I thought it best if I brought him inside," he said, halting in front of her. She could hear the condemnation in his tone and feel it emanating from his pores.

He spoke to her, yet still he did not greet her. Charlotte swallowed a lump of despair.

I cannot do this.

Nicholas tipped his head back and stared up at Alex, who at six-foot-two inches tall loomed above him like a dark angel.

"You have a son?" This time her sister's voice held more than a trace of pique and hurt. Briefly, Charlotte regarded Jillian, who appeared oblivious to the enfolding drama, her hazel eyes soaking in the grandeur of her surroundings with awe.

Angling her head over her shoulder, Charlotte met her sister's gaze. "Katie, I'm sorry." Explanations—as much as she could offer—would have to wait.

Truly, this was not how she had envisioned—had planned—the introduction of aunt to nephew.

"He's a handsome boy. I expect he looks like his father."

Turning back to him, Charlotte swallowed hard and felt the

burn of a guilty blush suffuse her face, not exactly certain how she should respond to Alex's remark. It was plainly spoken and lacking in artifice, some of which she might have expected given their history. But most people thought Nicholas resembled her with his dark blond locks and blue eyes. Most never bothered to look beyond those obvious similarities.

Alex was unlike anyone she had ever met, a fact she would be wise to remember.

"Yes, he does. Unfortunately, his father is no longer with us." There, she'd done it, the first lie, the seedling of a multitude more. But then it wasn't as if this was chaste, uncharted grounds. One would assume she'd be quite accomplished at it by now. She was unquestionably a connoisseur should lying be raised to an art form—if indeed it was not.

While her sister's indrawn breath scalded Charlotte's ears, Alex continued to stare at her, his thickly fringed eyes devoid of emotion, his expression positively deadpan. "So you married?"

Only the faintest inflection in his tone indicated it was a question, and nothing in his voice hinted that asking had caused his heart to contract in anguish, as hers had done. He sounded politely inquiring, expressing no great necessity to actually know.

But to utter that particular lie aloud—to Alex—was more than her conscience or heart could bear. There did exist a limit to her duplicity. Charlotte inclined her head in a jerky nod, unable to hold his gaze. But if she thought he might challenge her; that somehow he'd seen through the veil of her deception, she couldn't tell by his expression.

Alex glanced down at Nicholas and only then did she see an infinitesimal warming in his silver gray eyes. In a surprising move, he lowered to his haunches and extended his right hand to her son. Nicholas inched back against her skirts, shooting a quick look up at her as if to seek assurance that this strange man was indeed safe. Too bewildered by Alex's unexpected show of kindness to do anything else, Charlotte responded with another jerky nod.

Nicholas slowly lifted his hand to find it quickly enveloped in Alex's much larger one. "And your name, young man?"

Charlotte opened her mouth to answer, but it seemed her son had had the response primed and ready on the tip of his tongue.

"Nicholas."

"A pleasure to make your acquaintance, Nicholas," Alex said solemnly, giving her son's hand a firm yet gentle shake.

Who would have thought such an innocuous gesture could break a heart clean in two. Charlotte experienced the truth of it for herself.

"Thank you, sir."

"And how old are you?"

Charlotte's heartbeat thundered in her ears and her hand tightened on her son's slender shoulders. Before he could respond, she replied, "He will be four in July." Lie number two.

Releasing Nicholas's hand, Alex rose smoothly to his feet. "He's tall for three."

Her son was tall for four. He'd be tall like his father. A short silence followed his statement, as Charlotte could not bring herself to agree.

His gaze met hers. Guilt and a swell of wholly inappropriate emotions caused another wave of heat to flood her face in a mad rush.

Alex pulled out a gold fob and gave it a quick glance before returning it to his coat pocket. Inclining his head in a nod toward her son, he said, "It was a pleasure to meet you, Nicholas." He then directed his attention to Katie who had long gone silent behind her. "Good day, ladies."

The use of the term *ladies* should have signified her inclusion, but something in the fleeting look he gave her did not leave her with the feeling he wished her well at all. In fact, behind his impenetrable stare, she was certain he wished her a trip to hell and back—or perhaps he'd rather she not return.

For the second time in the span of a quarter hour, Alex took his leave of her and something inside her told her he'd do his utmost to avoid all future contact. She wanted to weep the same way she'd done when she had been the one to walk away all those years ago.

It was only at the distant click of the front door closing that Katie came to her side. "You were married and didn't say a word of it to me? Not in one of the twenty letters you've written over the years might you have mentioned a husband...and a son?" From her tone, it was difficult for Charlotte to discern whether her sister was more angry than hurt, but she estimated—or rather hoped—it was the former as that emotion was easier to deal with.

Nicholas turned and looked up to view his aunt. He became wide-eyed and began frantically tugging on the hand Charlotte had rested on his shoulder. "Mama, she looks like you," he exclaimed in a high voice.

With her eyes, Charlotte pleaded for her sister's understanding and cooperation. The last thing she wanted was to have *this* particular conversation in front of her son, her maid, and anyone else whose interest was piqued by a salacious bit of gossip.

Katie acknowledged her silent request with a terse nod before doing just as Alex had done by going down on her haunches in front of her nephew.

"Do you remember when mama told you that I had a sister who looked like me? Well, this is your Aunt Katie. Now be a good boy and say hello," Charlotte urged gently.

Tears gathered in her sister's eyes as she stared at Nicholas in wonder, completely enraptured.

"Hullo, Aunt Katie," he whispered, staring at her with the same sort of fixation.

Her sister's fingers skimmed his pink cheeks and chin in feather light brushes. "Hello, Nicholas," she said in a choked voice. "Would you mind terribly if I gave you a hug?"

Perhaps it was the familiarity of the face that eased

Nicholas's usual reticence with strangers, for he gave a shy nod of assent without seeking the assurance he'd sought from her when Alex had offered him his hand. Quickly he was enfolded in her sister's arms, his own trapped at his sides like a toy soldier. Nonetheless, he permitted her to hug him for a very long time.

The next hour passed in a blur of activity. Katie enthused over her nephew as if he were the greatest archeological find of all time. She hugged and petted him as much as Nicholas would permit, which was considerable given her son too seemed enthralled at the living and breathing creature whose face was the mirror image of his mother's.

Charlotte introduced Jillian to her sister. Relieved of her bonnet, the full glory of her maid's beauty caused Katie to halt and stare. A discernible blush appeared beneath Jillian's *café au lait* complexion. And Charlotte knew precisely what her sister was thinking; a servant that uncommonly pretty would be trouble in deuces and spades. But they would cope. They'd had to cope before.

Two footmen clad in liveries of the family colors, gold and green, were dispatched to collect their bags and trunks from the hackney. It was quickly determined that Nicholas would sleep in the nursery, and Jillian would sleep in the adjoining room until the children and their nanny returned. Charlotte would take her former bedchamber.

After they'd all eaten, Jillian insisted on putting a sleepy Nicholas down for his midafternoon nap. Charlotte dearly wished she could follow, but the look on her sister's face told her an explanation would not wait. The moment of reckoning had arrived.

Jillian and Nicholas had barely departed the small salon before Katie marched her down the hall and into the morning room. She steered her past the piano and harp, and dragged her down onto the chintz settee to take a seat beside her.

"You left because of what we learned about our mother, did you not?" No preambles. Her sister gave a whole new meaning to tackling difficulties head on.

Charlotte took a deep, fortifying breath, for she had to be convincing above all else. "That may have played some part in my decision to leave, but it wasn't the whole of it. I met someone two months prior to the wedding. We fell in love." In order to accurately affect the look of a woman in love, she thought of Alex.

Katie's jaw came unhinged, but soon shock gave way to disbelief. In the narrowing of her eyes, suspicion dawned clear and blue.

"I know it sounds extraordinary, does it not? I mean Alex had been the love of my life. But I realized what I felt for him was a blind devotion. A case of mad passion. Perhaps even the want of something I believed I could never have. I mean truly, Alex interested in me? I was not at all the kind of woman who could hold the attentions of a man like him for long. Peter—that was his name—was more…suited to me."

The disbelief faded from her sister's eyes and the puzzlement returned.

Relieved at the progress she'd made, Charlotte pressed on. "In the end, although I cared deeply for Alex, a marriage between us would have been a mistake. But I should not have waited so long to tell him and should have had the courage to tell him to his face. For that I will always be more ashamed and sorry than you can ever imagine."

"But how could you leave me? Have you any idea what we—what *I*—went through these past years without you? Without being able to even write to you? One-sided correspondence might suit your purposes but it didn't mine."

Upon her return to England, Charlotte had planned on telling her sister about the dowager's letter. But with the woman gone, what good would it serve? Whose good would it serve? Katie had had a difficult enough time in Society.

"If you only knew how much I regret what I did. But it had

to be that way. I knew if I told you of my plans, you would tell James. And if James knew, it was only a matter of time before Alex discovered. That wasn't a risk I could take."

"But even if Alex did discover you had fallen in love with someone else, it would not have been the end of the world. You didn't have to run away."

Charlotte couldn't very well tell her it would indeed have been the end of the world as they all knew it. Alex would have seen right through her lies and gently coerced the truth from her. Following would have been a Rutherford family scandal that would have sent earthquake-like tremors through the *ton*, and made their illegitimate birth a trivial matter by comparison. And Alex's titles would have been tarnished by his association with her. Everyone would have suffered. And then of course there was Nicholas....

"But why—"

"Katie darling," Charlotte implored, taking her sister's hand in hers. "No more questions on this subject for now. Please."

"Forgive me if I assumed as your sister, your *twin*, I would receive more consideration."

"Later, I will explain it all. Why I allowed so much time to pass. Why I didn't tell you about Peter and Nicholas earlier. I promise I will." Charlotte gave her sister's hand a gentle squeeze. "But please, don't press me on it now."

Impatience and exasperation flashed in Katie's eyes. A sure sign she would continue to press the issue. Surprisingly enough, instead of a relentless push for answers, a welcome silence pervaded the room.

"From your maid's accent, I gather you've been residing in America?"

Charlotte gave a brief nod, relieved her sister had opted for a safer topic.

"James had investigators searching throughout the Continent but I don't believe he ever thought to look there." Katie spoke as if to herself. "Have you come to stay?" she then asked, her cerulean eyes anxious and hopeful.

A heavy sigh escaped Charlotte's lips. That was a question she had yet to answer herself. She would like nothing better than to remain. The only person she would truly miss if she left America was Lucas, and he traveled to London on business often enough for them to remain in contact.

"I'm not certain."

Katie opened her mouth, and then quickly snapped it shut.

"Katie, will you tell me about Alex?" Charlotte asked in an abrupt change of topic. The question had festered inside her for too many years. She *had* to know.

Her sister's gaze sharpened just enough for Charlotte to don her mask and exclaim defensively, "What? I may not have married him, but I did care for him deeply. Naturally I care how he fared."

After a pause, Katie's features softened. "Well, to say your leaving hit him hard would be a vast understatement. He was like—well, like I'd never seen him before. Frankly, he turned into a man I never care to see again."

A needlelike sting of pain accompanied every beat of Charlotte's heart upon hearing those words. She'd wanted to know but now she wasn't certain. But her insatiable need to fill the gaps of those years without him urged her to delve in true masochistic fashion.

"What did he do?"

Katie swallowed, momentarily looking down at their joined hands. "The truth isn't pretty and may be difficult for you to hear. Are you sure you want to know?" she asked, looking Charlotte in the eye.

Charlotte held a breath and nodded, steeling herself for what was to come.

After a prolonged sigh, Katie began. "He was already at the church when James told him. He left soon after. Derek described him as catatonic. James was the one to inform the guests the wedding was off. Of course, he was also frantic with worry. We all were." Katie lowered her gaze as if reliving the pain of that moment. Charlotte gave her hand a comforting squeeze, attempting to convey just how sorry she was to have caused them even a moment of distress.

"After a day or so, Alex joined James, Thomas, Derek, Mr. Wendell and Lord Bradford in the search."

Charlotte briefly closed her eyes. These were the things she'd tried so hard not to think about. Her family, her friends searching for her. Worrying themselves over her. Only the knowledge that she'd saved them from certain social ostracism and grief made the ordeal bearable. And of course, then Nicholas had come, needing her just as much as she'd needed him.

"Oh, they were all quite discreet about the matter. To this day everyone believes you're residing somewhere in the north of England. James wanted it so. The gossip surrounding your departure must have kept every printing press running nonstop for well over a year. He had no desire to feed the frenzy by admitting that we had no idea where you were. In any case, when your first letter arrived two weeks later, Alex abandoned the search. I believe it was then he was convinced you had left of your own volition. It probably would have been easier for him if he thought you'd been taken by force."

Katie sighed and extricated her hand from hers. Charlotte instantly missed the warmth of her touch. "After hearing you were settling into your new home, he seemed to close himself off entirely. He wasn't sad anymore he was just...empty. Then he started drinking. And carousing."

Charlotte bolted to her feet, her skirt sweeping the low center table of knotted pine. She couldn't bear to hear anymore. The pain inside her was excruciating and blinding. "I see. You needn't tell me anymore," she said, trying not to choke on her words. She failed utterly.

Katie arose, regarding her with a look of concern. "It is difficult to hear is it not? It was even more difficult to watch, and I didn't witness the half of it. You have no idea how many years James, Derek and Thomas spent beside themselves trying to save Alex from himself."

The image of Alex lost in the stupor of drink as he caroused about town in quest of a warm, willing female almost brought her to her knees. And he'd no doubt found them to be had by the droves. But the images persisted unforgiving and relentless. She bit back a wave of nausea.

"Darling, you look pea green. Are you all right?"

Determinedly, Charlotte mentally shook it off, opening her eyes to take in the worried crease on her sister's brow. "You did warn me it would be hard to hear." Agonizing, excruciating were more apt terms.

"Alex loved you. He took it exceptionally hard."

"And now? How is he now?" Silly as it was, what she really wanted to ask was did he ever talk about her? When had he stopped missing her? Within weeks? Months? Years?

Her sister gave a wan smile. "Well, he does not drink spirits anymore. Not one drop. Gave it up entirely."

Thank God! Her guilt was suffocating enough. "Has he married?" Charlotte hadn't meant to ask, in her heart was afraid to know. But there it was, her insatiable need to know everything about him exerting its control.

"Would it assuage your guilt and make you feel better to know he's married with a brood of children?" Katie asked, compassion in her eyes.

God no. It would destroy her. But she had no claims on him. She was the last person who should begrudge him happiness, even in the arms of another woman.

Turning from her sister, Charlotte advanced to the bay window. "Perhaps a little." This time she couldn't look her sister in the eye when she voiced the lie. Moreover, it was how her sister would expect her to feel given she'd just admitted she hadn't truly been in love with him.

"Then you'll be disappointed to hear he remains unmarried. But the rumor is he will soon be paying court to Lady Mary, the Earl of Cranford's daughter. It appears not only are the earl and his wife keen on the union, but the duchess as well. They hope to see them wed before year's end."

Charlotte couldn't see the beauty in the profusion of budding daisies and violets landscaping the front lawn for pain and grief swelled her heart. Ready to send her to her knees. But truly, it was a small miracle he wasn't already wed with several children by now. Perfectly legitimate aristocratic children.

"I see." Charlotte paused. "Well I wish him well."

And she did. She sincerely did.

It would be utterly selfish of her to begrudge him happiness. And by God she wasn't selfish. Her absence from his life attested to that. *Marrying him* would have been selfish.

"Charlotte, do you know what I believe?" Katie said softly from behind. She hadn't even heard her approach.

Charlotte turned. Her sister took her cold hand in hers and looked her directly in the eye. "I don't for a moment believe there was ever another man—this husband. And I don't believe you left because you didn't love Alex."

Charlotte went stiff, her spine ramrod straight, feeling vulnerable and exposed. "What?"

Katie's mouth curved but it wasn't a smile. It was entirely too sad to be described as such. "My dear, do give me some credit. I've known you all your life. Perhaps, the story you've so convincingly rehearsed would have fooled strangers, acquaintances, and perhaps even James and Missy. But this is me. We occupied the same womb for nine months and bedchambers for fifteen years. You would have walked barefoot across the desert for Alex. And as for finding someone else? You had eyes for only him, which would have made that impossible. You loved him then and I'm quite convinced the years apart haven't changed that one little bit."

It should have been a diatribe, for Charlotte had lied to her, but it was not. Katie had exposed her web of well-rehearsed lies in calm, gentle tones, her only proof being her sister's intimate knowledge of her.

Thoughts of issuing an emphatic denial flitted through her mind but the lure of understanding in Katie's eyes had her head dropping as if her neck could no longer support its weight. Her admission conveyed the truth without a single spoken word.

"Nicholas is Alex's son, is he not?"

Chapter Three

Alex returned home and executed a swift change of clothes. His waistcoat suffered the loss of three of its four shanked, brass buttons. His rage ripped his linen shirt near the seam of the arm. He savaged the button closure of his trousers with his impatience. His drawers were the lone garment to survive the ordeal unscathed. He tamped down his anger long enough to ensure donning his riding clothes was a much less destructive affair.

He made good time getting to the stables, his long strides clashing with hard earth. Minutes later he sat bent over Shalais, his favorite Arabian mare, his gloved hands closed tight about the reins, flying across Reading's flat, grassy terrain with the wind at his back.

With his every labored breath and every stretch of dirt kicked up by Shalais's hooves, he tried not to think about *her*. But since the moment he'd left, his attempts at this had been wholly unsuccessful. Her image and the memories would not go willingly into the dark recesses of his mind, refusing to be bowed by the strength of his will.

Little by little, they seeped back into the forefront of his thoughts as his gray-stoned manor house shrank against the backdrop of a deceptively cloudless, sunlit sky. She had returned, bringing with her ugly and unforgiveable lies, effectively darkening the skies like a swarm of locusts.

Dusty-rose lips, just as soft and full as he remembered from countless dreams, looked too tempting to be the vehicle of such egregious lies. But those same lips had lied to him before. *I love you. Yes, Alex, I'll marry you. I can't imagine my life without you.*

With a squeeze of his thighs, Alex urged Shalais into a full-out gallop, trying to expend himself physically to quell the lure of oblivion a glass of alcohol could bring. He needed exhaustion enough to prevent him from the insanity of barreling a path through heavily wooded trees and underbrush to return to Rutherford Manor and force the truth from those same lying lips.

For years his feelings for her had drifted on the plane of indifference. He ceased to care where she was, what she did, and he never allowed himself to even venture near thoughts of with whom. Her return upended his long-dormant emotions. He'd never thought he'd ever feel this deeply again, whether it be in anger or love. Today she'd proven him wrong as she'd done so adroitly in the past.

It galled him that after all these years she still had *that* power over him. That despite everything she'd done, she was the only woman who could turn him inside out with just her presence.

But, he vowed, this time would be different. If the last five years had taught him anything, it was that only a fool didn't learn from his mistakes.

To his face and behind gloved hands and silk fans, he'd been called self-destructive, boorish and unfeeling. But they'd never accused him of being a fool and he'd make damn sure it remained that way.

He returned to the house two hours later sweaty and hot. He was greeted by his rather anxious-looking butler, Alfred, who approached him the moment Alex stepped a dusty booted foot in the corridor leading to the main part of the house.

Alfred's powdered wig and severe black garb should have demanded a mien of stoicism, instead of the wringing-of-the-hands look on his face.

"My lord, Lord Cranford is awaiting you in the withdrawing room." Alfred had a tendency to speak as if he'd lived a century ago.

Alex quirked a brow. "Pardon?" he asked sharply, taking a

moment to digest his shock. *What the hell is he doing here?* He almost blurted the question, but good manners—at least the vestiges of those he still ascribed to—prevented him from doing so.

"My lord, he was quite insistent on awaiting your return."

The Earl of Cranford, Lady Mary's father, wasn't someone Alex wished to entertain today of all days. He'd no desire to entertain a solitary soul, truth be told.

"Please tell him I'll be with him shortly. As you can see, I'm not fit for company," Alex replied with a dismissive nod.

"Yes, sir," Alfred said with a bow before he strode off.

Twenty minutes later, Alex presented himself in the drawing room, freshly bathed and dressed from head to toe in cotton and wool in a brown as somber as his mood.

"Ah, Cartwright," Lord Cranford said upon his entrance, slowly rising to his feet with the help of a wooden cane, his bare hand proffered in greeting. "I hope I haven't inconvenienced you by calling without an invitation." His jowls quivered from the force of his smile, which stretched across a small, narrow face unbalanced by the leftward hook of his nose.

Alex forced a smile, taking the earl's hand in a brief handshake. "I hope you weren't terribly inconvenienced by the wait," he said, smoothly evading the question.

"Think nothing of it. I passed the time comfortably. I hope you won't mind if I sit. My knees have been paining me all day. A sure sign of rain tomorrow." The earl renewed his place on the brushed-velvet sofa and although Alex would have preferred to stand, he followed suit and took up a seat in a wing-backed chair.

"Can I offer you something to drink or perhaps something to eat?" Alex asked.

Lord Cranford dismissed his offer with a negligent toss of his hand, the diamond on his signet ring glinting as it caught the sunlight pouring through the window behind him. "Your man saw to my needs. I could not eat another bite."

Which meant his wait had been considerable, possibly over an hour. "So to what do I owe this call, my lord?"

The earl cleared his throat, straightened his legs with a slight wince and shot a look about the spacious drawing room before returning his gaze to Alex. "Our families have been acquainted for many years now. Why, you've known my Mary since she was just a child."

"Almost her entire twenty-one years," Alex agreed blithely. Although the acquaintance had never been a particularly close one. He'd already been attending Eton when she was born. Their interaction over the years had been infrequent at best. It was only during the prior year that he'd taken any real notice of her.

But the earl confirmed that Alex hadn't been wrong in his thoughts. He'd come to press his suit on his daughter's behalf.

"Yes, yes indeed, a good while. My Mary is quite a beauty, is she not?" he asked, inclining his head toward Alex as if to compel him to agree.

"Yes, quite lovely." An inescapable fact.

Of late, his mother had become more insistent that it was time he married and produced an heir. Lady Mary, a dark-haired beauty whose lineage was said to trace back to William the Conqueror, had been selected as the ideal candidate to fit the future Duchess of Hastings role. Alex had given the matter great thought. A month ago, he'd decided to court her—had had every intention of commencing the courtship. But a day's delay had slipped quickly and all too easily, until soon he could count the delay by weeks instead of days. Now, given the change in circumstances, he was more than a little relieved he hadn't done a thing. A courtship and worse yet, a betrothal would have been a nightmare of a predicament to extricate himself from.

Lord Cranford made a pleased sound, like the purr of a tiger, deep in his throat. He smiled again, showing off a row of white, slightly crooked teeth. "It is your parents, mine and the countess's greatest wish that our families are united. We believe Mary would make you a wonderful duchess. And I'm sure you are aware that my daughter comes with quite a substantial dowry. Not to say, my good man," he hastened to add in a jovial tone, "that you are in need of it. Why, to your fortune, you no doubt see it as but a paltry sum."

Alex's mouth twitched, not quite a smile or a frown. The earl had flown through the courtship and spoke as if they were already betrothed. And truly, since when had thirty thousand pounds ever been considered paltry? Lord Cranford had all the subtlety of a mallet and wielded it with the grace of a lumberjack. But then he *was* well acquainted with the duke.

"My lord, are you asking me whether I have given any consideration to courting your daughter or demanding that I do in fact court her?"

A wash of red suffused a complexion that probably hadn't been touched by sunlight in years. The earl appeared taken aback and didn't speak for several moments, eyeing Alex as if attempting to gauge his true feelings on the matter.

"My daughter is much sought after. I'm merely urging you to strike while the iron's hot, as they say." He said it with all the pomposity of a father who knew his daughter's worth.

Indeed, thirty thousand pounds.

"Many men have already approached me for her hand," the earl went on to elaborate. "She would, of course, be partial to your attentions, which is why this would be a good time for you to press your advantage."

In other words, you have the advantage because you are excessively wealthy and heir to one of the oldest and most powerful dukedoms in all of England.

Alex had long since become familiar with aristocratic speak; the polite way to express one's single-minded ambition for money and position.

Alex tempered a wry smile as he was certain it would not be well received. "Then I would urge your daughter not to refuse any further marriage offers on my account."

Lord Cranford's brows lowered and his mouth flattened into

a line. His hand tightened on the curved ivory handle of his cane. What followed was a silence that strained every bit of civility in his narrow-eyed countenance.

"Are you telling me you have no interest at all in my daughter?"

"As much as I admire her, I don't believe we would make a good match." Another face appeared in his mind's eye. One with dark gold ringlets and eyes the blue of the Mediterranean Sea. How apropos she'd returned and resumed where she'd left off—wreaking havoc on almost everything in his life. But this time he was prepared. He'd not be fooled by her bewitching innocence that had so entranced him before.

Alex could tell by the dispirited look in Lord Cranford's brown eyes that the man would like nothing better than to be able to change his mind. "You won't find another better than my Mary," he warned, as if Alex had just turned down the treasure of a lifetime. "Your mother said as much."

Then perhaps my mother should marry Lady Mary herself.

"I shall consider that my loss." Lady Mary was lovely if somewhat frivolous and would have made an adequate wife, carrying out the duties of a duchess with aristocratic aplomb. But many others could fill the role just as nicely. He'd have to select someone after he'd concluded the whole affair with *her*.

"Mary is still young. Perhaps—"

"With all due respect, Lord Cranford, but on this matter, my mind is set."

"Your parents—"

"My parents do not have a say in who I choose to marry," Alex said, hardening his tone.

The earl stared at him and then as if realizing the futility of his mission, sighed and making full use of his cane, rose slowly to his feet.

"Very well. I shall take my leave. I have taken up enough of your time."

Alex stood, relieved the visit was at a close. "Then I shall bid you *adieu*, my lord." Alex turned to one of the footman who never ventured far when he entertained guests—although that itself was a rarity—and now stood framed in the opening of the drawing room. "Please see the earl out."

With a nod to Lord Cranford, Alex quietly departed. He then made his way to his study, a place where he could bar the outside world from entry. But he didn't bar the door, he merely closed it, instinctively crossing the room to the sideboard. He pulled himself up with a vigorous shake of his head just as his hand reached for the crystal decanter, the fingers of his other hand already curved in anticipation of the glass.

The decanter was empty. The glass was naught but a decorative piece of etched crystal. Both had gone unused for two years. Alex abruptly dropped his arms, curled his hands into fists and strode over to the black leather armchair.

Memories of why he sought comfort in this particular room assailed him. It was in this very room he'd so often found solace—oblivion—at the bottom of a glass of rum. When all the rum was gone, he'd start on the whiskey. He had spent hours in a day—days on end—sinking deeper and deeper under its spell.

But not anymore. But damn, he needed a drink.

Damn her!

Tugging off his necktie, Alex pushed himself back into the sloping pocket of the high-backed chair. The duke would think he's been handed heaven on earth when he learned about Nicholas. A living replica of his late beloved son would be like a dream come true. His mother, in her own dramatic fashion, would clutch her hands to her chest and cry copious tears. The *ton*, of course, would not only relish the scandal, they'd all but wallow in it. Something else to befall the future Duke of Hastings whose misfortunes had begun even before he'd been jilted at the altar. They'd practically rub their hands in glee.

Damn her!

This time, Alex refused to allow it to get that far.

"Alfred!"

Seconds later, his butler appeared in the doorway. "Yes,

sir?"

"Where is Conrad?" Alex inquired of his steward.

"He's—"

"Never mind that. Instruct him to arrange a meeting for me with Mr. Reynolds on the morrow. Tell him the matter is urgent." Bloody hell, at the moment not only did he require the counsel of a solicitor, he needed a vicar. Not to mention a constable to prevent him from wringing her deceitful, lying neck the next time they met, which would be soon enough.

"I shall inform him directly, sir," Alfred replied, but made no move to leave.

Alex shot him an arched look. The last time his butler had worn that particular look of consternation was two and a half years ago, during one of Alex's more memorable drinking episodes.

For failing to monitor the inventory of the rapidly diminishing alcohol closely enough, Alfred had suffered the indignity of having his capabilities, and worse yet, his hearing called into question.

Didn't you hear me when I told you I needed more rum? If you weren't so quick to run off, you'd take heed of half the things I ask of you.

Sober, Alex had apologized for his tirade. That had been three days later.

Now, Alfred never missed a word or a syllable, always fastidiously awaiting a nod of dismissal before departing.

Alex curtly obliged him.

Charlotte's chemise was not removed but caressed from her trembling body. Cotton linens woven so tightly, she thought it was satin or silk against her skin as she lay spread like a wanton on her back, her hands kneading and caressing sinewy muscles and damp flesh.

His finger traced her nipple in slow, delicious concentration. Her back arched as her fingers bit deeper into his shoulders.

Heat ripped a fiery path from her breasts, down the dip in her belly, and then set fire to the notch between her thighs. The wanting was excruciating madness, yet she knew she would die if he stopped.

"Does it feel good? Do you like it?" he asked, his voice rough with desire, his gray eyes dark with passion.

His breath fluttered on her nape and his finger continued its erotic dance with her nipple, reducing her to inarticulate gasps and moans.

She yearned. She writhed. So desperate was she to find surcease from the ache building and spiraling inside her, she was ready to beg for completion.

"Open for me," he said, before lowering his head and drawing a pink, beaded nipple into his mouth. His cheeks hollowed as he began to suckle. The chamber echoed her cry of delight and her moans of satisfaction. With knees bent and her feet flat on the mattress, her legs fell open in eager anticipation and welcome.

Easing his finger into her center, he found her slick, hot and tight. Soon another finger joined. Charlotte thrust her fisted hand into her mouth to muffle a scream. His withdrawal caused pleasure to scorch every inch of her sensitive inner flesh. Then he plunged back in. Helplessly, her hips began to move in counterpoint to his sumptuous thrusts. Soon his fingers weren't enough for either of them.

While he suckled her breast, pausing often to nip at her tip with teeth and tongue, he replaced his fingers with his erection. There was no easing or inexorable push, just a hard thrust, seating himself as far as he could go. Overwhelmed by the force of his possession, Charlotte whimpered, and then let out a gusty sigh of relief, of unadulterated pleasure. Her inner muscles clamped down on him hard.

He groaned low and long. "God, you feel so good." He wore an expression that ran the line between exquisite pleasure and torture. But Charlotte couldn't halt the undulation of her hips as she urged him deeper, hotter. Her soft pants filled the sex-humid air. His ragged groans joined hers as he set a rhythmic pace, thrusting heavily into her with long, smooth strokes. His tongue devoured her like a lusty invader, kissing her until he learned all the hidden crevices of her mouth. Charlotte reciprocated wholeheartedly, just as hungry for him as he was for her.

For endless minutes, they mated with the intensity and avariciousness of new lovers, or old lovers who'd been too long apart. The chamber walls echoed their whimpers, moans and the hard slapping of damp flesh, intent on the climb to satisfaction.

As the precipice grew closer, he tore his mouth from hers, panting and making guttural sounds deep in his throat. His hands made forays around her breast and belly, roamed down farther and found the hidden nub above her moist folds, and flicked it as he continued to pound into her, obliterating her every thought but the need for more. More of him. More of his touch. More of everything.

He shifted his hips, and the new angle and his finger on the source of her desire catapulted her up until she was soaring and exploding in a shuddering mass. She convulsed and heaved while he found his own release, before her glide back down to earth.

"Oh God, Alex. Alex," she chanted into his neck when he slumped atop her, his chest heaving for his next breath. Her hands clutched his muscled shoulders and slid down to the sweaty expanse of his back to pull him close.

And then he was gone.

Her arms lay empty on the tangled white bed sheets. Charlotte reached out again with an urgency that bordered on desperation, endeavoring to stop the panic from taking over. Again she found nothing. That's when the pain came and she embraced it with harsh, desolate sobs.

"Alex. Alex. Alex," she cried out in the dark.

Charlotte came awake with a start, her heart a stampede of horses thundering over America's wide-open plains. It took her a moment to get her bearings and catch her breath. She was in England in her old bedchamber. Tears wound their way down her temples.

She had dreamed him again. Alex and their last time together. The tears rolled their course faster. The dream now came with a frequency that frightened her. For two weeks now, it had made its nightly sojourn into her sleep.

She'd woken up hot, her senses acute and overwrought, but now the coldness seeped into every pore despite the warmth of her bedchamber. The dreams always left her this way, chilled and dissatisfied. But tonight there was something else, a prickly uneasiness. It was then she realized the source of her disquiet wasn't the residual effects of her dream but something based firmly in reality.

Charlotte heard a slight movement to her right. She bolted upright, her hands clutching the counterpane close to her chest. In the darkened chamber, she could only make out the shape of someone—a man—reposed in the chair close to the fireplace.

Fear so effectively gripped her by the throat, all she could manage was a gurgled exhalation, not the bloodcurdling scream that would bring in the cavalry.

"Don't scream," a male voice instructed her softly.

For a moment Charlotte was convinced her ears were playing some sort of cruel trick on her. Had she conjured his voice up from her dream? Was she that bad off?

He rose from the chair with an unmistakable ease and grace. Alex.

Seconds later, he was standing by the side of her bed, half his face illumed by the faint light from the fire burning on the grate. Not like the Alex of her dreams. This Alex was solid and real, and darkly forbidding.

"Alex—Alex what are you doing here?" Charlotte barely managed to croak out the question, hot all over once again.

She could feel his silver gaze scoring her, unreadable, unwavering. After a nerve-wracking pause, he asked in a voice both chilling and calm, "When did you intend to inform me that you bore me a son?"

Chapter Four

Charlotte didn't know what she'd expected him to say under such circumstances but what had emerged from his mouth did not even come close. The panic now flooding her left her disoriented, breathless, her mind spinning furiously as she debated how best to respond. Or rather, thought up a plausible lie.

How can he know?

While she sat staring at him in stunned silence, he casually lit the gas lamp on her bedside table. It was then she had a clear view of his face, his eyes burning into her when he turned from his task. Despite his tone, that calm masculine cadence, his form was taut and he stood too still. As if he was restraining some violent, volatile emotion from erupting and cracking his outward calm.

"I—I'm not sure what—"

"I swear, if you lie to me again, I'll make you pay in ways you could never imagine."

Such a threat should have been either raised in fury, or delivered low and menacing. Alex's voice rose not a notch while it maintained an even tone. His eyes, however, told an altogether different story. They flashed like lightning strikes displayed in the kind of thunderstorm that could split and fell a hundred-year oak and bring down rain enough to flood a town from cellar to roof.

How could he know with such unshakeable certainty? She had expressly told him Nicholas was three, which made fathering him impossible. But it was obvious he did not believe that.

With her eyes now fully adjusted to the gas light, she could also see his swarthy complexion held a dark-red hue beneath the surface. Charlotte swallowed as she debated how exactly she should respond. How *could* she respond?

"He—"

Alex must have sensed her coming denial because in the next instant he loomed above her, his proximity shrinking her back into her pillows. His face was all chiseled planes of rage, his lips curled back against his teeth.

"Don't you dare lie to me. Not again. Not ever again," he growled, deep and dark.

His tone frightened her, as if a mere gossamer thread of control checked a bottomless well of rage.

"Alex." His name emerged a whispered plea, a calming tone of reason.

He pulled slightly back, enough to bring the full of him into sharp focus. Drawing in a breath, his gaze raked her form and it was as if fire and ice had decided to do battle. In a rare show of glacial strength, ice won.

Charlotte shivered in response and the skin on her arms gave way to gooseflesh.

His mouth tipped at one corner but in nothing that came close to a smile. Perhaps its not-so-distant relation irony or mockery.

"Had Charles not been traveling the year we were betrothed, you would have met him," he murmured in the same conversational tone one might adopt when discussing one of life's mundane trivialities. "One day, I shall show you a portrait of him when he was Nicholas's age. Had I not known it an impossibility, I might have mistaken Nicholas for his."

Even if Charlotte had the ability to speak, she had no idea what she would say. Denial at this juncture would be pointless. She'd been found out.

"When was he born?" he asked quietly, bracing his hands on either side of her face and closing the gap between them. "And this time I want the truth."

As if the truth was alien to her tongue, she started to speak several times before the word finally emerged breathless and broken. "January."

He said nothing for several seconds, just held her captive in his flat, empty stare before lowering his head until his mouth brushed the lobe of her right ear. "See, that wasn't so hard was it?"

Arousal, razor-sharp in its intensity, cut her next breath as sensation spiraled at the fleeting touch of his lips and the warmth of his breath at her ear. Dear God, it had been so long since she'd been so intimately touched. Dreams were, after all, just dreams. Reality was...intoxicating.

He straightened and stood towering above her, his broad shoulders blocking much of the light. She felt his absence like a cold draft on feverish flesh. A sound, a mocking laugh, rumbled from his throat. "You've been back not yet one full day and you look starved for it."

The *it* being the cause of her quickened breath and the way her nipples perked to lurid attention. The act of sexual congress.

Not quite finished provoking her, he continued on, his voice all *faux* commiseration. "The journey back must have been long."

Despite his words and tone, his gaze ran hotly over her. She wasn't alone in her physical response. He was just slightly more adept at concealing his. Her gaze dropped to the discernible bulge in the front of his trousers. Or perhaps not.

Turning her head didn't stop the heat from flooding her face in shame. She hated that he knew. She hated that she'd reacted to him like a woman deprived of a man's touch for five long years.

"Were you dreaming of me?" It wasn't so much a question as a silky taunt.

Charlotte didn't answer and didn't dare look at him. She couldn't bear to see the smug smile accompanying his words.

"Did you know you cried out my name in your sleep?" No longer did his tone hold that thread of jeer, it was now dark and husky.

She edged her head in his direction. He was staring down at her, his eyes half-mast, his bottom lip shiny as if he'd given it a surreptitious swipe with his tongue. While he held her gaze, he lowered himself to her side, the rub of his thigh now pressed along the length of hers. Fine Indian muslin proved pitilessly insufficient protection against the senses-reeling effect of the contact, even with his leg encased in black wool.

"What was I doing in your dream? Was I kissing you like this?" His head ascended and his mouth rubbed gently over hers. Charlotte was too bemused and breathlessly aroused to do anything but part her lips.

What started as a soft rub became something more all too quickly. Charlotte barely had time to savor the ecstasy of tasting him again, the slide of his lips against hers, before his hands cupped her face, angling her for a deeper, more thorough kiss.

His tongue wanted more than her acquiescence, it thrust and parried, demanding full engagement. She gave that and more, twining hers with his, seeking, sliding, demanding, meeting him stroke for delicious stroke. He made a sound in his throat. Raw desire with a hint of impatience.

Charlotte surrendered to feeling, submerged in pleasure so deep, so completely consuming she couldn't think beyond the tangle of tongues and the hand that now moved from the curve of her cheek, gliding over the line of her neck, the hollow of her collarbone, to the swell of her breast.

Her nipple pebbled even further in anticipation of his touch. A whimper escaped her lips when it came, the flick of his finger over her nightdress. Moisture pooled between her thighs and heat washed her from head to toe, settling to torment the bundle of nerves where she needed him the most.

Suddenly his kiss grew fierce; he wasn't playing with her anymore—if he ever had been. His tongue swept her like a windstorm, his kiss wild and out of control. Charlotte welcomed the pressure, the scrape of his bristled cheeks against her sensitive skin, the clash of his teeth against hers. Pushing the barrier of the light blue fabric aside, he first cupped then squeezed the roundness of her breast. On a labored breath, he tore his mouth from hers, his attention now wholly focused on the white mound of firm flesh filling his hand. With a glazed look in his eyes, his head began to descend.

Then with the violent shake of his head that acted like a dousing of ice-cold water, he was on his feet. So swiftly did his expression change, Charlotte could hardly believe she was looking at the same man of seconds before. Alex was cold again; no give to his expression or form.

She wanted to sink inside herself, but instead made haste to right her clothing and conceal her breast. Her hands trembled at the task. And worse yet, she was still shamefully aroused.

"Were I the same fool for you as I was five years ago, I could not have stopped myself from taking you." He paused, his gaze drifting to her nipple, now covered but clearly outlined under the thin fabric. His mouth quirked. "And you would have allowed it, wouldn't you? Has it been that long, since you've had a man between your thighs?"

His words bit like gravel into her skin, as he'd no doubt intended them to, but she remained silent, accepting his treatment of her as part and parcel of her due.

"Don't think to seduce me. It will not work. But as you have *my* son, what is between us is far from over." If his words were not ominous enough, his narrowed eyes and rigid jaw punctuated his feelings on the matter.

Seduce him? It had been he who had kissed her. But for her own wanton response, Charlotte could do little else but swallow and nod in mute affirmation, embarrassment lingering in her fiery cheeks and lash-veiled eyes.

He turned to go and then stopped as if confronted by a wall. Angling his head, he pinned her with a stare as bitter and icy as the north England winters. "And by God, if you run again and make me chase you—because now that I know you have my son, I *will* chase you to the ends of the earth this time—I'll make sure you regret it for the rest of your days. Am I clear?"

Part of her wanted to do just that, run from the man he'd become. But an even larger part could not countenance the thought of being parted from him again.

"I'll not run." Her voice was scratchy and barely above a whisper.

"See that you don't." With that, he slipped from the room, disappearing into the dark hallway without hardly making a sound.

Another minute of silence passed before Charlotte looked down and noticed the stark whiteness of her knuckles as she clutched her bed sheets. Unclenching her hands, she forced herself to relax. She inhaled a deep breath and pulled the counterpane around her, enveloping herself in its warmth.

The risk had always been there that Alex would have deduced the truth about Nicholas. Her son could be a chatterbox when he got started and something—namely his true age—could easily have slipped. Hadn't her sister guessed the truth, repudiating the existence of her conveniently dead husband with facile confidence?

What had followed was Charlotte's retelling of those pivotal events that had forever changed their lives. A guilt-ridden tale ripe with omissions and half-truths.

She'd told her sister of the crushing weight of responsibility that had accosted her. When she'd agreed to marry Alex, he'd been the second son of a duke. But months after their betrothal Charles had died and suddenly she was to be a duchess. The culmination of it had all been too much. By the time she'd realized she was with child, she was so far from home and sick because of the pregnancy, she'd barely left her flat for four months thereafter. How could she return to England heavy with child? And then there had been her baby to consider. She could not have made the journey back pregnant and alone.

Charlotte thought her reasons all terribly valid and plausible. She certainly would not subject her sister to the truth, unvarnished and with the unsavory overtones of a penny dreadful.

But Lord, what was she to do now? Or perhaps a more fitting question was what would he do? Since he'd laid eyes on her, he treated her like something worse than leprosy. And then he had kissed her with a passion even he couldn't disguise. She desperately wanted the kiss to mean something; an instinctive reaction to a passion long denied. She'd settle for lust if she must.

But while her heart craved the happily ever after of reunited lovers, her brain, ever the pragmatist, told her he'd made his feelings for her clear. He despised her. He resented her. He would never forgive her. To him, not only had she abandoned him on the most momentous of days, but she was now the enemy who had denied him his child.

Alex exited the bedchamber and glanced around the dimly lit hall. He knew every nook and shadowed corner of the manor. He'd played in it often enough as a child, and had frequented it plenty in the years Rutherford had resumed residence there.

All was quiet, everyone asleep in their beds—save Charlotte. And if he'd joined her in hers, he'd have had her up until dawn attempting to slake five years of hunger. As it was, Alex would have a time of it himself when he returned to his bed alone.

Having managed his midnight *visit* without discovery, he ought to make his escape as quickly as he could using the most direct route. But imprudence won out over caution.

Silent as a thief, he made his way to the wing housing the children's rooms and paused in front of the nursery door.

Had the door been ajar, nothing could have stopped him from pushing it quietly open and peering inside to soak in the sight of *his son*, for Alex was certain Nicholas was asleep on the other side.

But he could only permit his imprudence to lead him so far

astray and Alex could not be selfish and risk waking him. Now that he knew of Nicholas's existence, they had a lifetime at their disposal to become properly acquainted in the manner of fathers and sons.

Alex turned from the door and soundlessly entered the narrowed hall of the servants' sleeping quarters and then proceeded down the stairs to the ground floor.

Five minutes later, he was riding down the narrow trail in the rear of the house that led to his property miles down the road. The night was cool, the air the kind one welcomed when drawing a breath.

She had cried his name in her sleep. God, he wished he'd never heard it. The sound had shocked him, and his heart had skipped a beat. For a moment, he'd been taken back to that time before she'd left him. He'd loved her mindlessly then, but his feelings had left him vulnerable, blind and weak. And what had he gotten for opening himself so completely? Abandoned and betrayed.

When he saw the light of his residence up in the distance, Alex spurred Shalais into a gallop with the slight pressure of his knees on his flanks. The greater distance he put between them, the better. He could already see—feel—the effect she had on him.

His mistake had been in kissing her, touching her. His mouth tightened grimly while his pulse reacted like a fickle lover, quickening at the memory. For the last two years, he'd prided himself on his control. She hadn't been in town for a day and he was instantly taken back to the one time in his life he'd ever gone *mad* over a woman.

One woman and his one big mistake. An ache started in his chest.

These past five years women had come and gone from his life without eliciting even a fraction of what Charlotte did with so little effort. Which made her dangerous in a way he resented deeply.

I should not have kissed her.

But there she'd sat, her fisted hands clutching her cover tight against her breasts, her mouth parted looking too rosy, her bottom lip shiny from the constant swipe of her tongue.

He'd kissed her to prove to himself she meant nothing to him. That after all these years, he *felt* nothing for her. Not even lust in its most basic form. Bloody hell, he hadn't expected her to kiss him back. Not to open up as she'd done.

The ache in his chest drifted lower until it inconveniently settled between his thighs. Alex squelched the memory of the kiss. He couldn't afford to dwell there.

What he'd learned tonight was that his feelings for her were complex as well as wholly unwanted and patently unfair. He did *not* like her. No, he wasn't that addled in the brain. But there still existed a physical attraction for her that frankly shamed him. After all she'd done, he simply could not believe his body had let him down. Hadn't God given man superior brains for precisely that purpose? Men were not animals, led about like a show horse by their cocks.

It would have been more merciful if she'd simply betrayed and abandoned him. Instead, she'd impaled his heart on the head of a very sharp pike...then wrenched it from his body because cleaving it nearly in two hadn't wreaked quite enough damage.

The air felt colder now and the night sky was relieved of complete darkness by the light of the quarter moon. Pulling up on the reins as they neared the stables, Alex brought Shalais to a sedate walk.

He'd let his heart and body rule him when he'd courted her, made love to her, gotten on his knee and asked her to marry him. He wouldn't ever be that naïve again. In all his future dealings with Charlotte Rutherford, they would play by his rules and currently the only thing he wanted from her was *his* son.

Chapter Five

"Did you not sleep well last night? Was the bed not to your liking?" Katie asked the following morning during breakfast. Without giving Charlotte an opportunity to respond, her sister rushed on. "Is it the mattress? We could easily purchase another."

"No, 'tis nothing, truly. The bed was par above the ones I've slept on since I left." Charlotte smiled her assurance and then commenced to eat her breakfast—or at the very least, attempted to.

"You are hiding something."

Charlotte might have taken her sister's statement as an accusation had she not glanced into her eyes, which seemed to plead, *Please don't shut me out.*

"I know something has happened since we last spoke, so you may as well tell me. You know I'm nothing if not determined. I'll discover it whether you wish it or not," she finished teasingly, but her eyes were anxious and concerned.

"I was thinking of Nicholas." Which was partly true. "All of this is so new to him."

Katie bit into a piece of buttered scone, chewed it slowly and then wiped the corners of her mouth with a linen *serviette*. "Nicholas, I imagine, will do quite well here. When James and Missy return with the children, he will acquire three exuberant cousins and playmates. You see how quickly he devoured his breakfast so he could go and explore the playroom? Did he at all appear like a child whose welfare you need fret about?"

Indeed he did not. Charlotte had joined him and Jillian this morning in the nursery, certain Nicholas's lack of familiarity with his surroundings would turn him into something akin to climbing ivy as it had for the past two weeks. She could not have been more wrong. He'd been like the proverbial child in a sweetmeat shop, awed at the vast array of toys in the adjoining playroom. Oatmeal porridge—which he'd never had a particular fondness for—and coddled eggs had been consumed in fifteen minutes flat, unlike the half hour it normally took to coax it down his throat. Bribery was always the last resort to achieve success.

After he'd finished, he'd scrambled from his chair, and with an absent smile in her direction, had hurried over to the shiny red train set spread out on the buffed wood floors. Charlotte had departed, assured he'd be occupied for the next few hours or more.

"No, I suppose not," she conceded.

"So, if my nephew's state of well-being is not a concern, what is it that has you looking strained and on edge?" Katie asked before taking a sip of her tea.

Charlotte added a lump of sugar to her hot chocolate and stirred it slowly. Just as slowly, she peered up at her sister. "Alex was here last night—in my bedchamber." She didn't speak loud enough to be overheard by the footman posted near the entrance of the breakfast room. However, the impact of her words were certainly felt if one could go by Katie's gasp as she jerked her hand and knocked over her teacup. The stain of the tea spread quickly, blemishing the white linen cloth covering the table.

"Oh botheration," her sister muttered as she righted the ivory cup.

At her sister's exclamation, the footman jumped into action, coming to the table to begin sopping up what little tea hadn't already soaked into the tablecloth. With a negligent flick of her hand, Katie waved him away. "You can do naught else. The linen must be removed but that will have to wait until we have finished eating."

The young man—quite young in fact, for his smooth cheeks said he'd yet to reach his majority—halted. "Are you certain, Miss Catherine?"

"Yes, you can tend to it later. Although, I'll need some more hot water."

Placing the towel, now soiled with tea, over the sleeve of his fustian jacket, he gave a short bow and swiftly departed toward the kitchen.

The moment he was out of view and earshot, Katie swung her gaze toward Charlotte. "Alex was here? Last night? In your chamber?" The questions came fierce and hushed.

Save the kiss that had only stoked her passions and kept her tossing in her bed until dawn, Charlotte told her of the night's events. By the time she was finished, the footman had returned and placed the piping-hot pot of tea on the table. With a nod, he resumed his post by the door, too far to hear their conversation if they kept their voices low.

"So Nicholas resembles his brother Charles?" Katie said in wonderment, her words part question, part statement.

"If I'm to believe Alex—which I have no cause not to— Nicholas is his spitting image."

Head tipped at an angle, Katie paused in the process of adding tea to her cup. "And he gave no indication as to what he intends to do? Do you believe he intends to acknowledge Nicholas as his son? Though that would be ruinous," she muttered, almost as an aside. "What else did he say? Have you truly told me the whole of it?"

Charlotte could barely keep up with the fury of questions being thrown at her. Questions she herself had no answer to.

"I've told you everything." The kiss was too private to be shared even with her twin.

A smile touched the corners of her sister's mouth. "I might have guessed he was Alex's straight away had you not lied about his age."

"That matters little. You guessed the truth in no time a'tall."

"Humph. I cannot believe you expected me to believe that ridiculous story of falling in love with someone else while still here in England. I'd have more believed it if you'd told me you'd been abducted by pirates," Katie scoffed. In the very next moment she grew serious, pinning her with a penetrating stare. "I wish you'd told me you were afraid to take on the role of a duchess. There was never a doubt in my mind that you would make a fine one. Better than any who ever held the role."

Briefly, Charlotte looked away. She couldn't help it. But came back, stolid as ever. "Sometimes I wish I had too."

Would things have turned out different if she *had* told her? Charlotte wondered. Well it did little good now to second-guess her decision. What was done was as good as engraved in granite. As if she'd had another choice.

"Did you fear Alex would discover the truth about you— about us?" Katie approached the question with the delicacy as one might a wounded bird. There was also a starkness in her expression that spoke of an inner anguish.

"I—I don't truly know," Charlotte said before quickly taking a large bite of her scone heavily laden with marmalade.

Her sister didn't resume eating. For long seconds she just watched her. "Mrs. Henley would never—" She broke off to correct herself. "What I mean to say is she never breathed a word of it to a soul."

Charlotte had never once considered Mrs. Henley to be the problem. But Katie did not know that for sure. Could not. "How can you be so certain? Have you any idea who she speaks to and what she says?"

"Lottie, Mrs. Henley died a month after you left." Katie added cream to her tea and then stirred it slowly as she stared fixedly into the swirling, hot liquid. When she swallowed, Charlotte could see what it was costing her to relay the information. And Katie had yet to meet her gaze.

"Oh darling, I'm so sorry." It appeared her sister had grown fond of the woman if her death years later pained her still.

When Mrs. Henley had finally tracked them down a month before her wedding, they hadn't precisely welcomed what she imparted to them. They'd been stunned not just to learn she had been a close friend of their mother's but rendered speechless at who exactly their mother was.

Instinctively, they'd both felt they could trust her. Mrs. Henley had known who they were for many years and by all appearances, had told no one. She'd merely kept a watch on them, relieved when she discovered their half brother had taken them in. And then upon deciding they were old enough to know about their mother, she'd told them. It had been *she* who had cautioned them to keep the information to themselves, fearing the grave repercussions of something like that becoming public.

Your brother need not know.

She'd said nothing of Alex but that had been inferred.

No, her sister was right. Mrs. Henley would never have told a soul. Had she wanted to ruin them, she'd have done so long ago.

Katie finally looked up and flashed a tight smile. "She was a good woman. She asked about you many times before she died."

Charlotte felt a pinch in her heart. It had been clear Mrs. Henley, seventy if she was a day, with fine, weathered skin and diminutive in stature, had formed a very strong bond with their mother.

Mrs. Henley had spoken of her in the fondest of terms, tearing up when she spoke of her death and when she'd lost track of her and Katie's whereabouts. When she had found them after a year of searching, they were living with the nanny and nursemaid their father had hired to care for them until they could be shipped off to boarding school.

Their mother had been like a daughter to her and hence the connection she felt to them.

"I'm sorry she's gone," Charlotte said and truly meant it.

With a small nod, Katie commenced drinking her tea. The silence following was stark with so many questions Charlotte dare not ask, at least not yet for it would only fuel questions she herself could not answer.

"You must go and speak to Alex—today," Katie announced

after a time.

This Charlotte knew. It's what was creating butterflies in her stomach and making her heart feel as if it were lodged in her throat. Her only response was a slow nod.

"You must tell him the truth," Katie continued, now looking at her direct.

The truth. Now that was a scary prospect and something Charlotte had considered only briefly after meeting Mrs. Henley. The letter had taken care of that unruly compulsion. How could she when the truth had the power to destroy lives if it fell into the wrong hands? Worse than that, should there be anything worse, the truth would make him look at her differently. It had made *her* look at *herself* differently since the day she'd learned of it. How could it not fail to do the same to Alex?

"I need to explain."

"If you lie to him, he will know."

That Charlotte also knew, which would only make him hate her more. Oh God, she could see she had no choice in this. She had to tell him the truth.

Days before, her sole concern had been her sister. Since the moment Lucas had told her, she'd made countless bargains with God to spare Katie's life. She'd been so scared, heartsick with it. Now she knew an entirely different kind of fear but one she felt just as acutely.

Charlotte arrived at Gretchen Manor an hour later and after spending two minutes in the foyer while the footman ascertained if his lord was in to visitors, she was finally led into the drawing room to await him there.

The manor house was smaller than her brother's but her entire residence could likely fit into three of the rooms with room to spare. The drawing room held two tan sofas, a settee, one rather lofty winged-back chair and a chaise lounge, which looked incongruously feminine amid furniture somber and square. Everything in the room suited Alex from the oil painting that hung like an island in the middle of an endless sea of wall, to the redwood center table and the oblong brown rug.

Charlotte had elected to wear her most flattering day dress, pale pink in color with a ruched neckline and an unadorned satin skirt. Amid tasseled gold and brown cushions, she was the brightest thing in the room.

She'd come here to bare her soul, as it were. However, when Alex arrived a full ten minutes later, his tight jaw, cold, gray eyes and thin-lipped expression did not invite her to remove her gloves—which she'd already done—much less bare her soul.

Nonetheless, her stomach went into a free fall and her equilibrium was duly tested. She imagined it would take time for her to see him again and not feel so completely undone. Like his appearance did not literally steal the breath from her lungs. That her pulse did not race like a raging river during a storm and every cell in her body did not immediately become acutely aware of him as the devastatingly handsome man he was.

Clad in nothing but shirtsleeves, black trousers and a pair of black scuffed boots, he hardly appeared ready for company. He stood at the entrance looking precisely the same as she'd first met him in the vestibule of her brother's home; unyielding and walled off. She willed her courage not to crumble and her speech not to declare mutiny in the face of his obvious aversion.

He moved toward the winged-back chair but did not sit, watching her all the while.

"Good morning, Alex." How perfectly rattled she sounded.

It should not have come as a surprise to her when he responded by lifting one eyebrow, a silent query regarding her presence there.

Heavens, this was going to be much harder than she'd imagined. Charlotte tried to steady her nerves with a lungful of air.

"I had to speak to you."

"Truly?" He dragged out the word to ensure it was infused with just the right amount of mockery to give her a taste of what was to come.

She didn't have to wait long.

"So after five years of absolute silence, suddenly you can't wait to speak to me. Should I be flattered?"

Alex wasn't merely going to make this difficult; it appeared he wouldn't be content until she crawled.

"Alex—"

"Tell me this, would you have told me had I not confronted you with the knowledge myself?" There was a steely quality to his tone.

His question was rhetorical, as they both knew full well.

"No, you wouldn't have done." His stare condemned her.

"Alex, I cannot begin to tell you how truly sorry I am." Her apology felt as if it had been wrenched from her throat and seemed to linger in the air long enough for the walls to throw her words back at her. But she knew if she stopped now, her courage would fail her completely.

Alex did not move, the thick lashes veiling half his eyes did not flicker. He didn't swallow. Charlotte couldn't even see a sign that he took a breath in the tortuous seconds that followed. She wasn't holding *her* breath that her apology would be so forthrightly accepted but she thought he'd say something, even if it was to deny her the very thing she craved most at that moment.

"Is that all?"

Charlotte could well imagine her own expression: her eyes wide with surprise and not blank as his own, her eyebrows in quest of her hairline, which was the polar opposite of his uncreased brow. She must look the way she felt, stunned and at an utter loss for words. She blinked like a dullard asked to explain the true meaning of life.

"Is that all you've come to say?" He expanded on his original question, his speech deliberately slower this time, as if

English wasn't the language she'd spoken since birth.

What she'd expected him to ask was *why*, but as it appeared this was not to be the course of the conversation, it was now up to her to set things to rights. "I would like to explain why I left."

His gaze became fierce, a fissure in his composure. "You would like to explain?" He paused and it wasn't apparent whether he'd intended it to be dramatic but it was the kind of pause that would make Edward Fitzball beam with pride. "You would like to explain," he repeated, seeming to enjoy savoring the words like one would a superior vintage of wine.

His hands glided over the wood frame of the chair while he remained an immovable figure behind. "Tell me, were you taken against your will?"

Charlotte shook her head. "No, but—"

"So no one held a pistol to you, no one had a knife at your throat?" His eyebrow rose. He was playing with her.

"Not physically, no," she said. This is what he would reduce it to? Her sister had been correct. It would have been better had she been captured by pirates.

The smile he flashed her was faintly smug and wholly dark. "So perhaps you would like to tell me a tale of how you left me on our wedding day with my son in your belly for my own good, eh? Let me see," he murmured, tipping his head to the side in a clear pretense to ponder the issue. "I imagine you will tell me how your uneasiness at becoming my marchioness and future duchess grew as the time drew near. Your lineage was uncertain, you were after all the by-blow of an earl, you had no knowledge of your mother and in the end you were leaving to protect me from the inevitable disdain of my peers?"

Although his statement resounded in the air with unerring accuracy, those reasons would not have been difficult to conclude to anyone who knew her.

And Alex had known her most intimately.

No, not even he could imagine what had really compelled her to leave.

"While all that is true, that wasn't—"

"No," he bit out sharply. All pretense of humor fled from his expression and his jaw and mouth turned as stony as his unwavering stare.

"Truth be told, you are too late for explanations, for excuses and apologies for there is nothing, *nothing* you could tell me that will change how I feel about you now and in the future. Nothing," he added for emphasis, as if she required it.

Charlotte's first instinct was to plead her case, make him listen. But his voice was as unyielding as the coldness etched in the chiseled planes of his face. His mind was set, he would not be moved. Trying to appeal to him now would be fruitless.

Her fingers absently smoothed her satin-trimmed skirts. What was she to say?

"I-I-I…" Words simply failed her. She fell silent.

"It is unpleasant, is it not?"

Charlotte lifted her gaze from her lap. She had been doing that a lot of late. She despised the habit for it was cowardly.

"To expect one thing and get something different entirely. You expected that after five *bloody* years, I would permit you an audience for you to tell me your woeful tale. You expected that I would sit here and *listen* to the reasons you kept me from my child—my son who should by all rights be my heir." His quickened breath spoke of rising anger tethered by a taut rein of control.

And then, as if he could not bear to be even that close to her, he crossed the room until the distance between them was as vast as it was unbridgeable.

"Alex—" she started, not even certain what she was going to say.

"There is only one thing I want from you and that is my son."

"I shan't keep you from him any longer. We shall make some sort of arrangement." The logistics of which would be a nightmare. Scandal was almost a certainty unless she took Nicholas to the country, away from the prying eyes and flapping jaws of the *ton*.

But what other choice did she have? Alex would not relent. That much was obvious. And she owed him this at the very least, unfettered access to his son. Of course that now meant she'd be remaining in England. There was no possibility of them returning to America.

"I am not proposing an arrangement." He spoke softly and an ominous chill swept the length of her spine, causing her to freeze. A sense of foreboding now permeated the air and her breath slowed to a halt.

She looked at him and he held her gaze. No one spoke but she could read his meaning in his eyes, in his wide-legged stance, his hands folded across the breadth of his chest.

"No," she whispered, barely able to speak, so horrified was she at what she saw in his emotionless eyes.

"I want my son."

"You can't mean to take him from me?" Charlotte's voice wavered as she clutched the arm of the settee.

"I want my son."

"Alex, please." She would unashamedly plead for Nicholas. She would give her life for him.

"I want my son. And I will use everything I have at my disposal—my rank, my fortune, and my family's considerable influence—if you dare think to fight me."

It was more than an implacable statement, it warned of a ruthlessness she'd never before seen in him—certainly not directed at her.

Alex knew the moment enough terror left her to allow room for anger to set in. Her lips thinned and her blue eyes narrowed. The only time her eyes turned this blue—the blue of tropical skies—was when she was aroused. She wasn't aroused now. Her expression said she would fight him, like a lioness guarding her young.

Good. He welcomed the fight for he'd no doubt this was one he would win. Even if winning called for bribery and coercion, even if it meant he'd have to bend the law to his will, he'd do so without a pang of conscience.

"You would be so cruel as to take a child from his mother?" she asked, her tone almost disbelieving.

"You kept his existence from me for over four years. Sadly, you are not inclined to my sympathy or lenience in matters pertaining to you."

"I'm not asking you for me, I'm pleading for *your* son."

Ah yes, Nicholas was now *his* son when it suited her purpose. There wasn't anything she would not do for him. Oddly, the thought was a comforting one.

"Can you imagine what it would do to him to be apart from me? As much as it must pain you to know, I am all he has. I am the one solitary familiar person in his life. I love him and he loves me."

"Oh, I have no doubt of that. But he now has me. His father," Alex said, lest she forgot that for even a fraction of a second as she'd conveniently done since his son's birth.

"Alex, he doesn't know you. You must see that any attempt to take him from me will cause him great pain."

Had he not experienced her treachery firsthand, her pleas may very well have worked. She had a way about her; the cadence of her voice, soft and lilting, the way her curled lashes created a shadow on the crest of her cheeks when she looked down. Even knowing her as he did now, all that she was capable of, he could see her allure. But seeing it didn't mean he'd ever fall for it again. And it certainly didn't mean he'd ever act on it.

"I think you misunderstand me. Unlike you, I'm not so coldhearted as to deny you contact with him altogether. Would I not be a hypocrite if I did the same to you as you did to me?"

Charlotte's face turned ashen. A direct hit. He ruthlessly quashed any twinge of consciousness that had the temerity to rear its head. He'd merely reminded her of the facts.

"But I never meant to hurt you. I never wanted to keep him—"

"Stop!" He made sure to keep his voice relatively low as he refused to actually shout at her. Raised voices conveyed too much emotion. But his tone was severe enough to halt her mid-word.

Eyes raised toward the ceiling, her furrowed brow gave all indications she was thinking…hard. When her gaze returned to him, she appeared resolute and calm.

"I would have cut off my right arm to spare you pain. Point in fact, that is precisely what I did. Yet you refuse to hear my reasons."

"Because they are at least four years too late in coming," he shot back. "You cared so much about my well-being, that I received not so much as a by-your-leave from you. No warning of what awaited me at the church. This was how much you cared for me?"

Charlotte looked stricken. "I sent a letter."

"A letter?" He rolled his eyes. It had been three weeks before he could bring himself to read it. He'd gotten very *very* drunk that day and stayed drunk two weeks thereafter.

"A letter is what you send a friend to keep them apprised of your goings-on when you live a fair distance apart. A letter is not what you send your fiancé when you intend to stand him up at the altar on his wedding day."

Abruptly, she rose to her feet, her gloves and reticule clutched in her hands and pressed tight against her skirts. "I will not allow you to take my son." But her words were all bravado for her voice shook with fear and uncertainty.

"Pray tell, did I hear you correctly? You will not allow me to have my son? Madam, you can hardly stop me."

Her plush bottom lip trembled and some long-suppressed and barely recognizable emotion caused his heart to contract and a stinging pain to pierce his chest.

Marrying her had meant defying the express wishes of his parents, which he'd done gladly. Most in Society had been aghast at his choice of bride. But she'd been the only woman he'd ever loved and no other would do for that kind of lifetime commitment. Who'd have thought they'd ever come to this? Why the devil had she run and ruined every good thing in his world?

No, he did not want to know. As he'd just told her, time for explanations was long past. The only thing that mattered was his son.

Alex rallied, determined not to permit himself to be misled by those quivering lips he'd kissed more in his dreams than in real life, and the torment in her eyes. The pain he felt was for all *he'd* lost—those years without his son. The pain had nothing to do with any lingering feelings for her. She meant nothing to him.

He should not have to fight against the urge to take her in his arms and kiss the frown from her face and touch her until the cause of her trembling was desire, not fear. Softening toward her would mean his experience with her had taught him nothing. Softening toward her would reveal just how weak a man he was in all matters concerning her.

With a quick pivot, he turned and strode to the entrance of the drawing room. He could hear the rustle of her dress as she followed. He had to get her out of his house. Her scent was so subtle, one could hardly detect it. But every time he inhaled, it felt as if the air around him was saturated with it, making breathing with relative ease difficult.

Bloody hell, he should be able to breathe in his own home. Was she determined to deny him that too?

"It is difficult to believe that you've altered this much. You never used to be cruel." She addressed his back with no malice undertones, just a bone-deep sadness in her voice.

Alex turned to face her. She halted abruptly. They stood as if the line between them wasn't made by the high-glossed wood planks of the floor but a line separating enemies during war. They watched each other; her warily, he, as if she'd just taken down his comrade in arms. At least that's how he felt.

"Cruel, eh? Well if I'm cruel then it is you who has made me so." Losing her had forever changed his life, he'd not deny

that. He would not even say he'd become a better man for it—
he had been told the contrary too often to delude himself into
believing that. It had, however, been how he had managed to
put her behind him; how he had survived.

"If you would just let me—"

"Simmons, will show you out." His frozen gaze met and
held hers for a breathless moment before he gestured with his
chin toward the footman in the hall.

Charlotte's throat closed up, making it impossible for her to
swallow. Never had a dismissal stung so.

Carefully, as to maintain a modicum of dignity, she walked
to the door as if she were traversing a field riddled with mines
unseen by the eyes, but felt in the very depths of her heart.

"And in the future, do not come to my residence without an
express invitation." This he said in a coolly detached voice as
she passed him.

She paused long enough to decide whether *to* respond. This
was the man who'd, only minutes before, threatened to take her
son from her. And she had no doubt he meant what he'd said.
He'd already proven he'd listen to naught she had to say.

What good would it do to respond to each and every one of
his barbs? If he took pleasure in hurting her, punishing her, so
be it. She'd survived his absence these last five years and she'd
lost his love. She could surely survive this too.

With eyes trained forward, Charlotte lifted her chin, exited
the study and permitted the footman to see her out.

Chapter Six

"How did things go with Alex? Does he intend to acknowledge Nicholas?" Katie's bombardment came the moment Charlotte entered the morning room. Her sister, regarding her expectantly, held a vase of large red roses in her hands.

Charlotte had given herself a full half hour—the time it had taken her to return home and freshen up in her bedchamber—to allow anxiety to have its way with her before forcibly reining it in. Nothing had happened yet, she'd had to keep reminding herself. All she could do at this point was pray Alex would come to see the folly of what he'd threatened to do.

"Yes he does," she replied shortly.

Katie placed the vase on a small round table near the window. "I imagined he would."

Not in the mood to discuss the particulars of their conversation, Charlotte gestured to the flowers and asked, "Did those come for you?"

"Pray, do not sound so hopeful. These are from yet another suitor who has lost interest. The flowers are merely an apology from Sir Camden that he will no longer be dancing attendance on me. I can now scratch him from the list of potential husbands," Katie explained with a light laugh as she arranged the roses to be displayed to their best advantage.

Either her sister was an actress par above the rest or the rejection didn't bother her in the least.

Charlotte quickly crossed the room to her. "Katie, I'm so sorry."

Flashing her an easy smile, Katie replied, "You needn't be. I'm convinced I would have perished of boredom."

But Charlotte wasn't fooled. Of course this had to sting. Katie herself had told her how if not for the dowager's maliciousness, she would have married years ago. The truth of it was no matter how beautiful or how large her dowry, every year that passed without a proposal and a marriage, the greater the likelihood her sister would not wed at all. And the inevitable scandal Nicholas's parentage would cause would help her naught. The sheer magnitude of *that* felt like a thirty-stone weight on her chest.

"Nonetheless, he should not—"

Suddenly, her sister pointed out the window and cried, "Lottie, they're here. They're here." The pitch of her voice rose at the repetition of her words.

Charlotte barely had time to register the landau in the drive before Katie practically dashed from the room.

A moment later, she heard a great deal of noise coming from the entrance hall—childish shrieks as well as one long, drawn-out wail. Then Charlotte heard the low pitch of a masculine voice. Anticipation was like a tight band in the pit of her belly.

James.

Trailing Katie out into the hall, Charlotte was met with such a sight it caused the cessation of breath to her lungs. For a moment everyone stood frozen, even the children—three in all—had ceased their crying and their incessant babble to stare at her.

Charlotte's focus began and ended at her brother's tall, leanly muscled form. When she'd been introduced to him at the age of fifteen, she'd thought him absurdly handsome, especially for a man of his rank *and* fortune—most weren't expected to be in possession of both. He'd been too young to be an earl at the age of twenty-eight and too much a bachelor to take on the care of his two half sisters. Or so one would have thought. However, one would have been mistaken.

But here he stood, if possible, looking more handsome than she remembered. He wore his maturity well, his dark hair showing no hint of gray, his eyes such a pale blue they sometimes appeared opaque. He smiled that wonderful smile of his—loving, tender, welcoming—and it was as if the place, once dark, was now bathed in sunlight.

That was all it took for Charlotte to rush to him. Moments later she was crushed in his hard embrace, inhaling his musky cologne and the scent of warm, masculine flesh.

"It's about damn time you came home," he muttered gruffly into her hair.

Hugging James was like embracing a rock, his chest solid and broad, and his arms like bands about her waist. "James. James," was all she was able to say so overcome with emotion.

When he finally released her, she resisted the urge to hang on to him in the same manner his twins used to. Like it was in his arms they felt truly protected.

"You will never do that to us again, do you understand?"

A hiccupping laugh escaped her lips as tears stung her eyes. "James, you look wonderful. How I've missed you." And she hadn't known exactly how much until that precise moment.

Pulling her close again, James affectionately rested his chin atop her head. Many of her hairpins surrendered under the pressure and Charlotte soon felt the heavy weight of her hair at her nape. Although it had taken Jillian over a half hour to style it that morning, Charlotte didn't care.

"Mama?" Her son called to her in a plaintive voice she was long familiar with. With that one sound it asked, *Mama, who are these people? Mama, who is that man hugging you?* Next, Charlotte felt the tug of his hands on her skirts. She quickly turned to him and spied Jillian lingering at the bottom of the stairs. The commotion must have brought them down from the playroom where Nicholas had been since her return.

"Come, darling, I want you to meet your Uncle James." She placed him in front of her.

Her brother wore a ready smile as if he'd been forewarned

of her little surprise. But his smile was transformed in a flash when his gaze settled fully on his nephew. It required all of approximately two seconds for his brain to make the connection, this Charlotte easily ascertained by the shocked expression on this face. His regard swiveled back to her, questioning, disbelieving.

"Alex," he said sharply on an inhaled breath. Apparently, that was the one thing Katie hadn't conveyed in her message to him.

It wasn't a question and Charlotte need not respond. James had known Charles and apparently Nicholas's resemblance to his uncle was such that one didn't have to ask.

Before her brother could utter another word, her sister-in-law, Missy joined them. "I've given you quite enough time to greet your sister, now it's my turn," she teased her husband lightly, her slender hand rubbing with warm familiarity on his upper back.

James quickly made room for her in their circle.

Missy was beautiful—tall, slim with wavy, chestnut hair streaked in russets and mahogany, which she wore up in loose bun today. Charlotte had instantly taken to the new Countess of Windmere when she and James had wed nine years ago.

Missy stared at her for a heartbeat before whispering, "Oh Charlotte—" Her slate blue eyes flooding with tears. They moved in accord to reach for each other, arms wide in greeting.

Silk tulle and Indian muslin crushed as they joyously embraced. And once again, for the last two days running, Charlotte shed another gallon of tears, although Missy may well have shed more.

Her nieces and nephew came next. The twins, Jessica and Jason, now eight years, had changed much since she'd seen them last. Gone were the round cheeks and sturdy bodies. Both had grown tall and slim, Jessica a lovely combination of her mother and father but Jason was all James with his light-blue eyes, dimples and dark hair.

Their youngest, three-year-old Lily, trailed closely behind

her older sister, and when Charlotte bent to kiss and embrace her, managed a smile around the thumb still tucked firmly in her mouth.

By the completion of the introductions, Nicholas lost all trace of his usual shyness and was soon giggling with his three cousins.

Along with the children's nanny, Mrs. Eldridge, a plump, middle-aged woman with kind eyes and a ready smile, Jillian ushered the children upstairs to the nursery. Never once did her son look back at her.

"Why don't we adjourn to the drawing room where we can speak in comfort?" James suggested mildly but his eyes were troubled. No doubt his thoughts were on Nicholas and Alex, and all that entailed.

Katie sent her a knowing glance. Missy clutched her husband's forearm, rose on her tiptoes and whispered something in his ear. The only part of her sister-in-law's statement Charlotte could make out was, "...wait until the morrow."

James responded by patting her hand solicitously. "Don't fret, love."

In the drawing room, her brother motioned for her to take a seat. It was clear it was going to be one of *those* conversations.

James waited until she and Katie had availed themselves of the sofa and he and Missy of the one opposite before he began. "Nicholas—"

"Is Alex's son," Charlotte concluded. "Of that I'm certain you're aware."

James exchanged a brief look with his wife. "When do you intend to tell him?"

"Alex already knows."

Her brother's brow rose. She'd managed to shock him again.

"Alex met Nicholas yesterday when he came by to pick up some papers," Catherine explained.

Missy's mouth formed a silent "o". James's gaze snapped to

Katie and then back to Charlotte.

"And?" he prompted.

All eyes were on her now.

"He wants him. He says he intends to take him from me." And that is when Charlotte's composure crumbled and a sob shook her. Broke her.

Alex was sitting at his desk in the study when the explosion came, disrupting the calm of the morning. Rutherford's pounding on the front door reverberated throughout the house. It was loud enough to send the servants scampering from their posts to discover the source of the commotion. Disturbances like these made excellent grist for the gossip mill.

A glance at the long case clock revealed it was almost half past ten. Yes, at least two hours earlier than Alex had expected. His friend's arrival had been a foregone conclusion.

A minute later, Rutherford swept into his study like a whirlwind or perhaps more like a volcano on the verge of eruption. Alfred trailed in his wake, an eddying mass of gesticulations, his hands moving about as if trying to rein in a fractious stallion with a feather.

"My lord, Lord Windmere to see you," Alfred finally announced when it became obvious Rutherford would not be restrained or controlled.

"So I see," Alex replied, his voice heavy with derision. "Thank you, Alfred."

His butler wasted no time in taking his leave. It was the fastest Alex had ever seen him move. Poor man probably didn't want to be witness to the bloodletting he thought sure to come.

Alex shifted his gaze back to Rutherford, noting the red slash of anger along his cheekbones. If his arrival at the front door hadn't all but advertised it, his expression surely said this was not to be a social visit. He'd come armed to do battle.

"Back from London so soon?" Alex asked, lifting a brow.

"What the hell are you doing? Have you deliberately set out to kill every ounce of affection I have for you?" Rutherford looked as if he wanted to hit him, the skin of his face tight, his pale eyes spitting fury.

The corners of Alex's mouth lifted ever so slightly. Glibness would not be appropriate at this time but his tongue appeared to have a mind of its own. "Yes, everything I do is for the want of your affection. I fear if I ever lost it, I should perish and die of longing."

Once upon a time—and under vastly different circumstances—such a response would have elicited a round of hearty laughter.

Today, Rutherford emitted something resembling a snarl and then lunged at him. But Alex knew him well enough to anticipate his reaction. He was out of his chair in a second flat while the earl caught himself in time to stop his forward momentum from sending him hurtling over the desk and into the now empty chair. Rutherford's solid weight against the desk sent papers sliding across the mahogany surface and onto the floor. The inkwell tipped precariously before landing upright with a distinct plop, thankfully not spilling its contents all over three shipping contracts Alex had been working on the week past.

Cautiously, Alex retreated, not stupid enough to turn his back to him and not stopping until he'd put half the distance of the room between them and several chairs and a side table.

"I see you've spoken with your sister." Alex didn't want to have to fight him but he would if Rutherford gave him no choice.

"If you believe I shall just sit idly by and do nothing while you attempt to destroy her, you don't know me at all." His friend issued the warning in the kind of threatening tone that buckled soldiers' knees and caused beads of sweat to spring up like geysers along their hairlines. He advanced toward him.

Alex gave a resigned sigh and met his friend's frozen stare, his hands also mirroring Rutherford's, curled as they were into tight fighting fists. Despite Alex's aversion to violence, there may well be bloodletting after all.

"You cannot take her son from her."

"You mean *my* son. The son of whose existence I knew nothing of until yesterday. Is that the son you're speaking of?"

"She's—"

"She denied me my son!"

And it was as if the full import of what she had done crashed into him just then. He heard the pain splinter his voice, peaking above the rage like the last note in a crescendo. The true enormity of what he had lost, all that he had missed and could never *ever* get back made his sight blur and caused his legs to wobble dangerously.

"She kept the existence of my child from me and yet she's the one you fight to shield from pain?" His question was low and gruff but yet not a question at all. It was an accusation meant to wound.

Silence blanketed the room as he and Rutherford continued to stare hard at one another. This was new, a novelty of the worst sort. Never had anything this contentious, this volatile and corrosive existed between them in the thirty-one years of their acquaintance. Betrayal could no longer be delegated to Charlotte and her alone, for it appeared her brother had picked up her baton.

His friend's betrayal stung, embedding itself deep under the surface of Alex's skin until it pierced his very soul. In many ways and for many years, Rutherford had been more a brother to him than Charles.

Rutherford halted just as suddenly as he'd burst into the room. He stood perfectly still for long seconds, then his chest seemed to deflate as he exhaled a long breath. It was as if the anger had drained from him. A sort of helplessness settled across his features and he appeared torn.

"While I understand your anger, this is not—"

"You cannot *ever* know how I feel," Alex replied, quick to disabuse him of the notion they would ever share any solidarity in this.

"I didn't say I know how you *feel*, I said I understand your anger. I did not meet my sisters—my flesh and blood—until they were fifteen years. To discover that my father had just *left* them in that school, knowing they had no mother, no adult who loved and cared for them, cut me to the core."

How like his friend to try to disarm him with sentiment by drawing parallels of their lives. Still it wasn't the same. "This was—is my *son*. A son who *should* be my heir. She didn't only deny me, she denied him."

"And for this, you intend to punish them both?" Rutherford asked, in a too reasoning tone. "You must see that you'll only be hurting Nicholas if you hurt his mother."

"I am not doing this to hurt her," Alex replied, knowing what he said was a lie. He wanted to wreak the same hell she had and *still* visited upon him.

Rutherford's face lost its hard edge. He slowly approached him, his hands up to indicate he had no intention of trying to beat him to a pulp. "I do not mean to excuse what Charlotte did. Believe me I do not. I don't know why she left you. I don't know why she stayed gone so long. But I'm glad she's back. And what I *do* know is that my sister does not have a malicious heart. For God's sake, she hasn't seen her own *twin* in five years."

Eyes softened and voice gentled, Rutherford continued to speak. "And given the circumstances of her own birth, do you really believe she would callously subject her child to the same? She *must* have had a powerful reason to do what she did, and I for one intend to find out what it was. Charlotte would never intentionally set out to hurt you or her family. That I would stake my life on. She has a generous soul and an even bigger heart. And if you weren't so filled with bitterness and this need to punish her, you'd see that."

Alex pivoted from his friend, dismissing his words with the sharp slice of an arm through the air while uttering a single vile epithet.

The very last thing he wanted to hear was excuses for her unforgivable behavior. He hadn't been keen to hear them from the liar herself and he was even less inclined to hear it from her doting brother. If she should suffer even a portion of the agony he'd suffered, that would be enough. Let her believe he had just enough vengefulness in him to take their son from her. Let her suffer the agonies of imagining that kind of loss. It couldn't come close to the loss he himself had endured.

"As I already said, this isn't some vengeful attempt to make her pay," he said, meeting Rutherford's regard direct without blinking.

Through narrowed eyes, the earl watched him in stifling silence, as if attempting to ferret out the truth with just one deliberate and probing look.

"So you have no intention of separating my sister from her son?"

"My son." He ground out the two words and it cost him everything to utter them with such restraint.

Rutherford sank into the nearby armchair and with a heavy sigh, dropped his head into his hand before running it wearily through his hair. "You're not thinking, man. There will be a scandal."

"Unless she returns to America, which I will not permit—at least not with my son—scandal is inevitable." Alex had already resigned himself to the fact. He certainly wasn't going to hide Nicholas like some shameful secret. He would claim him and damn Society.

Would that scandal stopped at Charlotte's doorstep and went no further, but scandal would play havoc on all their lives.

Rutherford knew this too and didn't speak for a good while, just regarded him, his expression a mixture of frustration, anger and pain. After too long under his friend's scrutiny, Alex turned from him and walked to the window facing the grounds in the rear. A drink would come in handy right at that moment. The thought was fleeting enough not to rankle.

"We have to do something."

"What precisely would you have us do?" Alex asked, shooting him a glance over his shoulder.

"I don't bloody know." Rutherford all but growled his reply, his hand tunneling through his hair again. "But the situation won't be helped if you're intent on going to war with her over your son. You have to try to put your animosity aside. You have to forgive her." From any other person it would have sounded like a plea, but from his friend it was all conviction.

"What would you do in my place?" he asked in a toneless voice. "Imagine that Missy kept your children's existence from you. What would you do?" Alex turned from the window to face Rutherford.

Such a look came over his friend's face, as if the thought unimaginable. And indeed it was for the love Rutherford shared with his wife made it so. Missy would never have kept his child from him. Alex hadn't been fortunate enough to fall in love with a woman like her. Instead he poured all his emotions into a woman to whom loyalty was a word tossed about when referring to countries and allegiances.

Rutherford's eyebrows drew together. "I know my sister and so do you. There's something else in play here. Something she's not telling us."

Alex wisely said nothing about Charlotte offering to divulge her reasons for leaving. No cause to incite his anger. But a small part of Alex—too foolish and sentimental for his own good—wanted to grab on to the notion that there was a reason sound enough to squelch his anger and ease his sense of betrayal.

But the sane part of him, the one that had eventually survived her stifling absence from his life, rebelled against it. Without conscious thought, his head began shaking in denial, his rejection of the idea unequivocal. There was no excuse to what she'd done to him, what she'd taken from him and he'd never permit her close enough to allow her to do it again.

"Do you not understand, Rutherford? I no longer care why

she left." As the words passed his lips, his certainty that he in fact spoke the truth, grew. He didn't *want* to care. That should be enough to make it so.

Rutherford let out a long breath as he shook his head slowly. "You can't fool me, Cartwright. You care. It's possibly the only thing you've cared about these last five years." He paused before saying, "And I think you still care for her."

Alex stiffened. His mind revolted against the idea. But his friend's words landed like a sharp blow to the gut—or perhaps it was his heart, they were after all close enough in proximity. His jaw went tight. In equal parts horror and anger, he stared at Rutherford.

"In all the years my sister has been gone, you've never married. Your personal life consists of a string of mistresses whom you discard within months of taking them. The month prior you were to start courting Lady Mary..." Another telling pause. A moment later, he continued on to finish Alex off in true merciless Rutherford form. "You have never truly moved beyond her."

The reason he hadn't started to court Lady Mary when he'd intended had *nothing* to do with Charlotte. And he *had* moved beyond her. It was her return that now dragged him back to the past. A past when he'd loved her.

Infinitely more appealing would have been if they'd had a good bring-down-the-walls brawl than Alex being forced to listen to *this*, for these were fighting words. He might not have been able to close his ears to them, but he'd be damned if he would remain and listen to another one.

Tamping down the rage broiling within him, he flicked a glance at his friend before starting toward the study door. "You can see yourself out," he said in parting, the words thrown over his rapidly departing back.

Chapter Seven

The man was punctual, Alex would give him that. His solicitor arrived promptly at quarter past eleven; ten minutes after Rutherford had gone. In his hand he clutched a tan valise, which looked as if it had just left the shop. The same could be said of his tailored suit and the glint from his black leather shoes had the power to blind. It was clear the man was being paid too much.

With polite greetings dispensed, Alex invited him to take a seat in the chair in front of his desk.

Mr. Reynolds's valise thumped to the floor at his side, his full bespectacled attention directed at Alex. "How many I assist you today, my lord?"

Always so eager to please when coin was involved. A jaded thought, but entirely factual.

"I would like to change my will."

"Indeed?" Surprise lit Mr. Reynolds's eyes and his brows rose accordingly. His hands reached for his case, managing the clasp with one hand. "What changes did you have in mind?" he asked, momentarily switching his attention to his valise as he rifled through its contents. Seconds later, he produced several sheets of paper. After a quick scan, he gave a satisfied nod and placed them on the desk.

"I want the sum of two hundred thousand pounds left to my son as well as the values of my stocks and securities put in trust to him until he reaches the age of twenty-five."

His solicitor's head jerked up. His eyes rounded, making them appear overly large behind the lenses of his glasses.

"I-I was not aware you had a child, my lord."

That makes the both of us, Alex was tempted to reply.

Judiciously, he kept the thought just that, a thought.

Instead, Alex acknowledged his statement with a brief inclination of his head.

"But surely you will marry, my lord. What of your legitimate children when that occurs? Do you not want to leave a portion of this to them?"

The gall of the man! He just assumed he'd been speaking of a by-blow. Some child he'd kept hidden away who, maybe now, Alex would attempt to carve a respectable place in Society.

This was how it would be going forward. And despite his exalted rank, he didn't fool himself into believing this would be an easy task. After all, he'd been the spare, the one dark presence in a sea of the golden beauty of his family. A fact his father never let him forget.

The thought of the struggle for acceptance in a spurious and merciless *ton* awaiting Nicholas overwhelmed him with a sense of helplessness he hadn't felt in years. If he could do anything, *anything* at all to spare him what was to come, he would.

"My lord?"

Mr. Reynolds's prompt pulled Alex back from his dark, frustrated thoughts.

He pinned the man with a hard stare but didn't speak. Could not in that moment, so great was his frustration at the whole affair. So great was his anger at her and the predicament she now placed him in. As the silence and stare stretched and breached the threshold of decorum, his solicitor began shifting in his seat, his gaze uneasy.

"You must think of your heir and your—er—other children, my lord." His solicitor's voice was calmer now. Thrown in too, was an extra dose of deference.

And it was that calm that unloosed Alex's tongue.

"He *is* my heir."

It was purely reflexive, his response. The man had practically goaded him into saying it.

Had the matter not been so serious, Alex would've thought

his solicitor's reaction amusing. He bolted upright in his chair, and apparently his sight wasn't as poor as all that for he tore his spectacles from his face. The man practically gaped at him.

Alex knew he should correct his outburst before Mr. Reynolds's heart gave out but he didn't. Something inside him stayed it.

"You married? But when? How? To whom?" his solicitor sputtered, bewildered.

The solution appeared to Alex in that instant. The one way he could set everything right. The only way he could make his son his legitimate heir.

"I married five years ago. How? Well, I would say in the normal manner of such things. My cousin married Miss Charlotte Rutherford and I in his parish situated on the grounds of my parents' country home." Alex felt no guilt for his monstrous lie. After all, it was done to right an egregious wrong.

Mr. Reynolds looked downright flummoxed, his sunken eyes bulging wide. "You me-mean, the earl's sister? The same one who—"

"Yes, the same woman who was to marry me again in front of a church full of people at St. Paul's Cathedral."

"Again?" Mr. Reynolds asked with a gulp.

"Yes again, Mr. Reynolds," Alex answered patiently, giving him time to adjust to the news.

Several times his solicitor appeared poised to speak, only to close his mouth as he continued to stare at him, his expression twelve leagues beyond confusion and shocked.

"Our marriage isn't common knowledge so I beg that you keep this to yourself until such a time that I wish to share it with the general populace."

It seemed that statement snapped him out of his stupor for Mr. Reynolds adjusted his necktie and cleared his throat. "This is most unorthodox, my lord."

Alex reclined in the chair and cocked his eyebrow, striving to appear his supercilious best. "I beg your pardon?" He stretched his legs out under the desk. "Pray tell me what's so unorthodox about me marrying and siring an heir?" There was no harm in having a bit of sport with the man.

Immediately Reynolds cowed, his Adam's apple giving a dramatic bob. Somehow Alex managed to suppress a smile.

"You misunderstand me, my lord. All I meant to say is that no one believes you to be married. Never once in all these years have you uttered a word about...well a wife. And talk about Town is that you are planning to marry."

It would appear even learned solicitors weren't immune to gossip.

"Talk about Town is obviously misinformed." Let him make of it what he would. On the path Alex had just committed to, he'd face greater opposition and scrutiny.

After several moments of silence, Reynolds pressed on in a clear attempt to fill the uncomfortable silence. "Given these unique circumstances, in order for your son to be recognized as your heir, you will be required to furnish proof of his legitimacy. No doubt your marriage papers are on file at the general registry."

His solicitor would never accuse him of lying to him—at least not to his face—but his tone conveyed a hint of skepticism at the validity of his claim. Which was good, as Alex had no tolerance for an eagerly trusting man, especially in a solicitor.

"Indeed they are," Alex replied smoothly. When the occasion warranted, he could lie with the best of them. Although when it came to deception, Charlotte had set the bar particularly high.

This would mean a trip to Yorkshire today. His cousin had better be about. "I shall request they send the verification to your office."

A look of surprise flashed in Reynolds's eyes as if he hadn't expected Alex to offer them up so readily. He'd no doubt expected him to hem and haw before making some excuse to explain the absence of said document.

"Good, good. Very well then, I shall go ahead and make the changes and draw up a new will. Your marriage papers *should* take care of the legalities concerning your title and entailed properties." Mr. Reynolds was all business briskness now. He rose from his chair.

Alex was not inclined to see him to the door, but those manners so strongly ingrained in him brought him to his feet. "And when can I expect it will be ready for my signature?"

In the process of collecting the papers from the desk, Reynolds glanced up briefly and said, "I can return in a week's time. Will that be sufficient, my lord?"

Alex inclined his head.

After Mr. Reynolds put the will back in his valise, he bowed just as Alex stuck out his hand. The awkwardness lasted but a moment before the men shook hands.

"Good day, my lord."

"It's still early, so that's left to be said," Alex replied dryly.

His solicitor made a sound in his throat as if he wasn't sure whether it would be in good form to laugh. Alex smiled. He supposed he'd tormented the man enough for one day.

The moment Mr. Reynolds departed the room, Alex gave an impatient yank of the bell cord on the wall behind his desk. The head footman, Simmons, appeared seconds later.

"Have the coach prepared. I want to depart for the train station as soon as it's readied. I will be traveling to Yorkshire."

"Yes, sir." Simmons gave a curt nod, turned on his heel and departed.

A time like this would normally be cause for celebration, Alex supposed. If everything worked out as planned, by the end of the day he'd be a married man.

Charlotte could tell by her brother's furrowed brows and the tight set of his lips things had not gone well with Alex.

James had stalked into the morning room where she, Katie and Missy were taking their midmorning tea—a practice

Charlotte hadn't realized how much she'd missed until her return. His dark hair was windblown and the buttons of his waistcoat were undone. He'd discarded his coat over the back of the armchair and now sat beside his wife, his hand covering hers, which rested with loving familiarity on his thigh.

The sight of the two of them together pinched at her heart. It always had.

"Were you able to sway him the tiniest bit?" Missy asked.

"He's as determined as I've ever seen him. He wants his son," James said, ending on a heavy sigh.

Wrenching despair gripped Charlotte, blurring her vision, and she could see only the bleakness of her future.

Instantly, Katie, who sat at her side on the sofa, clutched her hand and held it tight. "But of course we won't allow Alex to take Nicholas from you." She shot a pointed look at their brother. "Will we, James?"

Her brother's expression in no way served to alleviate Charlotte's worst fears. Worry etched fine lines about his mouth and futility clouded his eyes.

"But how can he? Legally, he has no claim on Nicholas."

Missy was correct as far as the law goes. Women retained full custody *and* responsibility of their illegitimate children. A punishment for their loose morals and poor character. Charlotte knew that much for a fact.

"He may not have any *legal* claim, but not many will dispute he *is* indeed the father. One only has to look at Nicholas. His resemblance not only to Charles but to the duke himself is striking. And given his rank, his wealth, the duke's considerable influence and the circumstances, there is every chance the courts would grant him custody."

"But—"

James held up his hand to stay Katie's protest. Grave-faced, he addressed Charlotte directly. "The truth of it is Cartwright had every intention of marrying you. You jilted him at the altar. Reports of the incident filled the papers for months. That you should return years later with his son…well this weakens your position—any defense you should choose to mount. The courts could logically conclude had you *not* abandoned him, he would have all the legal rights a married man has to his children."

Which was whole and absolute.

Good Lord, what was she to do? The walls closing in on her felt as high as the Himalayas and equally unscalable. "I must leave. Go back to America. I have no choice."

"No!" the three cried in unison.

Katie's grip on her hand tightened enough to impede normal blood flow.

"But what else am I to do?" Charlotte asked as she took in their stricken expressions. "James is correct. If Alex takes the matter to court he will in all likelihood be granted custody." She inhaled a deep breath. "And although I know I'm to blame for it all, I cannot risk losing my son. I simply cannot."

"Perhaps, if you went to Alex and explained everything to him. Told him your reasons. Perhaps that would sway him." Missy spoke calmly despite the loss of color to her face.

"Don't you think I offered—that I tried to? But none of it matters to him. Not anymore. He says it's too late for explanations."

James cursed and came swiftly to his feet. Missy laid a restraining hand on his arm. "Really, James. Such language."

In no mood to be scolded, her brother circled the chair and began to pace the length of the Oriental rug. "He is being spiteful."

"Well of course he is. But love, you must look on this from his view point. Naturally he feels cheated. He is only just learned of his son's existence. His emotions are raw which makes his reaction purely reflexive. He is hurt and now all he wants to do is hurt Charlotte in return. But it won't last—with Alex it never does. We just need to give him time."

Charlotte winced. Although she was certain Missy hadn't meant to, she made her feel like a villain of the worst sort.

Her sister-in-law's gaze shifted to her. "My dear, I hope you won't take that as a criticism. I'm merely voicing what I know Alex must be feeling. But I know him, and regardless of what he says, he's not the kind of man who could or would take a child from its mother, no matter the circumstances. It's simply not in his character. I'm certain that in a few days his initial anger will pass and another solution will present itself."

Solution? There was no solution to this. There was only scandal, ruin and complete social ostracism.

"In the meanwhile, let us not dwell on this when you've only now just come home. As the children are fully occupied, why don't we go into the village and shop for dresses? The girls are in need of new summer frocks and by the look of your wardrobe, you are in need of gowns which actually fit." A teasing light lit Missy's eyes.

"Yes, Missy, it's a lovely day to shop," Katie said, quick to agree.

Charlotte managed a small smile. Katie had never been altogether keen on shopping but she was trying so very hard. They all were. God how she'd missed them, loved them.

"But do you think it wise for me to be seen out so publicly?" Charlotte asked. She'd had to weather many hardships thus far in her twenty-four years, but she wasn't sure she was prepared for the storm to come.

"My dear, this isn't London. And all that happened so long ago. Most will have forgotten the incident by now," Missy said, all quite straight-faced and the like.

James stopped pacing and looked sidelong at his wife. Katie appeared mesmerized by the black-and-red pattern of the rug.

Charlotte arched a brow at her sister-in-law. The scandal she'd caused was like a book left on a shelf where it grew dusty in a dark, rarely tread corner until the author returned to cast light on its forgotten tale. Her return ensured the whole of London would vividly recall, in every salacious detail, the *incident* as Missy had so prosaically chosen to call it. Charlotte called it the worst day of her life.

"Come, as my mother used to tell Thomas and I when our

financial decline made us practically pariahs in Society, if you permit the weeds to grow underfoot, ridding yourself of them later will be all the worse."

This Charlotte took to mean, *Gird your loins, my dear, and jump into the fray.*

"If you hide yourself away, people will believe that *you* believe you have something to be ashamed of. And I know you, Charlotte, whatever your reasons, I know in my heart you never set out to hurt us." Missy reached out from where she sat in the adjacent chair, caught her hand and gave it a reassuring squeeze.

Charlotte swallowed hard. What on earth had she ever done to deserve such absolute loyalty and faith in her family? Whatever it was, she was glad of it and relieved she hadn't arrived home to find herself confronted by walls erected due to hurt, anger and resentment.

"Shall I call for the girls?" Charlotte asked, rising from her seat.

"Oh no, my dear, my daughters have no interest in shopping, which is why I must perpetually take these trips alone. Truth to tell, I have Miss Foster come to the house to fit them when I'm not in a mood to venture out."

Against a backdrop of neatly stacked leather-bound books on mahogany shelves, James watched her silently, intently. And then slowly, as if the sun nudged aside gray clouds of gloom, a comforting smile lifted the corners of his mouth. "Go and enjoy yourself. We'll have time enough to deal with the matter. Right now, I'm just grateful you've finally come home. And whenever you're ready to talk, I will be here."

If she spoke now, she feared she'd turn into a watering pot and she'd cried enough in recent days—weeks—to singlehandedly keep the flowers in Kensington Gardens thriving for a good fortnight. So she simply went to her brother and hugged him very tightly. And he hugged her back, just as tightly, whispering a heartfelt, "I love you too," in her ear.

They fully understood each other.

Chapter Eight

The dressmaker, a Madame Rousseau, presumably a French woman (because all of the truly talented *modistes* hailed from France), kept a small shop on Broad Street, the very heart of Reading commerce.

Two evening gowns, one a silk cream with lace *chevrons*, the other a blue satin, the underskirt of white silk flounced with dark blue lace, decorated the shop window. Included in the display were three bolts of expensive fabric artfully arranged to entice ladies content to window shop to come in, indulge their desire for the latest in fashion, and inevitably part with their coin.

"Oh, I believe that is new," Missy said, admiring the cream confection. "Come, Miss Foster is waiting for us. I sent word for her to expect us at two."

Although the sun shone brightly, the air was an icy reminder that winter wasn't finished with them just yet. Wrapped in their wool, silk-lined pelisses, the three women filed into the shop.

The tinkle of a bell announced their arrival. The women in the shop turned and stared as they entered.

Charlotte's eyes quickly adjusted to the dim interior lighting as she took in the neat orderliness of the shop. It hadn't appeared so spacious from outside. It smelled faintly of beeswax, wool and citrus. The floors were broom swept clean, and the bolts upon bolts of colorful fabrics lining two walls of shelves drew the eye and the reels of ribbon, lace and velvet conjured up countless trimming possibilities.

Everyone in the shop—eight women of varying ages and sizes—smiled and a staggered chorus of, "Good afternoon, Lady Windmere, Miss Catherine," rang out.

While Missy and Catherine responded in kind, Charlotte smiled pleasantly, meeting the women's gazes one at a time. She'd have to face them sometime; she may as well start as she meant to go on.

The woman Missy had greeted as Mrs. Moreland puckered her brows as her gaze swung like a pendulum between her and Katie. The other women in the shop quickly followed suit, watching them with creased brows. It was some moments before anyone spoke.

"Why Lady Windmere, is this—?" Mrs. Moreland broke from the group, her stride purposeful as the hem of her blue-and-green striped skirts flittered across the floor.

"Ah, Mrs. Moreland, I don't believe you have had the pleasure to meet Catherine's sister, Charlotte. It's quite astonishing how much she and her sister resemble, is it not?"

When Mrs. Moreland flashed a most disingenuous smile, Charlotte forced herself to rise above her fate of social pariah by feigning oblivion. "Mrs. Moreland, nice to make your acquaintance."

"Miss Rutherford. Oh yes, I've heard *much* about you." The way Mrs. Moreland spoke and the manner in which she perused Charlotte's form—from top to bottom and then reversing the direction—made it perfectly clear the things she'd heard had not been complimentary.

But *this* Charlotte had expected. She simply had to brave her way through it all. Mrs. Moreland was the first but certainly wouldn't be the last. And the others may not possess her particular knack for subtlety.

"Yes, and we are delighted to have my sister home." Even with a flash of white teeth, Catherine's smile didn't reach her eyes. Her voice was ostensibly pleasant but her tight jaw and pursed lips practically dared the woman to misspeak.

"Will you be visiting long?" Mrs. Moreland inquired. "I heard you do not frequent these parts much."

Missy and her sister closed in around her, a bastion of female strength and loyalty, intent on protecting her from all the evils that may befall her. At present, the most notable came in the form of one Mrs. Moreland.

"Our hope is that Charlotte remains." Missy's voice had gone from superficially warm to icily civil. "So if we can convince her to stay, you will no doubt be seeing much more of her."

"Oh how delightful." This time, the woman didn't make the slightest attempt to sound unaffected.

"Ah, there is Miss Foster. She is expecting us. Good day, Mrs. Moreland." Missy's dismissal was abrupt and unequivocal. Charlotte quickly found herself being steered toward the woman who had just emerged from the back, her arm now hooked through her sister-in-law's.

The other women in the shop, who had long gone quiet as they'd unashamedly listened as Mrs. Moreland had singled her out, resumed talking, although in decidedly more muted voices than when they'd first arrived.

She is the one who jilted the Marquess of Avondale at the altar. Of all the nerve! Really, who is she to stand up a future duke? Everyone knows she's barely deemed respectable herself.

Charlotte could practically hear them; certain that was what they were whispering behind their gloved hands as their gazes slammed into her like a runaway train and then cut away with a surgeon's precision.

"Lady Windmere, Miss Catherine. My apologies to have kept yeh waitin'."

Focusing her attention on the woman approaching them, Charlotte was shocked—but pleasantly so—to see Miss Foster was a mulatto. A fair one, her complexion a good deal fairer than Jillian's, but a mulatto to be sure. Her mixed race was evident in her high cheekbones, her fuller lips and the texture of her hair, though it wasn't as dark a brown nor did it appear as frizzy as her maid's.

Standing slightly above average height, Miss Foster wore a gray dress with pagoda sleeves that skimmed a slim figure. She was lovely and currently her startling green eyes were just as intent in their study of Charlotte as Charlotte's were of her.

"Miss Foster, I would like you to meet my twin sister, Charlotte. She's recently arrived in Reading and is in dire need of a new wardrobe."

The woman dipped a curtsey. "Pleased tuh meet you."

Charlotte responded to the genuine warmth in her voice with a smile. "Miss Foster."

They were immediately led into a private dressing room—which was a welcome relief given the furtive stares she was now receiving from the other women in the shop—where the three sat on cushioned chairs. They pored over fashion plates while Miss Foster paraded in and out of the room with bolts of fabric, swatches of French lace, corded silk and *poult de soie*.

Lord, Charlotte had forgotten what this was like; shopping without the need to watch her pennies. Being able to contemplate such lush fabrics. Not that she'd had this luxury all her life, but when she and Katie had come to live with James, he'd showered them with every possible creature comfort, clearly trying to make up for everything they'd ever lacked. But more important, he and Missy had made them feel loved for the first time in their lives.

"Lottie, do you not adore this color?" Her sister passed her a swatch, a silk velvet in a color one couldn't precisely call pink or salmon but something in between.

Charlotte studied it closely, handling it with care. "It's beautiful." After stroking the fabric a moment longer, Charlotte handed it back to her. Before accepting it, Katie grasped her hand in hers. "Isn't this so much fun?"

"The most grown-up fun I've had in ages," Charlotte said with a laugh.

Katie smiled and held her hand a moment longer before relinquishing it and accepting the swatch.

By the time they departed the shop an hour and a half later having ordered a dozen dresses in total, stockings and various undergarments, a fresh crop of women were milling about in the store.

Ensconced in the landau, Missy removed her bonnet and placed it on the seat beside her. "You will have to take care should you ever have the misfortune to run into Mrs. Moreland again."

"I believe they'll all be much the same."

Katie angled toward her on the seat. "Mrs. Moreland is Lady Mary Cranford's cousin."

Lady Mary. The woman the duchess wanted Alex to marry. Charlotte had to tamp down a stab of jealousy.

Missy's gaze flitted between them. "I presume you told her?" she asked, addressing Katie.

When her sister nodded, Missy exhaled a heavy sigh.

No one spoke.

Desperate to change the subject and cover the strained silence, Charlotte asked, "Where was Madame Rousseau? I thought I was to meet her." And she had thought it curious the shop's proprietor hadn't been the one to wait on Missy, who was, after all, the Countess of Windmere.

"Ah yes, Madame Rousseau. Well it would appear that the latest Madame Rousseau has left for a shop in London."

Charlotte regarded her sister-in-law, brows drawn. "What do you mean the latest? Do you mean there is more than one?"

"Actually, there have been three in the past four years," her sister said dryly.

"But—"

"Madame Rousseau is the name of the shop so every woman who purports to run it must assume the role of Madame Rousseau."

None of it made sense and Charlotte's confusion must have shown on her face because Missy went on to explain, "You see, my dear, Madame Rousseau is really owned by Miss Foster but very few people are privy to the truth."

"Then why doesn't she call herself Madame Rousseau?" Which would have been the most logical thing.

"Because most of the women in town wouldn't patronize the

shop if they knew she actually owned it instead of merely worked there as a seamstress," Katie explained in a subdued voice.

"I see." And she did. She saw it all too clearly now. How silly of her to not have grasped the reason at once.

"It is a sad fact, but one we must accept until things change." Missy spoke as if she had no doubt things *would* one day change. "I know you'll say none of this to anyone."

"But of course." Charlotte met her sister's stare. "And how did you all come to hear about Miss Foster?"

"I met her when she worked for one of the other clothing shops."

"Yes, but when Catherine learned of the deplorable conditions the poor woman had to work under, she appealed to James to find her employment elsewhere." Missy gave Katie an approving nod.

"But after speaking to her, she admitted to secretly wanting her own dress shop. Since James owns the building, he offered to lease her the space after the current tenant moved out," Katie said.

"I wouldn't imagine she'd have the money to open a clothing shop," Charlotte remarked. Miss Foster was a mulatto and a woman. Her disadvantages were many, her business prospects few.

"She didn't. Alex gave her the money," Missy said, brushing back wisps of hair from her forehead.

Charlotte knew her sister's reasons for doing what she'd done. However, Alex was an entirely different story. "But why would Alex give her money? Was he acquainted with Miss Foster?" Although, she couldn't imagine under which circumstances something like that would occur.

Katie shot Missy an indiscernible look before replying, "She once came to his aid and he never forgot her kindness."

What could Miss Foster possibly have done for Alex? But as it was obvious neither woman intended to enlighten her, Charlotte reluctantly allowed the matter to drop.

After a pronounced pause, Katie said, "I don't think Alex will court Lady Mary now."

"I shouldn't be surprised if he did not," Missy agreed.

"Well it is certainly none of my affair who Alex chooses to court and marry." Charlotte had no doubt Alex would agree with her on that.

"Are you saying you don't care?" Katie asked.

"No, because who Alex marries will affect me in regards to Nicholas. What I'm saying is I have no say in it."

"And your concern is only for how it affects your son?" Missy sent her a knowing look.

"My feelings in this do not matter and should not."

"But they are your feelings, nonetheless. And you're entitled to them without shame or guilt," Missy said.

The discussion was quickly going the way of all things melancholy and that Charlotte could not take. They were supposed to be trying to keep her mind off the more unpleasant things she may soon have to face.

Determinedly, she clasped her gloved hands together and plopped them solidly on her lap. It was past time to advance topics and she conveyed it with all the subtlety of a dinner bell; unflinchingly direct and impossible to ignore while not offending the ears.

"Missy, you must tell me about the children. I can hardly believe how the twins have grown. And Lily is truly a stunningly beautiful child." She felt no guilt in having taken such ruthless and unerring aim at Missy's Achilles heel.

The following silence spoke as words never could. Charlotte watched as the two women's gazes met and bounced. Katie delicately cleared her throat and pulled her pelisse tighter around her.

Charlotte breathed a sigh of relief—a faint mist of air in the chilly carriage—when her sister-in-law enthusiastically launched into an enumeration of all her children's accomplishments.

The scent of wood shavings assailed his nostrils as Alex followed his friend, Viscount Creswell, into his workshop.

Shortly after his wedding, Creswell's wife, Elizabeth had convinced him to turn one of the two still rooms at their residence into a room where he could comfortably work on his carvings.

In the years since, his friend's hobby had grown to include the construction of beautiful pieces of furniture and various assortments of toys for his two children.

Planks of wood in varying sizes were stacked against the wall and on the sawdust-covered floor. The only place to sit was the stool on which Creswell usually worked.

Alex left him to it, choosing to lean against the table holding four planks of unvarnished wood.

"You look serious. This must be important," Creswell said, settling onto the stool.

"Had it not been, I wouldn't have called on you with so little notice."

Alex had sent word to his friend by messenger, apprising him of his visit the day he'd set off to his father's seat in Yorkshire. The business with his cousin hadn't taken long but the journey there had taken the duration of an entire day. The following evening he'd arrived at Armstrong's residence in Devon with his marriage papers in hand, where he'd been able to convince Armstrong that although it may not be the lawful thing to do, his signature as a witness was the right thing to do.

This morning, Alex had made his way to Creswell's residence in Hampshire in Sussex. Upon securing his friend's signature as the second witness to his fictitious wedding, he would return home.

Pushing his shirtsleeves up above his elbows, Creswell placed a short length of board on the table before him. He then removed one of the many saws from where it hung on a hook on the wall at his side.

"Well, what is it? Has it anything to do with the woman you're thinking of courting?" his friend asked, glancing up at him.

"Charlotte has returned."

The saw blade, barely touching the edge of the wooden board, instantly stilled in Creswell's hand. Slowly, he placed it on the table.

"Charlotte?" he asked in a strangled voice.

Alex nodded as his thoughts flashed back to his own response when he'd first seen her standing in the foyer. He'd never come so close to being poleaxed in his life. His feeling of complete and utter euphoria had been so fleeting, it'd barely registered, was almost immediately replaced by rage.

"Yes, Charlotte. And she's returned with my four-year-old son, Nicholas."

Creswell's eyes went as wide as Alex had ever seen them. He came carefully to his feet, the movement appearing deliberately tempered.

"What did you say?"

"Are you certain you wouldn't rather remain seated?" Alex gestured to the abandoned wooden stool.

"No, I believe I'd be better off standing for this." Creswell's voice was firm.

Five minutes later, his friend knew everything.

"Did she tell you why she left?" Creswell appeared to still be suffering from shock as he sagged against the table and ran both hands through the sides of his dark hair.

"Why she left will not change a thing."

Creswell blinked. "What the hell does that mean? Are you saying *you* don't want to know?"

"It will not get me back the time I've lost with my son is what I'm saying." Why was that so hard to understand?

"Well, no it won't, but it would explain things. I would want to know. I know Elizabeth will want to know."

Ignoring his friend's remark, he asked, "Will you sign the marriage papers?"

Instead of answering, Creswell steadily regarded him with both hands braced on the edge of the table.

"Have you feelings for her?" he asked, breaking the silence.

Alex found himself shaking his head even before Creswell had uttered the final words.

"Are you certain?" His friends probing felt like the constant prick of a pin.

"Given what she's done, how can you even ask that of me?"

"Remember, I was there after she left. I know what it did to you."

"That was long ago." Alex didn't want to remember. He'd put that time in his life behind him. Why did Creswell have to bring it up?

"Good God, man, you almost—"

"*Dammit!* Can't you leave it alone? But if you want the truth, when I first saw my son, I wanted to wring her neck." He could *not* and would *not* feel anything else for her.

"Yet you are willing to marry her disliking her as you do?"

Alex didn't like the knowing look in his friend's eyes. He hated that Creswell knew him so well. Or at least thought he did. "I am doing it for my son. In the same situation, would you not also?"

Removing his hands from the table, Creswell stood up straight, his blue-green gaze level with Alex's. "Yes I would," he said solemnly.

"Then you will do it for me?"

"I will do it for your son." His mouth quirked. "Although, if not for you and Rutherford, I greatly doubt Elizabeth and I would have married. I'm still in your debt for that."

Alex offered him a faint smile. "Friends are never in debt to one another."

Chapter Nine

Two days later, Alex had yet to make an appearance. Charlotte was frankly shocked he hadn't come. For all his talk and threats of how much he wanted his son, he was being woefully neglectful of him.

With one final glance out the bay window in the morning room, which overlooked the drive in the front, Charlotte gave up her post, a place she'd become too frequent a visitor.

She'd spent two whole days half dreading his arrival and the upheaval it would bring. But she couldn't help feeling a certain amount of nervous anticipation when he entered her thoughts—if ever he was far from them. It was wretched, truly it was, to be out of sorts and anxious knowing her future was so uncertain.

Thankfully Nicholas appeared to be settling in well, his days spent running wild with his cousins. But there would soon come a time when she'd have to tell him about Alex. Who he was to him. And that wouldn't be an easy conversation—at least not for her. He may only be four, but as with most children, her son could be painfully direct in his questions.

Mama, do I have a papa? Nicholas had asked that at the age of three.

For the barest instant, she'd considered telling him the truth. But how could she when she was passing herself off as a widow? It was one thing to lie about a fictitious husband but her heart had balked, too pained by the thought of telling Nicholas his father was dead. So instead she'd told him his father lived too far away for either to visit the other.

He'd frowned at that but a minute later he'd been all smiles and playfulness as they dressed to go to the shop for a treat, the conversation all but forgotten.

Or so she'd thought until six months later he'd asked Lucas with a child's innocence if *he* could be his father.

How would you like it if I became your uncle instead? Lucas had suggested.

Nicholas had been more than satisfied with that and wasted no time in baptizing the title, his every sentence peppered with Uncle Lucas this and Uncle Lucas that. Charlotte had heard the newly anointed address of Uncle Lucas incessantly for three weeks straight. It had been heartwarming and agonizing all at the same time.

Now, all too soon she would have to tell him the man he'd spoken to ever so briefly when they arrived *was* his father.

Charlotte walked over to the tray of pastries the maid had brought in for the midday tea. She was on her own for the next few hours having declined her sister's invitation to take tea with her friends. James had taken the twins to the shops to pick out a gift for their mother with her birthday a week away. Nicholas and Lily were taking their afternoon nap and Missy was going over the weekly menu with the housekeeper.

As she sat down and reached for a crème puff, the low timbre of Alex's voice filtered in from the foyer. She'd recognize it anywhere, even from a fair distance and through four inches of solid wood. Charlotte put the pastry down, hastily wiped her hands with a serviette and then patted her hair several times while her heart slammed against her chest as though trying to break out.

Moments later the door opened and the head footman appeared in the threshold.

"Milady, Lord Avondale to see you."

Before Charlotte could open her mouth to tell him to see his lordship in, Alex was there beside him, all tight-lipped and hooded eyes looking as grim as the reaper himself.

It would appear nothing had changed. She'd receive no dispensation from him. In fact, if she were going just by his stance, legs spread, hands folded across his chest, she would say it appeared he'd come prepared for a fight and she was the perfect opponent to spend his anger.

Charlotte's stomach knotted and the urge to flee pummeled her, hitting her much harder than it had the day he'd made his intentions clear. It would be all too easy to pack up their clothes, take Nicholas and run. But she'd run before and that was no longer an option she could consider. Not anymore. They'd have to find a way to coexist, if not peacefully than without rancor.

With a nod to the footman, he departed and Charlotte turned her attention to Alex.

In silence, they regarded each other. Or perhaps, regard was too innocuous a word to describe the cold heat of Alex's gaze. It pinned and bore holes that had the power to sear her insides and make the skin on her arms prickle despite the long and luxurious sleeves of her day dress.

"Hello, Alex." She was happy to discover she spoke in an even, calm tone, the opposite of how she felt inside.

He gave a brief nod, uttering an excessively civil, "Charlotte."

"If you've come to see Nicholas, I'm afraid he is napping. But he should awake in the next hour if you'd like to wait."

"While I'd very much like to see my son, I came here to speak with you. May we sit?" He motioned toward the collection of comfortable chairs that comprised the room's seating.

Perhaps it wouldn't be so bad after all. Charlotte turned and made her way back to the sofa and sank onto the cushioned silken brocade, the shiny material cool beneath her palms. He ignored the armchair closest to her, choosing to take the one that put him just within shouting distance. Another pinch to her heart—and it did hurt. She just could not afford to let him see how much.

Seated, he faced her across the low center table. Charlotte's mind went blank to fill only with the sight of him. His chiseled features appeared harder today, which did little to lessen his appeal. Indeed it served to bring it into sharper focus. The hard cut of his jaw, the dimple in his chin and the fullness of his bottom lip made her belly knot, her pulse race and her throat dry. Under the circumstances, paramount in her thoughts shouldn't be the kiss they'd shared the first night of her return; the wet tangle of tongues as he'd caressed her breast, but oh dear God, it was.

Contrarily, Alex didn't appear the slightest bit consumed by such lurid thoughts. He watched her quietly between slightly narrowed eyes, the iris pewter in color, the brackets around his mouth, pronounced. Without removing his gaze from her, he extracted a folded sheet of paper from his navy coat.

"I believe I've found the solution to our problems," he announced with just the faintest touch of grandstanding. He flicked his wrist and the paper fluttered.

Charlotte stared blankly at the paper in his hand. She couldn't imagine anything could solve *her* problems if she remained in England. Not even the contents of the letter, whatever it was.

But if he'd hoped to stir her curiosity, he'd succeeded. "Pray, what is it?" Had he had something drawn up promising to never take Nicholas from her? Or was there a document in existence that would cause him to love her again? Did a document exist that would vaccinate her and her sister against Society's judgment? If not, there could never truly be a solution to her problems.

With a low, mirthless chuckle, he unfolded the paper. Charlotte was growing accustomed to his laugh, a mixture of wryness and cynicism. She recalled a time when it had always brought a smile to her face.

"Your return will cause a far greater scandal than your precipitous flight."

"Would you prefer I return to America?" Had he'd changed his mind on that score?

Alex sent her a sharp look, all traces of even feigned amusement gone. "You would leave your son?"

It appeared he had not. "Of course not," she replied, feeling a tad snappish. Why was he doing this? They'd gone over this before. She would not leave, of that he was well aware.

"Then you have no choice but to stay."

Charlotte wondered at the trace of smugness in his voice. Wasn't it his dream to evict her from England, leaving the sole rearing of her son to him?

"I thought you wanted me gone?" She tried to not sound put out by it.

"As I told you, unlike you, I wouldn't deprive my son of his mother if it was in my power to do so."

Charlotte didn't respond as it was apparent he'd use the same stone to bludgeon her time and time again. He'd forever see her as the heartless villain.

"Will you tell me how that paper is the solution to our problems? That is why you came, is it not?" she asked, suddenly tired of it all.

"Among other things." He held it out to her across the table.

"What is it?" she asked as she reached to take it.

"You must read it as it requires your signature."

She waited only a moment before he placed it in her hand. There was no conceivable reason for their flesh to make contact; why the blunt tips of his fingers should brush the back of her hand. But she felt the contact just as acutely as if he'd placed his mouth there. Then it was gone.

Nerves stretched taut, she began to read. It took several moments for Charlotte to comprehend what she was reading. Then like the click of a key in a lock, she understood. Her fingers froze, her indrawn breath ended in a gasp that ricocheted off the book-lined walls as her gaze snapped to his.

"But—but these are marriage papers stating we married five years ago."

"Correct. And with this document, in the eyes of the law, we will be as soon as you sign it."

Charlotte rose as she tried to collect her wits. "But we are not."

"Yes but we will be once you sign it." Not a hint of coercion lent the softening of his voice. He spoke with a steely edge of determination that indicated this was a command not a request.

Good Lord, he was asking her to commit fraud. People had been sent to prison for less. What did he hope to gain by turning them into criminals? "Alex, this is foolish."

His form stiffened. He came to his feet and circled the table to loom above her five-feet-six-inch frame. When he spoke, his voice was even and controlled. "Yes, in matters pertaining to you, I've been known to act very foolishly. That I wholeheartedly admit. But in this, you do not have a choice. It is either marriage to me or ruin. Take your pick. What chance do you think Catherine will have to make a decent match when the *ton* learns her sister bore a child out of wedlock? And have you no care for your brother and his family? Will you be able to sleep at night if you embroil them in scandal?"

He took a step closer and leaned down, his face hovering perilously close to hers. "And since I won't allow you to take my son from me *again*, this is the only course we have to save us all from scandal."

Instinctively, Charlotte took a step back. She couldn't think with him this near and the scent of sandalwood wafting in the air.

"Alex, this will never work. There is a church full of people who were witness to us *not* exchanging vows."

Alex folded his arms across his chest, his wool coat stretched taut about his shoulders. "Armstrong and Creswell have already signed the marriage papers and will swear we exchanged vows the week before. A formal church wedding I will say was for my mother, who wanted a spectacular and lauded ceremony to celebrate the event."

At his words, Charlotte's eyes shot to the bottom of the document and on the two lines designated for witnesses were Thomas's and Derek's scrawled signatures.

"They agreed to this?" she asked, astonished. Her brother's friends were fastidiously honest.

"It took a great deal of convincing, but they eventually relented."

Charlotte could well imagine what Alex had had to say to them to involve them in something like this.

"They did not do this for me or you. They did because they have sons of their own and in their heart they know this is what Nicholas deserves."

Because of course, it was she who would have denied him his title and everything it entailed.

"And the vicar who married us?" she asked after a pause.

"My cousin. He's been running the parsonage near our country home these past eight years," he replied smoothly. He'd taken care of everything.

"A man of the cloth aids in committing this kind of fraud?"

"I urged my mother to convince the duke to grant him the living so it's fair to say, he believes he's in my debt."

In silence, they regarded one another.

She would have to live with this decision for the rest of her days. There'd be no going back.

He emitted a weary sigh and shook his head as he continued to eye her. "Do you truly believe I'd be doing this if I felt there was another avenue? I no more want to break the law than you, but I will for my son."

"But—"

"I find it terribly ironic that you, who kept my son's existence from me for four years, have now become skittish when it comes to the particulars of honesty and integrity in this matter."

Alex should have been a marksman for he managed to hit his target every single time. But truly, she had no one else to blame but herself as she'd unintentionally made herself too perfect a target.

Alex walked to the desk in the corner of the room and plucked a pen from the inkstand. Turning toward her, he held it up.

"You know you have no other choice but to sign it. You

know it is the right thing to do not only for Nicholas, but for everyone—yourself included. I may be many things, but the last thing I want to do is to have this whole affair played out in court. I do not want to take my son from you—but if you leave me no choice, I will."

At his words and the sincerity in his voice, Charlotte glimpsed the Alex of old. As much as he hated what she'd done and as much as he'd altered over the years, he still possessed that innate goodness she'd so loved in him.

And of course, he was right. This was the only way to avert a scandal. Oh there would be talk to be sure. A great deal of it. But with one sweep of the pen, she could restore to Nicholas what she'd been forced to deny him; his rightful place as his father's heir. This was the least she could do. And for her troubles, she'd finally get to be what she'd always wanted—to be Alex's wife.

Charlotte affixed her signature below Alex's. There, it was done. She looked up at him to find him steadily regarding her, the tick of his jaw hinting at deeper emotions simmering inside him than his otherwise inscrutable countenance conveyed.

Calmly, he reached over and retrieved the document from in front of her. He gave it a cursory glance, and then with a tight smile said, "It appears now we are man and wife."

Yes they were. But what did that mean? "How are we to explain this to everyone?"

"We have been estranged and you've only now come home desperate to give our marriage a second chance."

If only that were true. At least then, there'd be some hope for them.

"And Nicholas, what will you say about him? Won't people find it strange you've never mentioned him?"

"Half my peers do not discuss their children. I won't be that much of an oddity," he replied wryly.

Charlotte rolled her eyes. He was deliberately being obtuse.

"Alex, you know this is different. First a wife everyone would swear you did not marry, and then a son—your heir—

you never once spoke of? You don't think people will question that? Even the most trusting of souls will find all this incredulous."

"They can question it all they like but I'll have marriage papers to support everything I say."

How utterly confident he looked and nothing in his voice gave the impression of hesitation or uncertainty. But then the world he'd been born into no doubt led him to believe he could commit marriage fraud with impunity.

"I heard there is talk you were to court the Earl of Cranford's daughter. Is that true? Had you plans to marry her?" It was a fair question but a small part of her wanted him to know she knew. Which was silly as it wasn't as if there had been any betrayal on his part.

His lips twitched. "My, my, my," he said in a deceptively soft voice. "Gossip is becoming more dependable than the papers. And travels ten times the speed of trains."

"I'm certain my sister did not know it was supposed to be a secret as your mother was said to be quite vocal in her approval of the match. I heard all parties involved hoped for a wedding by year's end."

"Heard?" he asked, his voice pitched low. A dark eyebrow rose and a faint smile curled his lip. "Can you truthfully tell me you did not ask?"

Katie, will you tell me about Alex? And now? How is he now?

Of course she had asked.

Charlotte averted her gaze from his too knowing one.

"I thought as much." The low pitch of his voice thrummed her sensitized nerves.

The tick of the clock had the power to deafen in the ensuing silence. Charlotte could *feel* his relentless stare. After too long under the crushing weight of his scrutiny, she waved a white flag of surrender and looked him directly in the eye; something she now tried to avoid at all cost.

That was all it took. Desire jolted her with the force of a

thunderbolt. Her nipples beaded, her stomach contorted itself into a knot and she felt the relentless throb of desire below.

Tension crackled the air. Her breathing grew ragged, her heartbeat erratic as she devoured him with her eyes. She had never wanted a man more—and couldn't imagine she ever would.

A look of pure want and need flared so hotly in his eyes, it burned her everywhere it touched: her parted lips, her breasts, her belly, her hips, the apex of her thighs.

For seconds, they hovered on the precipice of something raw and explosive, hot and all consuming. Caught up in a sexual haze, Charlotte stepped forward without conscious thought or will, mouth parted and head tipped back for the kiss she ached for so badly, she could already feel it on her lips. Taste it in her mouth.

But with her advance came his abrupt retreat.

"You want me," he said softly, running his gaze down her body.

A denial would be ludicrous all things considered and Charlotte was not about to admit to the obvious.

The only thing preventing the smile curving his lips from being completely overbearing was the rapid rise and fall of his chest as if his breathing wasn't under his control, and not even his mocking words could mask the desire in his eyes.

"I could stand before you now and tell you it gives me no satisfaction to know that you want me." His gaze lit her on fire as it lifted slowly, lazily, from her rapidly rising breasts to look her in the eye. "But that would be a lie. I want you to want me," he said, his voice silky and low. "I want you to want me so much you burn every night when you lie in bed and dream of me. Dream of all the things you want me to do to you. The things you want to do to *me*."

Fever pitch in intensity, desire coursed through her veins.

Charlotte thought of the five years' worth of sensual fantasies that often kept her awake at night and then followed her into her dreams.

"If you only knew what I dream of you, Alex, you might cease in your torment of me," she said in a broken whisper.

A flash of emotion darkened his eyes to the color of smoke. "You have no idea of torment." His voice became as frigid as the Arctic winds and as dark as a moonless and starless night.

"And you are determined I shall learn it at your hands."

"It isn't for me to mete out punishment."

Was it not? Did he not think threatening to take her child from her was punishment enough to last a lifetime? That his ill feelings toward her didn't slice at her already bleeding heart?

He cleared his throat and made a show of adjusting his necktie and checking the line of his jacket. When he finally looked at her, he'd fortified the wall of stony indifference around him, treating her to a blank stare.

"I never courted Lady Mary. I have, in fact, courted no one but you. It will suit our purposes if everyone assumes it was *our* marriage that precluded me from doing so. Now you'll understand if I do not wait about for my son to awaken from his nap. But I expect you to have him at my residence next morning." That said, he gave her a curt nod and started toward the door.

"Wait."

Alex halted mid-stride but kept his back to her. He kept her in suspense seconds longer before turning around, one brow raised in query. "It would appear you're loath for me to leave." His statement sounded more self-deprecating than anything else.

"As we are now legally man and wife, Nicholas will have to be told you're his father. I think I should tell him today."

His body went rigid. "No," he snapped.

Not precisely the response she'd expected. "But you agree he must be told."

All of Reading would know within days. If Nicholas's cousins hadn't already heard, she'd no doubt they would soon.

"I want to be there." Again he eyed her as if she were the enemy. "You will *not* deny me that."

As she'd denied him so much else. He didn't have to say the words aloud for Charlotte to know it was the constant refrain in his mind.

"Then, we shall tell him together tomorrow." Everything seemed to be moving at staggering speeds.

He glanced at the clock, suddenly looking as if he'd better things to do than converse with her. "Now, if that is all?"

"Alex." Her voice hitched on his name. "I want you to know I never meant to hurt or deceive you."

"Indeed?" His wry query was accompanied by a supercilious lift of his eyebrow. "Then I can only imagine how ruthlessly proficient you can be when you make a task of it."

He then bestowed upon her a bow fit for the queen. "Good day, *Mrs. Cartwright.*"

Chapter Ten

"Mama, why can't my cousins come with us?"

Charlotte stared at the wood door in front of her but couldn't quite bring herself to ring the bell. The thought of facing Alex had her nerves stretched as taut as a tightrope and her body stiff with tension.

"Because Lord Cart—Avondale wishes to see us alone," she replied for the fourth time in almost as many minutes. She could feel a dull throb commencing in her right eye. She'd have a fearsome headache before this was over.

With Nicholas's small hand clasped tightly in hers, Charlotte stood on the doorstep of Gretchen Manor, unmoving until he looked up at her again, his expression one of growing impatience.

Charlotte sighed heavily and rang the bell. The door was promptly answered by a man of middle age clad in black. He glanced down at Nicholas before his regard returned to her. "Lady Avondale," he greeted in a formal tone. "His lordship is expecting you."

Good Lord, Alex had just made her a marchioness and one day she'd be a duchess. It would take some time to not only digest it but accept it. In the meantime, she'd have to stop herself from looking about her like some gauche country girl when people addressed her by her new title.

They were admitted into the foyer. Her son tightened his grip on her hand. He too was nervous.

"His lordship awaits you in the withdrawing room."

After handing the attending footman her bonnet and cloak, Charlotte took her son's hand in hers and followed the butler, who announced them with a gravity that tragically suited the occasion.

Alex stood upon their entrance. Her heart leapt at the sight of him. In a word, he looked dashing. And in case her eyes had forgotten what a face as handsome as his could do to a body, her heart reminded her when it went from anxiously beating to furiously pounding. She wouldn't be surprised if he asked her to keep the noise down.

It appeared he'd spared nothing in his meeting with his son. Not the perfectly tied black necktie or the unadorned, dark green waistcoat, silk shirt and coat. No, today he epitomized the quintessential man about town; dressed to display his illustrious title and considerable wealth and success.

With a curt nod to his butler, Alex sent the man on his way. The click of the door closing was the only sound to be heard for many moments after.

Nicholas's gaze bounced between them. He too could sense the tension, which would have the opposite effect of putting him at ease.

"Hello, Nicholas." Alex's voice sounded impossibly deep but the way his somber expression transformed when he looked at his son squeezed her heart. In that moment she saw the old Alex: charming and engaging, so full of *joie de vivre*.

"Hullo." Nicholas's grip on her hand tightened.

Alex's eyes narrowed at her. He regarded her in that manner that urged—insisted—she put her son at ease. But he should know that Nicholas would never be at ease if he continued to glower at her as he was doing.

"Are you enjoying England?" Old Alex instantly materialized again when talking to his son.

Nicholas gave a shy nod.

"And do you enjoy playing with your cousins?"

Nicholas gave a much more enthusiastic nod. Several in fact.

"Would you like to sit?"

While Nicholas glanced over at the sofa feet from where they stood like two poor relations upon their first visit to the manor house, Alex shot her an accusing glare condemning her silence.

Pray, what did he expect her to do? This whole situation was difficult enough. He could at least pretend he didn't absolutely despise the ground she walked on in front of their son.

"Yes, let us sit." She tried to make her voice light but failed utterly, her words emerging in a strained rasp.

Once they were all seated—she and Nicholas on the sofa, Alex adjacent in a wing chair of Utrecht plush—her son finally relinquished the fierce grip he had on her hand and instead pressed up against her side and hooked his arm through hers.

It was clear from the tightness of his jaw that Alex was taking it all in. This would be no easy task, trying to extricate her son from her if that was his plan. The bond between them could anchor ships in the middle of the ocean. Any attempt to break it would evoke a battle of biblical proportions. And Nicholas, the most innocent in this affair, would be the one most hurt.

Alex cleared his throat. For the first time since she'd seen him again, he looked uncertain at how to proceed. And it was that hint of vulnerability in him that softened her and pushed her to take things in hand.

"Nicholas, do you remember when I told you your father was far, far away and that's why he couldn't see you?" She was looking at her son as she spoke, but from her peripheral, she saw Alex's jaw tighten. He'd never forgive her those lies.

Nicholas nodded mutely.

"Well, that's because he lives here, in England."

Her son's face brightened, a smile splitting his face. "Does that mean I can meet him?"

Charlotte glanced at Alex in time to see another flash of emotion flit across his face. This time she had no trouble pinpointing it. Anguish. She redoubled her efforts.

"Darling, Lord Avondale—Alex, he is your father."

With her words, a burden of five years in the making lifted

from her shoulders only to have nail-biting anxiety set in. She held her breath.

Nicholas's head whipped around so fast she feared he'd injure himself. Mouth agape, eyes the size of half crowns, he stared at Alex.

The silence was excruciating even if it lasted only seconds. The longest seconds in his life.

Alex eased his mouth into a smile, hoping to reassure and express his pleasure at the same time. His son didn't have to know that under his mask of calm, his nerves were razor thin and felt stretched to snapping.

Alex wasn't a poet and never purported to the artistic craft. But the light from the sun on the most beautiful summer day paled to the smile lighting his son's face. It brightened everything in the room, in the house, in all of England. More than anything, it lit up everything gray and shadowed in his life, giving Alex a sense of purpose he'd never had before. The care of this child—his wonderful son—was his. The notion was staggering and humbling.

"You are my papa?" Nicholas's voice trembled with excitement.

Alex began to speak but words failed him, caught somewhere between his heart and his throat. When they looked back on this moment, years from now, he prayed his son's first memory of him wasn't seeing him reduced to a blubbering mess upon their introduction.

He cleared his throat again. "Yes, I am your father."

As pleased as Nicholas appeared, he didn't so much as budge from his mother's side, although he'd given her back the full use of her left arm. What did he do now? Alex couldn't remember a time the duke had ever touched him in affection and while he knew his mother loved him, she simply wasn't the touching sort.

But he wanted to touch—hug—his son. Hold him long enough to make up for all the years they'd lost.

"Go on," Charlotte said, her voice soothing. "If you'd like to hug him, you can. I'm sure your father would like that."

Alex didn't want to feel kindly toward her. But for her, there'd be no awkwardness to overcome. Father and son would have long been acquainted to the sum of four years. However, he grudgingly conceded that she was trying to help. As well she should.

Nicholas slid from the sofa and took a tentative step toward him, his smile wavering. He glanced back at his mother, who nodded her encouragement.

Alex pushed from his seat and dropped one knee to the rug. He opened his arms and that was all the reassurance Nicholas needed, stepping into his embrace. His small arms encircled his neck, and Alex had never been so close to blubbering in his entire life.

"I always wanted a father."

Emotion constricted Alex's throat. He squeezed the little body to him and breathed him in. He smelled of soap and baby powder and felt sturdy and fragile at the same time. "No more than I wanted a son just like you."

Over the top of Nicholas's head, Alex met Charlotte's gaze. Tears streamed down her face. She quickly bent her head and snapped open the reticule she had at her side. Seconds later, a handkerchief materialized in her hand, which she put to immediate use sopping up her tears.

When Nicholas removed his arms from around his neck, Alex wasn't ready to release him. But because he didn't want to overwhelm him, Alex dropped his hands to his side, resisting the urge to snatch him back, hold on to him for dear life and never let him go.

Nicholas returned to his mother's side, his smile fairly triumphant and absurdly pleased. Smiling, Alex levered himself up and back into the chair.

That had gone well. Certainly better than Alex had anticipated given the rocky start.

Charlotte sent him a wistful smile and for a moment he was

transported. Back to a time of unbridled happiness when the future looked brighter than the sun and was a journey they'd take together as man and wife.

She'd been crying so in all fairness her face ought to be blotchy and her eyes red-rimmed. Instead, her creamy, unblemished complexion and blue eyes defied the ravages of tears as if to punish him. If only he wasn't still attracted to her, how easier his life would be. But better physical attraction than feel even a fraction of what he'd once felt for her. Loving her that much had nearly destroyed him.

"Mama, I'm hungry." Nicholas had resumed his seat beside his mother, his feet dangling over the lip of the sofa revealing blue stockings beneath navy trousers. He wasn't dressed like a proper English boy, a fact Alex intended to remedy straightaway. It was bad enough he spoke like an American, he couldn't have people mistaking his son for a foreigner, thus encouraging them to treat him as though he didn't belong.

Alex rose to his feet. "I will have Cook make you something to eat. What would you like?"

"I want to go to my cousins' home and eat with them," Nicholas blurted.

Home. A word that should have conjured up images of love, hearth and family instead represented nothing but division and strife. And suddenly Alex was consumed with a blinding anger. Gretchen Manor ought to be Nicholas's home.

No, this would not do. He, forced to call on his child like some interloper, or dependent on Charlotte to bring him by? He hadn't been willing to put his son through the trauma of being separated from his mother, but to have to live with her, share a roof with her...the prospect was as enticing as it was disturbing. And he resented her for that. That after so long, she still had power enough over him to entice. Adam had lost that battle with Eve but Alex refused to allow Charlotte to be his downfall.

"Nicholas, I am your father so do you know what that means?"

Two pairs of blue eyes snapped to his—one in question, the other warily.

"It means you—we will all live here. Together as a family."

Alex's announcement rattled her to the core.

"Mama, does that mean we're never going back to our real home?" Nicholas asked in alarm. The only reaction to indicate Alex was at all affected by his son's obvious distress was the tightening of his jaw.

Charlotte grew more annoyed by the minute. That he hadn't spoken of this with her, something this important, so life altering was simply beyond the pale. And the way things stood between them, living under the same roof was in no one's best interest. At least not at present.

"Nicholas, my housekeeper brought her grandson by for a visit. Would you like to meet him? He's just about your age," Alex coaxed with a smile.

"The cook can fix you both a snack and then you can play. Do you like trains?" Alex asked, continuing in his relentless pursuit to win his son's affections. "If you do, I believe there's a new train set upstairs in the playroom."

Toys. A child his age to play with. Food. They were all nirvana to a boy's ears.

"A train set? For me?" Her son was on his feet in an instant, his body taut as a harp's string with barely contained excitement.

Alex chuckled as he stood. "Yes, a train set for you. Let me call Mrs. Martindale." He promptly rang for the housekeeper.

Her son turned and beamed at her. Charlotte smiled stiffly. Apparently, the want of his cousins' company had soundly been trumped.

Five minutes later, a giggling Nicholas, his new friend Jonas, the housekeeper's five-year-old grandson, and Mrs. Martindale herself, departed the room.

The moment the door closed, Charlotte spun in a flourish of flounced skirts and flashing eyes to confront him.

"Alex, how could you?" she asked, her voice high and incredulous.

While she stood, her body tense, her composure shaken, the blasted man sauntered over to his chair and sat down. In seeming quiet repose, long legs stretched negligently out before him, he regarded her.

"I believe I told you I wanted my son with *me*." He spoke in a tone that made her grit her teeth.

"But you had no right telling Nicholas we would be living with you. That is something you should have discussed with me first. Have you forgotten he is just a boy and his whole life has changed? He'll require time to adjust."

"Did he appear distressed when he left?" he asked, gesturing toward the closed drawing room doors. "Believe me, children adapt better and faster than adults. Nicholas will be fine."

"How can you be so unfeeling? His excitement over the toy will fade and then where will he be? I shall tell you, he'll be fretting over the fact that he'll never see his friends in America again," Charlotte said, arms akimbo.

"As my wife—"

"Wife? Alex, you know as well as I that this marriage is a farce. You detest the fact that you must be married to me to legitimize our son."

His brows shot up and she wasn't sure if his surprise conveyed was at her obvious anger or her thoughts about their so-called marriage. A grimness settled over his features, and his gray eyes pierced her with an icy glare.

After the show he'd recently made of settling into the chair, he came to his feet slowly, like a lion preparing to pounce when it finally had its prey in sight. And he didn't commence speaking until his advantage was complete; in height, strength and fury.

"No, madam, it is you who should be the grateful one. This *farce* you so disparagingly call our marriage is the only thing standing between you and total ruin. This *farce* is the sole reason I'm not taking you to court for custody of my son. So unless you wish to jeopardize everything you hold dear, I suggest you climb down off that mountain you seem intent on pitching yourself from due to your own obduracy and thank God I deign to even speak to you, much less claim you as my wife and have you in my home. I doubt any other man in my position would be as generous."

Now Charlotte wished for a chair because her legs no longer wanted to support her. Blindly, she backed away from him until the backs of her legs bumped against the give of the brushed-velvet sofa. She didn't so much as sit as drop down onto it with a *whoosh* and fluttering skirts.

One would think she'd have grown accustomed to it by now. Yet still when she heard the contempt in his voice and saw the way anger lit his eyes, it felt as if she was floating outside of herself observing another woman. For the woman who elicited such violent emotions in him could not be her. The Alex she knew had been passionate, loving and kind.

She looked at him only after she could breathe without the stabbing pain in her chest.

At first glance, he appeared composed. But upon closer inspection, Charlotte noticed the tick of his jaw, as if he were grinding his teeth, and how he held himself absolutely still.

"Alex, this will never work, you and I living together in the same residence. Do you not see that? You despise me." Her voice caught on the word. "It will be a great miracle if we are able to persuade anyone we're happily reunited."

He took his time answering. "I said *you* were desperate for a second chance, not I. In any case, it's no business of theirs how we are in our private lives. The only thing that matters is we present a united front. Our happiness or lack thereof is no one's concern but ours."

She could believe he'd have no qualms about subjecting her to a life of misery, but himself? That she couldn't imagine. But there was one person whose happiness they both cared about.

"And what of Nicholas, shouldn't we try so for his sake? I should not like him to have to endure the kind of childhood where it's obvious his parents don't get on."

Endless seconds passed before he replied softly, "No, I shouldn't like my son to be raised in that kind of atmosphere. I know well enough what a trial that can be."

A tiny flame of hope flickered alive within her. Perhaps, she was getting through to him.

"What kind of marriage are we to have?" Charlotte refused to live in suspense, wondering and hoping, although yearning would be the worst. It was best she walk into this with her eyes wide open.

She hadn't thought the question impertinent or provocative, but suddenly he regarded her slyly, as if he found something in her perfectly legitimate question vaguely amusing. "What kind of marriage would you like us to have?"

"I-I should prefer we not constantly be at odds."

"I believe we can manage that. What else?" he asked softly, eyebrow raised.

"And that you not look at me as if you cannot bear the sight of me."

"I wasn't aware that I did."

She noticed he didn't deny that he could not bear the sight of her.

"Sometimes even *you* cannot hide *everything* you're feeling."

He smiled one of those cryptic smiles that spoke volumes but revealed nothing. He advanced toward her, until he stood over her, forcing her to crane her neck to meet his half-lidded gaze.

It became discomfiting to remain seated while he towered above her. On legs that now felt strong enough to support her weight—though only barely with him looking at her in that manner—she rose.

She hardly met him eye to eye given his superior height but it gave her—no matter how erroneous—the sense of a more equitable distribution of power in their discussion.

"Then I shall endeavor to gaze at you in nothing less than an endearing manner. Will that suit?" Another arched-brow look.

Charlotte was astonished. Not two minutes ago, he'd given her a sound dressing down in that icy tone of his and now on this matter he sought to bring levity?

"You are mocking me," she accused.

"Oh no, I would never do that," he said in a lowered voice. "In public we may be able to fool others, but our son is an entirely different kettle of fish."

"So what do you propose we do to ensure Nicholas believes we care for each other?" His voice dropped lower as his gaze fastened on her mouth.

Charlotte had seen that look in his eyes before. He wanted her whether he wished to or not. And she wanted him with a ferocity that was frightening in its intensity.

She gave a delicious shiver and watched mesmerized as he lifted his hand to her face and lightly, gently stroked her cheek with the backs of his fingers. It was barely a touch really, but it affected her more than if he'd cupped the whole of her face in his palms. Her breath caught in her throat as desire and a soul-deep need of him kept her rooted in place.

"Should I touch you like this?" Another stroke of her cheek followed. Charlotte had to stop herself from nuzzling her face into the source of such indescribable pleasure. She stifled a whimper as her arousal began to climb. And he hadn't *truly* touched her yet.

From her hot cheek, his fingers feathered along her jawline and then cupped her chin in his palm. With only the slightest bit of pressure, he angled her head before lowering his mouth to hers.

This was a prelude, his lips soft and coaxing, skimming and gently rubbing. Charlotte neither had the will nor the means to fight the tumult of passion that flared to full, blistering life within her. He drove her wild. She wanted more.

Her lips parted in eager response and she gave a breathy sigh when his tongue touched hers. And that quickly the kiss moved from gentle to wild and hungry. Then her body was plastered to his from thigh to torso, the spread of his fingers anchoring her head.

His tongue went on a greedy foray of her mouth, exploring her inner cheeks, the roof of her mouth and the sensitive underside beneath her tongue.

Charlotte needed to get closer, pressing—grinding—her hips against him. Her senses were filled with him. The scent of him surrounded her as heady as anything she'd ever inhaled. The taste of him, she couldn't get enough. Catching his bottom lip between her teeth, she ran the tip of her tongue over the full pink flesh. God, she'd been longing to do that.

She felt his erection hard against her belly. She squirmed to get closer but her skirts and petticoats were unwanted encumbrances to feeling him where she needed him most. Starting at his nape, she ran her hands up through the silky thickness of his hair until she was gripping handfuls and pressing him closer to her and feeding him her tongue in a maelstrom of greedy, hot, wet kisses.

The knock on the door, intrusive and unwelcome, startled them into action. They separated with a speed only the guilty could manage. Shaken, breathless and clenching her inner thighs together in hopes it would somehow relieve the throbbing ache between them, Charlotte gave her back to the door. Seconds later, she heard it open.

"Milord, would you like me to bring the tea?"

"No. And I will call you if I need you," Alex replied curtly.

The door immediately clicked closed.

Charlotte dragged draughts of air into her lungs, her balance not all it ought to be. It required a bit of time, but once her rampaging heart slowed to a regular *thump thump* and her breaths were not quite so excessive, she turned.

Alex too hadn't been unaffected, his breathing just as shallow as hers and the lust glaze still in his eyes. He stared at her and the next time he blinked, his expression transformed, becoming guarded.

"Do you think a kiss of that nature would convince him we

are on good terms?" He spoke in a tone uninflected.

"I believe a kiss far less substantial would have sufficed." She'd completely forgotten the discussion that had preceded the kiss.

He turned and crossed the carpet to the sideboard as if eager to put some distance between them. For the barest moment, his hand seemed to hover over one of the crystal glasses sitting atop.

It was then Charlotte remembered what her sister had told her about his drinking.

Well, he does not drink spirits anymore. Not one drop.

Abruptly, he dropped his hand to his side and turned back to face her. He made no effort to hide his arousal, which was making an impressive tent in the front of his trousers. The sight of it distracted her from her thoughts.

"Forgive me, I should not have kissed you as I did," he said evenly.

The last thing she expected was an apology. Surely he knew how much she liked it when he kissed her, touched her, made love to her.

"There's no need to apologize. The physical chemistry between us has always been..." How could she describe it? "Very good."

Explosive, wild, uncontrollable were words that better described what happened to her when he touched her. But they would also reveal to what extent he affected her. He had considerable control over her life as it stood and she refused to serve herself to him on a platter.

"It's obvious I still find you attractive and I admit I wouldn't mind having you in my bed. If I claimed otherwise, my body would already have made a liar of me."

Charlotte's gaze dropped briefly to the front of his trousers, where his erection emphatically confirmed the veracity of his claim. Her face was awash in heat.

"No," he continued as if nothing was untoward. As if standing in front of a woman whom he disliked with his arousal as visible as an elephant in a room was commonplace. "What I want understood is that I have no intention in getting more involved with you than circumstances warrant. We have a son and there is a filed document that binds us legally in marriage. But that is all we shall ever have."

Ever. Ever? The word sounded too concrete and final. It held no hope of possibilities. It conveyed years of…nothing. At least in America, he'd been out of reach. But to be married to him and living under the same roof and yet remain so far apart—would be a great deal worse.

"You expect us to live together, reside under the same roof and not…" How did one delicately phrase it? Make love would make a mockery of the term and many of the various terms she'd heard used would be indelicate.

Then she chanced upon it. "Have marital relations." A perfectly respectable yet staid way of phrasing. Quite devoid of the passion brought to the act itself.

A hint of humor flashed in his eyes and his mouth curled slightly up.

"I know it would be acceptable to you if we indulged in *that* aspect of our marriage."

When Charlotte failed to respond, his gaze narrowed and his mouth flattened into a thin line. "Or perhaps you've grown so accustomed to enjoying *marital relations*, the thought of doing without is making you queasy."

She could protest for he couldn't be further from the truth, but why should she waste her breath? He wouldn't believe a word she said.

"Do you mean for us to live a life of celibacy?" The notion was unthinkable.

This brought another of those wry smiles to his mouth. "Celibacy?" he asked, raising a brow. "I think not."

Charlotte swallowed. So that was how it would be. "If we are not to be faithful to each other, I insist we use discretion— for Nicholas's sake."

His form went ominously still and even his breathing

appeared to cease. Silence blanketed the room until the tension in the air almost stifled her.

"*We?* No my dear, *I* shall have a need of discretion. *You* will not, because if I ever discover you've taken a lover, I shall divorce you and scandal will follow you wherever you go. Do I make myself perfectly clear?" His words came out whisper soft but detonated in her ears with the force of a grenade. His nostrils flared and his eyes bored her in pinpoints of rage.

Charlotte hadn't expected such a reaction from him. It was illogical. Not that she'd intended to take a lover. She'd merely been reacting to the news he never intended to consummate their marriage.

"You expect me to go without physical intimacy for the remainder of my life?" she asked with unabashed incredulity.

"I expect you not to forsake your vows," he stated, his tone edged with steel.

Bewildered, Charlotte gave her head a hard shake. Had the man gone daft? "You forget, we made no vows to each other."

"Our marriage papers say we did, which is why I expect you to conduct yourself impeccably."

Alex wasn't making any sense. It certainly wasn't as if he could be jealous. What he appeared to be suffering from was an acute case of dog-in-the-manger syndrome. And at present, she hadn't the mental fortitude to take this on. Since there was not the remotest possibility she'd take a lover in the future, she remained silent on the subject and allowed the matter to drop.

"Are you saying you have no desire for more children?" She remembered when they'd talked of having children. Alex had said he hoped to fill every bedchamber in Fairleigh House, the home he'd bought for them in London. There had been six.

"Oh, I want more children," he replied softly, his gaze steady on hers. "I just don't want them with you. And as you are the only recourse I have to supply me with legitimate issue, Nicholas will be an only child."

Charlotte forced herself to breathe through the pain. He was deliberately trying to hurt her. She could tell by the look in his eyes, the provoking stare that dared her to respond. Willed her to give him further reason to despise her. Swallowing hard, she tamped it down, the pain, the hurt, all that he'd undoubtedly wanted to elicit in her.

Spine rigid and shoulders back, Charlotte collected herself, an internal feat that took much from her. "Very well, I believe we understand each other."

For a man who'd just made the rules and laid down the law, he didn't look particularly pleased as one would expect.

"I will make the arrangements to have your possessions moved here," he said briskly. "Tomorrow we must all go to London."

Charlotte shot him a sharp look, her brows arched. "Why must *we* go to London?"

"We are going because I will not allow my mother to learn of our marriage via the rags or the gossips. I also want my parents to meet their grandson. We will stay the night."

Charlotte had met the duke but once and it hadn't been a pleasant experience. He hadn't approved of her. The way his lips had curled and his eyes had perused her clearly stated he found her wanting. Only slightly less obvious in expressing her disapproval, the duchess had spent the majority of their visit to Alex's residence blithely ignoring her.

I'll grant you, she's a very pretty girl, but, my dear, must you marry her? His mother had remarked when Charlotte had left the drawing room, needing desperately to remove herself from an atmosphere brimming with civil hostility they'd made no effort to hide. The duchess hadn't stopped there. She'd gone on to elaborate her point:

For heaven's sake, do we even know who her mother is, what kind of family she comes from? They say blood always tells, and I should hate to discover she has even more a disreputable lineage than the unfortunate circumstances of her birth.

His mother's words had rung in her ears long after she'd departed. Those same words had pummeled her relentlessly after they'd spoken with Mrs. Henley. Those same words had chimed liked a death knell when she'd read the letter two days before her wedding day.

But the meeting with his parents would have to occur at some point. And she understood the reason he wanted it to occur as quickly as possible. They deserved to meet their grandson.

Charlotte nodded. "Then I best get ready. Will you have Mrs. Martindale bring Nicholas back?"

Alex walked to the fireplace and tugged the tasseled bell pull beside it.

"My carriage will pick you both up tomorrow at nine. I ask that you don't keep me waiting."

Charlotte nodded and turned to go. She was at the door when she heard him say under his breath, "Once this lifetime is sufficient."

Chapter Eleven

Charlotte returned to Rutherford Manor spent, completely bereft of emotion. Meeting with Alex now always seemed to leave her this way. The moment they entered the house, Nicholas was off running, shouting his cousins' names loud enough to wake the dead. Their response came from upstairs in voices just as boisterous, Lily's a shriek promising pandemonium.

Jillian came hurrying down the hall upon hearing all the noise. Today, she wore her hair up, her corkscrew curls secured in the back with strategically placed hair combs and hairpins. The dress she wore, light green with long raglan sleeves, was one Charlotte had never seen on her before.

Forced to wrestle her son's outer garment from him as he wouldn't remain still, Charlotte handed it to the attending footman and then watched as Nicholas scampered up the stairs where his cousins were playing.

She noted that she wasn't the only one looking at Jillian. The footman, a tall, strapping young man with hair the color of ripe wheat, seemed to linger on her maid a beat too long.

When Charlotte peered up at him, his gaze snapped back to her, a polite, deferential smile firmly in place. And he was a handsome one with his blue eyes and lashes thick enough to sweep.

Charlotte had a sinking feeling she was staring trouble directly in the face. She beat the feeling back. No use courting trouble when it had yet to rear its head. After handing him her bonnet and pelisse, he departed.

Her stomach growled her hunger but she hadn't the faintest

desire to eat. However, she best if she wanted to avoid a stern lecture from her sister. She'd put on a bit of weight since her arrival but not nearly enough to satisfy Katie.

"Jillian, is my sister at home?"

"No, Miz Charlotte, Miz Catherine is still out," she replied, coming to her side.

Before she'd left to see Alex, Katie had said she'd be calling on her good friend Lady Olivia Spencer, sister to the Earl of Granville.

"Come, we must talk." Hooking her arm through her maid's, Charlotte led her to the morning room.

Jillian hailed from America's south and had spent the first twelve years of her life on a plantation but had run away to New York with seven fellow slaves during an uprising. Unfortunately, her mother hadn't survived the journey, succumbing to a fever days short of their arrival.

It had been fate that Charlotte had come upon her the day the poor girl had arrived in New York, a frightened, bedraggled, half-starved child left to fend for herself taking refuge in the empty flat. Charlotte, already three months pregnant at the time, had been looking for affordable housing, conscious that the money she'd managed to obtain from her trust by forging her brother's name, would not last forever. But if she was frugal, it would last her a good many years.

Jillian's promise of great beauty had been evident even then. Charlotte had feared if she didn't take her in she'd end up spending her life on her back. The men had already been buzzing about her like swarms of mating gnats at dusk.

The land agent, a handsomish man of thirty or so, had insisted he'd take care of the problem, clasping Jillian by her thin arm. It had been the look of utter terror in the girl's eyes that caused Charlotte to intervene—that and a little of her own guilt, for in her she saw that same frightened child.

The land agent, a Mr. Overton, had been watching her too closely, with almost lascivious intent and Charlotte knew she couldn't allow him to take her. She'd asked her name and then offered her the position as her maid on the spot. Jillian had been nearly frenetic in her acceptance, latching on to her as if she were her savior—and perhaps Charlotte had been.

Lord, that had been five years ago and my how she'd grown. Jillian was more a little sister to her than servant.

"Are you being treated well?" Jillian may be beautiful but she was still the product of a Negro slave—had been a house slave herself—and many could not see beyond that and made certain she would never forget her place in Society.

This was the first time she'd been in a house of this magnitude, rubbing shoulders with so many servants. Charlotte prayed there wouldn't be friction.

"The men are nice," she said, her voice tentative as if taking undue care to choose her words carefully.

Charlotte thought of the footman. Of course they were. Jillian was young and beautiful and men had eyes.

"The chil'ren are kind."

"Has anyone been unkind to you?" Charlotte would speak to her brother if she got even a hint that Jillian was being treated poorly by the other servants. Women could be particularly horrid to one another. And as for the men, if any of them thought to take advantage of her, they'd have to deal with James directly.

Jillian shook her head, short, anxious movements, her hazel eyes round and pleading. She didn't want to stir the embers. "The women don't talk tuh me much, is all."

Some of Charlotte's anxiety drained. Better they ignore her than be vocal about their disdain—prejudice really, for that's what it was.

"Well you shan't have to deal with them much longer. We will be leaving to live with Lord Avondale. He owns the neighboring estate not far from here."

Some indiscernible emotion flickered across Jillian's face and was gone in an instant before she nodded. She'd always been like this, following directions without questions or resistance. Charlotte really wished she would speak up more or at least express some surprise, but she feared it had been beaten out of her long before she'd found her.

"Miz Catherine gave me dis and another of her ole dresses." She ran her hands lovingly over the light green skirt and the smile on her face made Charlotte misty-eyed. "She said you wouldn't mind if I took dem."

"But of course you may accept them." Since she and Jillian were approximately the same size, she'd always given her whatever old dresses she could spare. But Charlotte tended to keep her dresses for years, so she hadn't had all that many to pass on. She hoped her sister's lady's maid didn't mind. No doubt she was accustomed to getting her mistress's cast offs.

Perhaps it was a good thing they'd all be decamping to Alex's residence after all. His staff didn't appear as large, but then he was a bachelor and didn't require the number of servants her brother did. She'd seen signs of only two footmen, which was at least a quarter of what her brother employed. And as she would be the lady of the house—good Lord, she would, wouldn't she?—she'd be able to dispense Jillian's duties.

"Tomorrow, I shall be traveling to London with Nicholas— and my-my husband." If she wanted others to believe they were truly married, she couldn't choke on the word as if it was foreign to her tongue or freshly minted.

"Husband? You is married?" Arched eyebrows disappeared beneath of tangle of haphazard dark brown curls. Her maid looked bewildered, as was to be expected. If Jillian tended more to impertinency, she'd have saucily asked, *Are you a widow or are you not?*

"For the sake of my well-being and that of Nicholas, I felt it best to tell everyone my husband had died. I was alone and pregnant and there would have been too many questions if they knew who he was. My husband is a man of great wealth and his family is very powerful and influential."

In silence, Jillian took it all in, if appearing somewhat dazed. Then her forehead creased. Charlotte could tell she wanted to ask her the very question everyone would have asked if it had all been true. *But why would you leave such a man?* True to her nature, Jillian said nothing, merely nodding as if what she'd been told explained everything.

In this one instance, Charlotte was relieved at the girl's quiet acquiescence as she detested having to lie to her. But for five years now, lies—outright and those by omission—had become so integral to her life, they had no longer felt like lies.

The following day, Charlotte chose her gown with great care. The impending meeting with Alex's parents had her stomach threatening to reject the buttered toast, egg and hot chocolate she'd eaten at breakfast.

The duchess had the regal poise of a queen and the duke was all ducal hauteur. Together they were an intimidating pair. If five years ago, neither had thought her good enough for their son, today they no doubt despised her.

Since their visit to Miss Foster's, two of the five gowns she'd ordered had been delivered. Thankfully one had been Charlotte's favorite. The lavender complemented her complexion and brought out the blue of her eyes—or so Alex had once told her. She liked that the added fullness of the netted skirt didn't make her look quite so slender, which was also why she chose to have it constructed with a gore. To travel, she wore a comfortable dress with braided trimming, the skirt scalloped at the bottom.

Charlotte was shocked—and inordinately pleased—when Alex sent clothes for Nicholas. With so little time to prepare for the visit, there hadn't been time to order him new ones. Yet Alex had managed it. But more surprising was that he cared enough to make the effort. Now her son looked like the perfect English boy all suited up in a sailor blouse and knickerbockers. Well, perfect, save his pout. He hadn't been at all eager to be away from his cousins for *two whole days*. A veritable lifetime to a four-year-old boy.

When she and Nicholas finally made their way down the

stairs to the first floor, Alex strode from the entrance hall. Charlotte's heart seized. Every time she saw him, his beauty struck her anew, as if she were seeing him for the first time. Cleanly shaven, his dark hair brushed to a sheen, he could turn a nun into a wanton in minutes.

Alex's gaze flickered over her. If he found her appealing or wanting, she couldn't tell by his expression for it remained stoically blank. His gray eyes did light up when his gaze settled on their son, transforming his face into something truly breath stealing.

Charlotte was happy Alex was so taken with his son, truly she was. But she couldn't help a pang of longing for the time he'd looked at her with love and pleasure in his eyes.

"Good morning, Nicholas. Are you ready to meet your grandparents?" Alex asked as they reached the bottom of the stairs.

Nicholas, suddenly shy and holding tight to her hand, nodded as he looked at the floor. Although excited to have a father, Alex was still a stranger to him. Like everything, this too would take time.

Alex's hesitation was momentary, hardly noticed if someone hadn't been watching him so very closely. Would not even have registered had someone not known the circumstances.

"Charlotte." He gave her a stiff nod.

"Alex," she greeted in a low voice, all too cognizant of the vast difference in his manner of greeting when it came to her.

"Are you not traveling with your maid?"

"In America I did well enough without one. In any case, Jillian is not a lady's maid although she does sometimes help me with my hair. But I can manage that by myself as well."

"I see," he replied. Turning his attention to his son, he reached in the pocket of his frock coat and produced a whipping top and held it out to Nicholas. This had the desired effect for Nicholas's expression went from shy to exuberant in the blink of an eye. Riveted, he stared at the toy.

When he finally managed to wrench his gaze from the top, he peered up at his father and asked, "Is that for me?"

Alex laughed the kind of laugh that made her smile despite her dread of the meeting ahead. "If you want," he said, his tone indulgent.

Eagerly, Nicholas snatched it from his father's palm and at the same time released his hold on her.

Alex's hand remained outstretched, angled now in invitation for his son to take it. Charlotte's breath ceased, held in suspension just like Alex's hand. Nicholas's gaze darted between his father's hand and smiling face. Time itself seemed suspended. Nicholas slowly, almost shyly, placed his hand in his father's. Charlotte let out a breath and her heart resumed beating.

Alex looked both pleased and relieved.

Someone cleared their throat. Charlotte turned toward the sound and saw her sister, Missy and James observing them from a discreet distance just outside the dining room.

In short order, greetings were dispensed, and James pulled Alex aside for a brief word. Five minutes later, Missy and Katie waved them off with such ceremony, one would think they'd be gone a month instead of the duration of one full day and a night.

The clarence was spacious, easily accommodating four passengers. Charlotte had an entire seat to herself, as her son had opted to sit beside his father when Alex smiled broadly and patted the seat beside him.

Charlotte felt awkward in the silence as they sped along to the train station. Alex had barely looked at her since his terse greeting. She turned her attention to the window, pushing the curtain aside.

"You mustn't be nervous."

Charlotte's gaze snapped to his and his expression was not one that would bring her out of her current state of anxiety. It was in fact, one that only served to feed it. He looked hard and masculine and his steady regard caused all sorts of riotous flutters inside her.

"I'm not nervous." She wouldn't admit to anything else in front of their son.

Alex continued to watch her silently.

"Have you told your parents *anything*?" The question had been gnawing at her all night.

"My message only indicated it was imperative I speak with them. You needn't worry, they will be happy to meet him."

Charlotte hoped his confidence of their complete acceptance of Nicholas wasn't being misplaced. She didn't care if they disapproved of her but she couldn't bear it if they rejected her son—not to his face. How could Alex know with one hundred percent certainty just how they would react to the news of a newfound grandson—an heir to the esteemed Hastings dukedom?

"Do you intend to tell them about *the marriage*?" How difficult it was to have this sort of conversation with their son present, even engrossed as he was playing with his toy.

"I plan on telling them the truth," he replied smoothly.

Nicholas didn't look up, his hand turned up as he tried to keep the top spinning on the center of his palm with little success. Undeterred, he kept trying, his brow knitted in concentration.

While the thought of the duke and duchess in full knowledge of their deception made her hands clammy, Alex appeared unperturbed. But what could she say, they were his parents. If he felt this is what he ought to do, she couldn't change his mind.

"If you think it is best," she conceded.

It took her several seconds to realize he wasn't going to offer a response, just continue to treat her to one of his unblinking and enigmatic stares.

Charlotte endeavored not to appear as if his regard didn't completely upend her equilibrium and have all of her senses clamoring. Striving for an air of nonchalance, she turned to the window and pretended an interest in the sights of Reading's

rolling hills as they sped toward town.
Still she could feel his gaze upon her.
And the journey had only just begun.

Chapter Twelve

They arrived in London in the early afternoon, traveling from Paddington Station to Mayfair in a grand carriage stamped with the gold-embossed ducal family crest. They arrived at Alex's flat, a well-appointed bachelor's residence currently fully staffed. Her sister had told her he'd sold Fairleigh House two years after she'd left.

Nicholas had fallen asleep on the train to London, and didn't so much as open one eye when his father hefted him into his arms and carried him past the butler, who opened the door to them, and into the house. Charlotte followed closely behind. Accustomed to having full charge and care of her son, sharing in the responsibility was something she'd have to get used to. But she couldn't help feeling excluded from the bond budding to life between them.

"Will we be staying here tonight?" She'd thought they'd be staying at his parents' residence but was relieved that didn't appear to be the case.

"I never stay with my mother and the duke when I travel to London. My relationship with my father hasn't changed since you left."

Which Charlotte took to mean they could barely tolerate one another.

"We will change here before we meet with my parents," he said, shifting a still-sleeping Nicholas in his arms so his head rested more comfortably on Alex's shoulder.

Five servants—the butler, the housekeeper, the cook, the maid and the other footmen—stood in a line. The greeting party.

"Good day, milord. Welcome home." The sentiment was

echoed and was accompanied by formal bows and pretty curtseys.

"I would like to introduce you to my wife, the Marchioness of Avondale."

None of them even blinked at the announcement, which meant Alex had already apprised them of his marriage and the return of his erstwhile betrothed, who was suddenly his current marchioness. Though, she was sure he hadn't gone into quite that amount of detail.

After the introductions, Alex carried Nicholas to the nursery upstairs he told Charlotte he'd had prepared for him by converting one of the guest rooms. In the meanwhile, the housekeeper, a slender woman with the eyes of a hawk, took Charlotte to hers. The servants were no doubt speculating about the marriage and hers and Nicholas's sudden appearance in Alex's life. The gossip would commence in earnest now.

Charlotte sighed. She'd have to grow a very thick skin for it was something she'd have to become well used to.

Four hours later, Charlotte, Alex and Nicholas were admitted into the grand entrance of his parents' mansion on Park Lane.

Alex had watched Charlotte and Nicholas as their eyes rounded upon first catching sight of Somerset House from the street. He now tried to see it through their eyes.

While not as large as Rutherford Manor, rural Italian in design, the structure was impressively large by London standards with brick stone work and a low-pitched roof, Palladian style molding and pedimented windows and doors.

The interior could be said to be equally as impressive, the ceiling an elaborate and intricate design of decorative metal trimming, a design which was carried throughout the residence. Corinthian-style columns stood tall and majestic and the silk walls were the same cream color of the exterior.

But the house had always lacked something. Or perhaps it

just hadn't felt like a home. As a child, even when his father hadn't been in residence, Alex hadn't enjoyed staying there during many of their summers spent in London.

Alex turned to Charlotte, who was the picture of nerves. The stalwart smile she attempted to exhibit looked strained and unnatural.

"Go with Smithers. I would like a word with my mother and the duke alone." Charlotte did as he bid, following his parents' butler to *le petit* drawing room. Alex then made his way to the grand room. He found his parents seated opposite one another, his mother reposed on the settee and his father in a high-backed chair Alex referred to as his throne for its ostentatious gold frame and red velvet cushion.

"Hello, my dear."

Alex strode to his mother, leaned down and bussed her proffered cheek with a kiss. "Nice to see you, Mama."

The duke merely scowled at him. "I do not take to cryptic messages. If you've something to say, say it quick, I've better things to do with my evening."

Alex clenched his teeth. He'd expected nothing less from the duke, yet the man still managed set him on edge.

"Your Grace." Alex offered his father a formal bow for he knew how he disliked it.

Again, the duke scowled, dismissing the gesture with a flick of his hand. "You always were impertinent."

And no matter how hard the duke had tried, he could never beat it out of him.

"Now, Walter, let us strive to have a nice visit. Darling, you must tell us what all the mystery is about. Your father is correct, your letter *was* rather cryptic. I told your father this must be about Lady Mary. Have I finally convinced you what a fine duchess she will make?" she asked, a faint smile of satisfaction hovering about her lips.

At this point, Alex wagered his mother would be happy if he married any respectable young lady in Society, although she'd prefer it be Lady Mary. Every year that passed without a marriage and an heir, she'd despaired the dukedom would fall so far from the direct line, it would require an act of God himself to set it back on track.

"I have a son."

The announcement had the effect of propelling the duchess's back flush against the settee, her fingers spread flat against her chest. "Oh dear."

The duke didn't so much as twitch but leveled him with one of his imperious stony stares, his disdain evident. "I'd expect no less from you. But what are you telling us for? Is the girl a peer? If not, take care of the business yourself. You aren't the first peer to father a child outside of marriage."

No concern or interest in his grandchild. As expected. And the duke never failed to disappoint.

"Who is the mother? How old is the child?" His mother seemed to have regained her composure though her hand remained splayed against the neckline of her gown.

In very matter-of-fact tones, Alex divulged every pertinent detail. When he came to the part about the marriage, his mother gasped, horror plain on her face, and the duke bolted to his feet.

"No!" It was a roar sure to have the servants all a titter. But then, it wasn't as if they hadn't heard the duke roar before. At him.

"I will not condone it. And with that girl?" He huffed an incredulous laugh. "You'd make yourself a laughingstock. No, send her and the child somewhere else. Up north, Scotland, Australia, I don't care where as long as they're gone from here. They'll be no mention of it again, do you hear me?" The duke subjected him to the kind of look that used to have him cowering as a boy. It hadn't had the same paralyzing effect for well over a decade.

"I brought them here. They are in the drawing room," Alex continued as if they hadn't been obvious about their violent opposition to his plan. "I am going to bring your grandson in to meet you. You will not only be kind to him, but I will not have you treat his mother with any kind of discourtesy in his presence, do you understand?" The same sense of protectiveness washed over him as when he'd coached them for their initial introduction with Charlotte years before. He may not love her anymore but he wouldn't have her hurt and most assuredly, not in front of their son.

Alex could not remember ever seeing his mother's eyes quite so wide or the duke's face that particular shade of purple. He hadn't struck him since Alex's fifteenth year but he looked fit to resume the practice that very moment, his hands fisted, his form tighter than a drum. The duke practically shook with rage.

"Who the devil do you think you are talking to?" The duke continued to shout as Alex exited the room.

The last thing he heard was his mother saying, "Walter, for the love of God, please do sit down and pray, do not cause a scene."

When he went to get Charlotte and Nicholas, she looked fragile and frightened and lost. Another wave of emotion washed over him, this more acute and more terrifying than the last. One that didn't bode well for his derelict feelings.

"I told them we have reconciled. They'll never believe it if you meet them looking as you do."

She gave a nervous laugh. "At this moment, I'd rather be facing the wrath of the late dowager Countess of Windmere than that of your parents."

Alex looked down at his son, who appeared equally as nervous, blue eyes wide with trepidation. No doubt he'd taken the lead from his mother, mimicking her emotional frame of mind. This would not do at all.

Leaning forward, he kissed her on the lips. He breathed in a surprised breath of air. But all too soon, her mouth softened beneath his and what was intended as a simple kiss, to add a splash of color to her face and ease some of her anxiety, soon became something more.

She tasted sweet, her lips soft and receptive. Her mouth

opened for his tongue and just as he was about to take the kiss deeper and explore her fully, he heard Nicholas giggle. The sound was enough to bring him sharply back to the present. Alex peered down at his son.

"You're kissing Mama," Nicholas teased.

Charlotte's face turned a vivid shade of pink as she studiously avoided Alex's gaze. The heightened color in her cheeks made her look all the more appealing. One kiss, and one not even that long in duration, but that was all it took to make him forget...and want...and need.

"Indeed I am," Alex replied, smiling at Nicholas. He held his hand out to him and his son grasped it without hesitation.

"Mama, do you like it when Papa kisses you?" If nothing else, the kiss had certainly put Nicholas at ease for his grin went from ear to ear.

Alex looked over at Charlotte. If possible, her blush deepened. She returned his gaze and held it several seconds before softly replying, "Yes, I like it very much."

Alex briefly closed his eyes, his fight an internal war he wasn't sure he could win. It had been a mistake to kiss her. When would he learn? But the fact that he'd been unable to help himself concerned him more.

The first to break the stare, he said, "Come, they are waiting."

If he had kissed her to take her mind off the impending meeting with his parents, Alex had partially succeeded. Like a flame that never died, her desire for him needed only the smallest spark for it to ignite. Looking at him, dreaming of him, talking to him, being with him could do that effortlessly.

But all he had done was give her another cross to bear. One should never feed unrequited love. Although if she were smart, she'd refuse the meal. But then unrequited love and smart were innately at odds.

The walk to meet with the duke and duchess felt like the final walk of a prisoner to the gallows. Charlotte's dread climbed with every step.

Alex, acting the perfect gentlemen, held the door open for them and she walked into the room, clutching her son's hand tighter than he held hers.

They haven't aged a bit was her first thought when she saw them both seated in the kind of expensive sofa and chair one would expect to find in a house so well-appointed.

They also didn't appear at all pleased. And it was that second thought that increased the flutter in her belly and accelerated her breathing and pulse.

The duke, in fact, looked positively livid, his handsome face was not quite as handsome flushed so bright a red. His scowl he made no attempt to disguise. Perhaps his blond hair had grown grayer over the years, but his face had weathered the time well enough and he appeared fit and trim.

The same could be said of his wife, whose blonde hair was perfectly coiffed. But the nostrils of her aristocratic nose quivered as if something distasteful had just permeated the air. Charlotte could see the meeting would not be pleasant.

After the duke pronounced his displeasure at seeing her with one seething stare, which adequately expressed his contempt, his gaze then shifted to Nicholas.

It was extraordinary, really, what happened next. Such a look arrested his features, if it hadn't been so remarkable to see, it might have been comical.

The duke—and the duchess now—looked at their grandson as if they were seeing a ghost.

Her Grace's gasp was shortly followed by, "Oh dear Lord!" Her exclamation almost coincided with the duke's, "My God." But the sentiment was the same. In unison, they rose slowly to their feet, staring at Nicholas as if they dare not let him from their sight.

"Charles." The duchess's voice shook with emotion.

The duke swallowed hard, the action pronounced enough for Charlotte to note it. He then turned to Alex. "He is yours?"

Alex gave a terse nod but there was something in his

expression when he responded to his father's sharp query that told Charlotte something else was at play here.

"Charlotte, you remember my parents, the Duke and Duchess of Hastings." Given all that had just silently transpired, the introduction contained enough irony to sink a battleship.

"Your Grace," she said pleasantly and dipped in a curtsey, still gripping her son's hand. Or should she have addressed them collectively as *Your Graces*? Well, she couldn't worry about that now. If she'd somehow breached social etiquette, she was sure Alex would inform her of it later when they were alone.

"And this is my son, Nicholas. Nicholas, these are my parents, your grandmother and grandfather."

Responding to Charlotte's light squeeze of his hand—a silent communication to mind his manners and greet his grandparents like a proper young man—he replied in a low, nervous voice, "Hullo."

The duchess slowly approached, looking dazed as she continued to stare at Nicholas.

"He looks exactly as Charles did at his age."

A tall woman, the duchess stopped directly in front of them forcing Charlotte to peer up at her. No one could call her handsome, but her features combined in a way that made her striking. In a French design of ice blue silk that was all the rage now in London, she looked eminently polished and elegant.

"So Alex told me," Charlotte said but they were paying her no mind. Their too focused attention was on their grandson.

The duchess reached out and touched Nicholas lightly under his chin, so loving a gesture it nearly brought a tear to Charlotte's eyes. Nicholas stood perfectly still under the brief caress, looking up at Charlotte as if to draw support. She knew he was aware this meeting with his grandparents was important but he was still a child. He'd made it quite clear he'd rather be home playing with his cousins.

The duke cleared his throat, staring mutely at Nicholas.

Unlike his wife, he stayed back beside a high-backed chair, which boasted as regal a presence as the duke himself.

"Nicholas is my heir."

There was a hard edge to Alex's tone that made it more an edict than a statement of fact.

The duke did not confirm his son's claim nor did he refute it. Contrarily, the duchess turned to her husband and gave one affirming nod. It appeared her mind was clear on this particular issue. The story of their marriage would have her full backing and support.

To Charlotte, the duke had come across as the type of man who not only adhered to class distinction, but rank distinction as well, hanging fiercely to the notion that he had, by the nature of his birth, been born better than most.

At present, she saw uncertainty in his eyes, as if today some of his beliefs had taken a hard wallop.

When the duchess turned back to them, her attention centered on Charlotte. The softness in her face when she'd regarded her grandson vanished. Displeasure settled into the faint lines around her eyes and mouth.

"I should like to speak with the marchioness alone," she said in a tone clinging to civility by a hairsbreadth.

Alex came swiftly to stand at Charlotte's elbow. "You can speak with the marchioness in due time."

The duchess dismissed her son with a wave of her hand and a smile that was as genuine as the diamonds sold in Cheapside to the ladies of the evening. "You needn't fear your dear wife will come to any harm. She *is* mother to the future Duke of Hastings."

Her light response didn't appear to appease Alex nor did it come close to making Charlotte feel the tiniest bit more amenable to being alone in her company.

"I should like to show Lady Avondale the music room. If my memory is not failing me, you are quite accomplished on the pianoforte, is that not correct?"

Failing memory? The duchess' mind was as sharp as a tack.

It was doubtful she had forgotten one moment of their initial meeting when Her Grace had mentally measured and weighed her, and found her lacking in every conceivable way.

"I haven't had the pleasure of playing much on the piano these last few years." A piano was one of the luxuries she'd been ill able to afford and she'd refused Lucas's generous offer to purchase one for her.

"Then I should think you'd be eager to see one as grand as the duke gave me." With that, she turned and headed for the door, clearly expecting Charlotte to follow her.

She turned and saw Charlotte hadn't moved from her spot. Her lips thinned. "Come, we will leave the men to talk. I'm sure my grandson will be happy for the male attention." She looked at Alex. "You will stay and talk to your father."

The duke and his wife shared an indecipherable look. He then looked away, his blue eyes troubled. Alex didn't so much as glance in his father's direction.

"Let's give your mama and grandmama some time to talk," Alex said, taking his son's hand from her. Nicholas immediately latched on to his father.

Reluctantly, Charlotte followed the duchess from the room. The duchess led her down a long corridor lined with columns aplenty and stately furniture. The *click click* of their shoes on the porcelain floors echoed sharply on the otherwise silent walk to their destination.

The double doors to the music room stood open and a black lacquered piano sat in the middle of the room. The duchess glided in and waved her hands at the half-dozen armchairs and the three settees arranged to give anyone seated an unobstructed view of all the instruments situated in the front.

"Do have a seat."

Charlotte did so, choosing the chair closest to the door if by chance she was required to make a quick escape.

Her Grace chose to stand. Lord, it appeared she was to be lectured.

"I will come straight to the point, Miss Rutherford."

Charlotte noted she was no longer the marchioness.

"My son may have forgiven you for the spectacle you made of him five years ago, but I have not."

Charlotte didn't cringe or even wince. They had accepted Nicholas and right now that's all that mattered to her. Moreover, if she could survive Alex's wrath, his mother's frigid hostility hadn't the ability to break her.

"In case you were not aware, Her Majesty, Queen Victoria is the duke's third cousin once removed, and it was due to her considerable magnanimity that she agreed to intervene on my behalf and secure the cathedral for the wedding. That you should repay her largesse as you did is nothing less than disgraceful. The Duke of Wellington is buried there. Royalty is married there."

Charlotte wondered how long the duchess would stress the importance and sanctity of St. Paul's Cathedral, of which she was well aware. One of the many things she learned in the small rooms of Our Lady Fatima School for Young Girls.

"I do apologize, Your Grace. My intention was never to embarrass Alex or you and His Grace," she replied sincerely.

"I do not care to hear about what you intended if the result was precisely the opposite."

It didn't matter what she said, what apology she offered, it was clear the duchess wasn't of the mind to forgive her.

Charlotte studied her hands as the duchess stood court, standing regally next to the gold brocade settee. Silence fell and lengthened to such a degree, Charlotte finally looked up to find the duchess's gaze fixed upon her.

"I am waiting for an explanation," she snapped impatiently.

"Pardon?"

"Truly, Miss Rutherford, I know it has been some years but you didn't appear witless when last we met. I want to know the reason you ran out on my son."

For some inexplicable reason, Charlotte hadn't expected this question from her. The duchess carried herself in a way that suggested asking would be beneath her.

"I'm sorry but that is between myself and your son."

The duchess' spine lengthened, no doubt unaccustomed to being refused anything. If possible, she pinned her with an even colder stare, her displeasure further evidenced when a white line replaced the pink of her lips.

"Why are you here? Why have you come back after all this time? My son is no longer in love with you. He has been doing quite well without you."

Her words stung. But she understood the duchess' anger. A mother's love could cause any woman to become the most ruthless creature when protecting their child.

"I would have to be blind not to see your boy is a Cartwright through and through. And it is for the sake of my son and grandson that I shall go along with this so-called marriage scheme of yours. But take note, Miss Rutherford, if you hurt my son again, I *will* destroy you."

"I have no wish to hurt Alex. I care very much for him." She loved him.

"Then I must say you have an extremely curious way of showing it. I refuse to go through what I did when I was told he'd been fished from the Thames inebriated and half dead over a woman who would leave him at the altar. I warned him marrying you was a mistake."

Shock froze Charlotte in place as a sort of numbness stole over her.

Fished from the Thames inebriated and half dead.

The duchess's words echoed in her head until she could hear nothing else.

Over a woman who could leave him at the altar.

"*What?*" she asked in a strangled voice.

The duchess narrowed her gaze and regarded her in silence. She tipped her head to the side and said softly, "I see you were not told. I'm surprised. Your brother was one of the men who came to his aid."

"What happened?" Charlotte couldn't keep the distress from her voice, which wavered and shook. Her hands trembled uncontrollably in her lap.

The duchess' mouth curved in the facsimile of a smile. "If your own family and my son haven't yet shared it with you, I see no reason that I should."

That her heart could hurt so much yet still continue to beat in her chest must be one of life's great mysteries. Overcome, Charlotte forced herself to breathe slowly. She couldn't believe Alex would ever try to harm himself but if he had been drunk and not himself, accidents like that could occur. And if anything had happened to him it would have been *her* fault for it had been her abandonment which had driven him to that.

Had it been seconds or minutes, Charlotte didn't know how long she sat lost in thought, sorrow and regret relentlessly hammering her. A movement by the duchess drew her gaze back to her. The duchess' eyes had lost their faint glow of smugness.

"I cannot have you falling to pieces once we rejoin the men. Perhaps it'd be best if you forgot I mentioned it. I don't believe my son would want you to know."

No, Alex would not want her to know. But she did and the knowledge would haunt her.

"Will you require a moment alone to compose yourself?" the duchess asked, sounding the closest she'd ever come to expressing actual concern.

Desperate for it, Charlotte nodded.

"I will tell my son you required use of the retiring room," she said, inclining her head in a nod before taking her leave.

When her sister had told her how badly Alex had taken her flight, she could never have imagined the depth of his pain.

At least she'd had Nicholas, who had been too often her own raft in the stormy sea that had been America in the early days. It had been for his well-being she'd eaten on the days the very thought of food turned her stomach. So instead of settling comfortably into a state of melancholy and wallowing in heartbreak, she'd been forced to plan and keep herself strong for his arrival. Then after he'd arrived, his care had been paramount and that was how she'd coped.

Alex had lost himself in women and drink. But as her sister had informed her, he no longer drank. And given the fact he'd been contemplating marriage, it was obvious he'd wanted to settle down. And settle him down she would.

He now had a wife who loved him whether he wanted it or not and a son he appeared to want more than anyone or anything. She may not be able to give him back those five years but she was doubly determined to do everything in her power to make him happy. He deserved that and more. Perhaps they both did.

The hours following were—if not pleasantly spent—not as painfully taxing as Charlotte had anticipated they would be.

The duke tried to engage Nicholas, but his efforts were painfully awkward and the conversation, stilted. Charlotte tried her best to help the conversation along but *her* efforts were met with cold looks from the duke, which only served to make Nicholas all the more reticent to engage himself with his grandfather.

Supper was served in the formal dining room on a table intended to service guests greater in number. Allowances were made for the smallness of their party and Nicholas. Alex remarked that he and his brother hadn't eaten in the dining room until after their third year at Eton.

By the time they departed to return to Alex's residence, the city was cloaked in the dark blanket of night and Nicholas's lids were drooping closed, his head snapping up and his eyes fluttering open during prolonged periods of silence.

While Charlotte would not go as far as to say the duchess had been kind to her, she had made an effort—no doubt for her grandson—to treat her civilly.

Not even a minute after they boarded the carriage, Nicholas fell asleep in his father's arms. Alex appeared content to hold him. Again, she couldn't help thinking how normally it would have been in her arms that her son trustingly curled up to sleep. She should be happy that Nicholas had someone else to whom he could count on and look to for his physical as well as emotional well-being. But sharing him was new and it would take time to become accustomed to it.

The temperature outside had dropped over the last several hours, and the interior of the carriage bordered on winter cold. Charlotte clutched her cloak about her more tightly.

"Are you cold?" Alex asked politely.

"I will be fine. We won't be long in the carriage in any case."

Several moments of silence followed before she asked, "Is it Nicholas's resemblance to Charles the sole reason your parents so readily accepted him?"

The interior of the carriage was too dark to make out Alex's face but she saw the movement of his head when he nodded.

"Your father appeared most affected by the resemblance." While the duke's reaction hadn't been quite as overt as the duchess', his silence and the way his gaze had constantly volleyed between Alex and his grandson had been more telling.

"My father grieved my brother greatly."

Charlotte had been aware of Alex's estrangement from his father. But that had ended after Charles's death—at least for a time. But it was clear the men still didn't get on. She wondered if Alex had been jealous of his father's obvious preference for his older brother.

"Believe me, he will do everything in his power to ensure not only that Nicholas is my legal heir, but that he is accepted by his peers."

"And had Nicholas resembled you, would he have been as accepting?"

Alex's answer didn't come immediately. Charlotte so wished she could see his face.

When it finally came, it was cool and emotionless. "If he'd resembled me, my father would have continued on as before, firm in his belief that I am *not* his son."

Chapter Thirteen

Their arrival at his residence interrupted their discussion. Which was just as well as Alex no longer wanted to discuss it.

The only thing that would explain his reason for divulging the one thing he hadn't told even his closest friends was the feeling of triumph at being able to prove the duke wrong. In all the years he'd known Rutherford—and Armstrong as well—he'd never revealed the reason he and the duke were estranged despite being asked countless times.

When they entered the foyer, the footman relieved them of their outer garments. Before she could offer, as Alex knew she would, he said, "I shall put him to bed."

Charlotte looked as though she was going to protest but after a pause said, "If you wish."

Nicholas awoke while he was undressing him. Eyes half closed, he sleepily asked for his mother. Alex gave him a comforting smile and told him he would be putting him to bed and then proceeded to hunt through the chest of drawers to locate where the maid had stored his sleepwear.

Ten minutes later, Alex exited the room, his son changed and under the covers fast asleep. His nanny had always been the one to put Alex to bed. But he was determined to be a different sort of father than the duke had been to him. Even his mother, as much as she'd loved him, had never been able to stand up to the duke.

Normally, Alex wouldn't think of retiring before ten o'clock, but it had been a long day and frankly, he didn't want to chance running into Charlotte tonight. She'd looked beautiful this evening and she wanted him. Would gladly have him if he gave the word. And right now, that was a little too much temptation to resist. Especially now that much of the bone-deep anger he'd initially felt toward her had subsided, although not gone completely.

In his bedchamber, Alex shrugged out of his coat and was unbuttoning his waistcoat when a knock sounded at the door. It hadn't been the quick sharp knocks of his butler, but lighter, more tentative.

A feeling of unease crept up his spine. Alex stood motionless, hoping if he didn't answer whoever it was would leave. The knock came again, this time louder, followed by a hushed, "Alex, are you awake?"

Charlotte. Bloody hell! The last thing he wanted was to have to deal with her tonight.

"Charlotte, I'm going to bed," he said tersely. He hoped his tone was properly discouraging.

"Please, I'd like to speak with you. It won't take but a few minutes. May I come in?"

Her voice, soft and everything feminine, started his pulse racing and desire to unfurl in his gut.

Hastily, Alex tucked his shirt back into his trousers before going to open the door—but only halfway.

Alex nearly groaned aloud upon seeing her.

She wore a dark blue, silk dressing robe cinched at the waist with a sash. With her hair unbound falling down her back in a torrent of golden curls, she looked young and fragile and earnest. And beautiful enough to tempt the devil and make a mere mortal like him lose his head.

Which is precisely what will happen if I take up with her again.

He'd lived through the hell of losing her once—but just barely. And as he looked down into her blue, blue eyes, he very much doubted he could survive the thousand agonies of that nightmare again—or at least emerge the experience a whole man.

"Alex, I thought we could talk further." Her voice held a hint of the sort of tentativeness one used when uncertain of their reception.

The arousal he'd been suppressing since the kiss they shared at his parents' home flared back to life. He hated the inconvenience of it, wanting her and not being able to adequately control the wanting. He knew if he permitted himself to forget all the pain she'd caused, he was bound to repeat mistakes of the past, his biggest, in trusting her with his heart.

But they would be residing in the same house so he needed to face his weakness—build up his resistance.

"We can speak in here" He opened the door and motioned with his chin to the sitting area of the master suite. Everything would be fine as long as they stayed well away from the bed, which was separated by a wall that ran half the length of the room.

Although her smile was a slight curve of her lips, her eyes shone with what he could only take as relief.

Another shock of arousal pierced him, this one sharper, more acute than the last. He wished she wouldn't do that. He vividly recalled the smiles she'd bestowed upon him years ago. Smitten smiles, shy smiles that had grown passionate and more sensuous over the years. He'd relished those smiles and reveled in them for they had been his alone.

He would not encourage her. A kiss here and there to settle her nerves and give Nicholas the impression they cared for one another was fine. Anything more would be at his detriment.

The room was dark save the fire blazing in the fireplace in the bedroom area. Alex lit the wall sconce and a gas lamp on the side table. Charlotte took a seat on the sofa, the silk of her dressing robe pulling taut across her thighs.

Alex swallowed and hastily jerked his gaze back to her face.

"Why did your father not believe you were his son?"

Ah, that. He'd almost forgotten about their discussion in the carriage.

"Look at me," he said, sinking into the winged-back chair adjacent to her, deftly releasing the top two buttons of his waistcoat with one hand. "Both my parents are fair, as was my brother. When I came along, dark in hair and not fair in complexion, the duke accused my mother of cuckolding him."

"And your mother, what did she say?"

"My mother denied it. Told him she had Black Irish somewhere down her family line."

"But he did not believe her." She spoke softly, her eyes filled with sympathy.

"No he did not." Except for the one time at the age of seventeen, when his mother had finally told him of the strife between her and the duke, which then explained the duke's ill treatment of him, Alex had never discussed the matter again.

"Did you ever wonder if your mother was telling the truth?"

Unprepared for the question, Alex didn't have a ready answer. He loved his mother. She had been the singular light in his childhood, his only champion until he'd met the Armstrongs. She would never lie to him. But he *had* wondered at times. God, how many times had he hoped the duke *wasn't* his real father? Too many to count.

"Sometimes," he replied truthfully. "Sometimes, I did wonder when I looked at the three of them all together. My brother's resemblance to the duke was quite strong. He could never deny *him*. And the duke is such a rigid man, I often wondered if my mother hadn't grown weary of it and sought affection elsewhere. I wouldn't have blamed her if she had."

Charlotte nodded. "So the fact that Nicholas so resembles your brother proves to your father *he* must have sired you."

"Yes." Not only had it proven it to the duke, but it washed away any doubts he himself may have fostered. For the very first time in his thirty-four years, Alex was certain of his paternity and of his rightful place as heir to the Hastings dukedom. He wouldn't deny feeling a sense of relief to finally know where he belonged—that he did in fact belong.

"Now you both are assured of your paternity."

Alex nodded.

"I'm very happy for you." Charlotte also envied his sense of belonging.

He studied her intently as if trying to read her thoughts or trying to decipher more from her words.

"Do you often wonder about your mother?"

Charlotte blinked. They'd never spoken of this and he was now giving her the perfect opportunity to explain. Would he listen to her now?

"Yes I have."

He angled himself more toward her. "Would you like to have known her?"

Charlotte's throat closed up on her response and she felt the tears smart her eyes. "Yes, I would like to have known her." And that was the truth. She would have done, but had her mother lived, how different her life would have been. She and her sister would never have come to know James, she'd never have met Alex and she wouldn't have Nicholas.

For a moment it looked as if Alex would continue on in that vein of questioning, but he seemed to think better of it and fell silent, turning to gaze off in the distance at the fire burning in the grate. He looked unaccountably forlorn for a moment, his defenses down.

"Alex."

He turned to her.

"I did love you," she said softly, but unwilling to lay her heart completely bare to let him know her feelings had not changed. "Please believe me when I say I never meant to hurt you."

Some emotion flickered in his eyes. "What happened in the past is done. I accepted long ago it can't be changed no matter how hard I may wish it could."

Did that mean he now had it in his heart to forgive her?

"But we can't resurrect long-dead emotions. Our love affair was in the past and there it shall remain."

Charlotte bit her lip in an effort to override the pain of his words. While it appeared his bitterness was at an end, what seemed to have replaced it was indifference. He no longer felt enough for her to even elicit his anger. She'd never thought she'd ever prefer the former, but at that moment, she sorely did. Better he rage at her in anger and hurt than resign their *faux* marriage to the fate of complete indifference.

But he wanted her and that he hadn't been able to hide. A physical relationship would be better than nothing at all.

"I should like to have another child." If he would only but give her a chance, she was almost positive she could make him care for her again.

Alex's whole form stiffened at her words. "Another child? With you? I thought I made my feelings on that clear."

It wasn't so much his words but his tone that felt like blows raining down on her. Sharp blows that had the power to bruise a person's skin and destroy their soul.

"If we are to stay married…"

"Dear God, Charlotte, do not ask that of me. Even if we were to engage in marital relations, I fear another pregnancy would be too stark a reminder of everything I missed before, which would only cause me to resent you more."

As difficult as it was to listen to what he was saying, to hear the thread of anguish in his voice, his *if* gave her a renewed sense of hope. Perhaps, tonight could be a new beginning for them. But in order for that to happen, he'd have to know the truth. "If you would only listen."

Alex rose abruptly to his feet. "It has been a long day and I am fatigued." And like that he closed himself off from her.

A rigid mask had once again settled over his face, his jaw tight and his eyes veiled. He looked impenetrable now. Charlotte glimpsed her future in his blank stare and it loomed before her as arid as the Sahara. No warmth, no affection.

Charlotte rose from the chair and faced him squarely. "You refuse to listen to me because you want to hold on to your resentment and in some ways, I understand that. But I wish you would see that doing so will do neither of us any good and it certainly will be of no benefit to our son. Whether you believe it or not, Alex, I left because I loved you. I left to spare you the embarrassment and humiliation of a scandal. You and my family."

His too long black lashes flickered and his mouth tightened. He looked like a man struggling between two opposing emotions. The inner battle he appeared to be raging lasted several moments. Finally, but not in the manner of a man admitting defeat, he said, "Then speak. Go ahead and explain yourself for this will be your only opportunity."

Relief almost made her lightheaded. "May we sit?"

With a curt nod, Alex resumed his seat as did Charlotte.

Nothing about him suggested he would be receptive to anything she had to say. In fact, his eyes seemed to challenge her to convince him of something he already didn't believe.

Relief had been a respite for now she was doubly nervous not just in how he would receive the news but in whether he would understand.

"Months before the wedding, Katie and I were contacted by a woman, a Mrs. Henley. We would not have entertained her letter, except she said she knew our mother. She asked to meet with us." Charlotte paused to swallow as Alex continued to watch her somewhat passively.

"We met her in Cheapside. She'd insisted she didn't want anyone to see us together and when we saw her, we understood her reticence. She was a kitchen maid who'd once worked for the Earl of Forsythe. That is where she met our grandmother." She drew in a deep breath before confessing, "My grandmother was a slave." She paused a beat in order that the full import of her words would penetrate. Except for a blink, Alex appeared unfazed by the revelation.

"Both worked in the scullery. Mrs. Henley told us she was young at the time, they both were, neither not yet eighteen. Although, Mrs. Henley said she couldn't attest to it herself, rumor amongst the servants was that our grandmother had been born of a rape by one of the former Earl of Forsythe's peers during a house party. Many speculated it had been the late

Viscount Radcliffe."

It was the first time she'd ever relayed the story to anyone and she hadn't expected it to pain her as much as it did.

"Our grandmother was very pretty and attracted the eye of the earl's son, who made her his mistress the year following Mrs. Henley's arrival at the estate. She became pregnant with my mother. Lord Forsythe allowed her to stay and raise her within the kitchens. When my mother was eighteen years, she met my father. When she became pregnant with me and Katie, the earl had recently married and the new countess dismissed her without notice or recommendation."

The hardest part was out. Charlotte drew in a breath. Alex didn't appear in the least bit perturbed or distressed or really anything. He just watched her, his face wiped clean of emotion.

"So that is it?" he asked, unblinking. "You discovered you and your sister's blood is not as blue as you'd once thought?"

"That isn't it at all." He made her sound petty.

"And you thought that would matter to me? That I would learn of it and toss you aside?" His voice had taken on a hard tone.

"No," she protested.

"Then what was it?"

"The letter."

"What letter?"

"Two days before the wedding, I received a letter threatening to expose my mother's identity if I married you." There, he now had the whole of it. The truth she buried for years.

He didn't speak for what felt like a year, the silence stretching tortuously as the months flew by. "And where is this letter?"

The question took Charlotte aback. "I-I didn't keep it. I threw it away." The thought that someone would discover it had compelled her to burn it at the first opportunity.

"And you believed everything this Mrs. Henley had to say?"

"Yes, I believed her. Katie and I both did. She knew

everything about us. The home we were taken to after our mother's death. She knew the boarding school we attended. She kept track of us because our mother was like a daughter to her. She helped raise her. If you had met her, you'd not have doubted her either."

"She showed you proof?"

Charlotte nodded. "She had a miniature of the portrait painted of us just before we were sent to boarding school. You've seen it, the one James has up in the gallery."

Mrs. Doubletree, the headmistress at the boarding school, had had the portrait delivered to them—at James's expense, of course—when she'd discovered it in the attic where they'd stored it.

"For God's sake, Charlotte, why didn't you come to me?"

"If I had come to you—"

"I would have gotten to the bottom of it. I would have stopped it." Anger now laced his words.

"She would have ruined us."

"She? You know who sent the letter?"

"I believe it was James's mother, the dowager. She'd always despised us."

"That she did, which is why it doesn't make sense for her to keep something like that to herself. And she had no great affection for me, so why would she threaten you with that?"

"I don't know it was particular to you. I believe she would have done anything to cause us pain, thwart our happiness. Had I been marrying a viscount or the local butcher I'm sure she would have tried to prevent it."

"But if she could have ruined you both just like that, why wouldn't she just do so?"

"I imagine it is because it would have also caused considerable pain to her sons. I think she wanted to prevent me and Katie from being happy, from finding a place in Society without cost to James and Christopher."

Bracing his forearms on his thighs, Alex gave a heavy sigh as he looked off to the side and appeared to consider her explanation.

"And when did you realize you were with child?" he asked, directing his gaze back to her.

"Not until after I arrived in America. I don't know if I would have had the courage to travel that great a distance had I known. I attributed the sickness I was experiencing to the voyage. I'd never traveled by sea before. It was only when it continued after I arrived in New York that I realized." Oh the terror that had gripped her then. The prospect of managing in a country she didn't know by herself had been daunting enough, but a child added to the mix had at times seemed insurmountable. Jillian had helped and soon after, Lucas had come into her life.

"You should have come to me," he said with such ferocity she wanted to weep.

"I couldn't risk it. I couldn't do that to you. Your parents made no secret of their feelings toward me. James had to practically bully his peers into accepting Katie and me into their drawing rooms. We were already hovering on the fringes of Society as it was. This would have done us in and with us, you and James's family.

Alex came abruptly to his feet, plowing his hand through his hair. He circled the chair, his movements agitated, his lips tight and his eyes stormy.

He rounded on her. "Did you fear my reaction if you told me? Did you think I would reject you?"

If nothing else, she owed him honesty. Charlotte drew in a breath and expelled it slowly. "In truth, a part of me feared you'd no longer see me the same. And a larger part of me thought even if it didn't matter to you then, it would over the course of our marriage. I feared you'd come to resent me, resent all I had cost you. And that, Alex, I simply couldn't bear—to see the love you had for me—to see it die."

The silence that followed had never been louder. Charlotte could barely stand to look at him. It hurt too much to see the pain in his eyes, which he did nothing to hide.

"That is what you thought of me, that I would abandon you when you needed me most. That my love was so fickle that something beyond your control—as no one has control over the parents they're born to or the life they've been born into—would send me running?"

Alex tolerated the crushing pain of his heart because he could do little else but bear it. He had loved her with everything in him and she hadn't trusted in that love. Hadn't trusted that it could and would endure the travails of life, small and large. And because of that lack of faith, she'd abandoned him and stolen from him five years of his life, years without his son.

"Oh Alex." She was on her feet, her hand reaching out to him. He jerked sharply back. He didn't trust himself not to shake her senseless or crush her in his arms. Either response would be like playing with fire for he was certain to get scorched by the flames.

"I was so scared. I did what I thought was best for everyone. I felt I had no other choice. Surely, you understand the situation I was in?"

He understood that she must have been terrified. But to leave England? To bear him a child without sending word to him?

"I do understand fear and accept that one can act impetuously, but how can you possibly explain five years?"

Had she'd stayed gone only two years, he'd have forgiven her without question—such had been the depth of his love...and his pain. At three years, he'd been teetering on the brink of self-destruction and she'd been the oasis he sought in those dark and arid times. During the fourth year, he'd finally regained the lucidity and control he'd lacked for quite some time. Then, she might have found him receptive for without the panacea of alcohol, the pain of her loss had come rushing back full force. But this last year he'd finally accepted that his once-in-a-lifetime love was no more. Now, it would be like trying to resurrect the dead when there was nothing left in the grave but bones and ashes.

"You could have written to me and I would have been on the next ship to America. I would have given all this up for you if need be." He gestured widely, the sweep of his hand encompassing the well-appointed master suite equipped with the symbolic trappings of wealth and rank. An unsatisfactory affirmation of his station in life when compared to the love he once had for her.

All color drained from her face. Such a haunted look came into her eyes, one would think she had hell well within her sights. Tears glassed her eyes. One escaped and rolled down her cheek. She swiped it away almost angrily.

"Alex, I loved you too much to ask that of you." Emotion choked her voice. Another tear fell but this one she did not touch, allowing it to roll down and down until it clung to the edge of her chin. She turned her head and it lost its tenuous hold, sending it dashing onto the carpeted floor to disappear without a trace, as if it never existed. It was a pity feelings didn't behave in a similar manner. Instead they had a habit of forever making their presence known by staining everything they touched.

"You would not have had to ask." He would have given his life for her.

Charlotte looked away, briefly closing her eyes. After drawing a breath, she turned back to him. "I thought you'd understand, especially given your experience with your father. Can you even imagine what it would have been like for me and Katie? Despite everything James has done to protect us, everyone knows we are his father's by-blows. Can you imagine if they learned this too? How they would treat us? How it would affect you? You would have been tainted by association and our children would have been—" she choked back a sob, "they would have been shunned. That is what I saw in the future if I had married you.

Alex was torn. Part of him wanted to take her in his arms

and wipe away her tears and soothe her hurt. That and kiss her senseless—there was always that. But when he looked down at the entirety of all that had been stolen from him, he wanted to rail at her for not coming to him then. How could she think he'd not have stood by her and not once regretted the decision no matter the repercussions?

But the point was moot. She'd made her decision years ago. She'd chosen her path and that didn't change the present.

"Well it is done. You did what you did and nothing and no one can change that. We must just go forward." In the distance, he heard the tick of the clock he kept on his fireplace mantel, a stark reminder that the future was but a second away. So forward they went.

More tears fell, a steady stream of them, flowing silently. He hated to see her cry. Even her tears of joy had played havoc with his emotions. But how he'd loved kissing them away.

Alex walked to his bed and retrieved a monogrammed handkerchief from his coat pocket. He strode back and handed it to her. She took it and proceeded to dry her eyes. When she was finished, she didn't hand it back to him nor did he ask for it. Instead, she clutched it tightly as if holding on to something of infinite value.

"How shall we go forward?" she asked.

Was that hope he'd heard in her voice? "My knowing the truth doesn't change my feelings for you." Whatever they were. Only she had the power to confuse him like this. "No, that's not true. You have told me things I very much needed to hear and it has taken away much of the rage. But that doesn't change or bridge the years we've been apart. I meant it when I said whatever I felt for you is gone." Which wasn't an out-and-out lie.

Her blue eyes darkened with pain and she grew so still it was as if she was frozen in time. She wore defeat about her like a burden carried twenty years on an unpaved road stretching as far as the eye could see, and longer.

Slowly, she angled her head and stared at him. She looked

as if she was reading something in his eyes she hadn't seen before.

"You can't tell me there's no hope of getting back what we once had. You still want me even though I know you do not want to."

"I want you in my bed but that has nothing to do with love." He spoke in an even voice, the opposite of how he felt. Because there was a bed not but two dozen feet from where they sat in the seductive night darkness. It would be all too easy to succumb and feed the hunger that had been building for years.

"And I'd love nothing more than to be in your bed." Her voice held the allure of a siren's song.

Alex was immediately as hard as a bobbie stick. He retreated until his back met the wall and prayed she'd keep her distance. His physical weakness for her was something he'd have to deal with and would take a little time to get a firm handle on. In the meanwhile, all future encounters could not take place within fifty feet of a bed.

"I believe it's time to say good night. Good night, Lady Avondale."

"I want more than that from our marriage." Her eyes were luminous as she toyed with the sash of her dressing robe.

The way she slid the sash between her slender fingers was more fidgety than sensuous but he couldn't have found it more provocative.

The bobbie stick in his trousers suddenly felt like a cricket bat. Alex cleared his throat and forced his gaze from her. He stared blindly at the spot on the wall beyond her slender shoulder where a painting of a hunting scene hung.

Once he felt composed enough to speak, he returned his attention to her. "Well life has shown me sometimes we cannot get what we want. I wanted to be the one you turned to in times of crisis. I wanted to hold my son on the day of his birth. I wanted to hear his first words and watch as he took his first steps. I wanted the last five years with you."

The sash now dangled from her fingertip. He watched her lips quiver. The top was deep pink and bow shaped, the bottom more plush and wholly distracting. He refused to permit his gaze to drift any lower than her sweetly rounded chin. The shape of her breasts and hips were already burned like a brand in his mind.

"Alex—"

"I am a man who prides himself on learning from my mistakes, which means never making the same one twice. I gave you my heart but once and I won't give it again." This is what he'd been telling himself every hour since her return.

Hurt clouded her eyes and he held his breath, wondering just how strong he'd have to be this evening. God, don't let her weep again, he could only tolerate so much. And his damn erection showed no signs of flagging.

"I *am* sorry, Alex. So very sorry. You'll never know how much. But I promise I shall take better care of it in the future should you ever leave it to my safekeeping again," she said softly.

And then silent as a shadow, she turned and exited the room, leaving him shaken with a raging erection, ensuring he would not sleep at all that night.

Chapter Fourteen

Upon their arrival at Rutherford Manor next morning, Charlotte's thoughts were still on what had occurred between her and Alex last evening.

He finally knew the truth and she was truly glad of it. But his reaction had her doubting herself as she'd done many times in the past. Had she done the right thing? She'd truly thought so at the time. The crippling blow had come when he'd told her he'd have given up his title, his home—everything—for her.

When she'd first been introduced to him, he'd been more godlike than mortal; his masculine beauty only surpassed by his infinite charm. She'd immediately been drunk with a passion for him that hadn't faded a stitch over time.

When he'd proposed, he'd told her how much he loved her and she'd believed him. Now she wondered if she actually had at that. She knew she'd desperately *wanted* to believe him, counting herself as the luckiest woman on earth.

In her room at night, she'd pinch herself under the covers and pray to God that if she was dreaming, she'd never wake up. And now to discover, a man like *that* had felt all of *that* for her propelled her to dizzying heights of euphoria and then sent her plummeting to the earth like a falling star. For last night he'd vowed no chance existed for them, his heart securely locked away and out of reach from her.

She glanced across the carriage at him. He'd barely said two words to her since they'd departed London, giving Nicholas his exclusive attention then falling silent once their son had drifted off.

In minutes, two footmen were fetching their trunks into the house as they stood beside the carriage, Nicholas wide awake and happy to be back, but loath to be separated from his father.

"Why can't you stay here with us?" Nicholas turned piteous blue eyes up at him as he tugged on his hand.

Alex smiled and affectionately tousled his hair. "I must return home and have the house readied for you to move in tomorrow."

The quick look he shot her told her it had also been meant as a reminder to her. As if there was any possibility she might have forgotten. No, now it was something she anticipated like a child counting the days on a calendar as Christmas approached. He wanted her and that was something. Good, solid marriages had been founded on less. And given their unique situation, it might be the *only* place to start.

"May my cousins come and visit?" Nicholas asked, digesting the news without blinking an eye. Charlotte hadn't known how much he craved the company of other children until she'd seen him with her nieces and nephew. Alex had said there'd be no more children but in time she hoped he'd change his mind. Nicholas could do with at least one sibling and she'd certainly love another child.

"They can visit as often as you wish."

Charlotte smiled. It appeared he'd be the ever indulgent father. How quickly he'd learn the ways of boundaries when it came to their son.

"And I can come here to play too?"

"Of course," Alex said, smiling down at him.

His father's assurances brought a brilliant smile to Nicholas's face.

Alex's expression became unreadable when he lifted his head and regarded her. "I shall expect you by midday."

"Jillian will be coming with us."

He gave a curt nod.

"Very well, then we shall see you tomorrow."

Nicholas had been watching their exchange, his head turning with each volley. "Papa, are you upset with Mama?" he asked, his brow knit with worry.

"But of course not." Alex's denial came smoothly, his expression instantly brightening; the straight line of his mouth curving into a smile that brought Alex of old back to the fore.

Charlotte's heart must be controlled by invisible strings attached to his mouth when he smiled precisely like *that* for it swooned and leapt as if choreographed by a master director.

"Your papa is just frightfully busy and has much on his mind." She smiled in return while trying to wrestle her heart into abeyance lest it leap from her chest. "Come, let's allow him to return home. We shall see him tomorrow."

She took Nicholas's hand in hers and turned to leave when Alex asked softly, "Are you not forgetting something?"

Puzzled, Charlotte looked around. The footmen had already unloaded the trunks. That was the sum of everything she'd taken with them to London.

"No, I believe—"

Before she could finish, Alex's mouth was on hers. His tongue touched hers in a move too quick to satisfy, and then the kiss was over. But while the kiss was the briefest they'd shared since her return, it was its potency that proved so affecting, spinning her senses and making jelly of her thoughts.

"Tomorrow," was all he said before climbing back into the carriage. She heard two sharp raps against the roof and then the carriage was off.

Charlotte touched her gloved hand to her mouth.

"Papa kisses you a lot," Nicholas said, giggling, his eyes dancing and his grin wide.

If only her son knew how much she loved kissing his father, Charlotte mused.

"That is what married people do, my dear."

"I'm not gettin' mareweed if I have to kiss a girl."

"I should certainly hope not. You're entirely too young to get married," her sister chimed from where she stood framed in the front doorway.

And that was all it took. Nicholas left her side in a mad dash toward his aunt. He proceeded to greet her as if he'd known and loved her his entire four years.

They hugged for several seconds. Then upon spotting his cousins coming barreling down the stairs toward him, her son was gone.

Charlotte came to stand by her sister's side.

"It would appear things went well in London. I insist you tell me all about it and don't you dare leave anything out."

Two hours later, after Nicholas had been fed and was playing a game of rounders outside with his cousins, Missy, Charlotte and Katie sat in the parlor taking their midday tea.

Charlotte told them about the visit with Alex's parents and how quickly they'd accepted Nicholas into their lives.

"Frankly, I'm surprised," Missy said, pastry in hand as she sat poised to take a bite. "I met Alex's parents once, and they'd be the last people I'd expect to welcome an illegitimate grandson with open arms. Did you know that the duke is somehow related to Her Majesty or some such?"

Missy then bit into the pastry, closing her eyes and humming sounds of confectionary delight as she chewed. Her expression was rapturous enough to bring a smile to the dour countenance of *Monsieur Solielle* himself, their master baker.

"Indeed, she made it a point to remind me and berate me about it in the same breath. I thought to remind *her* she'd informed me of their intimate ties with Her Majesty during our initial meeting but thought better of it," Charlotte said dryly. "But they were swayed by Nicholas's resemblance to Charles. She made it very clear she holds no great fondness for me and I very much doubt that sentiment will ever change."

Katie made a face. "Wretched woman."

The sisters helped themselves to the same pastry Missy was consuming with such undisguised joy. Charlotte took a bite of the flaky apple tart and concurred with her sister-in-law; it was positively divine. They ate in companionable silence.

"I know, I shall throw a ball." Missy's sudden exclamation

came on the heels of having eaten every last morsel of the pastry. And then, armed with a serviette, she wiped her mouth of the lingering evidence of her indulgence.

"A ball?" Katie asked, making another face. "And how will a ball help improve matters with the duchess? I'm quite sure the duchess is invited to a plethora of social events."

"Simply put, I shall invite some of the most notable in Society. Once they've given Charlotte their stamp of approval, everyone will follow. It will be, in essence, Charlotte's reentry into Society. And once she's achieved that, much of the duchess' grievances against her will disappear."

"And if they don't give their stamp of approval," Katie queried, "what then?"

"Well of course I shall pick them with care. Amelia and Thomas, and Elizabeth and Derek will come I'm certain. I would invite the dowager Viscountess Armstrong but she's in America with Mr. Wendel and expected to remain until the fall. Needless to say, the guest list will be comprised of those most likely to be sympathetic to Charlotte's plight."

The pause that followed wasn't the least bit subtle in its invitation to come clean, divulge all. Charlotte remained mum. That Alex knew was sufficient for the time.

But a ball? The thought of being subjected to Society's scrutiny at such close quarters made Charlotte's stomach turn in on itself. She hadn't much liked it the year of her debut and, given the circumstances, was even less inclined to it now. But her sister-in-law did have a point. The Season was already upon them and she would have to face Society in the not-so-distant future. Best she get the whole thing over and done with and what better way to do so than with the full backing of support of her family and friends. Just the thought of her dearest friend, Elizabeth, the viscountess Creswell, made her wistful.

"I think that's a grand idea," Katie agreed. "Most will come once they get word of the marriage. And if that won't have everyone fairly champing at the bit for an invitation, then I guarantee when they hear about Nicholas, Missy will be besieged with people begging for an invite." The smug smile on Katie's face clearly showed she relished the thought.

"I shall book an appointment with Miss Foster as you will require a gown." Missy wore a calculating expression as if she was already going over the many details that went into the planning of an event of this magnitude. This would be no small undertaking.

"Tomorrow Nicholas and I shall be moving to Gretchen Manor," she reminded them. When she'd first told them, they'd looked at her, brows up, surprised she'd thought to have mentioned it when they'd assumed nothing less. She and Alex were, after all, man and wife.

Even still, Katie now sobered at her statement. "Well thank goodness Alex had the presence of mind to purchase an estate so close in proximity. I simply couldn't bear it if you were any farther away."

Charlotte too was glad of that.

"When I spoke to the duchess alone yesterday, she did tell me something I wanted to ask you both about. She said something about James having to fish Alex from the Thames."

Missy and her sister visibly paled.

At length, Katie said, "I wish the duchess hadn't said anything to you about it. It's an incident we'd rather forget."

"Well she did and I'd like to know what happened. It appeared from what she said, there were a number of people witness to it." She'd thought about it quite a bit last night while she tossed and turned, trying to fall asleep before the sun came up. She had failed miserably.

"Dearest, it happened a little over two years ago and at a time when Alex was not at his best. He was hurting a great deal," Missy said.

"Because of me." Although the duchess had told her as much, for some reason Charlotte needed it verified.

Katie's gaze dropped to her lap and Missy stared at Charlotte, stricken. After a pause she inclined her head in a nod. "He was devastated when you left and changed a great deal during that time. Unfortunately his drinking became excessive. I didn't actually see what happened, but I did see James and Thomas dive into the water to get him. We thought that was the end of it until days later he developed a fever." Missy grew misty-eyed and swallowed hard before continuing. "At one point, the physician advised us to prepare ourselves because he might not make it. But he did and we have Miss Foster to thank for that."

With tears but a blink away, Charlotte tried not to cry. She cleared her throat and asked, "Miss Foster? What did she do?"

"Miss Foster is very good with herbs. When she discovered Alex was ill, she arrived with a mixture she swore worked wonders on fevers," Katie explained.

"Since the physician told us no more could be done for him, we were willing to try anything. Hours after giving him the mixture, his fever began to abate. In two days' time it was gone altogether. Alex credits her with saving his life, which is the reason he was so willing to loan—well rather give her the money to open her shop."

Charlotte feared that if she spoke then, her words would jumble. Miss Foster had helped save Alex's life. Now she understood their affection for her and why they had all rallied around her. She too owed the woman a debt of gratitude she could never repay. While Miss Foster worked as a *modiste*, Charlotte would patronize no other.

"Did Alex say what happened—how he came to be in the water?" She knew Alex and she knew with utter certainty he would not have deliberately gone overboard.

"They discovered the railing had given way. A bolt holding it in place had rusted and become dislodged. Regardless, Alex blamed himself and said if he hadn't been drunk, he would not have stumbled against it. It was then he stopped drinking." Missy gave a sad smile.

"It was the one good thing that came of the horrible ordeal. I should hate to think what could have happened had he not stopped. But," Missy slapped her hands down on her lap, "everything is much better now. You are home and he has his son."

"Thank you for telling me." Charlotte couldn't think beyond the event and those that followed. Alex had almost died.

Missy picked up the teapot and poured the hot liquid into her cup. "I hope it helps you to understand him better. He has been through and endured much over these last several years."

All because of me. That was the part her sister-in-law was too kind to say aloud, but the truth of it riddled her with pellets of guilt.

"I shall do my best to be a good wife to him."

"It is obvious you still love him dearly, therefore I have no doubt you shall," Missy said. "Now, I must send word to Miss Foster to make an appointment to fit you for a gown for the ball. I shall have her go to you. You'll no doubt want some time to settle in first."

The need to be alone now clawed at her insides. Charlotte rose from the sofa. "I really must get our things together for our departure tomorrow. If you will excuse me."

Her sister's eyes looked suspiciously bright but she didn't try to stop her or offer a hand. She knew Charlotte needed time to herself to digest everything she had learned.

"You shall sleep here," Alex said, pushing open the door that led to the suite adjoining his.

As she preceded him into the room, Alex thought of her parting words of two evenings ago. And knowing she wanted him, would seek to win his heart was all he'd been able think about since she'd confessed it. Now from that night on, they would sleep a door apart. The image it conjured in his mind distracted from the marriage he sought to have with her: cordial, respectful, and one that wouldn't threaten the boundaries he'd set in place. So he forcibly thrust the thought of her lying with little more than a flimsy piece of fabric covering her as she slept from his mind. Night would be soon enough for that torment.

Charlotte surveyed the room, her gaze settling on a large wardrobe, a springlike scene painted on the doors, the sort of feminine things females adored.

"This is lovely," she said.

Alex's gaze strayed to the bed and then back to her. God she was beautiful, especially when she smiled as she was doing now. After all these years, an air of innocence still surrounded her like the clouds over a mountain. It had been one of the things he'd loved about her, because in bed she'd been passionate and insatiable.

That she could for even a moment think that he would not have loved her if she'd come to him still cut deep. Did he appear a man so fickle in his affections? What good would the dukedom have been to him without her? He shouldn't be in line for the damn title in the first place. But she hadn't wanted to test the bonds of his love, fearing they would fray and snap under the pressure of Society's judgment.

Advancing deeper into the room, her gaze slowly ran over the bedside table, the vanity, the wardrobe and bedstead until it halted at the door behind the dressing screen. "The dressing-room?" she asked absently.

Alex nodded.

She gestured toward the closed door located slightly adjacent. "Where does that lead?"

"To the master suite."

Her face flushed a brilliant pink as she immediately shifted her gaze from his. "Oh, I did not realize that…" Her voice vanished like a fine mist under the scorching heat of the sun.

"We are husband and wife."

He said it as if it explained everything. This from the same man determined not to have her in his bed. Again she glanced at the door. It was locked, she was sure.

His gaze flicked to the door and then back to her face. "If

you have any hopes I will ever make use of it, I fear you are sadly mistaken. As I told you before, while I may on occasion publicly express affection toward you, it will be to deflect suspicion from our marriage, which, as you know, will be under intense scrutiny. I will not go so far as to bed you in private."

Charlotte hated that he spoke as if the notion was unpalatable when they both knew he still desired her, that he wanted her just as she wanted him. But he wanted her against his will, which by the day was looking mightier than a Trojan suited up for war.

"Yes, you've made it very plain how you feel about me."

Except for the tightening of his jaw, Alex didn't react to her statement. She wondered what he'd do if one night when wanting him and not having him became too much for her to endure, *she* made use of that door. Would he turn her away? Of course she'd do no such thing. She simply hadn't the courage and couldn't fathom setting herself up for probable rejection. But that didn't mean she couldn't try to change his mind.

"I shall leave you to settle in. Dinner will be served at seven."

Charlotte didn't know whether to be relieved he'd taken the truth so well or angry it had mattered so little to him, he couldn't understand why she'd done what she'd done. Or forgive her.

"Thank you," she said and watched as he turned to leave. She hungrily took in the broad width of his shoulders, the narrowness of his hips to the long stretch of legs. Heat pooled between her thighs. God, how she'd missed him. God, how she wanted him.

So lost in her ardent perusal, she didn't notice he'd halted and was observing her reflection in an oak-framed floor mirror. His eyes darkened and the skin around his jaw grew taut as if he was clenching his teeth hard enough to hurt.

"Don't." The roughly muttered warning spoke not of his anger but of his inner turmoil.

Charlotte turned abruptly, her back to him. Blistering heat suffused her face. After an infinitesimal pause, she heard her bed chamber door click softly closed.

Alex quickly ducked into his room after escaping the alluring presence of his wife, his heart thumping wildly in his chest. He'd had to get out of there or he would not have been responsible for what would have happened next.

Good God, she'd nearly burned him with that look, so full of raw need and desire. And the response it had elicited in him had made him think that sanity was highly overrated. Would that he could forget the past, because only then could he allow himself to go down the very same path that had come close to destroying him before.

The future stretched out before him like a prison sentence in which he'd be forced to pay for crimes he himself hadn't committed. He wasn't naïve enough to believe that if he made the mistake of engaging in marital relations with her that it wouldn't leave him vulnerable to her charms again, that he wouldn't want her every day in every conceivable way as he'd once done.

That was not to say a woman couldn't hurt him again, but he'd be damned if he'd make the mistake of opening his heart to the *same* woman who'd broken it the first time. His pride alone would not permit that. The task before him—one that now seemed more daunting than recovering from his initial heartbreak—was in determining how he could live with her and not take what she so obviously wanted without going stark raving mad.

Or perhaps the true task was in determining if he in fact wanted to.

Chapter Fifteen

For the next two weeks, Charlotte accustomed herself to her new life, which at times was not an easy task. She looked forward to her daily visits with her sister, and Nicholas divided his time between going to Rutherford Manor to play with his cousins and spending time with his father.

Every day Alex had some activity planned for him and his son. An expert horseman, Alex was teaching Nicholas how to ride. The fear that had so consumed her on the day of their first lesson had receded considerably, but hadn't abandoned her completely. Her son was so young and her own riding skills could only be considered the side of passable that wouldn't get her thrown from a trotting horse. But her fear wasn't without merit for her father had died from a fall from his horse.

With the plans for the ball underway, Charlotte's anxiety began to climb. She hadn't attended a ball since the year she'd left England nor had she danced a step. There'd been no time for dances or balls with a child to care for. What there had been were countless sleepless nights. To make sure her finances would stretch another year, Charlotte had only been able to afford a cook, and Jillian, who served as a maid-of-all-work.

That was not the case here. Her husband employed a full staff and frankly there was very little for her to do much of the time and she wasn't accustomed to being idle. That evening she told him as much at the dinner table, on which she'd had the footman place two large vases of primrose and daisies from the garden. If she must endure yet another of those beastly, silent meals with her husband, it would be nice if she had something innocuous and pleasant at which to look.

"Perhaps you should speak to Missy and find out what wives do to pass the time," he advised as he cut into his roasted chicken. He spoke as if he found the topic pedestrian, which annoyed her to no end. Obviously the result of frustration.

Every night when she took herself off to bed, he went out to God knows where. She suspected he'd already taken a mistress. Or perhaps he'd always had one. And the thought of him with another woman tormented her, which had her twisting her bed sheets in her sleep.

He hardly spoke two sentences to her in a day. He was excruciatingly civil but coolly rejected any overtures of amiability on her part by excusing himself from any room she entered that he occupied. That was unless Nicholas was present, but then he'd direct all his attention to him. Charlotte could never have imagined she'd be jealous of her son, but during those times she'd smart in silence, wishing for a small fraction of Alex's attention. Lord, it wouldn't be so hard if she didn't have to live with him and see him every day.

Her knife sliced cleanly through her potato. "My brother and Missy have a real marriage. I'm certain our wifely duties do not coincide that much." Yes, she was feeling a bit peevish but her husband could blame himself for that, subjecting her to this untenable situation.

This got his attention. Slowly, he lowered his fork to his plate and observed her. A bolt of awareness coursed through her.

"Am I to take that as a complaint?" he asked quietly.

Would it change anything if it were?

"No, I'm simply stating that as we do not have a real marriage, it is unfair of you to in any way equate Missy's life with mine. Missy spends a great deal of her time with James when he's not working. Then there are the children. She has three and since we've been in England, Nicholas isn't so in want of my company. Now he has cousins…and you."

Continuing to regard her silently, Alex resumed eating. Charlotte did the same. Unfortunately the food was wasted on her. She found she could no longer enjoy her supper.

Neither spoke for the duration of the meal and Charlotte was happy to escape to her bedchambers once it finally ended. Alex did nothing to stop her, not that she'd expected he would.

Alex sat and watched his wife vacate the dining room. The feminine sway of her hips practically taunted him to take what his body desperately craved; a night between her thighs satisfying every lascivious thought he'd ever had about her. And there had been plenty.

Frankly, he was more than a little surprised he hadn't succumbed to drink by now. He could have worked off his sexual hunger between the thighs of his former mistress, who would have welcomed him and lived only an hour away. Instead he spent what remained of the evening playing cards in an exclusive social club in town surrounded by smoke, gambling and drink. If he desired a woman, one could be had easily enough. Much to Alex's chagrin, he'd discovered only one particular woman would do.

Living with Charlotte was enough to test his will as nothing else had done. When he returned home in the early hours of the morning, his eyes bored holes through the connecting door to their bedchambers as he lived in half dread and hope it would one day open. In the scene he'd play back in his mind when feeling particularly firm in his resolve, he'd refuse her and send her skittering back to her bed...alone.

But during the latter times—which far eclipsed the former in both frequency and breathtaking clarity—he'd resist but alas, lose his valiant fight when her female charms and innate irresistibility became too much for him. Then he'd take her in every conceivable manner and position, their release coming hard on the heels of another and another until exhaustion overtook them both and they collapsed in a tangle of arms and legs, their bodies replete with carnal satisfaction.

Alex, I do not have enough to fill my days, had been her comment without the faintest hint of provocation. Although, he had no doubt she'd not have minded if *he* filled *her* in the one way she'd love most. As would he. His mouth quirked at the thought but his erection had grown too pronounced—almost painful—to derive any real amusement from it.

Two days ago, he'd discovered her in the library on the step ladder reaching for a book. His arrival apparently had been too silent for when she sensed his presence, she gave a violent start, losing her balance, and would have tumbled to the unforgiving wood floors had he not caught her in his arms. Her supple curves had wiped clean his memory of the past and he'd seen only an infinitely desirable woman, her blue eyes darkened with awareness and passion.

To this very moment, he hadn't the vaguest idea how he managed to extricate her from his arms without the popping of ivory buttons and tearing of a rose-print percale, which comprised her morning dress. She'd been barely standing when he'd all but sprinted from the room, fearing if he remained the servants—or heaven forbid, their son—might have gotten an eyeful of things meant for the bedchambers…if that.

And this was how he felt after only two weeks. Yet he'd sentenced himself to a lifetime of this deprivation and torture. What the hell had he been thinking? Sleeping with her didn't necessarily mean he'd relinquish his heart as readily as his body had turned traitor.

Why should he suffer more because of her actions, well intentioned as she'd thought them to be? If nothing else, he deserved to derive not just the joy of having his son with him but the pleasures her body promised and had more than delivered in the past. Moreover, he was weary of denying himself. Weary of fighting himself.

He rose from the table and exited the dining room, only stopping to inform Alfred he'd not require his assistance that evening.

Before retiring for the evening, Charlotte checked in on Nicholas. Sprawled on his bed, he was the picture of innocence and serenity. Brushing a lock of hair from his forehead, she leaned down and kissed him softly on the cheek.

Ten minutes later, as she prepared for bed, a sharp knock sounded on her chamber door. Before she could wonder at the knocker's identity, it opened and Alex entered, shrinking it in size with his presence.

Without uttering a word, he latched the lock. He then turned back to her. His waistcoat was already off, and his fingers began to work the buttons of his fine cotton shirt.

Charlotte, who had just donned a night dress of a thin cotton that was fairly translucent if the light struck it just so, instinctively folded her arms over her breasts and exclaimed, "Alex, what are you doing here? Is something wrong?" His sudden presence made swallowing difficult. He looked dark and determined—and ravenous.

"Did you, not ten minutes ago, complain that we do not have a *real* marriage? Well, madam, you shall have a real husband tonight as it appears you require additional duties to fill your days. Now, if you'd be so kind as to remove your garments."

How entirely proper and reasonable he sounded while his eyes devoured her. There was something excessively primal about Alex tonight. He moved purposefully, pulling his shirt over his head, his hooded gaze never once straying from her. The heat in his eyes suggested he'd been stripped of his surface civility and now operated purely on his base needs and desires.

"Remove your clothes or would you rather leave that task to me? I know I will enjoy it." He had moved on to his trousers, unbuttoning and then pushing the superfine navy wool down over his hips.

Liquid heat pooled at her center as she watched in helpless fascination and belly-clenching lust as more of his taut, naked flesh was revealed. His legs were lean and muscled, dark hair covering flesh lighter in color than his face but that could never be considered pale. The muscles in his abdomen flexed and rippled as he bent to strip himself of his trousers completely.

His erection jutted out against his cotton drawers, demanding her exclusive attention, which it received most fervently.

Dear Lord, he was beautiful. She could never tire of looking at him.

Before lust completely overtook her fogged senses, it suddenly struck her that he hadn't gone out tonight. The first time since she'd moved in. Was his mistress not available? Nothing would be worse than to discover that's why he'd come to her.

"Couldn't she accommodate you tonight?" she asked, unable to keep the waspishness from her tone. The jealousy she was unable to hide.

He paused in kicking aside his trousers. "Exactly to whom do you refer?"

Charlotte crossed her arms over her chest. "Your mistress."

"I do not have a mistress," he replied calmly.

"I do not believe you." Although she desperately wanted to.

"I have no reason to lie to you. If you're referring to where I spend my nights, believe me it is not enjoying another woman's charms."

Shaking her head, Charlotte cried, "I don't believe you." Even as she discounted his claims of innocence, her fervid gaze couldn't help drifting down to peruse every inch of his exposed muscled flesh. His raging erection.

He stalked toward her and stopped no less than a foot away. "Well believe this, I haven't the desire to bed another woman, only you. If I could, believe me I would have weeks ago. Right now I want to be inside you more than I want my next breath." He pitched his voice very low. "Now, will you remove that or shall I?" He gestured to her nightdress.

At his words and the slumberous look in his eyes, a shock of relief, thrill and desire slammed into her with the force of a frigate. No respectable woman would be aroused by his manner—no wooing or gentle seduction. But as if to disprove any claim she had to respectability, her nipples peaked and moisture flooded her core. It was official, she was a wanton.

"Alex—"

He came closer, standing inches before her. With both hands, he grasped the hem of her nightdress and oh so slowly inched it up.

"Why must we deny ourselves when it is so obvious how much we both want it?"

Charlotte placed her hands on his shoulders, intending to get some distance and clarity but he released her nightdress and his hands were now caressing her calves, moving higher and higher.

She whimpered and then her breaths came in the form of pants.

We? It hadn't been she who'd wanted to deny them the physical pleasures of marriage. But this wasn't the right time to correct him of the facts.

Past her knees, one hand continued the climb along her inner thigh. Another whimper emerged and her breathing turned ragged and labored. Oh Lord, his hands felt so good. Thoughts of stopping him were fleeting at best, so quickly were they squelched by the sheer pleasure of his touch on her too-long-dormant passions.

Pale yellow muslin draped over his arms, the full length of her legs revealed. With a quick tug, he pulled it over her head, with barely any cognizant aid from her, to leave her without a stitch. Charlotte let out a gasp, her hands flying to cover her breasts, then realizing she was still bared to him, she slapped one hand over the nest of hair between her thighs.

Alex smiled at that, but it wasn't a smile of real amusement. No it was too hungry for that as his gaze scorched her bared breast. He then quickly removed his remaining garment, watching her narrowly as she watched him.

He was bigger was her first thought. Her second had her almost reaching out to stroke him—an inch closer and it'd be in contact with her belly. But it had been years since they'd made love last and as much as she wanted him, she suddenly felt shy.

"Beautiful," he whispered. He ran the tip of his finger over her ruched nipple and the areola surrounding.

Pleasure zigzagged through her like a lightning bolt, her knees buckled as the room tilted wildly. She wasn't sure if she reached out to clutch his shoulders to steady herself or whether the lure of his tanned flesh became too much for her to resist. Or perhaps it was both. Regardless of which, she was suddenly in his arms, the heat of him burning her.

He groaned long and low when their torsos met. She felt his erection, hard and hot on her belly and her body reacted accordingly, her center clenching in eager anticipation of his possession.

"This is what you want isn't it?" he whispered in her ear, his arms firmly around her waist while hers encircled his neck. "This is what you wanted from the start, isn't it?"

She sincerely hoped he didn't expect her to respond. After so many years of dreaming of this moment, the moment when she'd finally be back in his arms, her body's demands made speech impossible.

Instead, Charlotte tugged his head down for a kiss. But he would not relent and held himself back, his neck taut in resistance. Miffed, Charlotte retaliated by rubbing herself firmly against him, her breasts against his chest, her hips against his hard male member.

He inhaled sharply, his eyes closing as if he suffered the seven hells of agony and torment. "Don't," he groaned. "It's been too long and I don't want to be rough with you."

Now he decided he wanted to take it slow? After he'd barged into her chambers, stripped himself not only of his clothes, but her of hers as well and pulled her naked in to his arms?

"Kiss me."

His eyes blazed down at her. "We will have this but that is all."

At the moment, Charlotte ceased to care about the meaning of his words. She wanted one thing and one thing only, and that was to have him inside her. It had been so very long since she'd experienced this sort of pleasure, where her body had pulsed at the touch of a man's hands on her.

"Kiss me," she repeated, sifting her hands through the silky strands of his hair to press insistently down on the back of his head.

The speed at which his mouth came down on hers left her gasping. He kissed her like a man deprived of a woman for years. And Charlotte's mouth opened, welcoming the thrust of his tongue.

His hand cupped the back of her head, tipping it back as he fed on her lips like the greediest of lovers.

Charlotte closed her eyes as she clung tightly to him, helpless to stop the relentless surge of desire that coursed through her body. Their tongues traded thrusts and parries and then tangled in a kiss that worked like a drug running through her. Senses reeling, she rose on the tips of her toes and ground herself against his hard member; the head of it briefly touched the slick flesh of her center. She gasped and began to press against him in earnest.

Tearing his mouth from her sweet lips, Alex grasped her tightly by her bottom, blindly kneading the smooth, soft flesh as he stilled her movements before she sent him hurtling too soon and too fast to completion to satisfy her.

He buried his face in the floral-scented notch between her neck and shoulder, his breaths harsh and loud. "Stop. I don't want to come yet."

"Alex."

It was a plea that nearly undid him. But he wanted to do this right. To at least satisfy her first. It was clear he'd have to be quick for he didn't think he could hold on much longer. His cock demanded entry to her snug, slick center.

"Hold on," he said hoarsely. In a surprisingly smooth movement given his shaky control, he hooked his hands beneath her knees, hefting her up as he walked them to the bed.

But this position pressed his cock directly into her wet core. At the contact, he hissed and nearly dropped her.

"Damn it, Charlotte."

Her eyes were half closed and her mouth looked sweetly ravaged. When his upper thighs hit the edge of the mattress, he dropped her onto the bed and quickly lifted her legs up and apart. The sight of her, pink and wet, nearly undid him then and there.

With his finger, he traced the moist folds of her center. Excited, he parted her and found the engorged nub at the hood of her sex. He proceeded to toy with it, causing her back to arch off the bed as she moaned and bit her lip.

Alex simply lost what little control he thought he'd had. "I can't wait," he groaned, barely able to speak. With one hand holding her open at the knee, he used the other to guide his cock inside.

The first probe locked his jaw. His chest shuddered as he saw the head disappear. He caught her other knee in his hand and bore down with his hips. Charlotte's moans became pants and then whimpers. He slid into her until he was wholly and fully lodged. She felt like heaven, her sex clenching around him tightly.

"Char. Dear God," he groaned, briefly closing his eyes.

"Alex, please." The look in her eyes, blind with passion, and her quivering pink mouth started him thrusting. He hissed out his pleasure with every stroke.

"More. Oh, do it faster," came Charlotte's breathy command. Her hands, unable to reach him where he stood, feet braced apart on the floor between her legs, clutched fistfuls of the counterpane. She let out a low gasp every time he came into her and whimpered when he pulled out.

He spread her knees farther apart as his stokes grew faster until he was pounding into her. His release coiled in his belly. The incoherent sounds coming from Charlotte grew louder until she screamed, her hips high off the mattress, her back arched and taut as a bow. Her orgasm set off violent contractions of her inner muscles around his member. With three more hard thrusts as her sex continued to quiver around him, he roared to completion, spilling into her on a wave of ecstasy, eclipsing anything he'd ever experienced before.

Charlotte lay insensate under Alex's weight, the hairs on his chest abrading her breasts and belly. It felt divine.

It took another minute for her to resume normal breathing, which is when Alex rolled from on top of her. He pulled out of her and she immediately missed being connected with him in that way.

But he didn't go far. He moved her from the edge of the mattress and arranged her so she was lying flush against him, her back against his hair-roughened chest, his member against her bottom.

"I'll make it better for you next time," he said, his heated breath next to her ear.

She laughed lightly and pushed the tangle of her hair from her eyes. "I don't know I'd survive if you made it better."

A low laugh rumbled from his throat as he ran his hand over her long, tousled locks. The years apart hadn't changed *this* between them. In fact, their lovemaking had only gotten better, more intense.

"May I ask a question?" he asked after a minute of contented silence.

Angling her head around to regard him, she replied, "But of course."

"What was Nicholas like as a baby?"

Charlotte shifted in his arms until she faced him. Clasping the narrow indent of her waist, he pulled her until their hips were flush, his member lying just above the nest of hair of her sex. He was already semi-erect.

"He was a good baby. At four months he was sleeping through the night. By seven months he was crawling and he took his first steps at eleven months."

A faint smile curved his mouth; not in anger or sadness, it

appeared to be more one of regret. Charlotte looked deeply into his gray eyes and her heart ached for him.

"And when did he begin to speak?"

Charlotte found herself laughing softly, remembering the sweet sounds of Nicholas's baby babble. "The moment he came into the world it felt like. But if you're speaking of words one could comprehend, I believe that occurred when he was nine months. It's difficult to remember exactly when."

"He's a wonderful child," Alex said after a pause.

Her heart swelled and then lodged itself in her throat. In terms of compliments, it was the greatest he'd ever given her. "Yes he is. And Alex, he thinks you are wonderful too." Nicholas thought his father hung the sun, the moon and the stars. It did not hurt that Alex was making every attempt to win his son's affections. Two days ago, he'd begun to teach him to fish.

Alex swallowed and inhaled a prolonged breath. "Tell me about your life in America." He spoke quietly and watched her beneath a hooded gaze.

Lonely and wretched without you, she'd have said was she to be completely honest with him. But burdening him with her feelings of desolation given the circumstances would not be fair.

"Life there was very quiet. There was always much to do so Jillian and I shared the household chores. I became quite proficient with a needle and learned how to stretch our wardrobes by darning our garments."

"Were you happy?" he asked.

"I could not truly be happy being away from you and my family." It had taken some time, but eventually, she learned to bury her longings for him—at least during the daylight hours. A daily struggle, to be sure. But it was how she learned to cope.

"Did you not have close acquaintances? You do not expect me to believe that you, a beautiful, young widow, did not have gentlemen callers."

Charlotte wasn't fooled by the lightness of his tone or his not-so-subtle approach to seek the answer he craved. His gaze was fierce and probing. Possessive.

Her thoughts went briefly to Lucas. More than anything, she wanted Alex to feel secure in her affections. To that end, the mention of another man, regardless of the platonic nature of their relationship, wasn't likely to help at this particular juncture.

"I discouraged them. In any case, I had Nicholas, who required constant attention."

Alex's chest fell beneath her hand and the sound that whistled past his lips closely resembled a sigh of relief. His hold on her tightened as he rolled onto his back. She adjusted by resting her hot cheek on his chest. The steady drum of his heartbeat was loud and comforting in her ear.

In whispered tones, they spoke under the veil of darkness, discussing her and Nicholas's life in New York. At one point, he asked if she needed to return. She told him she'd recently written to the leasing agent to inform him she'd be giving up the flat. The furniture could be sold but she'd requested he have her personal items shipped there. This could be achieved with minimal fuss since, uncertain as to when or *if* they'd be returning, Charlotte had boxed up the remainder of the things she wasn't taking with her before she left.

Alex spoke not at all about his life during the same period and Charlotte was wise enough not to ask, fearing the topic would spoil the budding intimacy between them.

Eventually, their murmured voices gave way to silence. Alex broke it a minute later.

"Tonight I was careless. I did nothing to prevent pregnancy."

Charlotte's gaze flew to his face. She found it impossible to read his expression. However, she did remember his words, which were like a sharp nick on a not-yet-healed cut.

Oh, I want more children, I just don't want them with you.

The hurt was momentary. She'd not permit it to be anything

more. It was much too soon for him to have a complete change of heart on the matter. In time, she prayed he would.

She looked at him questioningly. Barring abstinence, the only preventive methods she'd ever heard of were French letters and Dutch caps.

"You needn't worry. I shall take care of it in the future. Until then, I shall take care not to spill inside you." He stroked the length of her arm, his touch both equal parts sensual and soothing.

A diversion from talk of contraception? Charlotte could only wonder. But what wasn't at question was how her body responded instantly to him. How her blood thrummed at his touch and the revival of his erection pressing stiff and hot along her inner thigh.

"I was so eager after so long, I fear I neglected these." His hands cupped her breasts and began playing with her nipples; lightly pinching, flicking and thumbing them into stiff buds. "I shall do my best to make it up to you," he murmured, his voice thick with lust.

The fire in her blazed back to life as if it hadn't been doused a short time ago. She was insatiable. She moaned and began kneading the outside of his thighs. Alex grew harder and hotter beneath her.

In a sudden movement, he went from being under her to over her, his mouth pulling her nipple between his lips. Charlotte's breath became choppy and she stroked his nape as he suckled her.

If he was determined to improve on the experience, who was she to stop him?

When Charlotte awoke the next morning, it was hideously bright. The sun in one of its more generous moods had decided to bless them with its singular presence.

The evening's events came instantly to mind and when she gave a lazy stretch, her body's pleasurable aches and pains further reinforced how deliciously she'd passed the night—and a good portion of the early morning.

Alex had been insatiable—and admittedly, so had she—taking her three times. The last time had been in the wee hours of the morning when he'd turned her on her side and taken her from behind. But as late as he'd stayed, he must have left her bed frightfully early.

But the sun proclaimed she had slept well beyond the hours she'd hence been accustomed to. A glance at the clock on the fireplace mantel indicated it was half past ten; she'd been well on her way to sleeping half the day away.

Alex.

She smiled at the thought of him. It was hard to believe he was the same man who'd, up until that very day, been determined not to make love to his wife. He was so good at it, his skill unparalleled—not that she had the intimate knowledge to make any comparison, but she knew.

Another stretch triggered the pleasurable soreness between her thighs. She'd been well and truly ravished.

Their lovemaking hadn't only satisfied a five-year longing, but it represented a change in the marriage Alex had so coldly laid out. They could not go back to that arid wasteland. The fire between them blazed hotter than ever before.

For the first time in too long, contentment seeped from her pores. Of course it would be better if Alex loved her in return. But he had softened, his manner a great deal more tender toward her. Now if they could achieve the same sort of intimacy outside the bedchamber, their marriage would have a chance.

Chapter Sixteen

Charlotte entered the breakfast room a half hour later and was surprised to find Alex sitting alone at the table reading the newspapers. Their paths rarely crossed in the mornings. When it did it felt like two strangers engaged in a waltz, each ever conscious that one wrong step would upset the precise rhythm of the dance.

The first thing that struck her when he lowered the paper was his smile. It'd been so long since he'd directed one at her devoid of mockery or derision. She became flustered.

"I see you've finally awoken." Folding the papers, he placed it on the table before pushing back his chair and rising to his feet. "I thought I'd perish of hunger."

It was only then Charlotte noticed that his silver utensils sat unused beside an empty bone white plate.

"Why have you not eaten?" Surely, he hadn't been waiting for her to join him.

His eyes trapped hers in his gaze. "I was waiting for you."

As much as Charlotte tried not to read too much into his meaning, it was impossible when he looked at her like that. As if he was remembering every second of the evening they'd spent pleasuring each other.

"Come, let's eat." He gestured toward the sideboard where they proceeded to serve themselves from platters holding thick slices of bacon, scrambled eggs, freshly baked bread and rolls, thick slices of cheese and kippers.

Once they were both seated, Alex said, "Shall I presume you passed the night agreeably?"

Charlotte, who had already commenced eating, nearly choked. Her gaze snapped to his. His expression was all feigned innocence.

The devil.

It took a moment to recover her composure and swallow. "I passed the night agreeably enough," she replied primly, suppressing a smile. Two could play at that.

With a brief nod of dismissal to the footman, when they were finally alone, Alex turned a heavy-lidded gaze back to her. "You do make a lot of noise for a woman who only passed it agreeably *enough*. You kept me awake with all your panting and moaning."

A shock of heat burned her face. Alex now watched her as if breakfast wasn't the only thing he was hungry for, which had her body instantly responding in kind.

"You are incorrigible." As reprimands went, it sadly lacked the proper reproachful tone.

Alex's mouth curved into a thoroughly wicked smile. "And you are insatiable. But don't fret, I shall do my utmost best to ensure you pass tonight far more agreeably."

An ice age had passed since Alex last flirted with her, since the full force of his charm had been directed at her.

"And I shall look forward to your most ardent endeavors." She spoke with a calmness and bravado she didn't feel. Fireworks of anticipation were going off inside her.

Chuckling quietly, Alex commenced eating, his gaze frequently returning to her flushed face.

Although she'd prayed last night would be a new beginning for them, this morning far exceeded her expectations. Being with him like this felt...right. It reminded her of how they used to be; how he'd once treated her. How special she had felt. How desired and wanted. It made her feel the same way now.

Alex broke the stretch of amiable silence. "I had your maid take Nicholas to your brother's until the afternoon. I thought you'd like to accompany me on my tenant visits. They have yet to meet the new marchioness."

Charlotte swallowed a mouthful of hot chocolate and placed the cup back in the flowered saucer. She met his stare and something warm passed between them. "I would be happy to accompany you. I would like that very much."

Rutherford Manor, Lucas Beaumont would admit, was an impressive piece of architecture.

So this was where Charlotte had lived before she'd gone to America. He recalled her small and fastidiously clean flat on Willow Street in Manhattan. The two dwellings were worlds apart. Not for the first or second time since he'd made her acquaintance, Lucas wondered what had really driven her from England. Her story of a husband who had succumbed to scarlet fever had never rung true.

Nonetheless, she'd been gone over a month and the letter she'd promised to send to let him know she and Nicholas arrived safely had never arrived. He was worried.

He rang the bell of the residence and waited. Seconds later the door was opened by a liveried footman. How the English did love the pomp and ceremony, especially when it came to their servants.

"Good afternoon, I am looking for Miss Charlotte Rutherford," Lucas said politely, remembering from his last visit that she went by her maiden name. A fact she'd yet to divulge to him.

Before the young man could respond, a woman appeared in the foyer behind him.

"Charlotte." Lucas smiled, relieved to see her looking so well.

But as she advanced toward him, he knew she wasn't Charlotte but her twin, Catherine, whom he'd met on his last trip to England. His feelings immediately shifted from one of friendly warmth to lustful interest.

Miss Catherine halted so abruptly he nearly laughed aloud. Her lips parted and her finely arched brows shot up. He hoped her shock was one of pleasure as he'd been looking forward to seeing her again.

A moment later, she seemed to catch herself and with a straightening of her spine and tossing back of her shoulders, composed her expression, although she didn't quite achieve the nonchalance it appeared she strived for.

"Mr. Beaumont." There was a slight inflection in her voice where one could have easily taken it as a question even though he knew it was not.

She quietly dismissed the footman as she approached him, stunning in a blue dress that lovingly adhered to her curves yet left much for the imagination. Lucas still found it surprising that although the sisters were identical in appearance, there was something about this one that had immediately, almost viscerally, affected him in a way he'd not felt before or since.

"Miss Catherine." He bowed formally, long familiar with English and how strictly they adhered to the formalities of aristocratic propriety. She hadn't struck him as that kind of person but when in England, etcetera, etcetera.

"Mr. Beaumont, wh-what are doing here?" A small, hesitant smile curved a pair of lush, pink lips. "Oh dear, how very rude of me, do come in," she said, opening the door to admit him.

Lucas smiled as he entered, finding her forthright manner refreshing. "I am looking for Charlotte."

Was it his imagination, or did her smile falter the tiniest little bit? Had she thought he'd come to see her? One could only hope.

"Charlotte? Does she know you're in England? I hadn't thought you'd be back so soon."

When Lucas had been in England last, he'd met Miss Catherine at Sir Franklin's supper party where he'd mistaken her for her sister. But when she'd turned and stared at him blankly, he'd known then Charlotte didn't just have a sister but an identical twin. Their resemblance was uncanny but discernible if one cared to look very close. He had.

He'd soon received an introduction and had immediately struck up a conversation with her. And the things he'd learned had been very informative.

Lucas cast an idle glance around. The house was typically English in appearance, as dwellings go, and a bit on the large scale. "I hadn't intended to come back until the fall but when I didn't receive a letter from your sister telling me she and Nicholas arrived safely, I thought it prudent to come early. I assume she did arrive safely, no?"

Her welcoming smile cooled by several degrees.

"Perhaps we should go to the drawing room to talk. I don't believe the entry way is the appropriate venue to carry on this sort of discussion." She spoke more formally now, her English accent crisp and more pronounced than her sister's.

Lucas removed his hat and followed her to the drawing room, while admiring the gentle sway of her hips and her nipped-in waist. God, he had almost forgotten how alluring she was.

The drawing room was like the many he'd seen in aristocratic English homes, although this one was less formal—not quite as stuffy. The sofas, two in number, were covered in a tan fabric and the fireplace was of a dark wood and very grand.

"Please, have a seat." She motioned to the sofas and armchairs. "And yes, my sister and nephew arrived safely some weeks back."

Lucas waited until she was seated before he chose the armchair closest to her. He placed his hat on his lap. "Good, she had me worried. I take she was surprised to see you on your feet and quite well. Did she happen to mention she'd come because she thought you were in failing health?"

Miss Catherine had the grace to wince. "No, she said nothing about it and should she ask, please tell her only that it was what you heard. You do not know the name of the person who relayed the information nor could you identify them even if they were thrust in front of you." She looked nervous.

During their initial conversation, he'd informed her he knew a woman who could be her identical twin named Charlotte, and Miss Catherine had nearly pounced on him—which he hadn't minded a bit. She pleaded with him to divulge her sister's location, explaining that Charlotte had fled England years ago and that she and her brother were worried sick about her. She'd indicated all she wanted was for Charlotte to come home, even for a visit so they could see for themselves that she was well. Miss Catherine hadn't mentioned her nephew and from that he'd taken she didn't know he existed and had decided it wasn't his place to tell her.

Lucas had listened with interest but hadn't wanted to betray Charlotte's confidence and reveal her location, remaining mute when her sister had repeatedly asked. What if the same family worried sick about her was the reason she'd left? That is when she had switched tactics, telling him Charlotte would return if she thought she was sick—perhaps failing. That would prove she loved her family and had nothing to fear from them. This had swayed Lucas and he'd finally agreed—she had pled so prettily—to tell Charlotte he'd heard her sister was very ill.

"I will not betray your trust. The truth of it is I had my own reasons for participating in the deception. Whenever Charlotte did speak of her family and England—which wasn't often— she became very emotional. I could see it pained her. I assumed she and her family were estranged. Then I met you and it became clear she was loved and missed. I thought this might help her."

Catherine couldn't decide whether to be miffed with Mr. Beaumont that he hadn't come to call on her or allow herself to experience that moment of pleasure that had all but consumed her when she'd spotted him across the front door.

Had he not felt the connection when they met? She had opened up to him as she had no other. And he had been utterly charming—and handsome. His voice, so different from English gentlemen, entranced her. And when was the last time she'd seen a man with hair the color of his eyes, the color of rich chocolate? God help the woman he fixed his gaze upon.

God help me.

Then a thought struck her. "I failed to ask you when we first met, but what kind of business are you in?"

Mr. Beaumont produced a lazy smile that only served to make him ever more appealing. Her heart skipped a beat.

"I dabble a little in this and that," was all he said.

If Catherine thought that in pressing him on the matter he would elaborate, she may have done but he appeared content to let his cryptic answer stand.

"Charlotte is home, so it appears I am in your debt."

His smile turned positively predatory, which normally would have dampened his appeal, but she felt her pulse quicken in response, her nipples pebbling beneath her silk chemise and dress.

"I believe I like the sound of that," he drawled in a voice that had the effect of reducing a woman to mush.

She rarely blushed but the heat flooding her face told her she was doing so now.

"Well, if you have come to see Charlotte, she lives on the neighboring estate with her husband."

No one could confuse the startled look in his eyes or the way his head snapped straight up for anything but surprise. And that is when the knot of dread wrapped itself about her stomach.

No. Oh no, please, let him not be interested in Charlotte.

"Charlotte is married?"

Catherine nodded. "Are you by any chance interested in my sister, Mr. Beaumont? It has just occurred to me that you've traveled a great distance to reassure yourself of her well-being." She quite literally braced herself for his answer, her hands lightly gripping the smooth edge of the sofa. She was and had been from the moment they met, wildly attracted to him.

He shook his head. "No. No, there is nothing like that going on between us. As I told you when we met, your sister and I are no more than good friends. I simply combined a business trip with my personal interest."

Since it would be unseemly at this point to reveal her feelings, Charlotte merely nodded for she did believe him.

"Charlotte is married to Nicholas's father."

Mr. Beaumont's eyebrows rose as if that was news to him. "Indeed?"

"Yes, indeed. If you'd like, I can accompany you to see her. As I said, she lives on the neighboring estate, which is only a quarter hour by carriage." She wanted his company, Catherine wasn't afraid to admit it—to herself. When was the last time she'd been this attracted and frankly intrigued by a man? Truth be told, never.

His smile returned like the sun's after being covered briefly by a cloud, full and winsome. "Thank you. I would like that very much."

Catherine's stomach became weightless as she stood. "Then I shall get a wrap."

Following suit, he rose to his feet and towered a good head above her. His eyelids lowered to half-mast, causing her stomach to plunge down to the soles of her feet. For a moment, she felt unsteady, a little lightheaded. With his hat in one hand, he reached out and caught her elbow with the other. The touch of his bare flesh on her sent a bolt of heat through her.

"Are you all right?" It came out *aw-right*, which she found positively delicious sounding.

"For a moment I thought you were going to fall." He didn't release her elbow even though she was in no danger of falling—at least from her feet.

"I must have stood too fast," she mumbled. No doubt he was well aware of the effect he had on women. If Catherine didn't know with one hundred percent certainty how much her sister loved Alex, she'd have thought better of his assertion that the two shared just a friendship.

He slowly released her, leaving Catherine bereft of his touch. When she'd first met him, she'd found him attractive beyond words but days later after she'd learned he'd returned to America, she'd questioned his appeal. Surely he could not have been everything she'd initially thought. She'd convinced herself it must have been the variegated lighting that made him appear more handsome and that in the cold light of day she'd feel much different should she see him again.

She could not have been more wrong. The light of day only further enhanced his appeal. The light of day also confirmed that she was more attracted to him than ever.

Catherine had never set out to attract a gentleman. Firstly, she'd never found one worthy enough to put forth the effort. Secondly, she'd always been wary of her brother's set, finding them to be a lofty lot. Lastly, she'd never felt like this, her insides tingling, her body coming alive at the thought of a man's hands touching her. Mr. Lucas Beaumont did that to her and it was an invigorating experience.

"Will you be staying long in London, Mr. Beaumont?" she asked, slanting a coy glance up at him.

"Lucas. My friends call me Lucas."

Even better. "Lucas."

His brown eyes heated as he peered down at her. "I believe I will, Miss Catherine."

"Please, Catherine only will do."

The first footman found Charlotte going over the menus for the week with Mrs. Henderson, the housekeeper, and informed her that Miss Catherine awaited her in the morning room.

The servants had been told Charlotte was always *in* for family and that they should be taken there and not the drawing room as with all other callers—not that they had many.

Charlotte immediately abandoned her task and made her way to the room. Although she saw her sister quite regularly, they hadn't spoken since the day before yesterday. And she could use a bit of company. Alex had taken Nicholas out for his daily riding lesson and once she completed the menus, she had very little to do. She had been seriously considering attempting a needlepoint sampler. She'd been reading so much her eyes were starting to cross.

But she couldn't be more pleased with the way things were progressing with Alex. He smiled more. Even Alfred had remarked in that very proper way of his, on how Alex's manner had changed; how happier and more at ease his lordship appeared.

Each evening for the past two weeks, he entered her bedchamber through the connecting door wearing a dressing robe, his body already stiff with need. The third night, Charlotte stopped donning her nightdress altogether, as he swiftly divested her of it not a minute after he arrived. True to his word, he'd begun using French letters. After five nights of that, they'd agreed she would try the Dutch cap, which proved to be a much more satisfactory experience for them both.

In truth, she didn't see him much during the day as he spent most of his time working or with Nicholas with whom he now shared a closer bond. As far as Nicholas was concerned, his father walked on water and could do no wrong.

To win back his heart, if that was at all possible, she needed to gain his trust and that would take time. Certainly more time than it took to inflame his senses.

"Katie, I'm—" Charlotte abruptly broke off speaking upon entering the room so effused in sunlight it took a moment for her to recognize Lucas standing beside her sister.

"Lucas!" she exclaimed and rushed to him. Arms wide and laughing, Lucas embraced her, giving her a tight, comforting squeeze before setting her away. How she'd missed the deep, rich sound of his laugh.

"It seems I was concerned for naught. When I didn't receive the letter you promised, I began to worry. As I was to come here on business in July, I thought I'd come and see for myself that you and Nicholas arrived safely." His smile was one of fondness.

"Oh dear, I should have written the week I arrived. I only sent the letter three days ago. I'm sorry to have worried you." Only the dearest of friends would have traveled so far to reassure themselves of her and Nicholas's safety.

Lucas gave a throaty chuckle. "No worries, I shall read it when I return home." He turned to Katie. "Your sister was kind enough to accompany me here. You never mentioned how exceedingly beautiful she was, you merely said she resembled you."

Charlotte let out a highly amused laugh. "You are incorrigible." Contrarily, her sister blushed the hot pink of desert flowers. Katie rarely blushed.

Interesting.

"How long will you be staying in England? Where are you staying?" Charlotte asked, motioning them to sit.

Just then the door to the morning room banged open and one golden-haired bundle of energy charged in.

"Mama, Papa let me ride the big horse by mysef." He came to a halt with an almost comical abruptness. The excitement in his blue eyes reached near fever pitch when he spotted Lucas.

"Unca Lucas." With the ease of a spinning top, he changed direction and ran full tilt into Lucas's arms, which were held outstretched in welcome. Nicholas was soon up high against Lucas's chest, his small arms wrapped tightly around his neck. "Mama didn't tell me you was coming."

It was at that moment that Alex entered the room. Charlotte felt his presence before she actually saw him. More than that, she felt his disapproval and his anger before she saw it in his severe square-jawed countenance, the dimple in his chin doing little to lessen the effect.

Nicholas looked over at his father, too excited to notice anything was amiss. "Papa, Unca Lucas is here."

Alex eyed the man holding his son and disliked him on sight. Never had he felt the physical urge to do a person such bodily harm. Had he been raised in the environs of St. Giles, no doubt he would have. Or ripped his son from his arms.

"So I see," he said coolly.

Charlotte stepped forward and laid a hand on his chest as if attempting to placate him. That she saw the need for that told him much about her relationship with *Uncle Lucas.*

"Alex, this is Lucas Beaumont, a friend from America. He has business in London and has called on us to make sure we arrived safely. Lucas, this is my-my husband, the Marquess of Avondale."

"It appears he is a *good* friend." Alex barely acknowledged the man.

And Mr. Beaumont, who would have to have been brain dead to sense Alex would have more welcomed the plague than his presence in his house, slowly lowered Nicholas to the floor then approached him, hand extended in greeting. More fool he.

"Lord Avondale." He gave a brisk nod and let his hand hover another moment before dropping it to his side when it became obvious it would not be accepted.

Both sisters emitted identical sounds of horror. The joy on his son's face quickly faded. Nicholas knew something wasn't right and could feel the tension in the room. Alex felt a pinch of guilt at that. His son's happiness was paramount but this man....

"Well as you can see, Mr. Beaumont, my wife and son are well." Now he hoped the man would take the hint and go back from whence he came.

"Er, yes, it would appear I have worried for nothing."

"And when will you be returning to America?" Alex asked baldly.

Charlotte eyes widened. *"Alex!"*

No one breathed and no one spoke. Even his talkative son was mute and wide-eyed.

Alex stared hard at Mr. Beaumont. He may have had their company these last five years but they were with him now. Moreover, Alex detested this practice of his son calling the man *uncle* as he was no relation to either Charlotte or himself.

With a delicate clearing of her throat, Charlotte said, "Alex, may I have a private word with you?" But she wasn't issuing a request, it was a steely demand sugar-coated in a soft, feminine voice.

Well that was fine with him. He had some things he needed to say to her, which didn't require an audience. They departed the room together and didn't speak until she'd closed the door of the library.

"Alex, you were unbelievably rude to Lucas," she said sharply. "He is a dear friend who has, at considerable effort and, dare I say, inconvenience, come to ensure mine and your son's safety. At the very least, I expect you to be civil to him."

"If he's such a dear friend, why have you not mentioned him before? Why was he not mentioned once when we've conversed about your life in America? You cannot possibly claim you hadn't ample opportunity to do so. We've been spending at least half the day in each other's company and *every* single night in your bed."

Charlotte opened her mouth as if to protest but after a moment snapped her mouth closed.

Her silence only served to fuel his anger, his sense of betrayal. "Was it because he was your lover in America?" Even had they still been estranged, their relationship not as warm as it currently was—or *had been*—no man would countenance his wife's lover calling on her at his own home. He would not tolerate such staggering degrees of audacity.

"Lucas is my *friend*. He has *never* been nor will ever be my lover."

And she addressed him as Lucas, *not* Mr. Beaumont. Another emotion he refused to identify seethed green and hot. Did she truly expect him to believe her? Despite the man being an American, Alex knew he was just the type of man ladies swooned over. He had a cocky air about him that some may mistake as charm and women fell like stones over his kind of looks. And as for Charlotte, there wasn't a chance the man hadn't found her desirable, hadn't tried to lure her into his bed. Not a chance in this world. He'd wager his entire fortune on that.

"Then let me phrase it differently. Is he interested in you or has he ever been?"

Her mouth opened and closed several times but no sound emerged. After more time elapsed with her stumbling about trying to find just the right thing to say, she said, "It is not like that a'tall."

"Then please do enlighten me," he invited on a mocking drawl.

"He may have been interested when we first met, but very soon after he realized we were meant to be friends and nothing more."

"And he came to this realization on his own?" he asked, folding his arms across his chest and widening his stance.

She averted her gaze and swallowed. "Perhaps my response may have had something to do with it."

"Not surprising," he murmured. He couldn't deny the feeling of relief that washed over him. He believed her when she said she'd never slept with the man. Not that it should matter to him, what she did and with whom when they were apart. But he wouldn't deny that it did. It mattered to him greatly no matter how irrational it may sound.

She returned her regard to him. "But that was almost five years ago. Now he sees me as a friend."

"So that's all it was, he expressed an interest and you turned him down. Nothing else?" he asked, continuing to probe.

Some emotion flickered in her eyes and she didn't respond immediately. She was hiding something.

She drew in a breath and confessed, "He did propose marriage once. But—"

"I want him out of my house." Alex spoke between clenched teeth as he tempered the impulse to bodily remove the man himself.

"But he only did that because he was concerned for my welfare. As far as he could see, I was a widow raising a baby on my own. He only asked to offer me his protection."

"And if you believe that, you are more naïve than most." No single gentleman could ever look at her and regard her merely as a friend. Her Mr. Beaumont hadn't given the appearance of a eunuch or a man who preferred the company of other men.

She frowned and looked properly affronted. "I'm not the least bit naïve."

"Really?" he asked archly. "So if I am to understand correctly, your *dear friend* Mr. Beaumont has expended considerable effort and inconvenience in tracking you from America to England to settle his mind that you arrived safely. This would be the same Mr. Beaumont who once expressed an interest in you, which you ever so gently declined. He then subsequently asked for your hand in marriage but only as a friendly offer of protection?" He paused to allow the absurdity of his words to penetrate. "And this is the same man you expect me to welcome into my home?"

The way he'd just enumerated the salient facts of her relationship with Lucas did make it appear somewhat suspect—at least on Lucas's part. But one had to know and understand Lucas to know as implausible as Alex made it sound, everything she'd told him was the truth. There hadn't been anything remotely romantic about Lucas's no-nonsense proposal. He'd been a friend with the belief he was coming to her aid.

Perhaps she shouldn't have been quite so honest with Alex. But if she wanted to earn his trust, she needed to tell him everything. Look how he'd reacted because she failed to divulge it earlier. God forbid should it have come out in the future.

"Alex, do be reasonable. Lucas is a friend and Nicholas is quite attached to him."

His body went stiff, his gaze narrowed and his gray eyes turned the color of night.

"If that man is not out of my house in the next ten minutes, I will be happy to perform the task myself, and believe me, it won't be pleasant."

Charlotte wanted to protest but thought better of it. Things between them had only recently thawed, although they had a way to go to reach the ideal temperature conducive to a truly happy and loving marriage.

But as much as she wanted things to work out, she *did* have her limits.

"I shall do as you wish. But understand this, Lucas is my friend and I shan't allow you to dictate with whom I can and cannot associate." With that, she turned sharply and marched briskly from the room, making sure to close the door behind her while exercising a bit more force than necessary.

Chapter Seventeen

Charlotte returned to the morning room where her sister and Lucas were preparing to leave. She didn't try to stop them but apologized for Alex's behavior. Lucas dismissed her apology with his typical insouciant smile but did say they would speak later. Nicholas, of course, didn't want him to go but Lucas promised him he'd see him again soon.

That night, Alex didn't come to her bed, which she'd half expected. However, it did anger her. Not that he denied her the pleasures of his body—although she would admit that had something to do with her anger—but that his actions effectively halted their growing intimacy. As much as she missed his lovemaking, she sorely missed the aftermath when they shared their thoughts, spoke of how they'd passed their respective days and laughed over tales of their son

But a part of her believed he'd not have reacted so violently to Lucas's presence if he hadn't cared about her more than he was willing to admit even to himself. They'd been apart five years and surely he couldn't rightly begrudge her a lover had she actually chosen to take one. It was not the sort of dog-in-the-manger behavior she'd have expected from a man who, if not for their son, would have severed her from his life completely.

She could only hope it wouldn't be too long before they put this incident behind them and continued forward in their life together—as man and wife in the truest sense of the term.

The day following, Miss Foster arrived at the house for the appointment when Charlotte would select a dress to wear to the ball—which was only three weeks away—on a day when

Nicholas was at home and feeling fractious.

The modiste and her assistant, Sally, were loaded down with swaths of fabrics and a book of fashion plates and some sketches Miss Foster had designed herself. Charlotte took them to the parlor, a quaint feminine room across from the library.

Before they could begin the task of selecting a dress, Nicholas dashed into the room breathless, his cheeks flushed, his locks tousled and his play clothes disheveled. Jillian followed seconds later, equally breathless and looking rather frazzled.

"Sorry, Miz Charlotte, but he got away from me. You know how he gits whenev'r visitors come a callin'."

"That's quite all right, Jillian." Charlotte caught her son by the hand. "Darling, Mama is busy. Now mind your manners and go with Jillian."

But her son wasn't about to pass up an opportunity to make himself known to every female he happened upon. "Who is that?" he said instead, directing his attention to Miss Foster.

Miss Foster sat frozen on the sofa, her gaze riveted on Nicholas. Frankly, she was staring at him as if she'd never seen a child before. Perhaps she didn't like children. However, her expression didn't convey any sort of aversion or dislike, more a wonder and yes, maybe even a twinge of sadness. Oh, dear Lord, perhaps she'd lost a child.

"This is your son?" she asked in such a way it gave Charlotte pause. There was something else in the woman's tone she couldn't place.

"Yes, he is mine. Nicholas, this is Miss Foster who has come to make Mama a beautiful dress. Now be a good boy and mind Jillian until I'm finished here."

Not unlike him, Nicholas did not budge from his place pressed against her side. "Hullo," he said, looking both at Miss Foster and her diminutive assistant.

"He's a handsome boy." Miss Foster hadn't removed her gaze from him since his unexpected entry.

The woman looked positively spellbound. Yes, her son was

a very handsome boy and charmed most people to pieces when they met him. But never had she encountered this sort of reaction from a stranger.

"Thank you," Charlotte replied politely, really at a loss to say anything else. "Now darling, go with Jillian." She spoke firmly, and with a gentle hand, urged him toward her maid, who quickly grasped him by the hand and led him from the room.

After they'd left and closed the door, Charlotte turned a curious gaze to Miss Foster, who now appeared a tad uncomfortable, as if she'd let some hitherto secret part of her slip. "I don't have any children. It is at times like this when I see a boy like yours that I wish I did."

Oh the poor woman. She was obviously alone in the world. At her age, which Charlotte guessed to be late in the thirties, the woman could very well have grandchildren of her own. It must be difficult to know she'd never have any.

"I'm sorry."

With a shake of her head, Miss Foster was the ever efficient *modiste* again. "Please forgive me, milady. No one need have to listen to the regrets of an aging dressmaker. Shall we begin?" She continued before Charlotte could respond. "I made several sketches of gowns sure to flatter your figure and selected some fabrics I think will look wonderful with your coloring."

Eager to proceed, Charlotte began poring over the sketches and samples, well on her way to selecting a gown to rival the best Worth had to offer.

Alex read the letter a second time before calling for Alfred, who promptly appeared in the library.

"Yes, milord."

"Please send Conrad," he said briskly, glancing down to look at the date of the letter for the third time.

"Yes, milord." With that he was gone.

Alex let out a curse. The solicitor's office had written to tell him that Mr. Reynolds had resigned his position the day before. The letter was dated three weeks prior, so why had it only now just made its way onto his desk? Conrad had better have a good explanation for that.

Also contained in the letter was the fact the changes he'd made to his will hadn't been properly drawn up—their humblest apologies accompanied that infuriating sentence. They'd require his signature *again*. If he could wait a fortnight, they'd send one of the other solicitors out with the new papers.

But Alex would have none of that. The matter should have been settled five weeks ago. He'd simply have to go to their office in London. If he left in the next few hours, he'd be able to go to their office when they opened in the morning and he'd be back home before noon.

"Milord, I'm unable to locate Mr. Conrad," Alfred intoned.

Alex sat up straight in his chair. "Not here? Where is he? I don't remember today being his day off."

"I knocked on his door but he did not answer."

"Did you go in?"

Alfred came as close to a gasp as he'd ever heard. "Milord, I do not possess a key for his office or his personal quarters."

Yes indeed, dare he forget. Conrad, as the house steward, had a set of the master keys and Alex had the other, which he kept somewhere in the master suite. But he didn't have time for that as it appeared he'd be taking a trip to London to get this whole mess with his will sorted out.

"Well when he arrives, if I'm still in residence, send him to me at once." Where the hell was he? He'd better not be lifting the skirts of one of the housemaids. Conrad knew they were off-limits. He was young and the women considered him handsome, so there was no reason he wouldn't be able to find his enjoyment elsewhere. During his work hours, he should be here and readily available when the lord of the house called.

Alfred gave a stiff nod and took his leave.

He'd have to inform Charlotte he was leaving. Not that it

would change her routine. It had been two weeks since Lucas Beaumont had arrived and since he'd last visited her bed. Sexual frustration was now his constant companion. And he had only himself to blame for that.

But by the time he'd gotten over his anger and jealousy—which he'd finally admitted to—they'd gone two nights alone in their respective beds. He'd stubbornly hoped she'd come to him, just once. He'd always gone to her and although she'd been eager—wild for it—he wondered if she'd ever come if he did not. He received his answer. She would not.

Now she barely spoke to him and had started coming down to breakfast long after he'd gone. Dinner was the only time he saw her, where she sat coolly polite, eating her supper and making no attempt at conversation. She didn't look as if she missed him. Certainly not as he missed her. Another thing he'd finally admitted to himself as he'd lain on his bed these past several nights staring up at the ceiling. And with each passing day, it grew harder and harder to remember the time when *she* wanted them to be truly man and wife.

All he knew was this impasse could not go on any longer. He was tired, grumpy and frustrated.

Bloody hell, he wanted his wife.

And as if he could conjure her up with his thoughts, she entered, saw him and said, "Oh, I didn't know the library was occupied." She moved to depart as if, apart from supper, they couldn't remain in the same room at the same time.

"Charlotte," he said, calling her back.

She turned to him and the sight of her started an ache he knew would take hours to subside. She wore her hair down, the curls falling about her face and trailing midway down her back. Her dress skimmed her hips and thighs, as it was obvious she wasn't wearing one of those crinolines or whatever they called them now. Her figure looked fuller all around, which would make her about the same size she'd been five years ago.

"I must leave for London today to take care of a business matter. I should return by noon tomorrow."

"Oh," she said, looking disappointed.

The most emotion he'd seen her express in little over a week. Progress.

"Have you forgotten Thomas, Amelia, Elizabeth and Derek are arriving today? The ball is next Saturday."

Damn, he hadn't intended to miss their arrival. It seemed a dog's year since he'd seen his friends for any great length of time. Calling to coerce them into helping him perpetrate a fraudulent marriage did not count. Hell, these days he barely spoke to Rutherford. And he'd freely admit the blame was his. When he returned tomorrow, that would all change.

"I shall call on them as soon as I return. Do send my apologies but this matter will not wait." He rose, circled the desk and strode to where she stood next to the door, her hand on the handle as if waiting to bolt.

She swallowed as he grew closer. "Was there anything else?" she asked, her voice even, her smile strained and her knuckles white.

She was affected. *Thank God for that.*

"I should like us to speak when I return." He watched her mouth as he spoke. So pink and soft, and exquisitely talented.

She caught her bottom lip between her teeth. And in her eyes, he saw what he had felt all those nights he'd spent alone in his bed. Wishing for her. Dreaming of her.

Her gaze flew to his eyes. "I should like that also," she said softly.

If he kissed her now, he wouldn't stop and the sooner he went to London, the sooner he'd be back home.

"Tell Nicholas I said goodbye. I will take him fishing when I return," he said, his voice gruff.

Charlotte nodded.

He stroked the flesh just above her elbow—it was the only place he'd allow himself to touch—and took his leave of the library.

When he reached the stairs and glanced back, she stood in the same place watching him, a mysterious smile on her face.

That look remained in his mind all the way to London.

When Charlotte arrived at her brother's house two hours later, after Alex had departed, she found the women in the morning room gathered around the fireplace in animated discussion.

All gazes swung to her when she entered and all conversation halted. Elizabeth sprang to her feet and rushed immediately toward her amid a chorus of cheerful greetings.

"Charlotte, you're positively glowing," Elizabeth said, hugging her tightly and pressing an affectionate kiss to her cheek. She smelled of gardenias with a hint of talcum powder.

Charlotte's smile widened. "And I must say motherhood suits you as I knew it would."

A more contented smile could not have lit her friend's face. "Today I was introduced to that young man of yours. Absolutely delightful. He and my Annabelle are getting on like a house on fire. But Johnny cries because he can't keep up with his older sister."

When he'd learned more children would be arriving the following day, Nicholas hadn't wanted to come home so he'd stayed the night at her brother's.

"Elizabeth, you mustn't keep Charlotte all to yourself. Ladies, do come sit down," Amelia called out from the sofa.

"Where are the men?" Charlotte asked, equally anxious to see them as well.

"Oh you know men, if they are not playing games or wagering money, they're not satisfied with their lot in life," Missy said with the cheek and confidence of a woman who knew her husband loved her to distraction.

Amelia, who hadn't changed a dot since Charlotte last saw her, sprang to her feet and embraced her. Raven-haired with eyes the color of sapphires, Viscountess Armstrong was beautiful. They'd become acquainted two years before Charlotte left when Thomas had brought her to Rutherford

Manor for Christmas. She'd quickly grown to love Amelia just as everyone else had—including her husband.

"Welcome home," Amelia said softly in her ear before releasing her.

Tears pricked the back of Charlotte's eyes. "Oh Amelia."

"Don't you dare cry," Amelia warned on a teasing note. "I cried quite enough when I was pregnant with Daniel. My poor daughter thought I was dying—or someone was dying. I had to hide in my chambers and lock the door so as not to distress her when the waterworks started."

Everyone laughed as Amelia resumed her seat and Charlotte sat beside Elizabeth on the sofa.

"Lottie, you needn't worry, I won't cry this time," Katie said from the balloon chair opposite.

The morning door opened and in forged—many would say—three of the most handsome men in all of London. Had Alex been present, he'd have rounded out the quartet quite nicely.

Thomas was the first to see her.

"Charlotte." It was a greeting and a hallelujah all rolled into that one word. His voice prompted Charlotte to her feet as she maneuvered the ottoman and the tea cart to rush into his arms much the same way her son had done to Lucas.

Laughing and smiling, Thomas caught her in his arms, pulling her into the strength and warmth of his embrace.

"Thomas. Oh, Thomas." Never had a face looked so golden and handsome. And welcome.

"How is it possible that you look exactly the same?" Thomas asked, his dimpled, lean-cheeked face beaming down at her.

"And how is it possible you grow more handsome every time I see you?" she asked, feeling perilously close to shedding still more tears. Goodness, since she'd returned to England, she'd turned into a watering pot; tears spouting at every turn.

"I suggest you check your vision because the man is as gruesome as they come," came Derek's wry rejoinder from behind them.

This brought a round of guffaws, chortles and raucous laughter from his friends.

"Don't listen to him," Thomas said sotto voce. "He's just jealous that of all your brother's friends, I am your favorite."

"I daresay, Cartwright would claim otherwise," Derek shot back smartly. Quirking his brow, he asked, "Do I not deserve a greeting even if you won't throw yourself at me and tell me I'm the most handsome man on earth?"

Giggling, Charlotte moved from Thomas's arms into Derek's. The same height as her husband, Derek encased her in his arms like a warm vise. After a prolonged embrace, he slowly released her.

"You look good," he said, suddenly serious. "We missed you. My wife missed you intolerably. We're glad you're back."

Charlotte's throat closed up. Her five-year absence came back in a wave of regret.

"Darling, I forbid you from reducing poor Charlotte to tears," Elizabeth lightly admonished her husband.

Charlotte quickly regained her composure. While the men took up seats in the unoccupied chairs, Charlotte went back to hers.

The conversation flowed easily, touching mostly on the growing broods they now all had. Elizabeth delicately asked about her time in America. *What is it like? Do all Americans really detest the English? Is it true they hide bars of gold under their mattresses?*

No one asked her the one question everyone wanted the answer to, all tiptoeing about the events that had sent her to the shores of America. No one that is until Elizabeth could tiptoe no further, making a cacophony of noise with her question.

"Won't you tell us why you left?" she asked quietly, refusing to release Charlotte from her gaze.

There had already been a lull in the conversation, yet silence still managed to descend upon the room with the force of an avalanche.

Necks swiveled, some not in her direct vision, craned. The cessation of breaths was a foregone conclusion.

Charlotte looked around the room and felt enveloped in their love, their utter acceptance. These were her friends, her family. They had never once judged her or Katie. They'd just opened their arms and hearts to two orphaned girls whose lineage mattered naught to them. And it was in that moment of complete clarity, like the sun casting its rays upon a place that had hitherto only known the dark, that she knew she could trust them with her most intimate of secrets. Whatever she said to them would never go beyond these walls.

She regarded her sister, silently seeking permission, for part of her revelation wasn't her secret alone and would affect her sister equally. Mute, Katie stared back at her, her expression anxious in her paled countenance. She gave a barely perceptible nod.

"I have told Alex why I left and now I believe you all deserve to know the truth," Charlotte announced.

More silence. She had their ever more focused attention.

Then the story poured from her and she felt none of the anxiety or fear of judgment and shame she would have a month ago. Once she finished speaking, she scanned their faces to take in their reactions.

Katie, Missy and Amelia had tears in their eyes. Elizabeth was openly weeping. Derek moved swiftly from his chair to comfort his wife.

Derek and Thomas were as somber as she'd ever seen them. But it was James, dear, dear James, who looked poleaxed. He swallowed, his pale blue eyes teeming with countless emotions.

"Charlotte." He uttered her name in a hoarse voice as if speaking no longer came easy. Slowly, he approached her. Once he stood in front of her, he dropped to one knee.

Tears stung the back of Charlotte's eyes as she stared into her brother's. She'd never seen him like this, so torn, so overcome. He swallowed and blinked rapidly. Slowly, he shook his head to and fro. Not speaking a word, he pulled her into his arms. Charlotte lost her composure then, sobbing against his shoulder.

He could have held her for seconds or minutes, time held no relevancy. Finally, when her tears ceased to fall and Charlotte lifted her eyes and looked around, there wasn't a dry eye in the room.

Thomas and Derek cleared their throats and set about straightening coats that required no attention and the women availed themselves to their handkerchiefs, dabbing tears from their eyes.

James came to his feet, his brows furrowed in concern. "But who would write such a letter. Who could have possibly known?"

"I believe it was the dowager—your mother," Charlotte whispered, as if that could reduce the impact.

"My mother?"

"His mother?"

Missy and James spoke in unison.

"She is the one person who despised me and Katie more than anyone I know. Who else could it have been?" Charlotte glanced at her sister, who stared back at her neither affirming nor contesting her assertion.

James gave a short laugh, but not one of amusement. "No, you don't understand. If my mother had had this kind of information in her grasp, there would have been no threatening letters, no warning at all. She would have used it to destroy you. And the way she was after my father died, she wouldn't have given a whit if she'd hurt me and Christopher in the process."

No. No. No.

Oh God, this was the last thing she wanted to hear. A niggling voice inside her head had told her very much the same thing, starting on her journey to America. The same whispers had started when she knew she had to come back. It was in learning of the dowager's death that she'd let other voices reassure her otherwise. Assure her that she was safe, that the threat was in the past.

"Are you certain?" Still hope prevailed in her whispered voice.

James looked grim but certain. "I know my mother and I know what she was capable of. And even if she had written such a letter, she would have tried to force you and Catherine from my life, not merely prevent you from wedding Cartwright."

Missy's grave expression said she agreed.

If what James said was true, that meant her nightmare wasn't over.

Who had written the letter and what had been the real intent behind it? If Alex had had other women, she might have thought it was one of them. But she hadn't heard a hint of anyone back then and now.

"That means whoever wrote the letter may still be out there," Charlotte said, regarding her sister. Now, Catherine looked as panicked as she herself felt. The feeling of security she'd had upon hearing of the dowager's death vanished like a wispy breath of air.

"But who would do such a thing?" Elizabeth asked, distressed.

"I think the real question is what is their motive?" Thomas interjected. "If their goal was to ruin you, why haven't they done so up to now? I mean, it has been five years."

"Perhaps they succeeded in their intended goal, which was to stop her from wedding Alex," Amelia replied.

The room fell silent as everyone seemed to consider this. Immediately Charlotte's thoughts went to the duke and duchess. Was that something either would do? They certainly hadn't hidden their feelings about the match. And they did have the money and influence to dig up that kind of information.

But Mrs. Henley had said she'd been the only person who knew of their relationship to the fifth Earl of Windmere. Their mother had been dismissed from the house when she was in her fifth month, just as she began to show.

Desperate and destitute, their mother had prevailed upon their father, who had put her up in a home in the country. Upon her death, he'd hired a nursemaid and a nanny, who had cared for them until he sent them off to boarding school.

Even the nursemaid and the nanny didn't know their mother's identity. Which left no one.

"Katie, do you think Mrs. Henley ever breathed a word of it to anyone?" Once assured of the woman's loyalty, Charlotte now wondered.

Her sister stared at her blankly, dazed for a moment before shaking her head emphatically. "No, she would not. Mrs. Henley was an honorable woman and fiercely loyal to our mother. If she said she shared this information with no one, then I believe it with all my heart."

"I shall get to the bottom of this." James looked quite determined.

"What are you going to do?" Charlotte hoped he wasn't about to stir the hornet's nest. Maybe the author was long gone and the threat of exposure gone as well.

"I'm going to find out who sent the letter," James replied.

Chapter Eighteen

Alex was weary of London and desperately wanted to return home. He'd expected the matter with his will to require his presence there for a day, two when he'd realized he hadn't made any provisions in his will for Charlotte.

But the solicitor's office hadn't received verification of his marriage papers from the general register's office, therefore his new will could not be drawn up. He didn't know what was taking the whole bloody thing so long. His cousin was to have sent the papers to London after Alex had them sent to him express. That had been four weeks ago.

It was on the third day that he'd been able to secure a meeting with Mr. Shelton at the register's office, and in whose small, cluttered office he currently sat.

"I'm trying to ascertain why the verification of my marriage isn't forthcoming to my solicitor's office. They requested it weeks ago."

Mr. Shelton pushed back into a chair that seemed too small for his rotund form. He inhaled a deep breath, straining the buttons of his black-and-blue striped waistcoat. "Lord Avondale, I too am trying to determine the problem."

"Do you or do you not have the papers?" Alex spoke in a level voice, trying his damnedest to not let his worry show. Rightfully, his response would be irritation if everything was above board.

"That is the thing, my lord, we do have them here. The problem is as far as I can ascertain, they've only been recently filed. When they were requested, my clerk searched the records filed in 1859. It was only today we discovered them filed only one month ago. We are in the process of contacting the parsonage where you married to discover if there was a delay in forwarding your papers. And if so why."

Alex breathed a little easier. Things weren't shaping up as badly as they could. When they contacted his cousin, Alan would merely state that given the confusion with the London ceremony, the marriage papers hadn't been forwarded. Hopefully, that would satisfy Mr. Shelton and his boss, Mr. Graham, who was currently the general register's head.

"Precisely how long will I have to wait for that to be accomplished?" Alex asked in a voice that suggested he was exercising enormous patience. "I should like to have the matter with my solicitors settled before I depart for home tomorrow."

Mr. Shelton angled his head and his meaty fingers stroked his fleshy cheek. "As your circumstances are pressing, my lord, I shall have my clerk draw up a letter that should satisfy your solicitor. In the meanwhile, I'll discuss the matter with Mr. Graham. I don't expect there will be a problem but one never knows."

Alex stood, placing his hat on his head as he grasped the wooden handle of his umbrella. For the last two days, so much rain had poured from the skies that he was sure the paired boarding of Noah's Ark was imminent. That afternoon, the rain seemed particularly relentless.

Hurriedly, Mr. Shelton clambered to his feet and with that the smallness of the office became more evident.

"What is of utmost importance to me is that my wife and child are properly provided for. I appreciate your help in this matter."

Alex stuck out his hand, which Mr. Shelton swiftly grasped, shaking it with deferential enthusiasm.

"The pleasure is mine, my lord."

Alex sincerely hoped that it would be. Things may have been settled for now, but he wasn't entirely in the clear.

For the next four days, Charlotte received daily notes by messenger from Alex. He remained in London, disgruntled by the tone of his messages, trying to settle business which involved a matter concerning his solicitor. He didn't say what, but he did say more problems had arisen.

Nicholas missed him dearly but he couldn't miss him half as much as she herself did. She'd been on pins and needles waiting for him to come home so they could *talk*. He did promise to be back in time for the ball, which was the following evening.

Charlotte had heard his parents were in town. Apparently they had a cottage—as River Court with its seven bedchambers was fondly called—in the vicinity. They hadn't called on them, which was just as well with Alex gone. In any case, she would see them at the ball.

Charlotte spent most of her days at her brother's house catching up with Elizabeth and Amelia along with Missy and Katie. She'd met their respective children that first night. She was now Aunt Lottie to the lot of them. The place sounded like a school yard most of the time, even when the children played outside. Their voices carried on a good wind and it had been windy the last few days.

James had hired an investigator to look into the matter of the letter. He'd assured her the man was discreet and he'd only asked him to look for a person who might have enough of a grudge against her and Katie to harm them.

Her sister didn't believe they'd ever discover who sent the letter. She thought James was wasting his money and told him exactly that. He ignored her, telling her it was his money to waste if he wished.

The day of the ball, Charlotte received another message from Alex assuring her he'd be arriving late afternoon—just in time to get ready. Which meant they wouldn't have time for their talk. But at least he was finally coming home.

As it was, it wasn't until just before seven that evening that her husband made an appearance. The housemaid informed her of his arrival while her sister's French maid, Esther—whose services Katie had so magnanimously offered as it appeared the girl must have dressed hair in another life (perhaps that of Marie Antoinette)—created miracles with her curly locks.

Her heart had gone from skipping a beat in anticipation every few minutes or so to thrashing about in her chest as if trapped and its only hope of survival was to escape. She willed herself to breathe in a normal manner but her body demanded autonomy from the more judicious aspects of her and so her breathing trotted gleefully along with her misbehaving heart. Charlotte could barely sit still such was the calamity going on inside her after the housemaid's announcement and subsequent exit.

Once her sister's maid skillfully coaxed the final hair into place, Charlotte admired the labor of almost an hour of work in the vanity mirror. With half the length of her hair pinned up at her nape in something that resembled an elegant chignon, the maid had managed to keep her natural curls in place. The resulting effect was breath stealing and Charlotte could not have been more pleased.

Profuse praise for her work was followed by equally profuse *merci mademoiselle* and *de rien*s. The girl departed shortly thereafter and with a happy sigh, Charlotte examined herself in the mirror one final time. She had gained back the weight she'd lost so her face no longer had that strained look. Her complexion was clear and her hair, glorious.

As for her gown; well Miss Foster had truly outdone herself. Her creation was sheer magic. It was certainly one of a kind, made of a pale green silk, the torso fitted and embellished with small, perfectly concentric pearls. The skirt was three tiered with a white chiffon overskirt. With the still-cool temperatures, they'd decided on pagoda sleeves capped at the shoulders and wrist-length silk gloves the exact color of her dress.

It had been years since she'd worn something like this— since she'd had cause to. She felt like a princess. Now it was time to go and meet her prince.

Charlotte was halfway down the stairs when Alex appeared in the foyer. Her next step faltered, forcing her to grip the railing more tightly. She hadn't prepared herself for the sight of Alex in black tails and tie formal wear.

Heat collected in her core where she felt the deprivation of the last two weeks and then some. The white of his shirt made his skin look all the darker by comparison.

He watched her intently as she descended the stairs toward him but his expression was closed. She couldn't tell if he approved of her appearance or not. Couldn't tell whether he was glad to see her.

Charlotte reached the bottom. "You look quite dashing." The lightness of her tone belied the mad pounding of her heart.

For a moment, she didn't think he'd return the compliment, although something flickered in his eyes. His gaze swept her, pausing here and lingering there before returning to her face. That is when she saw the heat smoldering in his eyes. Lust in human form.

"You look beautiful," he said, his voice slightly graveled.

"Thank you." Now she spoke as if short of breath.

"Come, the carriage is waiting," he said when it appeared they'd be content to stand forever practically eating each other up with their eyes.

In the clarence, they sat across from one another, he now sporting a black great coat and she having donned her new cashmere mantle.

"Were you able to get the matter resolved to your satisfaction?" Because of course they should speak and not just continue to openly covet the other. They were civilized.

His nod came in the shadow of a movement. "Indeed. It wasn't until after I arrived at the solicitor's office that I realized we have no marriage contract and I hadn't made provisions for you in my will. The initial changes only dealt with Nicholas. I've now taken care of that. You'll be happy to know, you shall be amply provided for upon my death."

For a moment, Charlotte hung suspended in a state between joy and horror. Horror won quite handily.

"Please, do not say such things. Not even as a joke." Her

thoughts immediately went to his unintentional dunking in the Thames and the fever that had come close to finishing what the river had not.

They could barely see one another for the sun had long sunk below the horizon and the moon had turned its dark side to Reading. But her sight adjusted enough to the dark to make out the varied gray outline of his form.

After a pause, he leaned forward and said in a low voice, "Do not worry, I don't intend to expire for a great while. My son is not fully grown and I expect to see him married with children of his own."

Charlotte knew she should have contented herself with that. Her heart should not twist like a pair of wringing hands because he neglected to mention her or future children. But then, he'd not long ago told her he wanted no more children with her and that his love for her was so obliterated, he could not will it back if he wished to.

Before she allowed it to spoil her evening, she forcibly thrust those thoughts aside. "Honestly, I hadn't given it a thought. Thank you for thinking of us."

A flash of white in the dark indicated he had smiled.

"I'd like to speak with you when we return." The timbre of his voice dropped to encompass ranges from enticing to seduction.

Charlotte instantly grew warm as her anticipation for the ball waned. Now all she wanted was to instruct the driver to turn back and take them home. Of course, Missy would never forgive her and neither would the guests, many who'd traveled a great distance to get a firsthand look at the couple whose wedding all had thought never to have occurred.

"Mightn't it be too late for that?" The coquette in her decided to make an appearance.

The sound of his chuckle, low and infinitely amused, filled the carriage. "Not the kind of discussion I hope to have."

Perhaps, it would be wise if they left the ball early was Charlotte's last thought before she realized they had stopped in front of her brother's estate.

They'd been instructed to arrive early and stand with James and Missy to greet the guests so it was no great surprise the circular drive was empty. Butterflies now collected in her stomach when she thought of the evening to come and its significance. Not that she cared so much for herself. No, her concern was for her family.

The door to the carriage opened and she sucked in a breath. Alex reached over and took her hand. "It doesn't matter what they say or think or do. You are not dependent on their patronage."

It was the closest he'd ever come since she told him the truth, to saying he understood, that he would stand by her no matter what. She couldn't afford to cry and found it impossible to speak. Instead she gave a tiny nod and curled her fingers around his gloved hand with the knowledge that no matter what happened tonight, things would be fine.

Halfway through the evening, Rutherford asked to have a word with Alex in private. Except for a brief conversation where his friend had approved the marriage solution, they hadn't spoken since Rutherford had stormed into his study months ago.

They adjourned to the library, where a fire blazed in the fireplace. His friend lit two gas lamps, bathing the room in white incandescent light.

"Charlotte looks happy," Rutherford said as he settled himself against the edge of the desk and crossed his feet at his ankles.

Alex smiled, inclining his head in acknowledgment of that fact. He was happy. Although he'd be much happier later on tonight in her bed with her naked under him—or on top—he wasn't the least bit particular on that score.

"She finally told us why she left," his friend continued. A frown settled on his brow.

Alex widened his stance and thrust his bare hands in to his

trouser pockets. "Ah, so she told you. Have we reason for concern? Charlotte is of the impression the culprit was your mother."

Rutherford was shaking his head even before he'd finished speaking. "It was not my mother," he said emphatically.

His friend's response did not come as a surprise. Alex had had his doubts about the dowager's involvement when Charlotte had informed him.

"Then who wrote the letter?"

Rutherford shrugged. "I don't know but I shall do my best to find out. I've hired a private investigator to look into the matter."

"But who would threaten them and then say nothing for five years? Surely this isn't something we need worry ourselves over any longer?" For Charlotte and Catherine's sake, he sorely hoped not.

Rutherford cast his gaze around the room as if deep in thought. He then directed his attention back to Alex. "It recently occurred to me that my sisters may not be the true targets of the threat."

"What do you mean?" Alex asked, removing his hands from his pockets.

"I mean what if it is your life they set out to destroy? Losing my sister devastated you. Everyone is well aware of that. It's only in the last year that you've managed to piece your life back together. And just when you started giving serious thought to marrying, Charlotte appears with your son. I don't believe it was merely a coincidence. We all would have been knee-deep in scandal if not for those marriage papers."

"Are you saying someone did this to make my life miserable?" The notion was absurd.

"I'm saying perhaps someone did this to ensure you did not marry. Haven't you a cousin or uncle who set to inherit should you not produce an heir? I'm saying, what if I've sent the investigator in the wrong direction. At present, he's looking for someone who has a grudge against my sisters when perhaps he should be looking for someone associated with you."

Frankly, the thought hadn't occurred to him. "My father's nephew, Henry Wentworth would have been my heir if not for Nicholas."

Although he and his cousin had never been close, Alex wouldn't have thought him capable of such deviousness—not that he could say he knew Henry all that well.

However, Rutherford's speculations did have merit. It was certainly worth looking into.

His friend gave a brief nod and said, "I'll give his name to the investigator. Have you given any thought to what you will do if the worst happens?"

"I will not have my wife and child treated as pariahs," Alex replied in a hard voice. "We'd move if we had to. Since America is familiar to them, perhaps we'd go there. Catherine could come too." Charlotte would insist on it.

Rutherford gave him a wry smile. "Let us hope it doesn't come to that."

Indeed, Charlotte's euphoria lasted two hours into the ball. The grand room had been transformed into something magical. Candles lit the place like a Christmas tree and the refreshment room held a steady stream of hungry and thirsty guests.

Which wasn't to say she had been received wholeheartedly by all of their guests. A few of the women had offered her stilted, sometimes even cold greetings, but thankfully she hadn't *actually* been cut. However, the evening remained young as it had yet to reach midnight.

She and Alex had danced the first dance, a quadrille, and were scheduled to perform the final waltz. Anticipation swirled within her at the prospect of being held in his arms, breathing in his singularly masculine scent.

The duke and duchess blessed everyone with their presence, arriving in grand style at the fashionably late hour of ten o'clock, causing a cyclone stir when they entered the ballroom looking every inch the highest-ranking peer in a realm of lofty nobles. Their manner toward her could be equated to a sunny day in the Arctic. They may have accepted their grandson but that didn't encompass her. Pleasantries—as Charlotte chose to call them—were blessedly short; truly the ideal duration when dealing with disapproving mother- and father-in-laws.

Suddenly alone for the first time that evening, Charlotte glanced around the domed room. Elizabeth had recently dashed upstairs to attend her fretful child. Missy was playing host and Amelia and Katie were on the dance floor enjoying an energetic polka. And James and Alex, having returned from wherever they had disappeared to a short while ago, appeared to be carrying on a friendly conversation with Derek and Thomas near the terrace doors. Charlotte couldn't remember the last time she'd seen her husband looking so at ease, his smile radiating a certain *joie de vivre*.

Just about to join Missy, who stood alone at the circumference of the dance floor, Charlotte saw him framed in the entrance. Had she held a glass in her hand, it would have shattered on the polished floors.

Staring at her, his eyes lit with pleasure, was Lucas Beaumont. Instinctively, Charlotte turned toward where she'd last seen her husband and found him boring holes into Lucas with his gaze.

Charlotte wasted no time rushing over to Lucas, arriving at his side at the same moment Katie did.

"Lucas, what are you doing here?" she asked, aware she didn't sound at all pleased to see him.

A lazy smile turned up the corners of his mouth. "Your sister invited me." He looked at Katie, interest blatant in his eyes. "And I hadn't the heart to refuse her."

Charlotte looked sharply at her sister, who was blushing profusely. So that was how it was. It was about time, her sister deserved happiness. She'd have to speak to Lucas in private, maybe tomorrow. She hoped he was serious about her for she would not have her sister's heart broken.

"Apparently you could not," Charlotte replied. "Listen, Alex has already seen you and he's hardly pleased. Katie, do make sure Lucas stays out of his way. The last thing I want is a scene."

A glance behind her revealed her husband shouldering his way through the crush toward them, his expression pleasant if one preferred storm clouds and pelting rain. "Hurry, the next set is starting. The two of you go dance."

Amused, Lucas proffered his elbow, which Katie readily accepted and they proceeded to the dance floor.

Moments later, Charlotte's arm was caught in a firm grip. She didn't have to turn to know it was Alex who held her. She felt his breath on her ear before he demanded in a voice that reminded her of icicles, "What is he doing here?" By this time, he began steering her from the ballroom, his smile frozen in place as he threaded their way through the throng of guests cluttering the entrance. In the hall, he glanced around and then urged her into her brother's study.

What had promised to be a wonderful evening vanished like a coin in a magician's nimble fingers. Alex looked fit to be tied.

"I did not know Lucas would be here. Katie extended the invitation."

He made a sound that sounded suspiciously like a growl. Spinning on his heel, he stalked toward the desk.

"Alex, there is nothing going on between me and Lucas. Truth be told, I believe he's set his sights on Katie and that his interest is returned. Let us just enjoy the evening without acrimony."

Alex spun violently back around. "He is interested in Catherine? Do you not find that at all rather distasteful? She *is* your identical twin."

Charlotte knew precisely what he implied and he couldn't be more wrong. "It isn't like that a'tall. You act as if we are the same person. If that was the case, then I would have to worry about you being attracted to Katie."

"Oh don't be ridiculous," he snapped. "I knew the two of you together. You are individuals to me. He met and was attracted to you first. It's only recently he's discovered there's another just like you."

"Even if he was once attracted to me, that doesn't change that we are only friends now. You are acting as if he is a threat to what you and I have, and you couldn't be more wrong."

"What we have?" he asked, lifting an eyebrow. "And what exactly do we have, dear wife?"

"Alex, don't do this. Don't be ugly," she whispered. "You said you wanted us to talk."

"What I wanted was you in my bed again. But that doesn't mean anything else has changed. You are in my house because of my son and you are in my bed because it's convenient for me. Why should I slake my needs elsewhere when you are more than happy to oblige me *every* night?"

"You'd like me to believe what is between us is just physical need and lust. But you know in your heart it is more." She refused to allow him to reduce it to that.

"Do not purport to know what is in my heart," he replied tersely.

"Then why do you care so much about Lucas? If I'm just a body, does it matter who I had in my bed when I wasn't with you?"

"I care because you are *my* wife. Your fidelity was the least you owed me. I wasn't the one who left you."

"I explained why I did." But as explanations went, she may as well have held her tongue for all the good it did.

"Did you take a lover at all in that time?"

Surprised, Charlotte stared up at him. She found her voice soon after. "No I did not. I had a son, and the rigors of raising a child on my own isn't easy and didn't leave me much time for anything else."

"That was by choice. You needn't have been alone. Your son had a father who'd have happily provided for him if only he knew his son existed."

Charlotte gave a weary sigh. "Nonetheless, I was on my own."

"So you wanted to take a lover?" he asked, refusing to let the subject drop.

How she wanted to tell him yes, she had wanted to take a lover. What she couldn't bear to admit was only he could ever have fit the role. Her body may have ached for the touch of a man but her heart had yearned only for him, and she had been unable to allow her body to go where her heart could not follow.

"No, I had no desire to take a lover," she said, unwilling to lie to him.

"Why?"

He wanted her heart bared. "Because of you that is why. That's what you want to hear, isn't it? I know you had no such compunction. I know you've had dozens upon dozens of women since I left."

The second the words left her mouth, she regretted it. Jealousy had its fangs in her when she had no right to feel it.

"What did you expect me to do, live the rest of my life like a monk, nursing my broken heart over your portrait?" he shot back.

"What has happened to you? The moment you saw Lucas, you changed. And things were getting better between us, you know they were."

Alex straightened to his full height and simply stared at her. He stood silent a good while, his eyes unblinking.

When he began speaking it was as if the anger had drained from him. "At times I believe I can live with what happened and not hold you in judgment over the choices you made. But there are other times when I can't see beyond your abandonment and what you took from me. How you leaving me changed my life, my whole world."

She approached him and gently touched the sleeve of his coat. All she wanted to do was hold him in her arms and kiss him deeply. Soothe the creases from his brow and wipe all traces of unhappiness from his beautiful visage.

"Alex," she whispered, heartsick.

"Perhaps we're rushing this." His tone was as serious as she'd ever heard it. Which said much.

It felt as if she was bleeding inside, but she wouldn't deny him his space if that's what he felt he required. And perhaps he was right. How did one heal five years of hurt within months? His wounds ran deep as would hers if their positions were reversed.

"We shall take it as slow as you'd like," she replied softly.

He took her elbow. "Come, let us return to the ball before the guests begin to comment on our absence. They are all here, after all, to celebrate your return." His mouth lifted at the corner.

As they rejoined the ball, Charlotte prayed that *not rushing this* didn't take on the connotation of stopping altogether.

Chapter Nineteen

When Alex returned from his morning ride the day following, Alfred informed him the marchioness and his son had gone to Rutherford Manor so he found himself alone.

It was funny, he'd lived there alone for almost three years and with his wife and son only the past two months. But when they were both gone, the house felt empty, too big for him alone.

"Milord, the duchess is here. Shall I show her to the drawing room?" Alfred asked after a brief knock on the study door.

His mother here? He'd thought they'd gone back to London. Then he remembered his mother owned a house nearby. But she and the duke rarely made use of it.

"Yes, do. Tell her I'll be with her momentarily."

"No need to inconvenience yourself, I shall be just as comfortable here," his mother said, appearing behind Alfred.

With a sigh, Alex waved his butler away. The duchess stepped into the study and looked around, taking silent inventory of everything.

"This room is so dark. Perhaps you might redecorate it in a lighter wood. All this redwood makes the place feel like I'm in constant mourning."

"Good morning, Mama. I should have thought you'd have slept till noon as late as you remained at the ball."

His mother advanced in, looking imperial and impeccable, her dress the sort that flowed easily when she moved. None of those stiff cages for Her Grace, she was too old for all that unforgiving rigidity, she claimed. But she'd been saying that the past fifteen years.

"I certainly would have done if the need to speak to you in

private hadn't been urgent," she said. It took her a moment to decide on which chair to sit and then she sank onto the sage sofa with the grace and elegance of a swan.

"And just what was so urgent as to disturb your beauty sleep?" Alex was certain it was some trivial matter.

"Well first and foremost, pray do endeavor to keep your feelings for your wife to yourself. The way you watched her at the ball last night...Well, my dear, it was hardly appropriate. Please do your best with that."

Alex sat up straight in his seat. "How did I watch her?"

The duchess' eyebrows rose. "Oh, I suppose you could not have known. Well it was the sort of look a man reserves for his mistress *not* his wife. It is such women gentlemen use to satisfy those sorts of carnal appetites. My darling, it was positively scandalous. I mean, truly, she *is* your wife. And since you are my son, I feared I'd have to hide my face. One might assume you'd picked that sort of thing up at home."

Did his mother think to embarrass him with her observation? Yes, he desired his wife. He wasn't ashamed of that. And he'd wanted her desperately last night, despite what he'd said about taking things slower.

"Oh, do not glower at me. I'm telling you for your own good. If the girl realizes how smitten you are with her again, God help us. Next time who knows what she'll do to break your heart. Thank you very much, but I have no desire to go through that again."

How like his mother to remind him of the past. As if it didn't weigh on his mind constantly as it was. "Is that all you've come to say?"

"No, of course not. That's hardly something I could not have waited to tell you." She harrumphed indignantly and lightly touched her coiffed hair at the side. "Your cousin has been making inquiries about your marriage. He had the temerity to come to our home and accuse us of participating in your deception. He says he intends to have the authorities investigate the legitimacy of your marriage papers."

Bloody hell! Just what he needed. But the more he thought about it, he should have expected something like this from Henry. Perhaps Rutherford *was* correct in his suspicions.

"He can look all he wants, he will find nothing out of order."

"The papers have only just been filed at the general register office in London. I would say their arrival five years late is enough to open an inquiry. If nothing else, it may well be enough to invalidate the marriage altogether. We do not want it to get that far. Therefore you have two choices, either marry the girl again and ensure the whole thing is legal and binding and then get her with child as soon as is feasible. If it's a male, an inquiry would be pointless for Henry would not be remotely in line to inherit."

"And the other choice?" he asked, his eyebrow propped high.

"You can allow the marriage to be declared invalid and marry someone else. Of course in the second case, Nicholas would not inherit. But he may not be able to inherit if your cousin is able to have your marriage proved invalid."

"Nicholas will inherit." He hadn't done all this to cave at the first sign of trouble. His cousin could do his worst but Alex would fight him every step of the way.

"Well then it appears we are to have a wedding." His mother spoke as if the matter wasn't up for further discussion.

"The sooner you get her with child, the better. I shall pray for male issue." She came smoothly to her feet—a clear indication the meeting was adjourned. "Leave everything to me. I shall make the arrangements. Of course, there are things I will have to discuss with your wife. Since holding the wedding at the Cathedral is out of the question, we shall have to settle for St. George's. Would a June wedding suit? Or perhaps July, right at the end of the Season?"

So he was to be married. This time for real. Strangely, he didn't believe he could feel more married than he already did.

"I suggest you discuss the matter with my wife," he replied.

"Well then, when you see her, please inform her I shall be in contact in the next several days. Your father and I will be staying at the cottage for two weeks. We are having the public rooms in town repapered and the floors in the library and drawing room buffed. I simply can't tolerate the dust. It plays havoc with my breathing."

The duke staying so close by. In the not-so-distant past, the notion would have filled Alex with dread and sent him to the other end of England. Now, he felt...nothing. The duke no longer had the power to hurt him or raise his ire. He had been noticeably quiet since his introduction to his grandson. Ordinarily, Alex would have received summons to attend him in London. The past five years, he'd blithely ignored them, only going to Somerset House at his mother's request.

"Your father would like it if you brought Nicholas to visit. And before you say no," she hastened to add, "I hope you can find it in your heart to be the bigger man. You know how much pride your father has. It would take an act of Parliament for him to admit he was wrong and apologize."

Alex didn't believe even that would do it. "And you expect me to forget a lifetime of abominable treatment by the duke because I happened to produce a son who looks just like him and his beloved son."

"Why must you persist in addressing him by his title? He is your father."

"He never appeared to mind it."

"Of course he minds. He believes the practice to be impertinent. And admit it, my dear, you do it to antagonize him."

That he did. "Why do you expect me to mend fences with him now? Because he believes me to be his son?"

"You are his son," his mother said sharply.

"I've been his son these last thirty-four years, Mama."

His mother sighed, her gray eyes troubled. "I'm not asking you to forget, for neither of us can. I'm just asking you not to deny him his grandson."

Only his mother could prick his conscience in just that way. She'd always had that ability. "I will think on it."

A smile wreathed her face. "Good. That is all I ask."

"And in return I ask that you be kind to my wife. I will not tolerate any mistreatment of her. I did not like your manner with her at the ball."

The duchess' spine lengthened and her chin lifted. She looked properly taken aback. This was a delicate dance to get his mother to see reason.

"Come, Mama," he coaxed, "I've seen you perform it more than a dozen times. You can be excessively charming when you want. Expend that gift on my wife."

A mix of concern and understanding flared in her eyes. "I believe I can manage that. I do hope you know what you're doing."

"I hope so too," he said gravely.

Alex stood and came from behind the desk to see his mother out. After placing a feathered bonnet on her head and settling a silk shawl on her shoulders, both which the footman handed her, she reached up and kissed Alex softly on the cheek. She wore the same exclusive scent she purchased in Paris as she had since he was a child.

"Give my grandson a hug for me and make certain he's in next I call," she instructed as he assisted her into the carriage.

Once she was safely ensconced inside, she gave a regal wave and then she was gone.

"Unca Lucas," Nicholas practically screamed before taking off down the corridor, his little legs pumping. With his customary enthusiasm and excitement, he pitched himself into Lucas's arms.

Lucas caught him up on his chest and then proceeded to hold him high above him, spinning around until Nicholas was thoroughly dizzy and giggling like a mad hyena.

"Do it again," he cried.

"All right, one more time," Lucas said, relenting. "Your mother will have my head if I make you spill your breakfast." He sent a grin her way.

"You are here early. Where are you taking Katie today?" Charlotte asked. The day after the ball, Katie had confessed he'd become a regular visitor at Rutherford Manor.

"Today, I'm off to London. I stopped by to bring Nicholas this." From his coat pocket, Lucas produced a small wind-up train, which had her son squealing in delight.

Snatching it from Lucas's palm, Nicholas took to the task of winding the red train. He then placed it on the wood floor and chortled with glee as it began rolling down the hall.

When the train came to a stop, Nicholas scooped it up and grasped Lucas's hand and began tugging him toward the stairs. "Come and watch me make it go on the train tracks up'tairs."

Laughing, Lucas allowed himself to be pulled along, turning to Charlotte with a helpless shrug. "All right, but just for a minute. Uncle Lucas has a train to catch."

Charlotte stood and watched the two until they disappeared upstairs before setting out in search of her sister.

Katie was where she always was at that time of the morning, in the morning room practicing on the piano. Her sister was determined to become passable on the instrument as it appeared being accomplished was too far out of her scope.

The playing halted the moment she entered the room. Katie twisted on the bench, a smile of greeting on her face.

"I didn't expect you at all today now that Elizabeth and Amelia have gone."

The Armstrongs and Creswells and their broods had departed for their respective homes the day prior, two days after the ball. Charlotte had been sad to see them go but had been there to send them off.

"My son simply wouldn't permit me to sleep a minute longer," Charlotte said, crossing the room to take a seat on the sofa. "In any case, I had already awoken and couldn't fall back to sleep."

In the distance, she heard the rumbling of a male voice coming from the entry way. Curious, she glanced out the window facing the front. In the drive she saw her husband's barouche parked behind the carriage Lucas had leased while in Reading.

Lucas was upstairs with Nicholas.

"Alex is here." Panicked, Charlotte sprang to her feet and rushed from the room and into the foyer. It was empty save the footman posted near the front door.

"Lord Avondale, did he arrive?" she asked breathlessly.

"He's upstairs looking for Lord Nicholas."

"Lottie, what's wrong?" her sister cried out from behind her.

"Katie, please remain here. I shall send Nicholas down to you," Charlotte said and hurried up the stairs, her skirts whirling about her like linens on a line on a day the air had a pleasant kick. The tale only got worse and worse.

She reached the second floor with her heart thundering loudly in her ears. Slowing to a quick walk, she started toward the wing that housed the nursery. Just as she turned the corner to the stretch of hall leading to the playroom, she spotted Alex looking the picture of a waxed image of him would have done. He stood utterly still and silent, staring through the partially opened door. As it was obvious he hadn't seen her, Charlotte pressed herself back against the wall to remain hidden from view.

Gingerly, she peeped at him around the corner wall and watched as he did nothing but stare into the room, his expression haunted. Nicholas's giggles and Lucas's deep-throated laughter filtered into the hallway. Charlotte had heard the exact sounds countless times over the years. But hearing it today was like the slash of a dagger on skin already open and bleeding, for she knew that was why Alex flinched.

He turned then, his face no longer in profile. And for as long as Charlotte lived, she would never forget the anguish in his eyes. Jerking her head back, she wanted nothing but to disappear into the walls. Tears pricked her eyes and emotion constricted her throat.

Had he seen her? He'd looked in her vicinity but his eyes hadn't appeared focused. Seconds later, he passed her at a brisk pace and soon after she heard his feet pounding down the stairs.

Slowly, carefully, Charlotte stepped out from her hiding place and the tears she'd tried to keep in check began to flow. Guilt, the likes she'd never experienced before in her life, consumed her whole.

How could she have been so utterly thoughtless to not have known the effect Lucas's presence would have on him? It was wrecking him through and through as evidenced by the tormented expression on his face.

After wiping the tears from her eyes, Charlotte started toward the playroom when Lucas and Nicholas emerged all grins, laughter and male camaraderie. How would they feel if they knew they'd just cut Alex to the quick with their easy familiarity and affection?

"Nicholas dear, Mama wants you to go downstairs and ask Aunt Katie to take you to the back where you can rejoin your cousins. I'd like to speak to Uncle Lucas before he leaves." Her voice held a firmness that immediately elicited results.

Clutching his new toy in his hand, Nicholas said goodbye to Lucas before dashing off, only slowing before he reached the stairs when she cautioned him not to run.

Lucas watched her, his forehead creased in concern. He'd known her long enough to know something wasn't right.

"Come, it's best if we not have this discussion in the hall," she said, and proceeded him into the playroom.

Once they were standing in what could only be described as a child's dream, the room spacious containing doll houses, train tracks and a plethora of other children's delights, Charlotte looked Lucas directly in the eye.

"Lucas, you must leave."

His brows drew together, surprise lighting his brown eyes. "Are you evicting me from your brother's home?"

Distressed, Charlotte shook her head, strands of hair floating about her face. "I mean we cannot see you anymore. At least for now," she added in an attempt to blunt the impact of her words.

"This is about your husband." His mouth was tight, his expression grim.

"I cannot put him through any more than he's already gone through. Your presence now and your relationship with Nicholas is tearing him apart. I should have been more sensitive. I should have known how much it would hurt him."

Lucas drew in a deep breath, his head tipped up to the painted ceiling of blue skies, clouds and stars. He idly studied the mural before he returned his gaze to her. "Dammit, Charlotte, you deserve better than this. If he doesn't trust you—"

"No, don't you dare criticize him. You have no idea what he's been through because of the decisions I've made. The truth is I left him on our wedding day. I gave birth to his son without his knowledge. He didn't abandon us, I abandoned him and now—" Charlotte lost the capacity to speak, emotion choked her words.

"You left him?" he asked, disbelieving.

"I'm surprised you haven't already heard. I thought for certain you'd have heard the gossip by now." No, truth be told, she thought Katie would have said something about it to him.

"You know I don't care for nor listen to gossip. Moreover, I'm a stranger here. Who would have thought to tell me?" He paused before saying, "This whole time we've been acquainted, you gave all indications that you were available for marriage. It came as quite a surprise when your sister informed me you were already wed." He appeared more hurt than angry at the deception.

"I'm terribly sorry for that but I had my reasons for not being truthful with you. I hope you'll find it in your heart to forgive me. The truth is I've loved Alex almost from the day I met him. He will and has always been the only one for me."

Lucas's mouth quirked in a half smile. "So I never stood a chance," he teased.

Charlotte shook her head and smiled.

"Which is just as well, you know as well as I that we are much better off as friends than we ever would have been lovers."

In that moment of clarity it struck her; the question she'd posed to him in the letter she'd sent after he'd already left for England.

"Lucas, who told you my sister was failing?"

Some unidentifiable emotion flashed in his eyes but vanished just as quickly. "I can't accurately recall her name. But she informed me she'd received the information on good authority. I believe she claimed a close acquaintance with the physician's wife. But as it's obvious she was misinformed, I believe she must have confused the names."

Of course Lucas had no knowledge of the issues she and her family faced, but Charlotte thought it too coincidental that the threat of exposure had sent her fleeing and then five years later, information of her sister's ill health conveniently found its way to her. Anyone the least bit acquainted with them would have known such information would bring her back.

This convinced her that whoever sent the letter was still about and it was through their machinations she was here in England. The knowledge sent a frisson of fear down the length of her spine. But she hadn't time to dwell on it now. She had more important matters at hand and she'd not worry him with her concerns.

"Well, I'm relieved she was mistaken. What matters now is that I have to make things right with my husband, and your presence here is making that impossible. I don't mean for you to remove yourself from our lives forever, just for now. I need to give Alex time to feel more comfortable in his role as husband and father."

"What of your sister? We've grown close." He appeared conflicted.

Oh God, she'd completely forgotten about Katie in that respect. This entire situation was more complicated than the written Chinese language. It was clear he had developed feelings for her sister and vice versa. But how serious were they?

"If your intentions are marriage, I will simply have to appeal to Alex's sense of family for I refuse to be estranged from my sister." If not, it was better he left now before her sister's heart became involved—if it hadn't already.

Lucas took his time responding as he studied her quietly. "After I've finished my business in London, I will return to America."

A sob caught in her throat.

"Please tell Nicholas goodbye."

Charlotte pressed her knuckle against her teeth and nodded, her gaze staring sightlessly at the floor.

Gently, he lifted her chin with his finger. "Don't cry, everything will turn out fine," he whispered.

"You are the dearest friend," Charlotte managed to choke out amidst a fresh well of tears.

Lucas gave her a sad smile and then planted a soft kiss on her forehead. "Be well."

Lucas descended the stairs stone-faced and grim. God save him from jealous husbands. Although he could well understand the marquess's reaction. He himself had reeled at Charlotte's confession. She hadn't been a widow, she'd been a runaway bride. If he'd thought she'd have shared her reasons for her flight, he'd have asked, but there'd been something in her tone that had told him that door was closed to him.

One thing was clear, he didn't know her as well as he'd thought he had.

At the bottom of the stairs, he scanned the empty foyer and thought briefly of seeking out Catherine. But what could he say? He lived in America and her place was here. He'd been fooling himself into believing he could have anything with her.

She wasn't the type of woman a man took as his mistress. For one, her brother would have his head on a pike. Secondly, she was the kind of woman one married, the kind of proper English lady who should wed a likewise English gentleman. He was not one nor would he ever be.

"Lucas?"

He felt that odd clenching in the pit of his stomach just hearing Catherine's voice. He stood unmoving as he watched her approach, his body immediately reacting to the vision she made. She was buttoned all the way up to her neck and covered down to her delicate wrists, but the cobalt blue gown she wore, lovingly outlined beautiful feminine curves.

The time he'd spent with her over the past weeks had given a whole new meaning to the term sweet torture. She moved like a dream and possessed a sensual allure few men could resist. He certainly hadn't been able nor wanted to.

"I didn't know you had come." She smiled and it was that sweet, shy sort of smile that did things to his insides. Softened the hardness there.

"Actually, I was on my way out. I just called to say goodbye."

Her smile became less certain. "Oh."

"I have business in London today."

"Will—will you be coming back?" she asked.

"Unfortunately, I am due back home the week after next so from London, I'll be returning to America."

Pain flickered in her eyes and he wanted to smash something. "I see." She drew in a breath and fixed a smile on her face that didn't reach her eyes. "Well then I shall wish you a safe passage back."

God, how he hated this. Hated himself in that very moment. She was hurt and there was nothing he could say that would make it better. Charlotte had said if his intentions were marriage, she would go back and plead her case with her husband. But he'd only spent the better part of two weeks in Catherine's company. He'd kissed her the one time—and what a kiss it had been. Yes, he was strongly attracted to her but he couldn't truthfully tell Charlotte he planned to marry her. The things separating them were too many.

"Catherine—"

"Goodbye, Mr. Beaumont." When she spoke her voice was too civil and much too polite to be anything but a dismissal.

"Goodbye, Catherine," he said softly, feeling more than a twinge of regret for what might have been under different circumstances.

Chapter Twenty

"Did you see him today?"

Charlotte started at the roughness of Alex's voice when she walked in to her bed chambers that evening.

She'd come back to the house around midday to find he'd yet to return. She'd consumed—although just barely—a solitary supper in the dining room and had spent the last hour with Nicholas getting him off to sleep. He'd demanded she read him two stories instead of the customary one.

"Alex. When did you come home?"

"Answer my question. Did you see *your* Mr. Beaumont today?"

He sat reclined in the chair by the fireplace, hands folded across his chest and a necktie draped loosely about his neck. He'd removed his coat, which hung over the back of the chair, and his unbuttoned waistcoat revealed a wrinkled, pale blue shirt beneath. A day's growth of whiskers shadowed the angular planes of his jaw. In a word, he looked a rumpled mess.

Charlotte knew she needed to tread with undue care. "Yes, when I called on Catherine this morning, Lucas was there but not at my invitation. However, Lucas is gone now. He's back in London and from there he will be returning to America. He came by my brother's house to say goodbye."

Alex uncrossed his arms and sat up higher in the chair. "Why?"

"Why what?"

"Why did he leave?" He asked as if he already knew the answer.

Charlotte swallowed hard. "Because I asked him to."

"And why did you ask him to leave? You yourself said I

was being unreasonable as he was just a friend. Why did you ask him to go if there was nothing going on between you?"

"Because I realized how unfeeling I've been. And today, I *saw* the effect with my own eyes. Saw that having him here was tearing you apart. And I simply couldn't stand to see you hurting like that." The words felt torn from her throat, acrid and raw like her emotions.

Alex stared at her and then cast his gaze off in the distance. Clasping his hands between his legs, he started speaking in a low voice fraught with emotion. "All those years, he had everything that was mine. My wife. My child. Everything. He knows things about my son I do not. Things I have yet to learn. Things I should know."

"Oh Alex, it wasn't like that at all. He never *had* me and Nicholas knows Lucas isn't really a relation. Your son loves *you*, his father. Nothing will change that." Charlotte vowed she wouldn't fall apart, but the edge was but a short step away.

Alex turned his attention back to her and rose from the chair.

"Did you tell him you loved me and only me? Did you tell him that you and Nicholas belong here with me?" he asked as he approached her, something dark and dangerous in his stormy gray eyes.

And just like that, the hum of sexual energy that had always existed between them became a roar. Like a storm that had been building for days, it rushed in with gale force winds.

His hand snaked out and snatched her to him, their bodies meeting like a magnet to the most powerful force field. His mouth all but crashed down on hers, but she welcomed the kiss, parting her lips for the sinewy thrust of his tongue.

He made quick work of her clothes, impatiently divesting her of her day dress and petticoats, without once removing his mouth from hers.

Charlotte drew his tongue into her mouth and proceeded to ravish it as he'd often done to her, eliciting a groan from him that originated deep in his throat. He tasted like brutish male strength and mint, and the scent of his cologne made her briefly think of heather in the spring. But he wouldn't be conquered for too long, taking the kiss back under his control by drugging her with licks, swipes and long, thorough strokes of his tongue.

Impatient, Alex finally broke the kiss to tug her silk chemise over her head. Her nipples puckered the second the cool air touched them. He instantly warmed them, cupping them in his large hands, where they pebbled further under his toying fingers.

"Oh God, Charlotte," Alex said hoarsely, staring down at her breasts, his eyes glazed with passion. Ducking his head, he touched her nipple with the tip of his tongue and slowly, with the fierce concentration of a child trying to paint within the lines, rimmed the rosy, ruched perimeter. A charring sensation coursed from her breast to her core, where she grew moist with need.

Suddenly, her head felt too heavy for her neck to support and she could do little else but sag forward, resting her forehead on the top of his head. She ran her fingers through the weight of his hair, tugging on the dark strands, urging his mouth closer. He was doing nothing but teasing her with his light caresses. She wanted him to take her in his mouth.

"Alex," she said, his name a breathless whimper. Why must he tease her like this? He knew what she wanted.

His only response was to transfer his attentions to her other breast, the stroke of his tongue on her nipple as if he had all night and wasn't in a rush.

Impatient and growing frustrated by the moment, Charlotte ground her hips against his and pressed hard on the back of his head to push her breast into his mouth. He emitted something between a grunt and a groan before finally drawing her nipple firmly between his lips. He began to suckle as he pressed his erection hard into the giving softness between her thighs.

Charlotte thought she would expire, the pleasure he ignited within her so intense it made her dizzy. God, how she wanted him inside her and clenched her inner walls in anticipation of his possession.

"Alex," she said, nearly sobbing his name.

With one last delicious draw on her nipple, Alex stood up straight. His slumberous eyes devoured her as he began pulling off his clothes.

Eager to aid him in his efforts, Charlotte reached out but he retreated a step, denying her the pleasure.

"My need is too great. If you touch me now, we won't make it to the bed."

"I don't care," she moaned, blind with need. She stepped forward and reached for him again.

This time he took two steps back. His waistcoat dropped to the floor and seconds later, his shirt joined the growing heap at his feet. "No, believe me. It is better this way. Once we start, I won't let you up until dawn. I want you comfortable."

His words, the hungry grumble of his voice and the lustful intent in his eyes caused another flood of moisture between her thighs. But heeding his wish, Charlotte stepped from the circle of silk and satin of her discarded gown and underclothes, and wearing a pair of pale pink stockings and garters, slid onto the bed behind her.

If she had to be content to merely watch him, she may as well do so in style and torture him just a little for his neglect. On her back, she scooted into the middle of the bed, propped herself up on her arms and allowed her legs to fall open just a little.

But enough.

Alex's expletive rent the air. Then in a flurry of movement, he pulled off his trousers and drawers. All this he did with his eyes locked on the one place on her currently demanding his undivided attention.

When he was fully unclothed, Charlotte pulled her bottom lip between her teeth and ran her tongue along the fleshy inside as she took in his thick erection straining against the hard, ridged flesh of his stomach where an arrow of dark hair thickened.

"You are playing with fire," he warned softly as he stalked toward her.

"I want you." It was as simple as that. And tonight she was going to get what she wanted.

Bracing his hands on the edge of the mattress, Alex levered himself above her. Charlotte dropped onto her back. She expected him to begin kissing her again, but he had other tortures in mind for her. The first kiss landed on the concave of her stomach. From there he proceeded down and farther down. The swirls of his tongue on the skin just above her center had her clutching the bed sheets in her hands and panting as if she'd covered the distance from the town square back home at a dead run.

"Alex," she pleaded but she wasn't precisely sure what she was pleading for. Relief. Yes, that's what she craved; relief from the need clawing at her insides.

"Shhh, my love, I'm coming to that." She could feel his breath at the heart of her. Then she felt the stroke of his tongue there and her body felt cleaved in two, the pleasure staggering. Her hips shot up, her body reacting as if struck by a bolt of lightning. She heard a woman cry out; the sound of someone being ravaged by pleasure.

Alex's shoulders shook. Was he laughing? Apparently pleased with himself was he? When he began licking her, toying with the folds of her sex, Charlotte lost all sense of reality, sent adrift into her own sensual world.

The pleasure built as he licked and sucked, parting her to delve into the very heart of her. She had no control of her body, her hips jerking, twisting and then undulating in time with how he was loving her. When he lashed the hard nub at the hood of her sex with his tongue, the culmination of need and want sent her rocketing toward release, and she was soaring.

It had been a little more than two weeks since he'd had her last and the need in him was ferocious. His cock was so hard it could split rocks. Surely a man could perish if the pain of this became too much to bear.

Charlotte lay beneath him, her body slack and replete with satisfaction, her breathing labored. She looked beautiful, her breasts reddened by his attentions, her lips swollen and tender from his kisses.

She was his and she'd never leave him again. He wouldn't allow it. He'd follow her right to the gates of hell if he must for he knew his life would be nothing without her.

Crawling from between her spread legs, Alex tamped down his voracious hunger, intent on bringing her to pleasure again. He started with her sweet mouth, the kiss drugging his senses and twisting his insides. Her tongue joined his in sensual play, her teeth nipping his bottom lip and then soothing it with the slash of her tongue.

Her hands kneaded his shoulders and then he felt her fingernails scraping down his chest until it came to his cock. She wrapped her hand eagerly around his length.

"Charlotte." It was a cry for mercy. It was a plea to continue.

She began stroking him, her touch wicked and right.

"No more," he groaned, grasping both her hands and pinning them above her head. "I won't last if you do that."

"Make love to me," she said in a throaty voice and almost unmanned him by wrapping her legs around his hips, leaving her open to him. His for the taking. And with a helpless groan, he took. With unerring precision, he slid into her sleek heat.

Snug and wet, she clamped on to him and he was certain he'd died and gone to heaven. The need to ride her hard was overwhelming. But he wanted to make it good for her.

Teeth gritted, he pulled out and then pushed slowly back in. Oh God, the most exquisite pleasure coursed through him.

"Harder," she moaned, her head twisting helplessly against the bed sheets. The moment he released her hands, she wrapped them about his neck to pull him closer. Her mouth found the sensitive spot behind his ear and he was lost.

He gave her precisely what she asked for, taking her hard,

his hips pummeling her like the frantic beat of a drum. She arched up to meet his downward strokes, gasping, urging him on.

The end came soon after, his groan, low and hoarse, signaled his release, which was the stuff of legends, decimating his insides as the inner walls of her sex milked him.

She let out something between a gasp and a shriek, her back bowed and taut. Seconds later, she collapsed limp and sated.

"Oh God, Charlotte," he said, burying his head in the crook of her neck. "God how I missed you." There he'd said it, and in the process, laid his heart bare for her to see.

Her arms instantly tightened about his neck. "Oh Alex, I love you. I love you. I never once stopped loving you. Ever."

Her body shuddered and he knew she was crying.

Alex lifted his head and stared down at her tear-stained face. "Shh, darling, don't cry." He kissed her gently on the lips. Her mouth opened to his instantly and soon the kiss of comfort he'd meant to give turned into something else all too soon, quickly giving way to another torrid, mutually satisfying joining.

Although they'd made love many times, this was the first morning she'd awoken beside him, his arms about her waist, her bottom pressed up against his thick member.

The closed curtains effectively kept morning at bay, shrouding the room in darkness but Charlotte could sense dawn hovered minutes away.

She thought Alex was still asleep until his hand softly stroked her stomach and began the climb to her breast. There he fondled the soft under curve before he caught her nipple between his fingers, where he teased and plucked until it pebbled in interest.

Charlotte bit down on her lip and hummed her pleasure, her bottom pressing back to rub against his growing erection.

"I didn't think you were awake," she said and released a low whimper.

"I was waiting for you to wake up so I could do this." His hand abandoned her breast for the place between her thighs.

"No, we can't," she said, even as she parted her legs to permit him more access to where she was already growing wet with need.

Alex kissed the column of her throat, his fingers strumming a wicked tune on her moist female flesh. "Why not?"

"Most mornings, Nic-Nicholas comes in the moment he wakes. And he-he usually awakens very early." It was hard to speak with his fingers plying her flesh, delving, coaxing a wanton response from her. Speak? She could barely think.

"Let your maid take care of him."

No sooner had he spoken, when she heard the door to the suite open. Nicholas was there, which meant they had seconds to make themselves decent.

Moving faster than she had since she'd had to scramble to catch her son from falling down the first floor stairs when he was two years, Charlotte hurriedly thrust Alex's hand from between her legs and yanked the counterpane to cover their naked bodies.

"Mama, I'm hungry," Nicolas called out, not yet in the bed chamber.

Charlotte could only thank God the curtains were drawn. Alex had left the bed and was scrambling into his trousers. He barely got them on before Nicholas appeared in the doorway, silhouetted by the light in the hall.

"Mama, it's dark. I want light."

Alex came around from the side of the bed. "Come, son, let's leave your mother to dress."

"Papa," Nicholas exclaimed, his sleepy eyes widening a little. But that was the extent of his reaction. Charlotte had been certain he'd pepper them with a dozen questions.

Instead, he silently took in the scene: his mother covered up to her neck and his father shirtless and barefooted in his mother's bedchambers.

"Let's go find your nanny," Alex said, offering Nicholas his hand. With one final glance at his mother, he took his father's hand and they left the room.

By the time Alex returned, five minutes later, Charlotte had slipped on her nightdress and was belting a silk blue dressing gown in place.

He grinned. "I was hoping to find you still undressed."

Charlotte laughed. "And risk a repeat of Nicholas barging in again. I think not."

Undaunted, he used the silk sash about her waist to pull her close. He was unashamedly hard and aroused. "And you don't think it's worth the risk?"

"I'd rather not have it be a concern when I make love to my husband," she whispered, feeling the tug of desire between her thighs.

Alex lowered his head and kissed her softly on the curve of her neck. "Then let's send him to your brother's or to my parents in London," he teased. "He surely won't disturb us then."

Then quite abruptly, he pulled back, his expression suddenly serious. "I almost forgot to tell you, my mother came to see me yesterday."

It took a moment for Charlotte to regain her equilibrium. He had that kind of effect on her.

"What did she want?" To remind him that Charlotte wasn't good enough for him?

Taking her hand in his, he led her to the armchair near the fireplace. He sat and settled her on his lap.

"She called to tell me my cousin is making noise about our marriage papers. He is talking about challenging its legality."

At his words, one of Charlotte's greatest fears was realized. "But you said—"

"Don't worry," he soothed. "I'm sure nothing will come of it."

"But what if it does?" she said, now heartsick with worry.

"Well my mother has advised we should marry to properly legitimize the union."

"But that won't make Nicholas legitimate."

"It would do so for any future children."

Her gaze snapped to him. "Future children?" Although things had changed between them, the last time she'd asked about children, he'd stated quite emphatically he didn't want another with her.

Dear Lord, was that what last night had been about, getting her with child to ensure the title remained in the direct line? She hadn't given a thought to putting in the Dutch cap.

"I know what you are thinking and you couldn't be more wrong. Last night we were careless. Just because my mother insists we rush to have another child does not mean we will. I feel more certain than she that Nicholas will inherit. Not only will I, but the duke will do everything in his power to make sure our marriage is upheld." He was all quiet intensity. "The other option was that I permit him to have our marriage be declared null and void and take another wife and get *her* with child as soon as possible."

Now *that* hurt. The thought of Alex married, making love, having children with someone else was like a knife in her heart.

"And how long did you ponder your choices?" she asked, almost afraid to hear the answer.

Wrapping his arms around her, he pulled her tightly against his chest. "Not one second," he assured her.

"Do-do you want us to marry—I mean without your cousin's threat to make our son illegitimate?"

"I will feel no more married to you than I do now. In my heart, you are my wife. You always have been. I just need your assurance that I won't be standing alone at the altar this time."

For a moment, she thought this was his attempt at amusement, but his solemn expression and unsmiling mouth stated otherwise.

Inhaling a sharp breath, she asked, "How can you ask that of me? Now that you know the truth, I have no secrets to hide."

"Are you certain?" he asked.

"Quite certain. Although I should tell you, James doesn't

believe his mother was responsible for the letter and I have come to agree with him."

"Yes, he mentioned that the evening of the ball."

So they had already discussed it.

"I was relieved you decided to tell him the truth."

"I was going to tell you but it appears my brother beat me to it." It was funny, now that she'd confessed all to family and friends, she felt less burdened by it and less ashamed.

"But you have my assurance, there will be a wedding this time."

Alex stared intently at her, as if trying to read her mind, see into the heart he'd claimed long ago. He may be willing to give their marriage a real try, but she could see he still didn't trust her—at least not fully—which meant he truly didn't understand why she'd left. And because he could not understand, he may not be able to find it in his heart to forgive.

But her assurance appeared to satisfy him enough for he pressed her head back against his chest and kissed the top of her head without saying another word.

Chapter Twenty-One

Alex rarely had cause to go to the back rooms. It was the servants' haven, a place they were assured their privacy; a place the master seldom tread. Today, however, he'd arrived home and Alfred hadn't answered the bell, which was rarer than a Whig at White's, and his housekeeper was nowhere in sight.

The hallway was narrower and darker in the rear of the manor. As Alex made his way toward his butler's office, he made a note to himself to have more lighting installed.

He passed the still room and business room and was passing Conrad's office when he heard a voice—feminine given the pitch—behind the solid oak door. He paused and listened. He cared little about how his employees conducted their private affairs when they weren't at work, but he wouldn't tolerate the man dallying about on the job. And over the last two months, Conrad's behavior had begun to make him uneasy. There had been one too many times he'd disappeared from the house and when questioned claimed he'd been in town on manor business.

The last time it had occurred, Alex had vowed to speak to the tailor, with whom Conrad had said he'd had to visit to settle a bill. But these last few weeks, Alex had opted to spend more time with his wife.

He heard it again, his ears confirming the voice was indeed feminine and it was soon followed by a masculine one. They were speaking low enough and the door was solid enough that he couldn't make out what they were saying, but he'd wager it had nothing to do with work.

Alex rapped on the door.

The voices stopped and the place fell eerily quiet. Alex rapped again, this time more forcefully. "Conrad, are you in there?" Which his steward would have been smart to translate as, *Open the bloody door.*

It was as if the sound of his employer's voice set the man in motion. Alex heard the sound of chairs scraping and a door closing before finally, and with what seemed the utmost care, the door slid open only wide enough to reveal his steward's pale face and sandy hair that looked as if it had been hastily finger combed.

"My lord, I did not know you'd returned." Conrad stood in the doorway, the whites of his eyes expansive, and a nervous ingenuous smile; sure signs of a guilty man, a man who's been up to no good.

Alex stepped forward, forcing the man to move aside or get run over. Inside the small office, he surveyed the room, noting the oak desk holding a stack of ledgers and two ink stands. Attached to his office was his sleeping quarters in the back.

"You there," Alex called out, "show yourself."

"Your lordship," Conrad protested.

Alex gave him a look he'd once been told made grown men quake. Beyond that, he ignored him completely.

"If you do not come out now, I will be forced to come for you and frankly, I'd rather not."

His steward made not a sound, or perhaps it was him whimpering. Alex had thought it was the woman. The door to his private room opened and a figure emerged. Alex started and blinked hard when the light revealed her face.

"Jillian?"

With her hazel eyes filled with fear, she stared up at him. "Please don't tell Miz Charlotte," she said before dropping her head.

Words failed him, something that appeared to be happening more and more. He spun to face his steward.

"We were just—I was showing her the office." His voice trailed off, ineffective and as weak as his pitiful excuse.

"You," Alex said sharply to Jillian. "Go to your room and be sure, I fully intend to speak to your mistress about this."

His wife's maid scampered from the office not giving him cause to repeat himself.

"And you." Alex returned his stony stare to his soon-to-be former steward. "You will pack your things and leave at once. Am I understood?"

As he'd been hit on his head hard enough to leave him momentary dazed, Conrad stared at him. "You cannot be serious?" he croaked, his expression one of utter disbelief.

Conrad had always been a touch arrogant.

"I assure you I am," Alex said between gritted teeth.

His steward blinked and shook his head as if trying to clear it. "Surely you are not going to dismiss me over *her?*" His tone made it abundantly clear in precisely what esteem he held the mulatto maid.

Alex seethed, barely able to hold his temper in check.

Conrad continued down his very short road to self-destruction unabated. "But, my lord, it was she who has been flinging herself at me. You must know how those woman—"

Lightning fast, Alex's hand shot out and clamped around his steward's throat. Conrad's eyes widened to the size of saucers and he made a gurgled sound in his throat, on which Alex tightened his hold.

"Finish that sentence and it will be the last thing you say."

After a pause, the terrified man nodded mutely.

Alex eased his grip. "Now I am giving you one hour to pack your belongings and vacate these premises. Should I hear you have spoken an ill word about that young woman, I ensure you will not even be able to find employment as a dockworker in all of England. Have I made myself clear?"

Conrad's head bobbed.

Dropping his hand from around the man's throat, Alex retreated a step and gave a curt nod. "One hour," he warned before departing the room.

Charlotte returned home late that afternoon to find Jillian hovering near the bottom of the principle staircase.

After Charlotte handed her bonnet and cloak to the footman, she approached her. Strangely, Jillian stayed back, not offering her usual greeting or smile. In fact as Charlotte drew closer, she saw the terror on Jillian's face. Her heart sank and landed with a splat.

"My dear, what is the matter? What has happened?" Charlotte could hear the panic in her own voice as she whispered fervent prayers that something untoward had not occurred again. The last time, Jillian had been lucky to escape with only her dress ripped at the shoulder as she'd withstood the pawing hands of the butcher's son. Charlotte should have known when he'd offered to deliver the meats directly to the house, he was up to no good. But then he'd been so mannerly and polite until the incident.

She'd been forced to switch butchers and insisted Jillian not appear when gentlemen called. Except for Lucas, of course. She'd actually been pleasantly surprised they'd had no trouble with the men here.

Jillian forced a wan smile and tugged the folds of her checkered skirts, but such a look of fear clouded her hazel eyes, Charlotte immediately took her by the hand and led her to the morning room.

After sitting her down and taking the seat next to her on the sofa, Charlotte took her hand in hers. "Now tell me what is wrong."

Nearly incoherent, Jillian, hands trembling uncontrollably, said in an equally shaky voice, "The master iz gonna send me home."

Charlotte might have laughed had the matter not been so serious. "Now what would ever give you such an idea?" she asked gently.

Jillian lowered her head, her dark curls veiling most of her face. "He found me in Mr. Conrad's room," she mumbled, her sun-kissed complexion giving way to the blush of red.

The knot of dread Charlotte had felt upon first seeing her grew so tight it cut her breath clean in half. She stared at Jillian's down-bent head.

Oh dear Lord, not again.

"He didn't—he didn't...?" Charlotte couldn't even get the words out, the thought so repugnant.

Jillian's head shot up, her expression horrified. "Oh no, Miz Charlotte, it was nuttin' like that," she cried. "I like Mr. Conrad. He wasn't trying to force me or anyt'ing like that. Not like the others. He treated me real nice."

Charlotte tipped her head back and closed her eyes. For a moment, she allowed relief to wash over her. But it was the minutest of reprieves for instantly her eyes snapped open. "What do you mean you like him? Has he—have you...?"

"No," Jillian denied, shaking her head. "He's only kissed me the one time."

"Oh Jillian." Charlotte moaned her name in despair.

"But, Miz Charlotte, he sed he likes me a lot. He told me I was beautiful."

She looked so earnest and innocent. And Mr. Conrad was much older. She'd hazard a guess he was close to thirty years if he was a day. Oh he was a handsome one all right. Charlotte had seen the female servants all a titter whenever he strolled by, light-brown hair, startling green eyes. Definitely the kind of face to turn a young girl's head—and break her heart.

"And my husband, what did he say?"

Jillian's face reddened as she ducked her head. "He sed he was gonna talk to you 'bout it."

"And Mr. Conrad?" How had he fared? Did the man still have his position?

Without looking up, Jillian shrugged her shoulders in a helpless, defeated gesture.

The whole thing was a mess. But of course she'd do her best to smooth things over with Alex, which was precisely what she told Jillian before she sent her upstairs to check on Nicholas.

Charlotte found Alex in his study. He sat at his desk rubbing his hands wearily over his face. His head shot up when she entered. Pushing back his chair, he came to his feet. "I've dismissed Mr. Conrad," he said tersely.

The situation had just gotten worse.

"You don't look surprised," he said, eyeing her grimly. "I take it your maid told you where I discovered her."

"That you found her in his rooms, yes she did."

Casting his gaze off in the distance, Alex's chest rose and fell on a heavy sigh. "I didn't even ask her. Did she tell you whether his attentions were unwanted?"

Charlotte could well imagine he'd no doubt been too angry to inquire about Jillian's well-being.

"No, going by what she told me, Jillian appears to be somewhat infatuated with your steward."

Alex emitted a humorless laugh and strode toward the window. "He had no right to carry on in my house with one of the servants."

Charlotte was taken aback at the hard tone of his voice and the impersonal manner in which he referred to Jillian. "Yes, while technically she is my servant and I pay her a wage, Jillian has always been more than just a servant to me," she replied in a tight voice.

Alex's spine stiffened as he angled a glance at her over his shoulder. "I am well aware you are extremely fond of her but that doesn't change the facts. She is your maid, she helps care for our child."

"She's a young girl whose head was turned by a handsome man. Such things are bound to happen."

His eyebrows shot up. He looked positively stupefied. "Are you condoning their behavior?" he asked.

"No, I am asking you to show a little compassion. Did you truly have to dismiss him? Jillian will be crushed when she learns. And I'm sure she'll feel responsible."

With a rueful shake of his head, Alex advanced toward her,

stopping just short of arm's length. "The man was playing with her. He would have seduced and left her to stew."

Ten minutes before, Charlotte had felt much the same but now hearing it from her husband's mouth, got her back up. "You can't possibly know that for certain."

His gaze narrowed. "Do you truly believe he intended to marry her?" He spoke as pigs flying or two-headed cows were more a possibility.

"I-I'm—"

"Because if you do, you are only fooling yourself. Men like Mr. Conrad—"

"What? Would never stoop to marry a girl like her, correct? She may be beautiful enough to dally with, but she would never be good enough for marriage. Isn't that what you mean?" she charged, fighting a tide of tumultuous emotions.

Suddenly his voice turned urgent. "Charlotte, our situation is not the same. I can't believe you would compare them."

"No? Isn't it the same? The only difference is that I look like this," she cried, pointing to the paleness of her skin, "and she looks like that."

"The biggest difference is that I love you and Conrad only wants her in his bed. He was dallying with her." Charlotte could tell he strived to keep a sensible, calm tone but frustration edged his voice.

Good Lord, she should be happy. He'd just confessed his love for her. Words she'd never thought to hear from his mouth again. But the situation with Jillian reminded her that sometimes love did not triumph in the end.

"But don't you see, Alex, should anyone discover the truth about me nothing else would matter. It wouldn't matter how I looked—that my skin and hair are this color. It wouldn't matter that my father was an earl or that my husband is a marquess and future duke. They would only see the part of me that's my mother. The part that will never be good enough." Charlotte willed the tears not to fall.

"I have never lived my life to satisfy those in Society or

elsewhere and I never will. I love you and everything that makes you who you are. And for that I will forever be grateful to your mother."

"Oh Alex, you say that now but you don't know what the future holds. They have always accepted you even when your father did not."

"Will you stop loving me?" he asked.

Startled, Charlotte responded without thought. "Of course not."

"Then why do you think I'll stop loving you should things get hard or unpleasant or scandal falls down on our house? Do I appear to be a man lacking in character? A man weak of mind as well as spine?"

"No, you are a good man. You are the best man. But can anyone be sure unless one's love is truly tested? Maybe I'm selfish, but we are finally together after five years and I simply don't want to risk losing you again. But I fear I shall in any case."

The person who'd written the letter was still out there. That she was sure of.

Alex's face was a myriad of emotions: frustration, anguish and love. He studied her a long time before saying in as defeated tone as she'd ever heard, "Charlotte, if you do not know me well enough by now, then I truly did lose you five years ago. If I don't have your trust in this, then we have nothing."

He remained there long enough for his words to settle in and drag her under like quicksand. He then turned and strode from the room, leaving her standing alone and numb. Moments later, she heard the hollow echo of his footsteps as he ascended the stairs.

Shaken, Charlotte made her way to a nearby chair and sat down hard. She pressed her hand over her heart.

Five years ago she'd crossed the Atlantic to America alone yet she'd never felt as alone as she felt at that moment.

Chapter Twenty-Two

After everything they'd been through, she still didn't love him enough to fully trust him.

The pain of it twisted his insides. Alex remembered the look in her eyes, the wrenching sadness in her face. He was no longer the man she once loved. Somehow, somewhere along their journey to this place in their lives, he had morphed into a man who would judge her and find her wanting. A sheep easily herded by rigid strictures of Society.

And there was nothing he could say, nothing he could do that would change her way of thinking.

Alex lay on his bed, his hands laced beneath his head as he stared sightlessly up at the ceiling. He thought of her maid, and his anger toward Conrad burned the length of his throat.

Alex could still hear the note in his former steward's voice when he'd referred to the maid. As if she was of such insignificance, he could hardly comprehend the manner in which Alex had spoken to him.

After pulling himself up by the bootstrap and working like the dickens, Conrad had made something of himself. Alex could spot and tag a man like him on sight. Handsome, ambitious, educated and meticulously good at his job, his eyes were far above his rank. He was always looking for something better, wanting more. And there was nothing wrong with that. It was one of the things Alex had admired about him, why after interviewing five other applicants, he'd chosen him for the position.

But with that ambition, came a cold ruthlessness. Conrad hadn't even believed dallying with the poor girl should have been reason for his dismissal. He'd had the audacity to blame her, a girl who hadn't yet reached her majority, barely the age when girls of his class were out of the school room. She could have little knowledge of men.

. Marriage to her, irrespective of her extraordinary beauty, fell well beyond the realm of possibility. He'd intended to seduce her and hide her away like a dirty secret, making sure no one would ever know.

What he'd done by dismissing the man was to save the girl from certain heartbreak and ruin. He had done the right thing, the just thing. And for this, he'd earned his wife's suspicion and distrust.

Alex angled his head to stare at the door connecting their rooms. What he wanted more than anything was to go to her, climb into her bed and slide into her. That is when all the rules and expectations of Society faded away and the only thing that mattered was the pleasure they found in each other. Just thinking about what it felt like when he thrust into her, her inner walls squeezing him, made him hard.

Alex tamped down his hunger. There was no use punishing himself for he wouldn't find relief for what he hungered for tonight.

She had overreacted. Charlotte knew that, although it had taken hours for her to admit it to herself. She'd allowed her emotions to rule her and her fears to cloud her judgment. Obviously, the knowledge that the person who knew the truth about her had that kind of power over her—over them all—was more than disconcerting, it was terrifying.

And just when she'd allowed herself to breathe more easily, true happiness within her grasp. To have that stripped away, wrenched from her like a buoy from someone adrift at sea.

But Alex wasn't to blame for this. And now she had what she never thought to have with him; a second chance. And if she mucked things up this time, she knew without a doubt, she'd not get another.

With that in mind, Charlotte rose from her bed. Not bothering to light the lamp, she padded across to the connecting door and opened it quietly.

Alex wasn't certain what woke him but he awoke hard as a rock, his cock stiff and already aching. This wasn't extraordinary or a new thing but the intensity of it was. Then he felt the soft brush of female flesh against his naked chest.

Fully awake and desire buzzing like a drug in his head, he turned to find Charlotte regarding him, her blue eyes hooded, her hair ripples of liquid gold on his pillow. Slowly, she ran her tongue along her full, pink bottom lip.

"I missed you in my bed." Her voice was all throaty seduction.

He took in her muslin white nightdress, translucent enough to render it inconsequential and wholly superfluous. Her nipples pushed impudently against the material as if begging to be feasted upon.

Saliva pooled in his mouth as lust spread through his body like liquid fire. "Then why are you wearing anything at all?" he asked in a desire-laden voice.

A siren's smile tipped the corners of her mouth. As she pulled herself up to a seated position, her thigh made startling, lust-inducing contact with his aching cock. Without the slightest hesitation, she yanked the garment over her head and then tossed it blithely on the floor beside the bed.

Hunger was practically consuming his insides. Her nipples were pointing directly at his mouth.

"I want you." And in a bold move, she ran her hand down his chest, her fingernails scoring the hot skin of his lower stomach.

His ribs jumped as she curled her slender hand around his erection. A breath hissed from his throat and ended in a drawn-out groan.

"Damn, Char." He fell back on the bed, pleasure making him weak and needy and demanding. "Do it harder."

Her clasp tightened on him and her hand worked him faster. Alex was certain he was going to explode. The sight of her dainty hand wrapped around him, pleasuring him, sent all the blood rushing from his head to his cock.

"You always take such care in pleasing me. Well I want to pleasure you tonight." Even as she spoke in that husky murmur, she didn't remove her gaze from his cock.

Alex's hips fell and rose under the urgent sweep of her hand. Blood roared in his ears.

Then she did something so shocking, he lost a foothold on reality. Bending her head, she swirled her tongue around the head of his cock. Had he the capacity to speak, he would have praised her but her tongue on him had left him without even the ability to think and his breathing was reduced to pants and groans.

"Ummm." He was officially incoherent.

Staring up at him through slumberous eyes, she enclosed the head of his erection in her mouth. His hips jerked clean off the bed. She smiled but didn't release him from her wet grip.

Pleasured seared him. But as good as it felt, this time he wanted to come inside her. Before he could explode, he hauled her up and flipped her onto her back. A startled gasp escaped her lips as he propped her leg over his shoulder, leaving her open to him.

Her desire glistened on the pink folds of her sex. He tested her readiness with a blunt probe. She was tight and wet, her body prepared for what she'd started.

Barely open, her blue eyes glazed with desire as she stared helplessly up at him. "Alex." His name came out on a breathy sigh, full of need and yearning.

Grasping his throbbing erection in his hand, he slowly pushed his way inside.

She closed around him, her feminine walls squeezing him. He halted midway home, the pleasure so acute he feared he'd spend himself before he could satisfy her.

"Alex." This time his name sounded something close to an urgent wail. She clenched him harder, tighter.

He gritted his teeth and then bit the inside of his mouth in an attempt to hold off his coming release. The last time he'd failed to bring a woman to completion during intercourse, he'd been all of seventeen and drunk on whiskey and rum.

Going slow may have seemed an achievable goal seconds ago, but it was clear he lacked the control to follow through. Thrusting hard, he buried himself to the hilt.

Her breasts bounced, her hips arched and her eyes fluttered closed as a gasp escaped her lips. He wanted to be gentle with her but his body had a mind of its own, immediately setting a brisk, urgent pace.

Her leg was malleable in his hand as he began thrusting, pumping into her with enough vigor to force her passion-glazed eyes open, and then pulling out so far only the tip of his cock remained inside her and she moaned in protest.

He may have made it another minute or two if she hadn't thrown back her head, lifted her hips as he buried himself deep in her and clutched his buttocks possessively.

The touch of her hands and the sight of him plunging inside her set him off like a rocket. The climb to the ultimate release was the most excruciating he'd ever had. And the explosion, when it came, ripped through him with such force his mind went blank.

But a part of him must have regained consciousness because he felt the moment her orgasm took her. She pulsated around him as her body went taut and the sound she emitted walked the fine line between a scream and a moan.

Wrung dry and utterly spent, he flung himself from atop her and onto his back. With his heart pounding loud in his ears and his chest heaving, Alex pulled her damp, limp body snug against him. Even now he couldn't bear to be apart from her.

"Alex," she said, her voice throaty and low, "I'm sorry for being such a goose. I do believe you love me. It's just—"

"Shh, I'm just glad you came to me tonight." His arms tightened about her, pressing her breasts together and forcing them up high on her slender torso. How he had done without this woman in his life for all those years was a mystery. But he had survived. Thank God for that.

Pushing damp strands of her hair back over her shoulder, he pressed a kiss on her neck. "Stay."

And that was all that needed to be said.

Charlotte had given up all say in the wedding, leaving all the planning in the duchess' capable hands. The only thing she wanted was one hundred percent say over who made her wedding gown.

That was when the battle had begun. Her Grace, who was making a grand attempt to be amiable, insisted she use her *modiste* in London. But in this Charlotte remained firm; Miss Foster would make her gown. The duchess finally relented when Charlotte forced Alex to take sides. Of course it had been a sneaky thing to do given Miss Foster had been responsible for saving his life, but Charlotte had learned if she was to win any battles with the duchess, she'd have to be properly armed while utilizing the appropriate ammunition.

Another glance at the clock indicated only two minutes had elapsed since last she'd looked. Miss Foster should have already arrived for their two o'clock appointment and it was now quarter past.

Katie paused to stare out the window of the morning room before resuming her restless pacing. "Where can she be? This isn't like her. She's always been punctual."

"Perhaps something happened to the hackney." Charlotte refused to worry until she'd been given sufficient reason. Carriages broke down and people lost track of time. The world wasn't perfect.

When the next fifteen minutes passed and Miss Foster didn't arrive, that proved reason enough.

"Something must have happened." Katie regarded her with troubled eyes.

"What has happened?"

Charlotte immediately turned at the sound of her husband's

voice. He strode into the room, his handsome face a momentary but welcome distraction to her mounting concern for the *modiste.*

"Miss Foster has not arrived. She was due to meet with Charlotte nearly a half hour ago. Oh, I just know something is wrong."

His easy smile slipped. "She sent no word?"

"No and she would never miss an appointment, not ever," Katie stated with all the conviction of someone who would know.

"Alex, would you mind going to her shop?" Nicholas was due to wake from his nap within the next hour and Charlotte knew her sister was hosting Lady Olivia and Lady Meghan for tea at Rutherford Manor. Neither of them, especially Katie, would rest until they knew all was well with Miss Foster.

"But of course," Alex said.

When Alex arrived at the *modiste's* shop, he was informed Miss Foster had not come into work that day and closing was only a few hours away. Unlike his wife and her sister, the woman in charge didn't appear the least bit concerned.

After securing her address, Alex drove his barouche to her residence.

Now he was concerned.

According to those who'd witnessed him in the throes of his near deadly fever, Miss Foster had saved his life. There wasn't much he wouldn't do for her. But to say they shared a close acquaintance would have been a lie. What he'd discerned from several conversations with her was that she was intelligent, ambitious and had a good head for money. A woman like that did not miss a scheduled appointment with a wealthy client.

He pulled up in front of her home and observed the narrow, brown-bricked structure. It was actually much nicer than he expected.

Alex leapt from his seat and onto the curb. Two wooden steps led to the front door where a worn, brown welcome mat marked the door's threshold.

"Miss Foster, it's Lord Avondale." Alex announced himself as he knocked on the door. He didn't want to frighten her.

Seconds ticked by. The door remained closed and silence reigned inside. Alex knocked again, this time louder and with more urgency.

"Miss Foster, it is Lord Avondale." No doubt, within hours his visit would be the talk of the town.

From within, he heard the squeaking of hinges as a door opened and then the shuffle of feet along hollow floors.

"Lord Avondale?" A weak cough followed the question.

"Yes, Miss Foster. My sister-in-law and wife sent me," he explained.

Alex heard the lock turn and then slowly the door opened. Miss Foster, wearing something that resembled a dressing robe, stood stooped in the doorway. Shocked by her drawn face and red-rimmed eyes, Alex swiftly entered the house and closed the door. It was colder in the house than the temperature outside. And the scent of sickness hung heavy in the air.

"You are ill."

A harsh cough wracked her slender frame as she held her hand over her mouth. When the coughing finally ceased, she said, "Do beg my pardon, my lord, but I forgot the appointment with the marchioness." *This* she appeared distressed over when she could hardly stand up straight and her every fourth word ended in a coughing fit.

Alex dismissed her apology with a negligent wave of his hand and took her gently by the elbow and started down the hall. "Never mind that, you should be in bed." Which was undoubtedly where she was before he came pounding on her door.

"This will pass. It always does." Her voice sounded as if talking required considerable effort.

"Have you seen a physician?" he asked. They passed a tiny parlor on one side and a dining room on the other. As Alex had guessed, both fireplaces in the rooms were unlit. Her bed chamber was probably in the back, as in most houses constructed like this.

Miss Foster's face was wan, her skin flushed with fever. Although she'd said she was fine, she was now leaning more heavily on his arm as if she welcomed the support. "I have all the herbs I need to take care of this cough," she replied.

They reached her bed chamber. Alex saw a sturdy-looking bed through the open door.

"Just because you managed to cure my hide, doesn't mean you do not need the attentions of a physician. I shall send for mine."

Another bout of coughing. "Please, my lord, that is not necessary," she protested once she managed to speak again. Her pallor frightened him.

"Come now, you must rest." She barely weighed a thing he noted as he helped her into bed. "I will also send a maid." The woman needed care.

Wearily, Miss Foster slid onto her bed, dressing robe and all. He shouldn't be alone with her in her personal chamber but that couldn't be helped, the woman had no one. She was mumbling something as her eyes fluttered closed.

Alex regarded her and the stirrings of compassion in his chest grew to encompass him entirely. He may have helped give her a better life than her station dictated she'd otherwise have had, but her life was by no means easy.

Far from it.

Despite the fairly decent living she made with her shop, most doors would never be open to her. A shop she could not even own openly. On the other hand, while slavery had been abolished since 1833, the enforcement of the abhorrent practice was sadly lacking in many areas of the country. She was certainly better off playing the assistant at her own store than toiling in someone else's kitchens.

Alex glanced around her room. It was a large space in comparison to the other rooms in the house, but it was compact and efficient. A lone brush sat on a vanity that looked as if it had seen better days. The rest of the furniture—a wood chest of drawers and a bedside table—looked worn but solid. Everything neat as a pin save the bed itself, whose lumpy mattress was covered by sheets thin and colorless.

On the floor behind him sat a portrait perched against the wall as if waiting to be hung. Initially, he'd given it a cursory glance, skimming over it before its familiarity struck him hard enough to send his gaze darting back to it and his mind reeling.

His gaze instantly swung to Miss Foster, whose eyes were now open and staring at him with trepidation. It was as if the realization of the portrait's presence had come too late.

With a sharp look back at the painting, Alex took in the two young girls who were the subjects—mirror images of each other. They appeared to be about five years and were simply dressed, their frocks plain and unadorned. The year at the bottom of the portrait indicated it had been painted in 1845. One very similar to this hung in the picture gallery at Rutherford Manor.

His gaze snapped back to Miss Foster, who clutched her counterpane up to her chin. There was only one question of which he required an answer.

"Why do you have a portrait of my wife and her sister?"

Chapter Twenty-Three

She was pregnant.

Having gone through it before, Charlotte recognized the signs: dizzy spells, nausea that could appear at any hour and the nearly crippling lethargy that sometimes made it hard to keep her eyes open long enough to get through the supper meal.

After emptying the contents of her stomach in the chamber pot, Charlotte hurried to the dressing room to rid herself of the evidence before the maid arrived to clean the room.

"Charlotte, I thought you might like to go riding with Nicholas and...."

Startled, her head whipped around to observe her husband, clad in his riding clothes and gloves in hand, standing in the opening that separated the sitting room from the sleeping area. He'd entered the room so quietly, she hadn't heard him.

His gaze darted to the chamber pot clutched in her hand. "Are you not feeling well?" His brow furrowed in concern as he immediately approached.

Charlotte shook her head, smiling up at him weakly. "It would appear the fish from last night didn't sit well with me. Just a small case of stomach illness. Nothing to concern yourself about."

"Are you certain?" His hand skimmed the bare length of her upper arm lovingly. But if one went by his expression, it didn't appear as if her assurance had eased his mind.

"Yes, I am quite certain. Now, I insist you go. Nicholas will be waiting. I shall come riding with you another day." Of all the mornings for him to come to her room. His return could not have been more ill-timed.

"Truly, Alex, I shall be fine," she urged when he hesitated.

In silence, he stared down at her, his gaze probing, questioning. Then with a heavy sigh, he leaned in and placed a tender kiss on her forehead. "If you insist. But *I insist* you rest today and eat properly. I shall check on you when I return."

Charlotte laughed softly. "I shan't be in bed because I am not ill. Now *go*."

After he exited the room, Charlotte sagged against the wall, chamber pot still in hand. She should have told him. But the unrelenting fear that she and Katie would be exposed made it difficult to completely enjoy the prospect of another child. Indeed, she found it difficult to look forward when it seemed she would always be looking over her shoulder. Waiting for the day her world would come tumbling down around her.

The irony did not escape her that history was repeating itself. She was practically in the same situation as she had been five years before; pregnant and about to marry the man she loved most in the world and facing a future in peril, fraught with so much uncertainty. This time, however, there'd be no running. This time she'd have to brave the storm head-on if she must. Conquer the weakness inside her that had sent her running the last time she'd been tested.

Would it truly be so bad if people were to discover?

Charlotte laughed to herself. It would probably be far worse. If they'd had trouble accepting her and Katie when they'd been thought to be the by-blow of an earl, they would find them far more objectionable were they to discover they had a slave's blood flowing in their veins. There'd be no magic wand to turn the men and women in Society into fairy godmothers and heroic knights. But this was the hand she'd been dealt and this time she had no choice but to join the game…and win.

She couldn't pretend it would be easy for any of them. Her husband, her children, her family. But the person it would undoubtedly affect the most was her sister. Her marriage prospects, which by Katie's own admission, hadn't been altogether bright to start, would be all but nonexistent.

Emotion burned her throat as she laid her hand on the flat of her stomach. The idea that her sister would never experience this, a baby and a husband she loved more than any other, pained her beyond comprehension.

There had to be something they could do—she could do.

An hour later, Charlotte sat in the morning room of her brother's home. Her sister had met her impromptu call with uncustomary reserve—or perhaps it was despair, Charlotte found it hard to tell.

The truth was, Katie had been withdrawn of late, her smiles now had to be wrestled from her. And in the rare times she gave them, they hadn't quite reached her eyes. Charlotte wondered if Lucas was the cause of her overall melancholy for as she recalled, Charlotte had noted the change in her shortly after his return to America.

"I am going to have another child," Charlotte announced.

For the first time in weeks, her sister's face lit with genuine happiness.

Charlotte rose to her feet as her sister rushed toward her. "Oh Lottie, I am thrilled for you," she said, embracing her warmly. "Does Alex know?"

"No, I haven't told him yet."

"What is it? Are you not pleased?" Katie knew her so well.

With a rueful shake of her head, Charlotte resumed her seat. Her sister immediately came down beside her on the settee.

"Of course I am happy, it's just hard to be truly happy with *this* threat looming over us. I keep thinking what if this person does expose us? What will happen to us?"

"Oh dearest, you cannot let that ruin things for you," Katie said, taking Charlotte's hands in hers.

"But surely the thought has crossed your mind?" Charlotte was certain that had been at least partially responsible for her sister's unhappiness.

"Lottie, it happened five years ago. And nothing was ever said, isn't that the most important part? I doubt very much if whoever wrote the letter will bother with us again." She spoke with such conviction, Charlotte desperately wanted to believe her. But if either of them believed that, there was also a real possibility pigs would fly.

"Why? Because now I am a marchioness and a future duchess? Don't you see, it's all the more reason for the person to expose us."

"Charlotte, we have nothing to be ashamed of," Katie said stubbornly.

What sort of world did her sister think they moved in? Women in their brother's set would cut another for wearing the wrong clothes, marrying the wrong sort of man. She and her sister would be lucky if they were only cut and not subjected to Society's own burning of the witches.

"They won't see it that way. You know that."

Katie glanced away briefly and then lowered her gaze. She couldn't deny it.

Then with startling abruptness, her head snapped up and her eyes were the size of quarter pennies. "You don't intend to flee again, do you?" Her sister's expression had gone from downcast to anxious and wary.

"Oh no, of course not. I would not do such a thing again," Charlotte said, giving her sister's hands a reassuring squeeze. "Alex acts as if we could withstand anything. But I guess that's what comes from living a life of privilege. Most think they are invincible, that nothing can touch them, no bit of talk can bring them crashing to their knees. I wish I had his confidence but as you can attest, we both know what it's like to live life standing on the outside."

"I don't believe Alex doesn't believe anything can touch him, I think the truth is what people think doesn't matter to him more than you and Nicholas."

Charlotte's heart swelled at Katie's words. "I *do* love him." He would stand by her come hell or high water. That spoke everything of his feelings for her.

"I know Alex will do everything in his power to protect us, as will James move heaven and earth to shield his family. But neither can adequately protect you, therefore you are who I'm most concerned for. What this kind of revelation would do to you. My greatest wish is that you were married to a man—a good man, a strong man—who'd stand by your side no matter the scandal."

As soon as the words were out, Charlotte wanted to call them back. Katie's face paled and a look of hurt flashed in her eyes.

"Darling, I'm sorry."

"You have nothing for which to apologize. You merely spoke the truth." Charlotte could tell she was being brave, her posture straight, her chin up.

"Is it Lucas? Is he the reason you've been cast down lately?" There hadn't been a day she hadn't suffered the guilt of sending him away when she knew of their growing attachment. But he'd all but admitted he hadn't been about marriage. She'd saved her sister the pain of heartbreak in the long run. Or so she told herself whenever she saw Katie moping about.

Her sister shook her head with more vigor than the question warranted. "Lottie, I barely knew him." She stuttered a bit before saying, "I admit I found him charming for an American, but my feelings went no deeper. I mean truly, he lives in America and I am here. There was no future in it even if my feelings fell along those lines—which of course they do not."

Charlotte wondered what Gertrude in *Shakepeare's* Hamlet would have thought of her sister's protests, which were a little too emphatic to strike a believable note. But Katie had her pride and she'd leave her to it. She'd not bring up the subject of Lucas again.

When Alex had wheedled the truth from Miss Foster, the woman had begged him not to tell Charlotte and Catherine. He'd finally relented but only on the condition that *she* be the one to tell them. This was a secret he refused to keep from his wife. She and her sister had a right to know more than anyone.

Miss Foster had promised to do so when she was up and about. Well that had been a week ago and Miss Foster had been declared fit enough to return to work on the morrow. She was to come to the house the same afternoon.

His most pressing concern was his wife. She had become withdrawn over the last two weeks. Over a month ago, they'd begun to take breakfast together in the mornings. Now, it appeared she deliberately waited until he and Nicholas left to go riding before she came down for hers.

When he searched his brain to determine what had changed, he could think of nothing. If not for her recent mood shift, he'd have sworn things could not have been better between them. In bed she was still as passionate and out of bed, still as in want of his company as she'd ever been.

Could she be missing America? It had been her home these last five years. Or perhaps she missed her friends—

Beaumont!

Could it be? Alex thought back to when he'd first noticed signs of her withdrawal. It had been shortly after the bounder's departure. Alex was sure of it.

But that couldn't be it. He believed Charlotte when she said she hadn't had that sort of relationship with the man. Although, Alex couldn't deny that she cared for Beaumont. She'd said it often enough for her words to still ring in his ears.

And despite the fact she'd sent Beaumont away for him, Alex couldn't bear to think that the man's absence had such a dispiriting effect on her. Several times when speaking with her, he turned to catch her staring off in the distance, her mind so obviously preoccupied, he'd had to repeat himself.

Had she been thinking of Beaumont?

That evening as Alex watched her push her food around her plate like a game of ring-a-ring a rosie, he debated how to approach the matter. How to ask her without starting a row. He decided he wouldn't mention the man directly.

"What is the matter? You appear distracted and you have hardly eaten more than two bites of your meal."

Charlotte halted and lowered the same fork she'd been using to push the roast pork around the white porcelain plate. "I ate a small meal earlier so I fear it's spoiled my appetite." She laughed lightly but the hollowness of the sound confirmed his fears; something was wrong. And once again, she refused to share it with him.

His expression must have conveyed his doubt for her lips curved in another forced smile. "Do not worry yourself over me, I'm simply tired is what it is. What I need more than anything is more sleep."

Liar. What ailed her had nothing to do with lack of sleep. It was much more heartfelt than that. He could see it in her eyes. As much as she tried to hide it, it was obvious she was suffering.

Alex hadn't felt this helpless since…the last time she'd left him.

That night in bed, she was more passionate than usual, clinging to him as if she couldn't get enough. When his release came, the explosion seemed to go on forever, not abating until the tremors of the aftermath shook his body. Afterward, he held her tight in his arms, hoping that spent and limp in the haze of passion, she would confide in him. He wanted to know, even if the truth proved painful.

Instead, she reached up and pressed a kiss on his lips, her touch both sweet and sensual as her tongue tangled briefly with his. Then quite abruptly, she'd tucked herself tightly against him, damp skin against damp skin and promptly fell into a deep sleep.

Her lovemaking had been needy and tinged with a sort of desperateness one may feel if they were making love to their lover for the final time.

A sense of foreboding swamped him and crept under his skin. Something unpleasant loomed in the horizon and he felt helpless to do anything to prevent it.

❖

The wedding was four weeks away and the London Season was in full swing. In two weeks they would make the trip into town. Charlotte wasn't looking forward to it. Alex had become withdrawn and her early pregnancy symptoms had not yet abated; the chamber pot now her closest friend.

Nicholas, cheerful and full of energy, was the one truly bright spot in her life. Today Jillian had taken him, as she tended to do with regular frequency, to Rutherford Manor to visit with his cousins. Charlotte was expecting Miss Foster in just fifteen minutes. The fitting had had to be postponed due to the *modiste's* illness. Alex had assured her Miss Foster had fully recovered. He'd had his own physician tend to her.

Charlotte was making her way to the morning room when Alex appeared in the entrance hall. She hadn't expected him home for another half hour, his daily rides usually at least an hour in duration.

"Alex, that was—" Her voice broke at the sight of her sister and Miss Foster trailing not far behind him. Katie stared at her wary-eyed, looking about the place as though she'd never been there before, which was absurd. Miss Foster wore a simple tan chambric dress under a fringed shawl and clutched a handful of swatches. But she looked as if her head was next up for the guillotine, not as if there to take final measurements for the wedding gown.

What on earth was going on?

"Shall we repair to the morning room?" With a sweep of his hand, Alex gestured to the open door.

Charlotte's gaze flitted from Katie to Miss Foster and back. She then regarded her husband. "Alex, what is this all about?" Something was definitely awry.

"You will discover soon enough," he said cryptically, taking her elbow and leading her to the room.

"Yes, I would certainly like to know what this is all about," Katie echoed as she preceded them in. Miss Foster complied without a word, the dread on her face becoming more pronounced with every passing second.

Once they were all in the room, Alex closed the door, then turned and addressed the *modiste*.

"Miss Foster has something to tell you."

Katie's eyebrows dove together furrowing her smooth brow. For Charlotte, the sense of unease pricking at her became a full-fledged stab. She regarded Miss Foster intently, noting the nervous manner in which she rubbed her gloved hands against her sides and how she couldn't seem to hold her gaze nor anyone else's.

"Miss Catherine, milady, if I had my way, you would never learn of this. I stand here at the insistence of Lord Avondale."

Thoughts of the letter instantly came to mind. Charlotte's disquiet grew. What she'd heard thus far had all the telltale signs of a confession.

"I knew Mrs. Henley," Miss Foster continued in a soft, shaky voice. "Fact is, she helped raise me, she did."

Charlotte felt the breath leave her body and heard her sister gasp.

Oh dear Lord. Oh dear Lord.

Dazed, Charlotte studied the woman, this time with the scrutiny of a magnifying glass. She noted the high yellow tone of her skin—so much lighter in color than most of the mulattos she'd seen in America. High cheekbones, full lips and a nose not quite as slender as hers and Katie's clearly spoke of her heritage. Her eyes, however, were a clear, distinct green and faintly tipped at the corners. The shape of the *modiste's* eyes were as familiar as the perfect oval of her face. Charlotte had seen it in the mirror and in her sister these last twenty-four years.

That is when the truth crashed down on her with enough force to have her reaching for the support of something. She immediately felt the solid warmth of her husband's arm.

"I am here," he whispered gently. Charlotte could see in his eyes that he knew.

"Are you our mother?" In a barely audible voice, Katie asked the question before Charlotte could.

With a shake of her head, Miss Foster managed to stupefy her once more. "No, I am not your mother," she whispered, looking first at Katie and then shifting her gaze to her. "I am your mother's younger sister," she concluded, succeeding in jolting her all over again.

If she did not sit down, Charlotte feared she would find herself a crumpled mess of yellow muslin on the rug. As if sensing the effort it was taking her to remain upright, Alex led her to the closest chair and then sat down beside her, his strong arm wrapped around her shoulders.

Worried, Charlotte glanced at Katie, to see her standing motionless, staring at the woman with wide eyes, her hands clutching her waist as if she was warding off blows.

Shrugging Alex's hands from her, Charlotte hurriedly went to her and pulled her sister's trembling frame into her arms.

An eternity elapsed. Alex rose to his feet, his worried gaze settling on both her and Katie. Miss Foster stood, head bent, eyes downcast, tears tracking their way down cheeks void of color.

"Is our mother dead?" Charlotte had the presence of mind to ask.

Miss Foster's head jerked up. "Oh yes. 'Tis the only way she'd have left you. The two of you meant the world tuh her. She'd have done anything for you," her aunt was quick to reply.

"When our father cast her from the house, your mama went to your father for help. He set her up in a small house and I visited her there until her death. After she died, I wanted to take you, but I was too young—only thirteen years at the time. At first, I didn't know what'd become of you girls. It took Mrs. Henley a whole year tuh find out you were being cared for by two women in Kettering. When she tole me, I left my position and moved there. I found a job working for a dressmaker and became friendly with Mrs. Turner, the woman in charge of your care. I sometimes offered her my sewing services free of charge. I was able to see you on the days I delivered her garments."

At this point, she and Katie slowly made their way to the sofa positioned in front of Miss Foster and sank onto its cushioned seat. That appeared to be the cue for the woman to sit in the chair behind her and clasp trembling hands on her lap. She boldly held their gazes, but Charlotte could see by the large expanse of whites in her eyes, what it was costing her.

"I didn't know where you were until Mrs. Henley found out you was at the school. I could only afford to move to Chesterfield, there being no work for me in a place like Bamford. But I would try to visit 'bout three or four times a year. I jus wanted tuh make sure you were getting on well, that they were treating you right."

"So you knew who we were when we came to live with our brother?" Charlotte asked, her suspicions rearing up again and coming full circle. She simply could not bear it if all this time it had been her own aunt responsible for the misery of the last five years.

Miss Foster affirmed her question with a nod. "Mrs. Henley tole me. She loved me and your mother like we was hers. She had no children of her own and was there when both me and your mama was born. She said when our mama was dying, she promised her she'd take care of us. And she did. She never left us."

Mrs. Henley. She had been utterly devoted to them just as she'd said. Charlotte wished she had gotten to know her better. Wished she could have stayed.

"Did you tell anyone about us?" Charlotte asked, approaching her suspicions cautiously.

With tight lips and guileless eyes, Miss Foster shook her head and Charlotte believed her. But that didn't mean she hadn't threatened to expose them. Of course it made no sense why she would do such a thing but who else could it have been?

"Did you send me a letter threatening to expose the truth about us if I married Lord Avondale?"

Miss Foster's eyes widened in horror. "Oh dear Lord, no!"

Although it appeared her mortified reaction was genuine, Charlotte couldn't be certain she was in fact telling the truth. It didn't matter that she desperately wanted to believe her, wanted to know that all their life, while they'd felt unloved and unwanted, there had been someone—two people—who had always loved them, looked out for them.

"But—"

"She didn't send the letter." Katie's voice was like a dash of cold in the discussion, for until then, she hadn't spoken a word. Unfortunately, her sister had a weak spot for the woman and couldn't be counted upon to remain objective.

"Darling, you cannot know—"

"I do know." There was such conviction in her voice, Charlotte turned to her.

"How? How can you possibly know for certain?"

Katie closed her eyes tight but the tears squeezed through. She averted her face and came slowly to her feet.

"Because I wrote the letter." Katie whispered the barely audible words but they rang out as loudly as the report of a rifle and caused just as much destruction.

Chapter Twenty-Four

For a brief moment, the room tilted wildly as a wave of dizziness came over her. When her vision righted itself, her sister was staring at her with wide, guilt-stricken eyes, a river of tears running down her face. With her hands fisted tightly at her sides, Katie backed away from her slowly, one wobbly step at a time.

The truth rendered Charlotte mute.

No, a plaintive voice in her head cried. She could not have possibly heard correctly.

Alex bolted to his feet and uttered one single epithet that had Katie stumbling back as if she'd feared he would physically accost her. Charlotte knew he would not but he looked as close to violent as she'd ever seen him with his jaw tight, his gaze narrowed and his lips peeled back from his teeth.

Charlotte lifted pleading eyes to her sister, willing her to tell her it wasn't true. "You?" The word caught in her throat, so difficult was it to speak.

Sobbing and now nearly doubled over, her sister moaned, "Lottie, I am sorry. Lottie, I am so sorry." Her heart-wrenching apology was nearly incoherent.

"B-but why?" None of this made sense. Katie adored Alex.

Oh dear Lord, perhaps she had feelings for him? The thought was intolerable.

As if reading Charlotte's mind by the horrified look on her face, her sister shook her head furiously. "I know what you're thinking but it was nothing like that."

Katie glanced at Alex, who watched her with cold eyes. "I adore Alex but he's always been like a brother to me."

Had her sister loved him, although it would have been excruciatingly painful, it would have made sense.

Dazed, Charlotte could only shake her head from side to side. "Then why?"

Supported heavily by the desk behind her, Katie tried to hold back another sob but it broke forth and shook her frame. "I didn't want you to marry Alex. I didn't want you to leave me. That's why I sent the letter. I knew you'd never go through with it if you thought it would ruin everything." Her chest rose sharply as she inhaled a deep breath. "Now you know what a horrible, terrible person I am."

Memories came flittering back, scenes of the past. Her sister rolling her eyes when she'd gone on and on to her about Alex. Charlotte remembered how desperately she'd tried to discourage her, assuring her Alex would never think of her in *that* way. That had been the reason Charlotte had stopped confiding her feelings about him to her.

"But I never meant that you should leave and not come back. Oh God, Lottie, when I read your note, I wanted to die. What I did, the way I acted so utterly selfish and I couldn't take it back. You don't know how much I wanted to find you, write to you and tell you it was safe to come home. But you refused to tell me where you were."

It was obvious guilt had been her sister's constant companion over the years. Her eyes looked hollow and haunted. Pained. Yet nothing could absolve her of the pain she'd caused.

"I cannot believe you would do something so cruel."

Katie's head hung low in shame. Another sob wracked her body. "Lottie, I do not know what to say except that I am so very, very sorry. I would beg your forgiveness if I thought I had the right to ask for it, but I don't because what I did cannot be forgiven. I can only pray that one day you won't think as ill of me as you do now."

It became all too much to take in. Charlotte rose from the sofa, her hands and legs trembling. If she did not get out of there that very moment, she feared she'd do something rash. Betrayal wrecked her from inside to out. The foundation of the things she'd been so certain of before in her life had been rocked with such force, the ground felt as solid to her as quicksand.

The one person she'd loved all her life, depended upon and trusted had done the unthinkable. It was all too much.

"I must go." Sightlessly, Charlotte started toward the drawing room entrance.

Alex's arms closed around her as he pulled her tight against his side. Charlotte allowed herself to lean on him, breathe in his masculine scent and draw strength from his support.

"Lottie." It was a tear-choked plea. If not for forgiveness, Charlotte couldn't fathom a guess. Well Katie would not get either from her—at least not now. Everything was too fresh and her wounds too raw.

Angling her head in her sister's direction, she briefly met Katie's tear-soaked, wounded gaze. She slowly shook her head. "I can't."

Alex's initial burst of anger had been explosive and blinding. But it eventually passed once he looked at his sister-in-law's face; the anguish, the torment, the guilt. She was suffering a thousand deaths, her arms wrapped tightly about her waist and weeping even harder than when Charlotte had left five years ago.

"Watch her," he said tersely, directing his attention to a bewildered-looking Miss Foster.

Without waiting for a reply, he led Charlotte from the room and up to her bed chamber. She was leaning heavily on him but didn't speak. Her sister's revelation had shaken her to her core that much was obvious.

He wanted nothing more than to absorb her pain and wipe the disillusionment from her eyes.

At her door, she peered up at him, glassy-eyed and a tear hovering on the tip of her lashes. "Please, I would like to be alone." Her voice was choked with emotion.

Alex didn't want to leave her, but she deserved time to

herself. She—they—had been dealt a terrific blow, worse when the betrayal came at the hands of her twin.

"I shall be here," he promised solemnly and it was a promise he meant to keep forever.

After she entered the room and closed the door behind her, Alex wasted no time returning to the morning room where he found Miss Foster holding a weeping Catherine in her arms.

"Miss Foster, I shall have my driver take you home," he said. Right now he needed to speak to his sister-in-law.

Alex thought he saw Catherine's arms tighten around the woman's neck before loosening and then slowly dropping to her sides.

Miss Foster's gaze darted between them, her expression uncertain.

Aware he probably appeared grim and forbidding, he kept his voice even and calm. "I would like to speak with Catherine."

"Yes, of course, milord." She gave Catherine's trembling shoulders a reassuring pat and then made her way to the footman awaiting her by the door, his posture military erect.

Seconds later, the click of the door indicated they were alone.

Alex allowed the silence to stretch and lengthen until Catherine raised her head to peer at him. He trapped and held her gaze. She didn't look away.

"Did you dislike me so much?" he asked softly.

"No, Alex, that wasn't it at all. I did like you. I wasn't lying about that. I liked you very much, it was just that…."

"Just that what?" he prompted.

"She always preferred you. The minute she met you, you were all she thought about. It was as if I was no longer as important to her. All our lives, it was just the two of us, and then she met you."

Jealousy. All this time her sister had been jealous of him and he hadn't known it, hadn't once guessed the truth. "Catherine, she loves you. I could never, nor would I ever want to change that."

A laugh that sounded more like a sob escaped her lips. "I know that. I knew I'd made a big mistake the day of the wedding but by then it was too late. I tried to find her and tell her she had nothing to fear. But she had already gone. I never meant for her to go. I don't even know I actually wanted to prevent her from marrying you forever. I thought the letter would just give me more time with her before you married her and moved away."

Alex found the whole thing hard to fathom. Could not believe Catherine would have done such a thing. And even worse, he had a hard time wrapping his head around the fact that he'd been the cause.

"Pl-please don't hate me," she begged with big, sorrowful eyes. "I know I deserve it, but I don't think I could bear it if you hated me."

Only a man with a heart of stone and ice running through his veins would not be moved by her entreaty. And he wanted to be angry at her for she deserved it more than his wife. But he'd spent five years with bitterness and anger flowing more easily through him than the blood in his veins. He was tired of being angry. More than anything, all he wanted to do was to enjoy his life with Charlotte and their son—and any more children they'd be blessed with.

He sighed heavily and reached for her, pulling her into his arms. Her body trembled as she laid her cheek on his chest and her arms circled his torso.

"As much as I hate what you did, I could never hate you, Catherine. You were young and scared of losing her. That I understand for I've experienced it a time or two myself."

A sob broke from her lips. It was quickly followed by a hiccup. Alex's mouth curved up at one end.

"Does that mean you have forgiven her?" she asked, looking up at him.

Her question was so unexpected, Alex took a moment to respond. Had he forgiven Charlotte? If anyone had asked him the question the week before, his answer would have been an unequivocal yes. After all, they'd been living as man and wife in the truest sense.

But as he had watched her crumple before him a short time ago, watched as she'd experienced the same sense of betrayal he himself had felt, he realized he hadn't—not fully. It had only been when he'd heard Miss Foster explain why she'd stayed away, had never told her nieces who she was that he truly understood what Charlotte must have been going through when faced with the threat of exposure.

Her aunt had never come forward to claim them, and selfish bastard that he was, he thanked God she hadn't. He could never fault the woman for the sacrifice she'd made that had brought Charlotte into his life.

Ironically, Charlotte had been forced to make a similar choice and she, like her aunt, had chosen to sacrifice her happiness to spare those she loved pain.

"Yes, I have forgiven her," he replied softly, knowing with all certainty he truly had. "She was young and scared just as you were."

Catherine looked relieved. A moment later, she frowned. "I don't think Charlotte will ever forgive me."

"She will in time."

She drew herself from his arms and took a step back, her eyes haunted. "I don't know. What I did has cost you both so much."

"But we've been given another chance and our love is stronger for what we've gone through."

Tears filled Catherine's eyes. For several seconds she merely stared at him, a myriad of emotions flitting across her face. When she spoke, her voice was choked. "Lottie could not have chosen a better man. I envy her that."

"I was wrong," Charlotte blurted the moment Alex stepped into her bed chamber.

Her statement pulled him up short. He halted and angled his head quizzically. "Wrong about what?"

"I should not have left. When I received that letter, I should have come directly to you." And she would always regret that she hadn't.

"I have forgiven you that," he assured her.

"It wasn't that I didn't love you enough to tell you the truth. I don't want you to ever think that. The truth is, I didn't believe you could ever love me enough for the truth not to matter. The way I felt about myself back then, where I stood in the eyes of my brothers, in the eyes of Society, I just couldn't believe I was worthy of your love."

He strode to her where she sat on the edge of the bed, came down beside her and pulled her into his arms in one smooth motion.

"How could I not love you? You were everything I ever wanted in a woman, a wife, a lover and the future mother of my children. When I proposed to you, I had no title and earned a living dabbling in trade. I was the fortunate one."

Charlotte's heart swelled three sizes too big for her chest as she pressed her cheek against the wide breadth of his shoulder. The scent of his Aleppo soap assailed her nostrils and she breathed it in deeply.

"I too wish you had come to me but I understand why you did what you did."

She laid her soft hand against his bristled jaw. "Do you really?"

Alex brought her hand up to his mouth and kissed it gently. He then moved to her lips, taking her mouth in a deep, drugging kiss. His tongue swept her mouth and he probed, licked and sucked. When he had completely mastered her and she was returning his kiss with hungry abandon, already wet and aroused, he pressed one hard kiss to her lips before lifting his head.

"I do." He spoke in a voice husky with desire.

In looking into his gray eyes and hearing the sincerity in his voice, she knew he meant it.

"I don't want to keep looking back at what I—we lost. I'd much rather us live in the present and look forward to what's ahead. I have you and I have my son. That's all I can ask for right now."

Charlotte took his large hand and laid it on her stomach. "And our baby."

Alex went stiff, his eyes instantly widening in shock. He swallowed and stared down at his hand. "You are with child?"

"Yes. I know you said that you didn't—"

"No," he said sharply, halting her before she could finish. "So many of the things I said to you, I said out of pain and anger. But I never truly meant them—not in my heart."

Charlotte cupped his face in her hands. "Oh Alex, I do love you."

Taking one of her hands in his, he placed a tender kiss on the center of her palm. "I love you. Now, I want to see."

"See what?" Charlotte asked with a laugh.

"Remove your dress. I want to see where my child will grow."

"Is that truly the only reason you want me to remove my dress?" she teased.

"Of course. What else could I possibly want with my beautiful, naked wife?" he asked, arching one brow. "But your pregnancy does explain things."

"Really? Pray, what would that be?"

"Why you refused to rise until I left the room. Or why you suddenly weren't in the mood to make love in the mornings but by noon, you were rubbing up against me like a cat in heat."

A blush suffused her cheeks. "I am so happy I'll be sharing this and all future pregnancies with you."

"Yes, and I want a houseful of children with you as I've always done. When I said otherwise, I did so out of spite."

"In my heart, I believe I knew that."

"But in hurting you, I merely succeeded in hurting myself,"

he said solemnly.

"I think I knew that too," she replied with equal solemnity.

"Good," he grunted. "Now remove your dress." His gaze raked over her, already anticipating getting her naked and under him.

Her eyes clouded with desire. "I shall need some help. The buttons..." She gestured to the back of her gown, now all coquettish helplessness.

Alex had her out of her clothes—stripped naked—in less than thirty seconds and out of his own in the ten following.

The only evidence of her pregnancy was the additional fullness of her breasts, and pressing her down onto the bed, Alex made sure he paid special attention to them, circling her nipple with his index finger until it stiffened into a hard nub before drawing it slowly between his lips and sucking.

Charlotte arched beneath him, causing him to groan and smile around her nipple. He loved that he could so easily bring her to this state. Levering himself up onto his elbows, he stared at the flatness of her belly. His child grew there, he mused in wonderment. He covered her warm, pink skin with his hand.

"Mine."

"Yours." She regarded him through half-closed eyes, tilting her hips to encourage his hand to venture lower.

Alex needed no further encouragement, his fingers finding her wet and welcoming. Her legs fell open to his touch as he tested her readiness.

She was ready. And hot.

He was inside her within seconds and groaned at the snug, wet heat. Somewhere in the back of Alex's mind, he knew he should take it slow given her condition. But being inside her felt too good, too right. So while his mind told him to be gentle with her, his body urged him to take her hard and fast. His body won.

And Charlotte wasn't content to merely be on the receiving end of his hard thrusts and deep strokes. No, she gave fully in return, her hips thrusting back with just as much rigor to meet his thrusts dead-on.

The pressure in his cock grew and the pleasure became nigh on intolerable until she shuddered in release beneath him, her sex pulsating around his. An orgasm wracked his body with an intensity that wiped his mind blank of everything but sensation.

The next thing he knew, he was on his back trying to catch his breath. God, had he actually passed out?

"I love you."

Alex turned his head at the throaty declaration. She looked well-loved and sated. Naked and flushed, just the way he liked her—and on her back.

"Not nearly as much as I love you," he replied pulling her to him for a soft, lingering kiss.

Charlotte could have lain like this with him forever, aglow in the aftermath of their exquisite lovemaking. She was certain it couldn't get better than this.

"Catherine is hurting."

Why must he bring that up now? "She hurt me," Charlotte countered.

"She deeply regrets what she did."

"How quickly you are able to forgive her," she groused, only slightly aggravated by the fact.

"That's because I'm not in love with her. Had I felt like she'd ripped my heart from my chest and left me a broken man, believe me I wouldn't be so kind." He tweaked her nipple with his thumb.

She gave a low moan. The surge of heat between her legs was positively shameless. Had he not just pleasured her unconscious?

"You know I cannot remain upset with her forever. Though I can't find it in my heart to forgive her just yet. What she did wa-was so very wrong. I never imagined she'd be capable of something like that."

"I don't imagine she did either," he said, stroking the under curve of her breast.

It was damnably difficult to think when he insisted on touching her like that. Still she angled toward him in hopes of encouraging him more.

Chapter Twenty-Five

Alex sat in the drawing room of his parents' cottage, River Court, and cursed the day he'd listened to his mother. When his father had summoned him, Alex had remembered the promise he'd made to his mother. And since, according to Charlotte, his mother's attitude toward her was ten degrees warmer than civility, he'd acquiesced without a fuss.

But she'd assured him she would be in residence when he arrived. That had been a barefaced lie. The duke was his only parent in attendance. Alex had almost climbed back into the carriage once he realized there'd be no buffer between them as there'd always been in the past.

It had been the look in the duke's eyes that had stopped him. For the first time in his memory, the duke hadn't looked as if he couldn't wait to see the back of him. His neutral expression may very well have been taken for unadulterated giddiness so severe was it usually.

With a tumbler of rum in hand, the duke crossed the dark planked floors to recline in the armchair closest to where Alex sat on the sofa.

"How's the boy?" the duke asked and took a drink from the glass.

"Nicholas is adjusting well."

Pleasantries. This was uncharted territory and Alex wasn't quite certain how to maneuver these unfamiliar roads.

The duke gave a grunt and nodded. "Your cousin will let the matter of your marriage papers die if I give him five thousand pounds."

Alex wasn't the least surprised at his cousin's demand. Henry had always been a money-grasping little worm.

"I hope you don't intend to pay him one shilling."

"If I believed it would save us the ordeal of a public trial and my grandson his future title, I would. But I know my nephew. He'd never be satisfied with that. He'd only come back for more. So I am prepared to do whatever else I must to ensure your marriage is upheld and your son remains your heir. Mr. Graham is a decent chap and very ambitious. I've had him over for supper several times. "

Ah! So his father had befriended the register general, the man in charge of the registration of births, deaths and marriages in England and Wales. That explained why, thus far, there didn't appear to be any problems with his marriage papers. This kind of support from the duke was rarer than a solar eclipse, the last which occurred some thirteen years ago. Alex couldn't remember once in his thirty-four years ever being offered it. But, he reminded himself, this had more to do with his brother than even Nicholas or himself.

Alex shifted in his seat, unaccustomed to going this long in his father's company without anger and animosity overtaking the discussion.

"I pray that also means better treatment of my wife." For her, he'd risk breaking the tenuous cease fire that currently existed between himself and the duke.

However, his father was intent on surprising him on all fronts today, merely grunting before taking another drink of his rum. As it wasn't an out and out refusal, that meant he'd agreed. Had Alex not been sitting, he might have fallen over.

The next ten minutes were the most excruciating Alex had ever experienced. Their conversation went in fits and starts like a rail train that hadn't enough steam to propel it along. They spoke of nothing of consequence: the duke's seat in Yorkshire, how the cost of upkeep on his various properties had almost doubled in the last ten years. As he could find little in the way of adding to the conversation, Alex remained silent much of the time.

Finally, his father, who too appeared fatigued from the effort, rose to his feet to signal the end of the visit.

Relieved, Alex stood. His father stuck out his hand. For a brief moment Alex stared at it, so unexpected a gesture was it. He couldn't remember ever voluntarily touching his father much less shaking his hand. But he did and in two short pumps, the contact was over.

His father's hand wasn't as soft and clammy as he'd always thought it would be.

"Good day, Father," Alex said with a curt nod.

His father nodded in response and Alex started toward the door.

"Next time you come, bring the boy."

"Make sure you have toys for him to play with. He likes trains," Alex tossed over his shoulder as he exited the room.

The following week, Charlotte, unable to sit, stood in her brother's drawing room. She would admit to being nervous—an unheard of occurrence when pertaining to calling on her own twin sister. But they had been at an impasse the past week.

Katie had called upon her three times after sending two letters begging an audience. Charlotte hadn't been prepared to speak with or see her. Her betrayal had more than wounded her, it had crippled her.

But with the wedding two weeks away, she hadn't been able to bear the thought of her marrying with the two of them estranged.

The last word she'd ever use to describe Katie was timorous but that was precisely how she would describe the manner in which her sister entered the drawing room. Anxious and looking as woebegone as a child newly orphaned. She offered a tentative smile as if terrified anything broader would be rejected out of hand.

"Hello, Lottie. I've missed you."

Charlotte felt a pinch in her heart. She hated to see her sister so heartbroken knowing the strife between them was the cause. Which was silly since it was Katie who had set the whole thing in motion.

"I do not want to fight with you. I shall be getting married in two weeks and being away from you for five years is long enough."

As if she'd been thrown a life boat, a relieved smile spread across her sister's face. "I hate it when we aren't speaking."

"I love you dearly, but I'm still angry with you. I don't know when I shall be able to forgive you."

"I understand." Katie spoke softly, glancing down at the floor. "I'm more than a little ashamed of myself and have lived with the guilt and regret since that day. I don't know that I shall ever be able to forgive *myself*."

"Oh Katie." Charlotte's heart softened completely, unable to steel herself against her sister's anguish. She closed the distance between them—literally and figuratively—and hugged her.

"As Alex said, we cannot go back and it won't do us any good to live in the past. Let us move on from that unfortunate time. We were both young and reacted too rashly. I must shoulder at least a portion of the blame. I should never have run or remained gone so long."

"You were doing what you thought best for all of us. I shan't fault you for that and neither should you." Katie had always been her staunchest defender.

"Miss Foster has come by the house twice this week. She's shared many stories about our mother." Charlotte was trying to get her to come around more. She desperately wanted to get to know her better.

"Yes, she told me. I called on her at her shop yesterday. I'm trying to convince her to move in here with us—tell everyone we loved her designs so much, we decided to keep a *modiste* as part of the staff. She simply will not have it. She claims to love her dress shop and her independence too much."

"You know she will never let us claim her."

"I know," Katie replied. "I just wish it didn't have to be this way."

"She is doing what she believes is right for us, which I understand."

Her sister nodded.

A beat passed before a thought suddenly occurred to her. "Katie, I returned to England because Lucas told me you were failing. At one time I thought the person who wrote the letter also fabricated that story to get me home. But if it was you who wrote the letter…."

Her sister lowered her gaze and her cheeks flushed a crimson red. She opened her mouth and a confession emerged in halting tones. Charlotte learned how Katie and Lucas had conspired together to get her to return to England.

"I was extremely fortunate to have met Mr. Beaumont when I did. I was quite terrified that Alex would marry Lady Mary and all would be lost. I had to get you home. I think I would have done anything shy of murder to give you and Alex what I'd selfishly stolen from you. A chance to be together." Katie held her gaze and Charlotte could see the guilt and despair, and the love in her eyes.

"In this instance, I shall forever be grateful for your scheming and interference," Charlotte said softly. She hadn't slept properly those weeks she'd feared she'd lose her sister and had cried until not another tear could be wrung from her. But Charlotte would gladly go through it all again to have the life she presently had. A life with Alex and their son.

Katie blinked rapidly and gave a delicate sniff. "It is the very least I could do. All I want is for you to be happy."

"I want you to be happy too. Oh Katie, I do worry about you," Charlotte admitted, hesitant to broach the subject.

"Do you fear I will be the maiden aunt with no husband or children of my own?" she replied lightly.

"I want you to be happy. The men in Society are obviously blind."

"I have a confession to make."

Charlotte stared fixedly at her sister, a sinking sensation in her stomach. What would she tell her now?

"I actually haven't been the pariah I made myself out to be. I have had my share of suitors but I have done my best—and was very successful at it I might add—in discouraging them." Her sister then listed three eligible lords most mothers would do a jig and kick their heels up to have them courting their daughters, who had courted her.

"But why would you discourage their suit?" Charlotte's mind boggled.

"How could I marry and have a family when I denied you yours because of my childish jealousy? After what I did, I didn't deserve to be happy."

A swell of love so big her heart could hardly contain it flooded her. It was just the sort of logic her sister would employ. And the sort of punishment she would deal herself.

"Well, I am home and I have everything I ever wanted and more so you can stop punishing yourself and finally get the happiness you deserve."

Charlotte could tell by her sister's faint smile that still she didn't believe she deserved it, but Charlotte was determined that in time she would—no matter how long it took.

Alex stood at the altar of St. George's in Hanover Square waiting for the wedding march to commence. His new valet, whom Charlotte had insisted he hire now that the household had grown and Alfred had additional duties to manage, had tied his necktie too tight.

Armstrong stood at his side, he swore, wearing the exact clothes he'd worn five years ago. Nicholas sat in the front pew flanked by Missy, Amelia, Elizabeth and Creswell. His parents, Rutherford's younger brother, Christopher and Armstrong's younger sisters, Sarah and Emily sat in the pew directly across. Jillian and Miss Foster hovered in the wings of the church, both refusing to join the guests fearing the scandal it may cause. Charlotte insisted they would attend a more intimate wedding breakfast at Gretchen Manor when they returned home. All parties had agreed on that.

The music commenced and Alex saw only Charlotte walking toward him, as beautiful as he'd ever seen her in a cream silk wedding gown, on her head a veil artfully attached to a flowered bonnet. He took scant notice of Rutherford, who escorted her, or Catherine, who followed behind.

Whispers immediately abounded in the boxed pews as guests murmured, nodded and smiled their appreciation. *Absolutely stunning. What a beautiful duchess she will make. Is it true she is with child?*

Some needed to master the art of the whisper.

Alex didn't care, all he cared was that today he'd marry the woman of his heart, the woman of his dreams, the woman who would bear all his children. Today he would marry the woman he'd love for the rest of his life.

Ten minutes later as he looked into her beautiful blue eyes, held her trembling hands in his and after they'd both recited their vows, he did.

Epilogue

"I suppose you'll have to try for another." Elizabeth smiled down at the latest addition to the Cartwright family curled up in her arms. "She's breathtaking. And doesn't look a thing like you."

Charlotte gazed lovingly at her two-month-old daughter, Rose, taking in her inky-black hair, pink cheeks and silver gray eyes. "No, she looks exactly like her papa. And don't think he doesn't crow over the fact.

Already three months pregnant with their third child, Elizabeth hadn't been able to come see Rose sooner until her morning sickness had abated sufficiently for her to travel. She and Derek had arrived earlier that day, braving the icy February winds of Reading.

The men had recently adjourned to the billiard's room, Nicholas was playing upstairs with Elizabeth's children, and she and Elizabeth sat on the flowered chintz sofa with the winter sun flooding the morning room.

"And the duke and the duchess, have they gotten over the disappointment of a granddaughter?"

"For the duke, it may take a bit more time, although he's happy Mr. Graham has authenticated our original marriage papers. Mr. Wentworth will not be filing a claim in court to challenge its validity, so Nicholas will inherit."

There had been much joy in the house when the duke had delivered the good news in person.

"The duchess believes she now has the girl she'd always hoped for. I fear she'll spoil the children dreadfully."

Charlotte smiled, still amazed how hers and the duchess's relationship had changed over the course of the year. They would never be the best of friends, but they rubbed along well enough. The duke still held himself aloof from her and it appeared that wouldn't change but his relationship with Alex had vastly improved and for that she was grateful.

Charlotte reached for an empty cup on the tea cart and noticed the letters Alfred had delivered earlier sitting on the side table. She'd put them aside with the intention of sorting through the various invitations that arrived daily at a later time. But the handwriting on the envelope on top caught her eye. She recognized it instantly.

Lucas!

It had been so long.

With anxious fingers, she peeled the envelope open and drew out the letter. She read it quickly and gave a small gasp upon reading what he'd written in closing.

Elizabeth raised one finely arched brow. "What is it?"

"It's Lucas. He's returning to London next week."

20191128R00173

Made in the USA
Charleston, SC
29 June 2013